Also by Jennifer L. Armentrout and available from Hodder

# JENNIFER L. ARMENTROUT

# Fire in You

HODDER

First published in Great Britain in 2016 by Hodder & Stoughton
An Hachette UK company

First published in 2016

A CIP catalogue record for this title is available from the British Library

ISBN 978 1 473 65690 1

Typeset in Plantin Light by Hewer Text UK Ltd, Edinburgh
Printed and bound by Clays Ltd, St Ives plc

Hodder & Stoughton policy is to use papers that are natural, renewable
and recyclable products and made from wood grown in sustainable
forests. The logging and manufacturing processes are expected to
conform to the environmental regulations of the country of origin.

Hodder & Stoughton Ltd
Carmelite House
50 Victoria Embankment
London EC4Y 0DZ

www.hodder.co.uk

*"I survived because the fire inside me burned brighter than the fire around me."*

—Joshua Graham (*Fallout*)

# Chapter 1

I was going to kill Avery Hamilton.

Sweaty palms gripped the steering wheel as I told myself I needed to get out of the car. It was way past time, but I knew I'd rather walk barefoot across broken, heated glass than go into that restaurant.

Sounded excessive even to me.

But all I wanted to do was go home, change into a pair of leggings that were probably not suitable for public viewing, curl up on the couch with a bowl of sour cream and cheddar potato chips (the ruffled kind) and read. I was currently going through this weird stage where I was devouring historical romances written in the eighties, and I was about to start a Johanna Lindsey viking romance. There was a lot of bodice ripping and alpha men on steroids awaiting me. I *loved* it.

But then, Avery would kill me if I bailed on tonight.

Well, okay. She wouldn't kill me, because who would babysit Ava and little Alex so she and Cam could have a date night? Tonight was a rarity. Cam's parents were in town, so they were watching the babies, and I was here, sitting in my car, staring at one of the Japanese maple trees that lined the parking lot and looked like it was seconds from toppling over.

"Ugh," I groaned, tipping my head back against the seat.

If I was doing this any other day, it wouldn't be so bad, but this had been my last day at Richards and Decker. There'd been so many people in and out of my tiny office. Balloons. An ice cream cake that I may have had two . . . or three slices of. I was all peopled out.

Leaving my job of five years had been weird. I'd convinced myself for so long that I'd loved it there. I went to work, closed my door and, for the most part, was left alone while I processed insurance claims. It was a quiet, simple job I could lose myself in, and I had no risk of ever bringing it home with me at the end of the day. It paid for the two-bedroom apartment and covered the loan on my Honda. It was a quiet, boring, and harmless job to go along with a quiet, boring, and harmless life.

Then my father had finally, literally, made an offer I'd be an idiot to walk away from, and that offer had unlocked something inside me, something I'd long since thought was dead.

The desire to start really *living* again.

Yeah, that sounded cheesy to even think it, but it was the truth. For the last six years, I'd existed from one day to the next. Not looking forward to anything. Not doing any of the things I used to dream about.

Taking the offer my father made was the first step—the biggest step—in finally moving forward with my life, but I still couldn't believe I was doing it.

My parents hated . . . they hated how things had turned out for me. They had all these dreams and hopes. I had those same—

A tap on my car window startled me and I jumped. My knee cracked off the bottom of my steering wheel as I looked to my left.

Avery stood outside my car, her hair a fiery red in the fading evening sun. She wiggled her fingers at me.

Cringing because I felt foolish, I reached over and hit the button. The window slid down silently. "Hey."

She leaned over, resting her forearms on the door and all but stuck her head in the car, speaking directly to my left side. Avery was a few years older than me and had two kids, one of them less than a year ago, but with those freckles and warm brown eyes, she still managed to look like she was barely in her twenties. "So, whatcha doing?"

I glanced from her to the windshield and then back again. "Um, I was . . . thinking."

"Uh-huh." Avery smiled a little. "Do you think you'll be done doing that anytime soon?"

"I don't know," I murmured, feeling my cheeks heat.

"The waitress just took our drink orders. I got you a Coke," she offered. "Not diet. I'm hoping you'll join us before we order appetizers, because Cam is talking soccer and you know how my attention span is when he starts talking soccer."

The right corner of my mouth curved up a little. Cam had played pro soccer for several years. Now he'd moved on to coaching at Shepherd, which meant he got to be home way more often. "I'm sorry to leave you hanging like that. I wasn't going to bail."

"I didn't think you would, but I figured you might need a little coaxing."

Peeking up at her again, the small half-smile slipped from my face. Letting Avery talk me into this was also a part of the whole getting out there and living again thing, but this also wasn't easy. "Does . . . does he know about . . . ?" I gestured at my face.

A soft look crept onto Avery's face as she reached inside and patted my arm. I was back to gripping the steering wheel like a freak. She nodded. "Cam hasn't gone into detail, of course, because that's not our story to tell, but Grady knows enough."

Meaning he wouldn't have that "WTF" expression on his face when he saw me.

Granted, he probably would still have that expression at some point. From a distance, there didn't appear to be anything *off* about me. It was upon closer inspection that my face just didn't add up.

And that's what I was dreading about tonight, what I dreaded whenever I met anyone for the first time. Some people just blurted it out, having absolutely no care if the question embarrassed or bothered me, or made me think of a night I'd rather forget for a multitude of reasons. Even if they didn't ask what happened to my face, they were thinking it, because I would think it too. Didn't make them terrible people. It just made them *people*.

They'd stare, trying to figure out why my right jaw looked slightly different than my left jaw. They'd try to hide that they were looking, but they'd keep glancing at my left cheek, guessing about what could've left such a deep notch just below my cheekbone. Then they would wonder if the deafness in my right ear had anything to do with what was going on with my face.

No one had to ask those questions, but I knew that was what they were thinking.

"He's a really great guy," Avery continued, squeezing my arm gently. "He's super nice and very cute. I've told you how cute he is, right?"

Ducking my chin, I smiled—smiled as best as I could, which always looked fake or like I was smirking. I couldn't get the corner of the left side of my mouth to work right. "Yes, you've mentioned that a few times." I sighed as I forced my hands off the steering wheel. "I'm sorry. I'm ready."

Avery stepped back as I hit the button, closing the window. Turning my car off, I grabbed my burnt-orange purse off the seat. I had a thing for purses. Truly the one thing I splurged on, and I could throw down some ridiculous money on a purse. As in, that autumn-themed Coach purse was by far not the most expensive one I'd bought.

I stepped out into the cool, late September evening air, wishing I'd worn something heavier than the thin black turtleneck, but the light sweater looked good with the black, knee-high boots, and I was actually trying tonight. You know, putting effort into how I looked, which meant I would hopefully put effort into this date.

"You need to stop apologizing." Avery looped her arm through my left one. "Trust me. Take it from someone who used to be a habitual apologizer of the secular order. You don't need to apologize when you haven't done anything wrong."

I lifted my brows. I knew Avery had a pretty messed-up past. For the longest time, I'd had no idea what had happened to her, but about five years ago, she'd confided in me. Hearing what she had gone through, even though it was vastly different than what had happened to me, had helped. Especially seeing her moved on from such a traumatic event, happy and healthy, and in love.

Avery was the proof that scars, whether physical or emotional, could be not just a representation of survival but also a story of hope.

"Yeah, but you guys have been waiting for me," I said, reaching around my neck and gathering up the long strands of hair. I brought them around my left shoulder, so the thick curtain of hair fell forward. "I'm almost twenty-seven years old. You shouldn't have to come get me out of my car."

Avery laughed. "There are times that Cam has to come get me out of the closet and pry a wine bottle from my fingers, so this is nothing."

I laughed at the image those words created.

"I'm glad you agreed to come out tonight." Avery slipped her arm free and opened the door. "I think you'll really like Grady."

I hoped I did.

But I didn't have the highest expectations, mainly because I had, well, not the best of luck when it came to the opposite sex. I'd only been super interested in two guys. I didn't even want to think about the first one—about *him*—because that was a pit of despair I was not going to fall back into. And there was this guy I dated three years ago, but Ben Campbell had treated me like he could deduct dating me from his taxes under charitable donations.

Other than that, I was sort of dateless and I truly believed my mom feared I'd end up unmarried, childless, and alone for the rest of my life, living in my apartment with a dozen exotic birds.

"You ready?" Avery asked, snapping me out of my thoughts.

I nodded, even though this wasn't what I wanted to be doing. I lied, because sometimes lying was like surviving. You were doing it without even realizing it. "I'm ready."

# Chapter 2

Stomach churning, I followed Avery toward the back of the restaurant with my gaze trained on the pretty green sweater she wore so I didn't get distracted. Crowds were weird now, because the chatter made me feel off-balance. Like I was only capturing half of what was going on around me. Keeping up with conversations in large groups or when there was a lot of noise was often as successful as using my forehead to bang a nail into the wall.

Avery's steps slowed as we neared a table, and Cam looked up with those extraordinarily bright blue eyes of his. The first time I'd met Cam, I'd been struck tongue-tied and unable to formulate simple words. He was that gorgeous, and he was so much in love with his wife that at times I felt a little jealous. To be on the receiving end of that kind of devotion and acceptance was something I'd never felt. Truthfully, I didn't think everyone in the world got to experience that level of love. It was as rare and beautiful as an albino alligator.

"You've found her." Cam leaned back against the chair, grinning up at Avery. "Good job, wife."

She grinned as she slid into the seat beside him.

"Sorry," I said, slipping my purse off my shoulder while I ignored the pointed look Avery shot in my direction. "I was running late."

The man with his back to me, who I knew was Grady, rose and turned. With a bit of relief, I realized he would be seated to my left. Looking up, I found he was a few inches taller than me and was just as cute as Avery had said. His sandy brown hair and light blue eyes reminded me of the beach. He was smiling, and it was warm and friendly.

"That's totally okay," Grady said. "It's good to meet you."

"You too," I replied, flushing slightly as he pulled my chair out and waited for me to sit down. I did just that, carefully placing the strap of my purse on the back of my chair. No way in hell was my Coach purse sitting on the floor. I glanced around the table. "So, um, have we ordered food yet?"

"I put in an order for spinach artichoke dip." Cam curled his arm around the back of Avery's chair. "And cheese fries . . . with extra bacon and cheese."

"Someone eats like they run up and down a field for a living," Grady commented, grinning as he glanced over at me. "Unlike the rest of us."

Cam chuckled. "Don't hate."

Picking up the glass of Coke, I took a sip to ease my dry throat and calm the nervous buzz trilling in my veins. "So, Avery was saying you work at Shepherd?"

Grady nodded and spoke directly facing me, obviously aware of my partial deafness. "Yes, but my job is nowhere near as entertaining as Cam's. I teach chemistry."

"He's just being modest," Cam said, waiting until I turned to him before he continued. "He's the youngest professor in the science department."

"Wow. That's impressive," I commented, wondering if he knew I'd dropped out of college and what he thought about that. You had to be pretty smart to teach chemistry. "How long have you been there?"

As he answered my question, I saw his gaze drop from mine, flickering over my cheek, but his expression didn't change, and I wasn't sure what that meant. "They were telling me you attended Shepherd?"

I nodded, glancing at Avery. "I did . . ." I closed my mouth, not sure of what else to say. Silence trickled out, and I grabbed my glass again.

Cam came to the rescue, bringing up the subject of seven-year-old Ava's fixation with soccer. "She's so going to play."

"She's going to dance," Avery corrected.

"She could probably do both," Grady jumped in. "Couldn't she?"

It took me a moment to realize he was talking to me. "With her energy? She could do dance, soccer, *and* gymnastics."

Avery laughed. "Our girl is . . . well, she's a handful."

"It's so strange that Alex is the mellow one out of the two," Cam mused. "Would've expected him to be all over the place."

"Give him time," she replied dryly. "He's only eleven months old."

"He'll be playing soccer too." Cam leaned in, kissing Avery's cheek before she could respond. "You'll be carting them both around to practice in a minivan."

"God help me," Avery laughed.

The waitress appeared at our table then, stopping abruptly when her gaze roamed over Grady and then halted on me. I hastily looked at the menu, settling on the roasted chicken and potatoes. I didn't look up at her when I placed my order because I didn't want to know if she was staring at me or not.

Once she left to put in the order, the conversation picked up again, and I loved listening to Cam and Avery banter back and forth with one another. Those two made me smile even when I wasn't comfortable with the way it felt or looked.

I was quiet while the appetizers arrived, murmuring my thanks when Grady offered to load up the small plate for me.

"Cam was saying you're starting a new job on Monday?" he asked, genuine interest shining through his eyes.

"I totally told him who your father is." Cam's grin was sheepish. I wasn't surprised. Cam was a total Lima fanboy. "Sorry."

"It's okay." And it really was. Even though I'd distanced myself from my father's profession, I was still thoroughly proud of what he and his brothers had accomplished. "My last name kind of gives it away."

"I wouldn't have known," Grady admitted, his cheeks turning pink when I looked at him in surprise. "I mean, I don't really follow the whole mixed martial arts thing."

That *mixed martial arts thing* had been a part of my life for a long time.

Dad had been at me for *years*, especially once he opened his new state-of-the-art mixed martial arts and then some training facility in Martinsburg, less than fifteen minutes from where I'd been attending college at Shepherd University. God, I'd been so pissed when I'd discovered that my family had practically followed me to college. Dad would've stayed at the Philadelphia location, but one of my five thousand uncles would always be with stalking distance.

Dad had wanted me to come back home and work at the center in Philly, but he'd finally caught on about two years ago to the fact that was never going to happen. Ever. There were too many memories there, too much that reminded me . . . reminded me of *him* and of the way I used to be.

But about six months ago, Dad started on me again. So did my mother. So did Uncle Julio and Dan and Andre and, oh my God, the Limas were like mogwai fed after midnight. The pitch had started off differently this time. Andre, who was currently the General Manager of the Lima Academy in Martinsburg, wanted to move back to Philly by the beginning of October, because I guess West Virginia just wasn't cool enough for him. Dad wasn't offering me the GM position, but the position of assistant to the GM—a manager position that hadn't existed before at the Martinsburg location. The assistant manager would oversee the day-to-day functioning of the Academy while helping expand services. He wanted someone he could trust and who knew the business while he found a new GM. The offer was, well, very tempting, but I'd turned it down.

Then Dad showed up at my apartment and handed me a piece of paper that had my salary written on it, along with a slew of benefits, and I would be the stupidest and most stubborn person to refuse that, but even though the offer was amazing, it wasn't the real reason why I finally accepted it. He just came at the right moment, when I just . . . just was so damn tired of the windowless room and working a job I didn't give two craps about. The offer poked and prodded at the Jillian I used to be, and a part of me knew that was who Dad had been trying to reach this entire time with one crazy job offer after another.

"I do," Cam confirmed, breaking me out of my thoughts.

"We know." Avery sighed. "We all know."

"So, you . . . you really have no clue what my last name means?" I asked, finding it somewhat freeing that there was a red-blooded man who didn't secretly wish he could climb into the Octagon and walk back out in one piece.

"Not really. Is that a bad thing?"

"No." I dipped my chin as I smiled and peeked back up at him. "It's a . . . a good thing."

His gaze met mine. "I'm happy to hear that."

My face heated again, so I focused on my plate. I poked at the cheese fries as my stomach grumbled. If I was at home, I would've already consumed half my plate, but I forced myself to not eat like I hadn't seen food in a week.

The dinner went . . . surprisingly smoothly.

Cam and Avery kept the conversation flowing naturally, picking up whenever the gaps of silence started to stretch out too long, which didn't happen often. Grady was easy to talk to, guiding me into conversation. There were only a few times when Cam or Avery had spoken to me and I hadn't heard them, so Grady had to catch my attention. This didn't seem to bother them, which made it easy for me to gloss over it.

Our main dishes arrived while Grady was telling me about a new art exhibit that had come to Shepherd. The way his eyes lit up as he talked about the exhibit, you could tell *that* was the kind of stuff he was into.

And it was cute.

"Sounds like it's an amazing thing to see," I said, picking up my fork. "I haven't gone to many art exhibits recently." Or ever. Like, seriously. I didn't go look at art. Not like I saw anything wrong with doing that, but it just wasn't something I did.

Then again, there wasn't much I did.

"I can take you," Grady offered, grinning. "I'd love to."

My lips parted at the unexpected offer. We were getting along well, so I wasn't sure why the offer caught me off-guard, but it did. I started to respond, but realized I didn't know what to say, because I wasn't sure if I was excited about what seemed like a genuine offer or if I was wholly unmoved by it.

An all-too-familiar feeling swept through me, the one that usually hit me in the middle of the long night, keeping me awake.

It was how I had felt when I'd been dating Ben; it was the feeling that had kept me with him, because I didn't see anything better for myself. Not because I didn't deserve better, but I . . . I gave my heart so completely, so fully to someone else, that when my heart was broken, those pieces I'd freely given away weren't mine any longer.

My heart wasn't complete.

And that might sound silly and overdramatic to some, but I didn't care. It was the truth, and I wasn't sure I could ever feel that way about someone else again. So I had settled with Ben. Would I be doing that again with Grady, if it got to that point? Settling?

Oh God, wait a second.

Was I really sitting here and thinking about settling after I just met this guy an hour ago?

I needed to get a grip.

"Jillian?" Grady said, and I guessed he thought I hadn't heard him.

"T-that would be nice," I managed to force out.

He studied me for a moment too long, and I wondered if he could sense my growing nervousness.

"I'll be right back." Placing my folded napkin onto the table, I rose and stepped around the chair. I could feel Avery's concerned gaze on me, and I didn't want to make a big deal out of anything, but I assured her I was okay.

I just needed a minute.

Or three.

Making my way through the narrow pathways between the tables, I headed back toward the bathroom. Only once I pushed open the double doors and stopped in front of the water-spotted mirror did I realize I'd left my purse at the table, so there'd be no reapplying my lipstick.

I pumped soap onto my hands and waved them under the faucet. Water flowed, washing away the suds as I slowly lifted my gaze to my reflection. Normally when I looked at myself, I didn't really pay attention longer than was necessary to put makeup on without ending up looking like a tutorial gone wrong.

Standing here now, though, I really looked at myself.

I used to wear my hair up all the time, but I'd stopped doing that every day. My hair now hung in waves and the ends curled over the tips of my breasts. I also used to have heavy bangs, but thank God they were long gone. I'd finally learned how to put on eyeliner. *That was another miracle.* The slight flush of my face darkened my naturally tan skin. My lips were fuller and my nose straight.

My hair was parted to sweep to the left so it shielded my cheek . . . and my cheek didn't look that bad, especially considering how it looked the first time I'd seen it after . . . after days in the hospital.

Hell, my entire face had been one hot mess.

There was a deep indentation in my left cheek, almost like an icepick had been shoved in there, and as I stared at my right jaw line, I was still amazed by what reconstructive plastic surgeons could accomplish. Half my face had literally been pieced back together with an iliac crest graft with a reconstruction plate and a crap ton of dentistry to give me back a full set of functional teeth.

Plastic surgeons didn't have magic wands, but they *were* magicians. If you weren't looking at me straight on, you'd have no idea that my right jaw was thinner than my left.

You'd have no idea what had happened to me that night.

Now I stared back at myself just like I had done that night, six years ago, standing in a bathroom, mere *minutes* before my entire life came crashing down.

It wasn't that I hated the way I looked now. The fact that I was alive meant I was one of those rare, walking and breathing statistics.

But even knowing how lucky I was didn't change the fact that I felt . . . deformed. That was a harsh word to use. I didn't like to whip it out often. Doing so on what was so far a pretty good date was probably not a good idea.

Taking a deep breath, I shook my head. I didn't need my thoughts going in that direction tonight. So far, the dinner had been amazing. Grady was nice and he was cute. I could maybe see myself going out with him again, to an art exhibit, and maybe coffee.

And that was what had freaked me out.

I was not going to let *living* freak me out.

Nope.

I could give him a chance and not worry about whether or not I was settling.

Turning from the sink, I dried my hands and then readjusted my hair so it fell forward, over my left shoulder and cheek. I walked out of the bathroom and into the narrow hall, gaze trained on the floor as I took about two steps before I realized someone was standing right outside the door, leaning against the wall. Before I nearly plowed into him.

Gasping, I took a step back. All I could see were finely cut black trousers paired with . . . with old black and white Chucks? What an odd combination, but those shoes reminded me of . . .

I gave a little shake of my head and stepped to the side. "Sorry. Excuse—"

"Jillian."

I stopped.

Time stopped.

Everything stopped except my heart, because it was suddenly pounding in my chest too hard, too fast. That deep, rough voice. I recognized it all the way to my very core. Slowly, I lifted my gaze, already knowing what I was going to see but refusing to believe it.

Brock Mitchell stood in front of me.

# Chapter 3

Shock held me immobile as I stared up at Brock, stunned into silence, because I couldn't believe what I was seeing. There was no way he was standing in front of me. As far as I knew, he never came to Martinsburg. Ever. Because *I* was here. He had the entire world. I only had West Virginia.

Those were the unspoken rules.

Maybe I'd fallen and hit my head in the bathroom.

Sounded unlikely.

Because it was Brock, and he was so close I could smell the familiar cologne, the fresh mixture of burning leaves and winter wind.

How in the world was he in this restaurant and I hadn't seen him? Then again, I never was all that observant, even more so now. But that didn't explain how Cam, who was majorly obsessed with Brock, hadn't zeroed in on his presence.

Cam was going to be so disappointed in himself.

"Damn," he rasped out.

My lips parted, but I was at a loss for words. Brock looked the same as he had the last time I'd seen him, several years ago, but he was more . . . refined, more . . . well, *everything*. He was still a foot taller than me, but he was broader in the shoulders. The gray button-down pulled taut across his chest. Sleeves were rolled up, revealing those powerful, tattooed forearms. There was new ink on his forearm. New color. His waist tapered in and those pants were tailored to fit what I knew were still strong, muscled thighs.

I dragged my gaze back to his face. Gone was the spiky hair of a man in his mid-twenties. Now the dark brown hair was calmer, cut so that it was styled back from his forehead, and there was a day or two worth of scruff along his jaw and cheeks. He was older.

Well, duh. He would be thirty-four now.

Faint lines were etched into the sandy-colored skin at the corners of his eyes. His face was still all angles. High cheekbones and a full, sensual mouth. The scar on his lower lip was barely noticeable now, after all these years. The one under his left eye still stood out, the one his father had given him the night he'd run away, sending him on a collision course with my life.

Those eyes, the color of warmed chocolate, were just as I remembered, heavily lashed and sharp, and right now he was doing the same thing I was doing to him. Brock was checking me out.

His gaze had started at the tips of my boots, had traveled up the dark denim jeans and over the thin turtleneck. Over the years, my body had evened out. I'll never be considered thin. My body was rather average, and I didn't have the desire or willpower to spend two hours a day trying to shape it into something that resembled the women in magazines. I liked my fatty food, and I also liked lounging around and reading in my spare time.

But I remembered quite painfully the kind of women Brock had been attracted to when we were younger. Women with flat stomachs and toned legs. The type of girls where guys could wrap their hands around their waists. Someone who'd spend hours working out alongside him and still somehow looked sexy and amazing when they were sweaty and flushed red in the face. That was what he'd been drawn to. Still was, considering I knew who his *fiancée* was.

Then I stopped thinking about what I looked like compared to the random chicks he'd hooked up with—to the woman I knew he was *engaged* to, because yes, I did know that about him. None of that mattered now, because he was staring at my face, and it struck me that he hadn't seen me in six years without my face being swollen or bandaged. Other than what my family had to have told him, this was the first time he was seeing me since I wasn't a fan of pictures. Never had been, but even more so now. Any time he would've seen me would've been a rare glimpse from a distance.

His eyes were slightly wide as his gaze drifted from the left side to the right side of my face. The way he looked at me, a mixture of surprise and an emotion I didn't want to see, something that turned the blood in my veins bitter, snapped me out of my stupor.

"What are you doing here?" I demanded sharply.

Brock's gaze flew to mine. "Like, right now? Well, I was actually out here waiting for you."

"Outside the ladies' room?"

"Yeah."

"That's . . . that's next level weird," I muttered, glancing at the end of the hall. Avery and everyone had to be wondering where I was. "But what I *meant* is what are you doing in Martinsburg?"

"Having dinner," he replied, his gaze never straying from mine. He held my eyes with the intensity that I found more than just unnerving. "You look . . . look amazing, Jillian."

My breath caught at what appeared to be genuine sincerity in his voice, but then I realized that, compared to what he had seen, I looked like a million bucks. "So, you're randomly in Martinsburg having dinner at the same restaurant I'm having dinner at?"

Brock blinked, obviously surprised by my snappy tone. Couldn't really blame him for that. Back in the day, I pretty much smiled and nodded at whatever he said, so much so that my middle name could've been "Brock's Personal Doormat. Welcome."

And thinking that, I was suddenly thrust back to the night at the bar, when I stood in front of him in the dress I'd felt so grown up in, so hopeful, so in love, and so incredibly *foolish*.

One side of his lips kicked up, and it was that half-grin, the one that pretty much got Brock whatever he wanted. "Are you insinuating that I somehow found out about your dinner and purposely came here tonight just to see you?" He paused, eyes glimmering in the low light outside the restrooms. "Like I'm some kind of stalker?"

Well, that did sound ridiculous but wasn't impossible. Mom knew I had this date tonight. I'd told her where we were going. Though I doubted she would've told Brock.

She had better not have told Brock.

"Or maybe not a stalker, but someone who is desperate to catch a glimpse of another person who has been avoiding them for years?" he suggested smoothly. "Six years this December."

I blinked once and then twice. "What?"

That half-grin grew as he eyed me. "Or someone who just happens to be having dinner with a friend who also happens to live in the same vicinity as you?"

My cheeks started to heat.

"If I was stalking you, I'm doing a really bad job at it since I waited for you to come out of the restroom," he continued on, obviously amused by my observation. "From what I know about stalkers, and trust me, I've had a few, they tend to be a little more inconspicuous."

Anger flushed through my system. Did this amuse him—did I? Of course it did. I had always amused Brock. "I'm pretty sure most of the stalkers you've had in the past would've walked right into the men's room instead of waiting for you outside, and you wouldn't have had one problem with that."

"Damn." Brock tipped his head back and laughed. Air punched out of my lungs. God, I'd forgotten how his laugh sounded. Deep and infectious; he laughed without a care. He handed those laughs out to anyone and everyone while I thought they were just for me. A smile played at his lips. "You are not the Jillybean I remember."

Brock using my nickname did funny things to me. Threw me back in time, to *years* ago, when we'd sit side by side on the old swing out in my parents' backyard. Reminded me of how Brock would listen to me ramble on and on about all the places in the world I wanted to visit. It made me think of the way things used to be, and nothing could ever be like that again.

"No," I told him, lifting my chin. "I'm not her."

He dipped his head so he was suddenly in my space, his mouth nearly lined up with mine. "I know that."

A startled gasp left me.

"I think I like this Jillian," he said as if he were sharing some highly kept secret.

I stared at him, unable to process what that meant.

Brock's head tilted to the side. "Who is that guy you're with at the table?"

Jerking back, I about toppled over backward. "I . . . I can't even believe you're asking that question."

His brows furrowed together. "Why? It's a valid question."

My eyes widened. "That is so *not* a valid question."

Straightening, he leaned against the wall like he had all the time in the world and we weren't standing outside of the restrooms. "Is he your boyfriend?"

Struck speechless once more, all I could do was stare at him while one half of me wanted to point out it was none of his damn business and the other half wanted to demand to know why he was even asking that question.

I did neither of those things.

"Excuse me," I said, stepping around him. "I have to get back to my table."

"Seriously?" He pushed off the wall, wrapping a large hand around my arm, stopping me. "We haven't seen each other in years and you're just going to walk away? No hug? No 'how have you been?' Nothing?"

"Sounds about right." I pulled on my arm, and after a few seconds he let go.

He studied me for a moment and the teasing smile faded away into a grim line. "I guess I can't really blame you."

Every muscle in my body tensed. *This is so wrong.* I couldn't help but think that, because Brock and I . . . we used to be inseparable despite the age difference. It was always us—me chasing after him, tagging along, and clamoring for his attention, and it had always been him letting me chase, including me in everything he did and focusing on me like I was the only person in the world.

Until that night.

Until I realized it had always been me wanting him and him wanting everyone but me.

"No," I whispered, hating myself a little for what I was saying. "You can't blame me."

A muscle flexed in his jaw as he nodded. Heart pounding, I turned around and hurried back to the table without looking behind me. I had no idea how long I'd been gone, but guessing by how everyone was staring at me when I slid into my chair, it had been a little too long.

Avery smiled tentatively at me.

"Is everything okay?" Grady asked, touching my arm.

I started to respond, but before I could, I heard only part of what Cam said, "Holy shit."

A shadow fell over the table, a shadow that originated directly from behind me. Avery's eyes widened and her mouth formed a perfect O. The tiny hairs along the back of my neck rose.

No, he didn't.

He *so* didn't follow me back to my table.

Cam was rising from his chair, a look of pure adoration etched into his handsome face. "Holy shit, man. It's been a long time since I've seen you."

Yep.

He'd followed me to my table.

Looking to my right, I watched Brock clasp Cam's hand and then they exchanged one of those one-arm man hugs. All I could do was sit there as Brock and Cam spoke to one another. I had no idea what they were saying, and it probably had nothing to do with my hearing. I was concentrating on not standing, picking up my chair and tossing it at Brock.

Then Brock was standing to my right, looking directly at Grady. He held the man's stare like he used to hold the stares of his opponents during weigh-ins and before the matches, smiling narrowly.

Clearing his throat, Grady removed his hand from my arm.

My hands slipped off the table and fell into my lap.

Brock's eyes were cold and flat as he extended his arm over *my plate*. He spoke, but it sounded muffled since he was speaking to my deaf ear.

"Grady Thornton," I heard from my left, and I realized Brock had introduced himself. Grady's hand was all but swallowed by Brock's much larger one. "You know Cam?"

"We've met a couple of times." Brock placed his hand on the back of my chair, the gesture oddly intimate and possessive. "I met him and his lovely wife through Jillian."

I stared straight ahead, counting under my breath.

"Really?" Curiosity filled Grady's tone. "How do you two know each other?"

"He works—well, *worked* for my father," I answered before Brock could.

"Ah, come on, that's not the whole story." Brock chuckled, and I widened my eyes. "We actually grew up together. There's barely a thing I don't know about *Jilly*."

What in the actual hell of all nine circles of hell was this?

"And how do you know everyone here?" Brock asked, and since he shifted closer, I could hear him even though it sounded like it was at the end of a tunnel.

Grady's gaze darted between Brock and me. "I'm a friend of Cam's. We work together."

"Interesting," Brock murmured, still smiling. "You're coaching soccer now, right?" When Cam nodded, Brock turned back to Grady. "Are you also a coach?"

"No." Grady sat a little straighter. "I teach chemistry at Shepherd."

The smile on Brock's face went up a notch, and I wanted to slip under the table. "A professor? Wow. And how do you know Jillian?"

Oh my God, this was an interrogation.

Grady picked up his bottle as he smiled at me. "We just met, but I think we're . . . going to be pretty good friends."

"Good friends?" Brock chuckled, and my hands tightened into fists. "Sounds about right. Anyway," he said in a way that dripped dismissiveness, "I don't want to keep you all from your dinner. Just wanted to stop by and say hi. I'll hit you up later," Brock said to Cam before focusing on me in that intense way of his that made you feel like there was no one else in the entire world but you.

He tapped the tip of my nose.

I blinked.

Brock grinned. "I'll see you again soon."

He then stalked away, drawing attention from nearly every table as he made his way toward the front of the restaurant.

"That was unexpected," Cam said with a laugh. "You didn't know Brock was in town?"

I shook my head. My father had to have known Brock would be here, and he hadn't warned me. Then again, my dad didn't know what really had gone down between Brock and me. All he knew, all my family believed, was that Brock and I had simply grown apart from one another.

But I could never tell my parents, and I demanded of Brock that he didn't, because if my father had known why I'd been where I had been and how I . . . how I got hurt, he would've straight up murdered Brock. It wouldn't have mattered that my father treated him like a son or that he'd invested hundreds of thousands of dollars of time in Brock.

Brock would be a dead man.

"You have no idea whose hand you just shook, do you?" Cam laughed again with a shake of his head, sitting back in his chair. "That was Brock 'The Beast' Mitchell. God, he's like, what, Jillian? Heavyweight Champion twice? Then once at Light Heavyweight. Damn." Cam looked like he was about to pass out. "I can't believe he's not fighting anymore. Watching him in the ring was like seeing a damn Titan throwing a punch . . ."

I shifted in my chair, uncomfortable for a thousand different reasons as Cam updated Grady on the awesomeness that was Brock. Someone must've said something to me, but I didn't hear them until I looked up at Avery.

Suddenly, I couldn't do this.

I didn't *want* to do this.

Not with Brock sitting in the same place as me, not after all these years, and all I could think about was that night.

"I'm sorry. I'm not feeling well." Catching Grady's startled stare and Avery's concerned one, I hurriedly picked up my purse. "I have an upset stomach—a sensitive one."

Oh my God, did I seriously just say that out loud?

I did.

There was no taking *that* back, like, in forever.

Cheeks blood red, I put some cash on the table, more than enough to cover what I had ordered, and rose, mumbling my goodbyes before I speed-walked my way out of the restaurant. It wasn't until I was sitting in my car, the engine running and my hands gripping the steering wheel, that I realized what Brock had said to me before he sauntered off.

He'd be seeing me again.

*Soon.*

# Chapter 4

Rhage, named after my most favorite brother in all the *Black Dagger Brotherhood*, stared up at me with the cringe-inducing judgment only a cat could master from where the brown and white-striped little devil was perched.

Which was on my calves.

Sighing, I turned my head and glanced at the clock on my nightstand. It was almost eleven o'clock on a Saturday morning . . . and I was still in bed.

Rhage was probably hungry for fresh kitty food, because whatever was in the bowl now was obviously not good enough for him.

I'd found the guy when he'd just been a kitten, hidden under my car at work one evening during winter. Snow had started to come down, and the poor thing was shivering and hungry. I'd taken him in and pretty much immediately regretted doing so.

The cat, even as a kitten, didn't like humans eighty percent of the time, including me. He seemed to only tolerate me because I gave him food. He spent most of the time hiding somewhere, waiting patiently for me to walk by and be caught off-guard by his Godzilla blitz attack.

The cat was the devil.

But I sort of loved him anyway, because when he was being nice, that rare twenty percent of the time, he let me cuddle him, and there was nothing better than kitty-cuddles.

"Stop staring at me like that," I muttered, narrowing my own eyes at possibly the meanest cat in the whole world. "I'm getting up in a few minutes."

The cat's ears flattened.

I tipped my head back and sighed again. Sleep had not come easily last night. Brock's unexpected appearance had tossed me headfirst through a loop. It didn't help that Avery had called three times to make sure I was fine, not giving up until I answered the phone. Of course, I lied again, claiming it was just an upset stomach. I doubted she believed me, but Avery didn't know a lot about Brock, as far as I knew. She hadn't lived where we grew up. So unless she heard something from one of the other girls, then she didn't know the details.

Groaning, I placed my hands over my eyes. I still couldn't believe I stood in front of her, in front of Cam and Grady, and basically said I had bowel issues.

God, I shouldn't be allowed out in public.

Even thinking about it now caused the tips of my ears to burn. So embarrassing.

Based on the way I'd left dinner last night and how I acted, I doubted I'd hear from Grady again. To be honest, I wasn't sure how I felt about that. If I truly cared or not. We had hit it off, I supposed, and he also didn't seem bothered by . . . well, anything about me. He was cute and intelligent, but I just didn't feel anything.

No spark. No catch of the breath. No anticipation or yearning. Nothing.

Looking back, it had been the same with Ben. He was the first guy to be interested in me and actually want to have sex with me, and I'd just been so . . . so damn lonely. I just wanted to be *wanted*, and I stayed with him well past the expiration date on that romance just because I so desperately wanted to feel again.

This was a consequence of reading way too many romance novels, because I wanted what the characters I read about had. The mind-blowing, all-consuming attraction like I had for—

I cut those thoughts off, opening my eyes. I was not going down that road. No way. No how. I'd been doing so good for the . . . for the most part.

Okay. I was kind of lying to myself.

Truth was, there wasn't a week that went by where I didn't think about Brock. It used to be not a day would pass. Sometimes even an hour. Making it to a week without wondering if he was happy was a major life improvement, so I wasn't going to go backward just because he randomly appeared at the restaurant last night.

*I'll see you again soon.*

A shiver danced over my skin. What the hell could he mean by that? Unless he was planning to hang around town and make use of the training facility here, there was no reason our paths should cross. Even though he hadn't mentioned the fact that I would be working for the family business, I wouldn't be at all shocked if Dad had mentioned it to him.

Knocking a strand of hair off my face, I thought about the first time I'd seen Brock. It had been in the middle of the night and I'd woken from a nightmare. Whatever I'd been dreaming about I couldn't remember, but I had been thirsty, so I'd left my bedroom.

*Cold sweat dotted my forehead as I held onto the railing, quietly creeping down the staircase. Hearing my father's voice, I stopped a few steps from the bottom. Daddy sounded weird to me, his tone tense, like I sometimes heard him speak to my uncles.*

*"When's the last time you ate, boy?"*

*"I . . . I don't know," an unfamiliar voice, filled with hesitation, responded. "The night before last, I think."*

*Curious, I tiptoed down to the last step and peered around the wall. I saw my daddy standing in the center of the room, arms folded across his chest. Then I saw a boy several years older than me, sitting on the edge of the couch.*

*I placed a hand over my mouth when I saw his face. There was a gash on his forehead and a horrible cut under his lip, one that looked angry and raw. An eye was swollen and black.*

*He looked like one of the men Daddy sometimes fought at work, except Daddy would never fight a kid. Never.*

*"Is that why you tried to rob me?" Daddy asked, and my eyes widened.*

*The boy shrugged a shoulder.*

*"I'm a patient man. I can stand here all night. I can also call the police and have you thrown into jail. Would you like that? Or, you can get to talking and I can get to feeding you. It's your choice."*

*Pressing against the wall, I watched the boy glare up at my daddy mutinously. He was crazy! I would never look at my daddy like that. Several moments passed and he demanded, "Why would you not call the police?"*

*"I've seen you around, hanging outside the Academy for a while. You didn't look like this last time. You also never tried to rob me before, so I'm figuring something about your situation has changed. That you're not a bad kid about to embark on a life of crime."*

*The boy was quiet again.*

*"I was once in your position," my daddy said after a moment. "Having to fight and steal food just to survive. I know what it's like to try to survive on the streets."*

*The boy's wary eyes closed and he seemed to shudder. "I left home a couple of nights ago. Couldn't deal with it any longer. My father . . ."*

*"He do that to your face?"*

*He didn't answer, but my daddy seemed to know what that meant, because he barked a bad word I was never supposed to use. Then he knelt in front of the boy, speaking too low for me to hear. I had no idea what he was saying, but then my father spoke louder, "Come on. Let's see what we have in the kitchen."*

*As my father turned, the boy with the bruised face looked up, looked right at the stairway, and saw me. I didn't understand how, because in a house often filled with voices and people and even when it was silent and nearly empty, no one really saw me.*

*But this boy did.*

I dragged myself out of the memory, shaking the image of the scared and lost boy he'd been, because he wasn't that boy anymore, just like I wasn't that girl.

As much as I tried not to learn anything about Brock, it was hard not to know what was going on with him. I could resist the urge to internet stalk him all I wanted, but whenever I visited my family, at some point, someone would inevitably bring him up.

I knew Brock owned a home outside of Philadelphia, not too far from Plymouth Meeting. According to my Uncle Julio, he had it built to his specifications, and included a home gym. I assumed his fiancée lived with him there, and I tried not to think about his fiancée.

Mainly because I sort of knew her.

Kristen Morgan.

And she had been there the night he broke my heart and everything changed.

Sucking in a sharp breath that did nothing to ease the burn now traveling up my throat, I pressed my lips together as I stared at the slowly churning ceiling fan.

"I'm not doing this." I spoke out loud, causing Rhage to squirm on my legs. "I don't care why he was here last night. It doesn't affect me anymore. *He* doesn't affect me anymore."

Sounded like a plan.

Deciding it was far past the time to get my butt out of bed, I sat up and reached for Rhage. Just before the tips of my fingers brushed his soft fur, he flew off my legs and darted across my bedroom, running like a pack of wild dogs was chasing him.

I shook my head. "Ass."

Wondering why the cat even bothered sleeping next to me, I reached for my cellphone. Hitting the screen, I saw I had a missed call from my friend Abby. "Shoot," I murmured, remembering I'd turned the phone on silent after I'd gotten done talking to Avery last night.

Weeks had passed since I'd last spoken to Abby, and it had been almost a year since I'd seen her. When I headed back home for Thanksgiving, we were going to have to get coffee and catch up. Since she and Colton married a few years back, they'd been in the process of renovating an old, nineteenth-century home they'd bought.

There was also a missed call and message from a local number I didn't recognize. Curious, I hit the message button and waited.

"Hey, Jillian, this is—um—this is Grady. We met last night?" There was an awkward laugh. "Well, of course you probably remember that. Anyway, I hope you don't get mad, but I finagled your phone number from Avery, because I wanted to know if you'd like to check out that art exhibit I was telling you about. I'm going to be out of town this weekend, but I would love to show it to you when I get back."

Eyes wide, I stared at my phone in disbelief as Grady rattled off his phone number and then laughed again when he realized I'd have his number because of caller ID. His constant laughing at himself was . . . it was cute.

Grady wanted to see me again after I insinuated I had an uncontrollable bowel or something? For real?

A shocked laugh burst out of me. I didn't even know what to think of that, and I felt like I needed a gallon of coffee to truly process it.

I threw the covers off my legs and rose from the comfy bed, padded across the plush carpet, and made my way down the narrow hallway, into the sunlit kitchen and living area. The hardwood floors in the main part of the apartment were cool under my bare feet.

Rhage was sitting on the kitchen island, his bushy tail swinging to and fro as he watched me shuffle toward the coffeemaker.

"There's food in the bowl," I told the cat, placing my phone on the counter. "You can eat the dry kibble and it won't hurt you."

As I turned around, Rhage hopped off the island and pranced out into the living room, his furry butt high in the air. A second later I heard one of the thick pillar candles hit the floor and roll across it.

"Ass," I muttered and then said louder, "You're eating the food in the bowl."

Another candle hit the floor.

I folded my arms across my chest. "Throwing a temper tantrum is not going to get you anywhere."

There was a moment of silence and then the loud thump of the wooden candleholder joining the candles on the floor. Then the remote hit the floor, and I knew he'd move on to bigger and more fragile things, like the blue blown-glass bottles situated on the center of the coffee table.

"What a diva."

Sighing, I pivoted around and went to the narrow pantry. I opened the door and grabbed a small can of wet cat food. The tinny sound of the lid peeling open was like ringing a damn dinner bell. Tiny cat paws scampered off the floors and Rhage came slipping and sliding into the small kitchen. I raised a brow as he crashed into his water bowl. Water sloshed over the side, spreading across the mat the bowls sat on.

Rhage stared up at me with yellow eyes, ears perked, and I'd swear, if I didn't know better, the damn cat was smiling.

I was such a pushover.

Seriously.

My gaze drifted to where my phone sat. Grady's laugh was . . . it was cute. Maybe I would call him back and take him up on his offer.

Maybe.

Later that day, after reading what had to be every article on Buzzfeed, I picked up my phone and called Grady.

And I made plans to see him next weekend, when he was back in town.

# Chapter 5

I spent the rest of Saturday and most of Sunday absurdly proud of myself, because agreeing to go out with Grady again without Cam and Avery was a good step—a great step, because what else would I be doing?

Living like a hermit in my apartment, arguing with my asshole cat while trying not to drop ice cream on my Kindle and using my stomach as a table for my bowl? Yep. That sounded *almost* right.

Sunday night, I spent an ungodly amount of time going through my closet, plotting what I would wear on my first day at work at the Academy. That time was interrupted by a call from the mothership.

"Are you excited about tomorrow?" That was what Mom said when I answered the phone.

I grinned. "I am. I'm a little nervous. I'm trying to figure out what to wear."

"Honey, it's a training facility. You could probably wear jeans."

"I cannot!" I shook my head as I rummaged through the stacks of black work pants and then eyed the skirts and dresses I never wore. "The staff in Philly don't wear jeans. Unless that's changed?"

"Your father owns the company. You can wear whatever you want," she replied dryly.

That was not true, not even remotely. The fact that my father owned the company and the assistant-manager job had been created out of thin air was probably going to be an issue with some of the staff at Martinsburg, but I was trying not to dwell on it.

"So, how did your date with your friends go?" Mom asked, changing the subject.

"It was good." I plucked out a pair of pants and held them to my chest. "Speaking of my date, you'll never guess who I ran into."

"Santa?"

I rolled my eyes. My mom was weird. Loved her, but she was so weird. "Um no. I ran into Brock."

Mom was silent.

My earlier suspicion blossomed. "You didn't happen to talk to him recently?"

There was a pause. "I talked to him about a week ago."

I turned as Rhage darted in front of the closet door, chasing what I hoped was some invisible insect. "Did you tell him where I was Friday night?"

"No," Mom said immediately. "I know how you feel about him. I wouldn't tell him where to find you."

That was a weird way of answering the question, but then Mom asked carefully, "Did you talk to him?"

Walking out of the closet, I placed the pants on the chair by the door. "Yes. For a couple of minutes."

"And . . . and how did that go?"

"It was okay," I answered hesitantly, not wanting to give her any false hope that Brock and I were suddenly going to reconnect and become best friends forever. "Do you know why he was here?"

"So you guys talked and it was okay?" she asked instead. "Jillian, this is the first time you talked to him in how many years?"

"A lot of years, but do—"

36

"I'm sure it was more than okay," she said. "I'm sure that there was probably a little part of you relieved to have actually spoken to him?"

I started to tell her "hell no," but was there a part of me that was relieved? I wasn't sure. What did I have to be relieved over?

"Honey, I know this is an old conversation, but you two were so close. From the moment your father brought him into the house, you were his little shadow. You thought the world of him at one point, and I know he still thinks that of you," she said, and my free hand clenched into a ball so tight my knuckles ached. "So talking to him had to be more than okay. You were *that* friend to him, Jilly, and because of that, perhaps one day, you two will find your way back to each other."

I sucked in a shallow breath, reminded of another person saying the same thing to me. "I'm not that friend anymore, Mom. It's not like that. It will never be like that."

"Maybe not, but the future isn't written in stone."

This was not what I wanted to talk about and this conversation was pointless, because I didn't plan on seeing him again. "Look, I've got to go. I'll call you later, okay?"

Mom sighed, and it was a sigh of someone who was worried and not annoyed. "Okay. I'll talk to you soon. I love you."

"I love you, too."

Hanging up the phone, I sat on the edge of my bed and found my mind wandering once more into places I'd rather it not, but it was something Mom had said—something that my friend Katie had also said to me hours before every aspect of my life had changed.

*"You're that friend, Jillian."*
*I felt like that wasn't really something I needed pointed out, but I stayed quiet as I listened to Katie Barbara break down the last*

37

*decade of my life with the wisdom only a psychic stripper could lay upon you.*

"*You're the friend who's always there, no matter what. Even if you don't want to be there, you're still there.*" *She pointed the strip of extra-crispy bacon in my direction.* "*You're so that friend.*"

*I glanced down at my scrambled eggs and sighed. How had this conversation even come up, because if I was in the possession of a Time-Turner, I would so go back and stop this from being the topic.*

*Beside me, Abby Ramsey shifted forward, dropping her elbows onto the table. I lifted my gaze, searching for the waitress. This would be a great time for her to ask if we wanted our checks. Problem was it was Saturday morning at IHOP and the place was ... well, hopping.*

*Katie bit into her strip of bacon, which had actually been the last piece of bacon she'd swiped off my plate.* "*Like this weekend, for example. You haven't been coming home during the summer. Not really, and you only have a couple of more weeks before your fall semester starts, right? But you're here today.*"

*I started to defend myself, but Abby spoke up.* "*Katie, she didn't leave Shepherd just for him.*"

*Well ...*

*Sitting back against the booth, I kept my mouth shut. Of course Abby would defend me. I was closer to her than I was to Katie. Abby and I had first met years ago at a book signing, and our mutual love of reading had spawned what I like to think was a pretty epic friendship, considering there was a ten-year gap between us.*

*But love of books knew no age.*

*Growing up, I'd always known of Katie. Even in a city as populated as Philadelphia and its surrounding suburbs, everyone knew Katie. And it really wasn't because she was a stripper at the club across from the bar called Mona's. It also wasn't because she claimed to be psychic, a side effect of falling off a slippery pole.*

*It was just that Katie was a friend of everyone. I didn't think there was a person out there that Katie hadn't befriended at some point.*

*But right then I was kind of wishing I hadn't agreed to this break-fast when I'd told Abby I'd be coming up for the weekend.*

*"You know damn well that's why she's here," Katie retorted, finishing off the slice of bacon before flipping thick blonde hair over her shoulder. "He's the only thing that brings her back here at a snap of a finger."*

*"I wouldn't say it's the only thing," I reasoned, picking up my glass of soda. "I came home last month."*

*"For the Fourth of July," she returned.*

*Abby's sigh was nearly swallowed by the sip of coffee she took. "I think what Katie is trying to say—"*

*"She knows what I'm saying." Katie slid the sleeve of her neon purple shirt back up her shoulder. Her bright, ocean-colored eyes met mine. "He treats her like a little sister/slave. He's not worth it. Not yet."*

*Every part of me stilled and then stiffened. Muscles along my back locked up. Skin prickled like a swarm of fire ants. I was a pretty level-headed person. So much so that when I died, I was pretty sure that "calm and collected" would be etched into my gravestone, but nothing, nothing made my head want to spin three-hundred-and-sixty degrees quicker than someone talking smack about him.*

*"Don't say that about Brock." My voice was cool, but fire was sparking deep in my belly.*

*"He's a grown adult." Katie shrugged a shoulder, ignoring my warning. "And he's making his own decisions. Has been for as long as all of us remember, and you've been his little shadow."*

*"Well, it sounds kind of pathetic when you say it like that." I placed my glass back on the table before it accidentally slipped out of*

*my fingers, and my epitaph changed to "ill-tempered and impulsive."*

*"If the shoe fits . . ."*

*My mouth dropped open. Everyone knew Katie could be as blunt as a two by four, but Jesus, that was a little unnecessary. "Katie," I said, eyes wide.*

*"You went grocery shopping for him," she pointed out.*

*I knew the time she was talking about. Roughly a year and a half ago. "He could barely move," I protested.*

*"You did his laundry," she continued, and the bright purple shirt slipped off her shoulder.*

*I gaped at her. "He'd had surgery on his chest wall muscle!"*

*"You actually cleaned his apartment for him," Katie finished with a clap of her hands. "And who does that? Like, I don't have a single friend, not even a special friend, who would clean my apartment. You are that friend."*

*I snapped my mouth shut. "Maybe you need better friends."*

*Katie tilted her head to the side and raised her brows.*

*"What Katie is trying to say is that you've always been there for Brock. You've gone out of your way to be there for him," Abby tried again, and this time Katie didn't interrupt her. "And he's . . ."*

*Abby didn't finish.*

*She didn't have to.*

*Because she was too nice and Brock was just . . . well, he was Brock.*

*I drew in a deep breath as I met Katie's stare. "I did those things for him because he was really injured, and I was just helping him."*

*"And he's all better now." Katie tugged the sleeve of her shirt up again. "Next weekend is his big return to the MMA scene."*

*My stomach knotted, like it did every time I thought about his upcoming fight. He'd been training for his big comeback since the moment the doctor cleared him to return to the cage—the Octagon.*

*It would be okay though.*

*Because my father wouldn't have backed Brock if he thought for a second he wasn't ready. Not when my father was* the *Andrew Lima, a ju-jitsu and mixed martial arts expert.*

*Dad had discovered Brock when he was just a teen, fourteen years old. Brock had a natural talent when it came to mimicking moves. When he was younger, every kick, submission hold, and skill had been self-taught.*

*I was eight years old when my father brought him into the Lima fold—into our family—and under my father's tutelage, Brock quickly became the next big thing once he was old enough to compete. Everyone wanted him. Endorsements. Pay-Per-View fights. He was on his way up, and I'd been so happy for him, because Brock hadn't had an easy life up to that point, and no one—no one—deserved it more than him.*

*Almost two years ago, while he was working with one of the new recruits at the Academy's main facilities in the city, he'd suffered a pectoralis major tendon rupture, a serious tear of the interior muscle of the chest. The horror and helplessness I'd felt when it had happened resurfaced. It took no effort to see him falling to his knees, clutching at his chest as pain etched into his striking features. It had been so bad he'd been rushed into surgery, but with rest and rehab, he'd been able to return to top fighting form.*

*Shaking my head, I refocused on the present. "I did those things for him because he's my friend. I'd do them for any of my friends."*

*Katie looked like she wanted to say more, but decided against it, and I shifted uncomfortably on my seat. Katie never held back, so if she was holding back now, it couldn't be good.*

*Then again, none of my friends really got the whole Brock situation, and not a single one of them thought it was a good thing.*

*I took a deep breath and lifted my chin. "And Brock did ask me to come home this weekend. He wants to go out to dinner tonight, just him and me—an early celebration in honor of his fight next week since he leaves tomorrow night with my dad to train there."*

*Abby's eyes widened. "What? You're just now telling us this?"*

*Biting down on my lip to stop myself from grinning, I shrugged. "I really didn't get the chance to explain since someone—" I paused, shooting Katie a pointed look "—has been lecturing me for the last thirty minutes."*

*"I am not ashamed of this piece of knowledge," Katie replied.*

*"Is this a date?" Abby demanded.*

*My stomach tumbled again. A date? Oh God, just thinking about tonight like it was a date made me want to laugh and vomit at the same time, and that would be rather impressive . . . and gross. "It's not really a date. I mean, he didn't call it a date, but it is just us."*

*Abby opened her mouth and then looked over at Katie. I waited, knowing that whatever Katie was about to say, I probably didn't want to hear it.*

*Katie plopped her arms down on the table, rattling the silverware. "If you don't know if it's a date, it's not a date."*

*The grin I'd been fighting slipped away. "I don't think it's a date, Katie."*

*She sighed heavily. "Sometimes I really hate that man."*

*I deflated like a balloon that had been pricked. Katie didn't understand. Time to change the subject. I glanced over at Abby. "Are you and Colton still planning to go to the Poconos for your anniversary?"*

*"Yep. Next weekend. I can't believe it's already been two years." Her lips curved up into a pretty smile.*

*"Time for you to start popping out some babies," advised Katie.*

*Abby's eyes widened. "I don't know about that."*

*I grinned, thinking a little. Abby and Colton's baby would be adorable. I was absolutely fascinated with how the two had reconnected. It was like something straight out of the romance books Abby edited for a living. They'd known each other in high school. Abby had innocently crushed on Colton even though she'd married her high-school sweetheart, but her husband had sadly passed away. Then, years later, Abby had run into Colton after witnessing a murder—a freaking murder that Colton ended up investigating.* The odds! *Seriously.*

*"What about you?" queried Abby, her stare pointed. "When are you going to give up the pole and have some kids?"*

*"Give up the pole?" Katie tipped her head back and laughed. "If and when I have kids, that doesn't mean I've got to give up dancing."*

*I pressed my lips together to stop the giggle building in the back of my throat as I pictured a pregnant Katie working the pole. If anyone would strip while obviously pregnant, it would be Katie. She'd work it, belly and all.*

*The waitress finally arrived with our checks and we headed out into the bright August morning sun. As I pulled the sunglasses off my head and over my eyes, I promised Katie I would try to visit her tonight at the club.*

*I always promised her that.*

*I never went to the club she worked at.*

*Not because I had anything against strip clubs. I just knew, knowing my luck, I would run into a family member and that would be about seven different kinds of awkward.*

*My family was so large, you couldn't throw a rock and not hit a Lima. Cousins and nephews and nieces, and—oh God—uncles were literally everywhere. It was like a higher being threw up, spraying Limas all over the city of Philadelphia. Once, I went to a gyno appointment and my Uncle Julio was in the damn waiting room with his much, much younger wife.*

*Younger, as in Nicole was only six years older than me. Brock's age. She was a ring-card girl. It was love at first booty shorts and bikini top sight. Nicole was super sweet. Super hot. And super pregnant. Like, every time I saw her, she was pregnant again. During Christmas I always managed to almost forget one of their kids. They had an entire litter. Julio was one of the middle brothers, younger than my father, and in his early forties, so you'd figure at some point he'd run out of active sperm.*

*The answer was nope.*

*Anyway, the gyno appointment run-in had been horrifying. Since Julio believed that I had to be a virgin, he hadn't understood why I would be at the gynecologist. As if women didn't have any other reasons for visiting the gynecologist outside of having sex.*

*I loved my uncle, but he was an idiot sometimes.*

*He'd promptly called my father and insisted that I must be sexually active, and when I'd gotten home that day, it was like A&E had showed up and an intervention was about to go down.*

*So, yeah, I knew if I went to where Katie worked, I'd probably end up sitting next to an uncle or a cousin while boobs were jiggling in my face, and that would lead to therapy.*

*Abby lingered by the driver's side of my used Camry, watching Katie fly out of the parking lot in a new Mustang. "She's nuts and she's an acquired taste." Abby turned to me, squinting. "But I love her."*

*Smiling, I leaned back against my car as I brushed my heavy bangs to the side. I really needed to let them grow out, because I was getting so sick of them, especially in the summer. Something I'd been telling myself since I was, oh, about fourteen. But I always cut them, the same way I'd always cut them. Straight and thick, brushing my eyebrows.*

*Maybe I'd let them grow out this time.*

*Maybe.*

*Or maybe I'd cut my hair like Abby's. It was dark and brushed her shoulders. Mine was the color of milk chocolate and long, all the way down past my bra strap. I never wore it down though. Not anymore. It was always up in a bun. So why keep it long, especially when it was such a pain to dry and style?*

*"Jillian?"*

*Realizing I was staring at the road, I turned my attention back to Abby. She smiled at me again. Abby was a pretty woman, but when she smiled, she was stunning, and she smiled a lot more since reconnecting with Colton. "Yes?"*

*She studied me closely. "You know Katie meant well, right?"*

*My shoulders tensed. "I know."*

*"She can just be a little . . . brash at times," she continued, stepping closer. "But it comes from a good place. She worries about you. So do I. So does Stephanie."*

*I frowned as I shifted my weight from one foot to the other. "Why would any of you worry about me? I'm a hundred percent fine."*

*Abby tilted her head to the side and the smile slipped a little. The look that crossed her face was full of doubt and then she exhaled slowly as she nodded. "Okay," she said after a moment, and then hugged me, giving me a quick squeeze before kissing my cheek. "We're still on for lunch tomorrow with Stephanie?"*

*Relieved she wasn't going to push it, I hugged her back. "As long as Nick and Colton let you two out long enough."*

*Abby laughed as she stepped to the side, hitching the strap of her purse up. "As if they could stop us."*

*Considering that both couples—Abby and Colton, Stephanie and Nick—were experiencing an extended-honeymoon period, I really couldn't blame them if they'd rather hole up in the house all weekend.*

*"See you tomorrow." I wiggled my fingers and then pivoted around. My cell dinged as I climbed into my car, alerting me to a text.*

*Cranking the air conditioner up, I reached into my purse and pulled out my cell. My breath caught and my stomach took a pleasant tumble as I saw the name on my screen. I couldn't stop my lips from curving up at the corners.*

*Brock.*

*Opening up the text, I felt a silly little grin tugging at my lips when I started reading his message.*

Hey Jillybean, change of plans. A few guys are in town. Meeting up with them at Mona's for a bit. Can you meet me there at 7?

*The smile slipped a bit. Who was in town? I gave a quick shake of my head. It didn't matter. He still wanted to do dinner at the intensely popular steakhouse not too far from Mona's. Dinner was still happening. Tonight was still happening.*

*Texting him back that I was okay with it, I placed my phone in the cup holder and then let out a shaky breath. Tonight was going to be the night I proved to Brock I was no longer a little girl.*

*Brock would no longer think of me as a little sister.*

Dragging myself out of the memory, I stared down at my phone. My eyes began to burn and blur. God, I had been such a foolish love-struck idiot back then, but even so, I'd been *happy*. I'd been willing to take risks.

Because falling for Brock had been a risk. Love was a risk no matter what, and I had been brave—dumb and blind—but brave. When it came to Brock, I dove in headfirst and didn't come up for air.

And I had *lived*. Sure, I'd been shy and sometimes over-whelmed by my large-ass family, but there were all these things that version of me had done—collecting books obsessively, going to signings and meeting authors, conning friends into taking trips to New York City, and spending every Sunday morning eating breakfast with the best people in the world. There was so much that I'd wanted to do back then. I'd wanted to travel. To write a book! I'd wanted to meet my ultimate author crush, the Queen known as JR Ward. I'd wanted to stand next to my father during a televised match, knowing I had a hand in bringing that talent to the ring. I'd wanted . . .

I'd wanted so much.

I barely recognized that girl with the thick bangs and wide smile, but sometimes I wasn't sure if not being her anymore was really a good thing, because I didn't do any of those things I enjoyed anymore.

I didn't collect books.

I didn't go to book signings.

I sure as hell didn't travel.

I still hadn't met JR Ward.

I had nothing to do with my family's legacy until recently.

And I never once attempted to write a book, but that was probably a good thing.

This version of me, the one from the last six years, went to work, came home, and then lost herself in fictional worlds that were far, far more exciting than mine. I lived through characters that weren't real, but they still lived more authentic lives than me, and how . . . how was I supposed to keep going like this? How was I supposed to continue when living among pages held more appeal than living in real life?

Dropping my phone, I clapped my hands over my face and rubbed at my eyes. I felt like I was seconds from shattering all over again, and the good Lord knew I'd already done that once before.

But I couldn't let myself do that.

Because tomorrow I was starting a new job and it was one I would care about, because it was a part of my blood. And I was going to go out on that second date with Grady. Not only that, but when Avery invited me to Sunday breakfast, and she would, because she texted nearly every Friday and asked me to go, I wouldn't come up with an excuse to not go like I normally did. I would go. These were small but impressive steps, and maybe I could be a little of that old Jillian.

Maybe that wouldn't be so bad.

# Chapter 6

My stomach was churning and full of knots the entire drive to the Lima Academy on Monday morning. I didn't even know why I was so nervous. I knew how to manage the Academy. I'd grown up looking over my father's shoulder as he ran the business.

Today was such a big deal.

I could buy so many more purses with my new salary.

And Rhage could start eating Fancy Feast.

But I was still as nervous as a cat in a room full of rocking chairs. I'd woken up about an hour earlier than necessary, which meant I had time to style my hair, something I normally didn't do when I went to work. Dressing in the wide-leg black trousers I'd picked last night, I paired them with a deep maroon blouse with lacy sleeves I found this morning. I still had more than enough time to make the drive from my apartment off of Del Mar Orchard Road to where the Lima Academy was situated a few miles outside of Shepherdstown, between the University and Martinsburg.

The Academy was located about a mile off of Route 45, beyond a sub-division and a small farm. I'd seen it a hundred times since it opened, but I couldn't help but feel awed when the sprawling, three-story building came into view.

This was my father's, but it was also *mine*.

The first floor was the state-of-the-art gym open to public membership. It came complete with separate rooms for classes, an indoor Olympic pool, sauna and whirlpool rooms, childcare for those working out, and of course, several tanning rooms, because why have all those sleek muscles and be pasty white? I rolled my eyes at that.

The second floor was dedicated to various martial arts classes, ranging from classes for kids who were interested in karate, to those serious about learning jiu jitsu, grappling (both standing and on the ground), striking, and so on, and of course, a training center for those looking to pursue a career in the mixed martial arts. Self-defense classes were also held on the second floor. There was a lot of available space on the second floor, and that was what my father had wanted me to focus on.

The top floor was offices—where *my* office would be located.

This was my family's legacy.

And it was a part of mine.

I'd once told my friend Abby that I didn't want to do what my family did, but that had been a lie in the end. Maybe at that time I was going through some stage in life where I wanted to rebel against everything and everyone, but deep down I always wanted to be a part of it. So pulling into the parking spot was almost like I was finally, *finally* coming home.

I opened the back door and grabbed the box of personal items I'd placed on the back seat. I hadn't brought much with me. A candle from Bath and Body Works that would make my office smell like a pumpkin had thrown up all over it. One framed photo of my parents from a couple of Christmases ago. A hot pink stapler that Avery had given me a year or so ago, and my Sam and Dean Winchester Funko Pops, because they went everywhere with me.

Feeling more ready, I rode the elevator up to the third floor, my sleek black bag dangling from my forearm since it had slipped down my arm. I nibbled on the inside of my cheek as the elevator slid to a gentle stop and the doors glided open.

Just like at the Academy in Philly, a sea of cubicles greeted me. They were all empty as I walked past them. It was still about an hour before the sales teams and trainers would arrive.

I walked toward the closed offices, my steps slowing as my uncle, Andre Lima, rounded the corner. With slightly graying hair, he was still more fit than most men in their twenties.

"Jilly!" He strode forward, his short but powerful strides eating up the distance. Grasping the box from my arms, he placed it on a nearby desk and then wrapped his arms around me. I squeaked as he spun me around like I was twelve. When he placed me back on my feet, I felt like I'd just gotten off a merry-go-round. "Look at you, all dressed nice and stuff."

Andre was wearing khakis and a Lima-branded polo.

"You look nice too," I told him, brushing my hair back from my face.

He laughed as he picked up my box. "This is my *I'm almost out of here* clothing attire."

"You really want to get back to Philadelphia, don't you?"

"I miss it. So does Tanya, and you know what they say. Happy wife, happy life." Andre winked at me. "Aren't you here early?"

"I figured I'd get myself settled before everyone started showing up."

"Smart idea," he replied. "Well, let me show you the office. It's new since we didn't have a manager position before."

Moving so he was to the left of me, I peeked over at him. "Can I ask you a question and you give me an honest answer?"

Grinning, he nodded. "When have I ever lied to you, Jilly?"

"Does the staff think this position is unnecessary?" I asked.

He started to frown. "I'm not sure I understand what you mean."

I guessed I couldn't beat around the bush. "What I mean is, do they think Andrew Lima randomly created this position for his daughter?"

"What?" Andre laughed. "No. Not at all. They actually think it's a good idea. Trust me, I needed the help, and more than once I had to have one of my sales reps join me in meetings—spending extra time on the job in a way that's not necessarily going to make them money. Now they'll be able to focus on their accounts and training sessions while you'll be accompanying the new GM to meetings."

That made sense. "Well, I'm relieved to hear they think it's a good call."

"They do. So we had a contractor come and carve out a new office for you," my uncle explained, stopping in front of an office that had a glass front. "The office furniture just arrived. Never used, and it's all yours."

The office reminded me of a partial fishbowl. This was nothing like my tiny office with walls that weren't see-through, but it was definitely nicer than I realized as I'd stepped inside.

The large, dark cherry wood desk was spotless—not even a fingerprint marked the shiny surface. A new desktop computer sat to the right. Beside it was a NASA-level phone system. Two chairs were stationed in front of the desk, and the chair behind it looked like it would be more comfortable than my bed. There was a credenza against one wall, and on the other was a large potted plant with palm leaves. Blinds covered the wall facing outside.

"What do you think?" Andre placed my box in one of the chairs in front of the desk.

"It's great."

"My office—well, my *old* office—is right on the other side of the sitting area." He gestured to his right, and since I had glass walls, I looked past the sitting area, and saw the fully *walled* office of the GM.

"Has a new GM been hired yet?" I asked, wondering if another one of my uncles would be coming down in the interim.

His dark brows knitted. "You don't know who's replacing me?"

I placed my purse on my desk. "So the position has been filled?"

"Yes. It was filled quite some time ago," he said as I turned around, moving toward the blinds. *Been filled for quite some time?* My father hadn't mentioned that. I opened them as Andre said, "Actually, here he comes now. Earlier than I expected. Not that I'm surprised. You're early, so of course, he'll be early too. Just like old times."

Just like old times?

I froze.

My fingers were wrapped around the little knob connected to the blinds and I simply stopped moving as a series of shivers crawled across my shoulders.

*I'll see you again soon.*

No. No. No.

Everything started to click into place, but I refused to believe it, because I couldn't fathom how or why. In a state of utter disbelief, I let go of the knob. It swung back toward the blinds, clanging off them. I slowly turned around.

Brock Mitchell stood in the doorway of my brand new office, his lips curved into a half-smile. "Good morning, *Ms.* Lima. I hope you like your new office."

# Chapter 7

"You've got to be *fucking* kidding me," I gasped.

Brock's eyes widened and then he threw back his head, laughing loudly and freely. "Ms. Lima, *language*."

My face turned blood red. Did he seriously just say that to me?

Andre's smile was a bit sly as he eyed the both of us, and I knew—I just *knew*—he was fully aware of the fact I had no idea Brock was going to be here. Just like my mother had to have known and just like my father had failed to mention.

My family was a bunch of assholes.

"Okay, I'm going to go—uh, pretend to do something," Andre said.

Brock's brown eyes were trained on me as he stepped aside and clapped the shorter man on the shoulder.

"Good luck," Andre said to him, and my hands balled into fists.

The half-grin appeared on Brock's mouth and he waited until Andre had disappeared. "I don't think I've ever heard you use the word 'fuck' before." His gaze flipped to the ceiling. "Well, there was the one time you tripped over your own feet and banged your knees off the pool deck. Pretty sure you yelled 'fuck' then."

"This is not happening," I murmured, heart thumping heavily in my chest.

"Actually, I think you yelled 'fuck' when your Uncle Julio caught you trying to sneak out of the house. You remember that, right? You were trying to follow me—"

"You can stop," I snapped, "with the walk down *Fuck* Lane."

That grin increased, spreading into a full smile that caused my stomach to dip. I placed steadying hands on my desk. "Please tell me I'm dreaming right now."

"If you were dreaming, I'd hope we'd both have less clothes on."

"What?" My jaw hit the top of the table. Was he flirting with me? Not entirely surprising. If you looked up "flirt" on the internet, I was sure it had a picture of him grinning the panties right off of some chick, so I guessed a fiancée wasn't going to change that.

Chuckling, Brock leaned against the door and folded his arms across his broad chest, stretching the material of his white button-down. My gaze dropped. Yep. He was wearing the damn Chucks. "You're not dreaming, Jillian. I'm the new General Manager and you're *my* assistant manager."

"There is no way," I said dumbly.

He glanced around, arching a brow. "Is it really that surprising?"

I wanted to scream yes, but I should've guessed it the moment I saw Brock Friday night. Anger swept through me. Not only did I feel incredibly stupid for not figuring out Brock was my new boss, I was extremely pissed everyone in my family had basically set me up.

Taking a deep breath, I asked, "Can you give me a second? Please?"

Brock didn't move for a moment and then he unfolded his arms. "Your wish is my command."

My fingers curled around the edge of the desk to stop myself from throwing something at him. The moment he stepped out of my office, I hurried to the door and closed it behind him. Storming back to the desk, I pulled my cellphone out of the little slip inside my purse and jabbed my finger on my father's contact.

He answered on the third ring, his accented voice way too cheery for this time of the morning. "Jillian, my baby girl, are you—"

"Brock is the new General Manager?" I whispered-yelled into the phone.

"You're at the office already? It's not even eight-fifteen— Wait, Brock is already there too?" He laughed. "That *is* surprising."

"That's not really important right now." I took a deep, calming breath. "Brock really is . . . he's the GM?"

"I don't think you really need to ask that question," he responded. "Especially when you know the answer to it."

Closing my eyes, I held the phone so tightly I was surprised it didn't shatter into a million pieces. "Why didn't you tell me?"

"Would it have a made a difference?" he asked.

Yes. A thousand times yes, but I didn't say that. I refused to admit that. "Why didn't you tell me?"

"You're going to have to ask him that." There was a pause. "I didn't offer you this job because I thought you couldn't handle working with him or that you would be calling me on your first day, thirty minutes before you should even be there."

*Ouch.*

"And I'm not saying that to hurt you, hon. You know that. Hurting you is the last thing I'd ever want to do." There was another gap of silence while I contemplated knocking the computer off my desk with a ninja kick, and then Dad said, "You can do this."

Then he hung up on me.

*What in the hell?*

For a moment I didn't move and then I lifted my chin and saw Brock waiting outside the office. That grin was back on his face as he raised a hand and crooked his finger, motioning me to come out of the office, to come to him.

My temper flared. Seconds away from flipping him off, I forced myself to gently place my phone on the desk.

There was a huge part of me that couldn't believe this was happening, but I had to face the fact that Brock—one of the main reasons why I'd left Philly, the man I'd loved with every ounce of my stupid little being and the man who broke my heart—was not just back in my life, he was also my *boss*.

Holy crap, this was like worse than a nightmare.

I had two options at this point.

Option one included me grabbing my purse, walking out of the office, whopping Brock over the head with the thing, and then driving straight to the unemployment office and then on to an epic job search. That option scared me, because hello, being jobless was not exactly a smart move, but having to see Brock five days a week also wasn't a smart move. And his hard head would probably damage my purse.

Walking out of here meant no more wet food at all for Rhage. Or new purses for me.

Option two required that I gain some lady balls and deal with the cards dealt, and I'd obviously done that before, to some extent. I was standing here today, and even though my life hadn't panned out exactly like I'd expected it, I was a walking *miracle*. Dealing with Brock was by no means the hardest thing I'd had to stare down. I was finally where I *felt* like I needed to be.

I was finally starting to live outside the pages of my favorite books.

Brock had chased me out of my home, away from my family and friends, and out of my family business.

*No*, I told myself. That wasn't exactly true. I made the decision to run from my home, away from my family and friends, and from my family legacy. That was all me.

Choosing to stay meant Fancy Feast for Rhage, a new purse or two for me eventually, and a job that would actually mean something to me.

But this option, staying here and working for Brock, terrified me. Not just because it truly forced me to move on from the mess that was our past, but also because it would inevitably require that I actually *face* it.

Obviously, I admittedly had a habit of not doing that.

There was a third option, I realized. I could stay and do this job while looking for a new one if being around Brock was just . . . well, too much.

Squaring my shoulders, I decided I was going to exist somewhere between option two and three and I walked around my desk and to the door, joining Brock.

"What?" I asked, my tone sharper than I intended.

One eyebrow arched. "Watching you in there, it seemed like you were deciding between toppling the desk and breaking a window or walking out here and staying, working for your family like you always wanted to."

I sucked in an unsteady breath, split between wondering if I was as transparent as a glass door and being extremely uncomfortable with the reminder of how well Brock knew me.

"So," he said, dipping his head slightly as he stepped in. He was so close I could feel the heat from his body. "What did you decide, Jillian?"

Forcing myself to hold his gaze, I ignored the way every inch of my body was immediately aware of Brock, like it had been the moment I started seeing him as more than just a boy who was supposed to be like a brother to me. "I'm staying."

"Good." His smile was slow and soft. "That's what I was hoping to hear."

"Really?" I couldn't believe it, because I would think he'd find this just as awkward.

He studied me a moment and then said, "Let's chat."

My mouth opened, with my initial instinct driving me to refuse, but I snapped my mouth shut and nodded. I may have been a coward when it came to Brock and all that, but I wasn't stupid. He was my boss now, and I wouldn't get myself fired. I wouldn't embarrass my father like that.

Brock stepped aside and then moved to my left side as I followed him to the GM's office—to *his* office. He held the door open for me, and waited until he was back on my left side before he spoke. At dinner Friday evening, he didn't seem to remember or realize I couldn't hear half of what he'd been saying. Did someone remind him?

"Have a seat," he offered.

Looking around the office, I realized today was not Brock's first day here. No way. It wasn't the fact that his desk was covered with neat stacks of paper or that a gym bag rested in the corner, next to a pair of sneakers. It was the pictures on the fully stocked credenza—framed photos of Brock proudly holding a champion belt high. Another photo of him with his arm around my father, both wearing sponsor shirts and beaming at the camera. Several more photos of Brock with my uncles—

My breath caught.

There, in the middle of all those photos, was a picture I recognized immediately, because it used to be mine. It used to sit on my nightstand back home, because it had been my favorite picture of Brock and me.

Brock was in a tux, his hair a spiky, glorious mess, and I was standing next to him, in a deep red ankle-length gown with a heart-shaped neckline. It was from my senior prom, and I couldn't stop staring at it, because that night, I felt *beautiful*. I felt like I belonged on Brock's arm. But it was more than that. That night, I'd been confident. I'd been strong. I'd been full of possibilities.

Without realizing what I was doing, I walked over to the credenza and reached out to pick up the photo, but stopped short of touching it. "How . . . how did you get this?"

"You left it behind the last time you left." There was a constricted pause, and then he said, "Considering what you said to me the last time we were standing this close, I figured you wouldn't care if I took it."

A knot of emotion formed in my throat and I had to look away from the photo. He'd been in my old bedroom? Obviously. I had no idea why he had that photo here, but I couldn't focus on it. My gaze focused on a large flat-screen TV hanging on the wall opposite the desk. Why in the world did he need a TV in his office?

Wait.

A more important observation kicked in, and my head flew back toward the credenza. There wasn't a single picture of his fiancée or them together. I glanced at his desk. Nothing there.

Interesting.

Wait again.

Not interesting. Not at all. Not even remotely.

I cleared my throat as I walked back to the chair and sat down. "When . . . when did you start here?"

"Three weeks ago." Instead of walking behind his desk, he leaned against the front of it, lazily crossing one ankle over the other as his hands clasped the edge of the desk. "But all of this isn't officially mine until Andre leaves at the end of the week."

My jaw was probably on the floor. "And when were you hired to become the GM?"

He eyed me curiously. "About a year ago, when Andre first announced his plans to return home."

I would've fallen out of my seat if I weren't sitting down. "And no one thought to tell me this?"

Brock inclined his head to the side. "Well, before you took the position, why would anyone tell you? Now, let me finish." He held up his hand when I opened my mouth. "You and I might not have spoken in years, but that doesn't mean I haven't been around. You know that. So you know I've been aware that up until Andrew convinced you to take this job, you've completely distanced yourself from the Academy."

Okay. He had a point there. "But he could've mentioned the fact that you were the new GM for *months* now. Or you could've said something Friday night."

"I could've." Brock gave me that grin, the one that used to make me blush and act like a fool. My eyes narrowed now. That grin increased. "Actually, I asked Andrew not to tell you."

That was an unexpected answer. "Why would you do that?"

"Because I knew you'd never agree to coming on board if you knew," he answered with some hesitation.

My hands opened in my lap as I tried to think of something to say, and I finally settled on, "I have no idea how to respond to that."

Brock's gaze flickered over my face and the line of his jaw softened. "It's been a really long time since you and I have sat and talked to one another. I know you have every reason to hate me. I don't blame you."

"I don't hate you." That twisting motion in my chest picked up. What I had said was true. Maybe at one point I did. Okay. I'm sure I had, but I'd never been one to hate anyone. It just wasn't in me. Well, I hated plenty of fictional characters, but some people would claim they didn't count. I drew in a shallow breath and repeated, "I don't hate you."

Brock was still as he stared at me, a flicker of surprise and relief mingling across his chiseled features. "I'm . . . I'm glad to hear that."

I pushed all that mess aside and focused. "Why are you even the GM? You've probably made enough money to live a very, very long time without having to worry about a paycheck."

"I have. When I retired from professional fighting two years ago, I could've lived quite comfortably for the rest of my life."

I wanted to ask why he'd retired so young. At his age, he still had a couple more years left, but I resisted the urge. "So why take this job?"

A frown started to appear. "Do you really need to ask me that?" Before I could respond, he lifted a hand, thrusting his fingers through his hair as he said, "Your father saved my life. That's not an exaggeration. You know that. If it hadn't been for him, I would've died on those streets. The Academy became my life and it is a part of me. This company is important to me, and even if I'm not fighting, representing the Academy, I still need to be a part of it."

Lowering my gaze, I squirmed in my chair. Of course I knew that. No matter what had happened, that would've never changed for him.

"I love scouting, looking for fresh talent," he continued. "As the GM, I can still do that. I can give back to your father for everything he did for me. I need to do that. Especially considering how badly I let him down."

"How in the world did you let my father down?" I asked, genuinely curious. "You've won championships for him. Brought so much attention to the—"

"That's not what I'm talking about." Tone serious, he held my gaze. "You never told him why you were at Mona's that night."

I stilled.

"If you had, he would've—"

My eyes snapped to his. "Brock."

"And I would've deserved everything I had coming to me," he continued, leaning forward. "And the only reason why I never told him you were there because of me was because you made me promise not to."

Closing my eyes, I pressed my lips together. I had made him promise not to say a word. I'd begged him, because I knew what would happen if he'd been honest. Brock would've lost everything.

The knot was back, expanding in my throat. I couldn't sit here and think and talk about these kinds of things if I was going to be able to make this job work. Curling my hands together, I opened my eyes. "What happened back then has nothing to do with now. It can't."

Brock leaned back and straightened.

"And I don't want to talk about it," I continued, struggling to keep my voice steady. "We don't need to talk about any of that for us to work together."

He was silent for a moment, his body deviously relaxed, but he was like a coiled cobra, and could strike at any moment. "I don't agree with that, but I'll let it go."

Some of the tension seeped out of my shoulders even though I had a feeling there was an unspoken "for now" at the end of what he said. "That's all, then? I would like to get my office set up and get to work."

Brock nodded and pushed off the desk. Walking around it, he scanned the paperwork on his desk. "I do believe we have a meeting today with the sales team. Two o'clock."

"Sounds good." I rose on oddly shaky legs and turned to the door. Everything felt surreal.

"Jillian."

Stopping, I faced him. "Yes?"

His shoulders rose with a deep breath as his gaze drifted over my face once more, and I wondered what he thought about how I looked now. "I really want this to work for us, Jillian," he said, and I felt the very sharp twisting motion in my chest give one powerful stab. "It's a second chance for us."

# Chapter 8

"Are you sure that'll be okay?" Avery asked as I watched Rhage prowl across the living room floor. "I just feel like I'm not giving you a lot of notice."

Readjusting my phone to my left shoulder, I picked up my feet and curled them under me before Rhage decided that whatever he was doing wasn't as interesting as attacking my legs would be. Sometimes I thought he mistook my legs for scratching posts. "I don't have anything planned for Friday. It's fine. What time will you guys be bringing Ava and Alex over?"

"You're amazing. You know that?" Avery paused, and I could hear Cam yelling Ava's name in the background. The child was probably racing through their house or jumping from the top of the staircase. A second later I could hear peals of Ava's laughter. "How does seven sound?"

"Perfect."

The sound of Cam and Ava's girlish giggles faded. "So, tell me all about the new job while I have a few minutes."

"It's been good." It was the following Wednesday, and I'd been at the Academy for a little over a week. Things were going surprisingly well. Mainly because I rarely saw Brock. He was either in his office, door closed, and when he wasn't, I made an art form out of avoiding him unless I had to deal with him during a meeting. Both of us were pretty busy, and I was focusing on advertising and renting out the additional spaces we had on the second floor. "I'm still getting adjusted, but I'm . . . I'm happy to be working there."

And that was the truth.

"I'm so happy to hear that—oh, by the way, before I forget, Brock ended up meeting up with Cam on Monday. They had lunch," she told me, and I guessed that explained why Brock was gone half the afternoon that day. "I think Brock made Cam's year. So you can thank him for that."

"Sure," I murmured.

There was a pause. "So, I know you guys kind of grew up together, but I would've never guessed it based on the way you acted toward him when he showed up at the restaurant."

Unsure of how to answer that question, I watched Rhage drop to the floor and then raise his fluffy behind. He was staring at the wall. When I talked to Avery last week when she called to invite me to breakfast, which I'd ultimately bailed on like a freak, she hadn't really touched on Brock. I skated by during that conversation without having to talk about him.

"I was just thinking about it, because I was chatting with Steph last night," she continued, and I let my head fall back against the couch as I swallowed a groan. Steph worked in the Philadelphia Academy, and when I first met her several years ago, I'd been outrageously envious of her. She was everything I'd wanted to be back then—beautiful, intelligent, kind, beyond confident, and strong, so strong. "She's coming home to visit her mom soon and we talked about getting together. Anyway, she asked about you," Avery said.

"Did she?"

"Yep," she replied. "She wondered how you and Brock were getting along. It wasn't like she was gossiping or anything like that," Avery quickly added. "I even asked why she was asking that question, and she really didn't answer, so it made me super curious."

While I stared at the ceiling, I saw the framed photo in Brock's office. Why did he have that photo in his office? The urge to talk about him, to talk to someone, rode me hard. Ever since I left Philadelphia, I never spoke to anyone about Brock. Not even when I saw Abby and Katie, two people who knew just how much I cared for him.

Talking about Brock brought forth a lot of wonderful memories at the same time that it dragged up things I didn't want to deal with.

Right at that moment, I heard a thump and looked over, brows snapping together. Rhage was by the wall, shaking his furry head. Obviously he'd attacked the wall and the wall won that battle. What a dumb cat.

"You still there, Jillian?"

"Yeah. Sorry." I wrapped an arm around my knees. "Brock and I . . . Well, we were really close, but we kind of grew apart." Okay. That sounded lame and clichéd, and I could do better. Avery deserved that. "All right. If I'm going to be honest, I was—I was in love with Brock and he thought of me as a little sister. He didn't feel the same way, and our friendship . . . eventually imploded because of it."

"Oh. Wow. You know who this reminds me of? Teresa and Jase."

One side of my lips twitched. "It's nothing like that."

"Well, yeah. Kind of. You know, Teresa was super in love with Jase when she was younger, and he wouldn't dare touch her because Cam would've murdered him in his sleep." Avery laughed. Teresa was Cam's younger sister and Jase had been his best friend since they were kids. "Anyway, look how that turned out. They're married and—"

"And Teresa is about to pop out a baby," I said. "I get what you're saying, but Brock was never secretly lusting after me like Jase was for Teresa."

"How do you know?" she asked.

I rolled my eyes. "Trust me, I know."

"Hmm. I don't know—wait. Wait. I better go. I hear Ava shrieking." Avery sighed. "You're going to come to brunch with Teresa and me on Sunday? You can tell me all about your date with Grady Saturday."

"Wow. News travels fast," I said, jolting a little at the reminder about the art show with Grady. I'd actually forgotten about that. It was on the tip of my tongue to tell her I had plans, but Avery knew I never had plans, and I remembered I'd promised myself nearly two weeks ago that I could turn her down. I did that once since then. I wouldn't do it again. "I will do brunch on Sunday."

"Really?" Avery's voice pitched with surprise.

"Yep. Looking forward to it."

"Awesome. Okay. I'll see you on Friday. Love ya!"

Saying my goodbyes, I lowered the phone and placed it on the end table. I was about to pick up the remote when there was a knock against my front door that sent Rhage darting under the coffee table.

Having no idea who could be here, I rose and walked the short distance to the door. Rhage peeked his head out, ears flattened as I rose on the tips of my sock-covered toes and peered through the tiny hole . . . which showed me nothing more than maybe a distorted view of a chest, but who really knew?

Peepholes were so pointless.

Settling back on my feet, I threw the deadbolt and cracked the door open. My stomach immediately pitched.

Under the bright overhead light, Brock stood in front of my apartment door. "Hey." He planted a hand against the frame of the door and gave me that half-smile while he kept his other hand behind his back. "You busy?"

For several seconds, I couldn't even find the words to formulate what I needed to say and then I blurted out, "How do you know where I live?"

"You're my employee. I have all your tax information, which has your address," he explained. My gaze snagged on the thin silver chain hanging from his neck, disappearing under the collar of his gray Henley. "And if I didn't have that, pretty sure Andrew would've given it to me."

My dad so would have, too. "Can I just point out that showing up at my apartment unannounced is kind of creepy?"

The look to his lazy grin said he probably hadn't thought of that and he also didn't care. "You going to let me in?"

I gripped the door handle. "Why are you here?"

"I wanted to talk to you."

My brows flew up. "And you couldn't have done that at work?"

"Nope," he replied.

"And since you've been looking at my employment documents, you would've seen my phone number. So you also couldn't have called me?"

"I don't like talking on the phone."

I narrowed my eyes. "Are you for real?"

"As real as a heart attack."

Jerking my head back, I stared way up at him. "Did you seriously just say that out loud?"

"Maybe I did." One shoulder rose as the grin reached his eyes. "Are you going to let me in, Jillybean?"

"Not if you call me that," I shot back.

He tipped his head down, and there was a soft flutter in my chest. "Why do you have a problem with me calling you that?"

"Maybe because I'm not twelve years old anymore?"

"Hmm." Brock straightened. "I doubt that's the reason."

"Whatever," I muttered. "What do you want to talk about?"

"I'll tell you if you let me in." His gaze turned shrewd. "Would you be more open to letting me in if you knew I brought something for you?"

The center of my cheeks heated. "You shouldn't have brought anything for me."

"Well, it's too late for that, because I did." He cocked his head to the side. "And I think once you see it, you'll be really, really happy you let me in."

"I don't care about what you've brought."

"I don't think you'd say that if you knew what I have."

I shifted my weight from one foot to the other as I glanced behind him. Cool air was drifting into my apartment, and if I weren't careful, Rhage would sneak out. I nibbled on my lower lip as I weighed my options. Letting him in wasn't like I was opening myself to anything other than having a conversation with him.

"Decisions, decisions," Brock murmured.

Rolling my eyes, I stepped back and grumbled, "Come in."

Brock dropped his hand and walked inside, his head turning as his gaze swept over me. I closed the door.

"Nice socks," he commented. "You know, it's like you're recognizing two seasons right now—summer *and* winter."

I glanced down at myself. Oh crap! I'd forgotten I was wearing cotton sleep shorts paired with knee-high socks. And these were *short* shorts. Grateful that I was wearing a long cardigan over my shirt, I self-consciously tugged on the hem of my shorts while he looked around the apartment. I saw he had a little brown bag dangling from his fingertips.

"So," I said, fiddling with the sleeves on my cardigan, "what did you bring me?"

"Oh, so now you're curious about what's in the bag?"

Crossing my arms, I stared at him while I hoped it wasn't obvious that I wasn't wearing a bra, because I could feel my nipples pressing against my shirt.

Brock chuckled as he lifted the bag and reached inside, pulling out a small white carton. He then turned, spying the small kitchen. "So, how long have you lived here?"

"Um, I don't know." I watched him walk over to the island and place the carton and bag on it. "I think I moved in here about four years ago."

"Nice place." His gaze strayed to the stack of books on the other end of the island, and a fond smile appeared as he started to open the carton. "It's safe here?"

"Yeah. There have never been any problems here." I crept closer. "Most of the people who live here are married or work in D.C and commute." My gaze dropped to his back. Did he ever get the large phoenix tattoo colored and filled in? I bet he did and it looked amazing. Then again, his back with all those ropey muscles always looked amazing. "So, where . . . where do you live now?"

"I bought a house outside of Shepherdstown," he told me. "Got an amazing view of the river. You need to see it."

I stopped walking, thinking his fiancée might not be too keen on that. Then again, I doubted she would see me as a threat.

Brock turned sideways, sliding the carton toward where I stood. I glanced over, and I stopped thinking when I saw what he'd brought.

"Glazed doughnuts," Brock said. "Just glazed. Nothing weird hidden inside them. I know how much you used to hate biting into something and having no idea it's filled with cream or fruit. They're fresh, too. Picked them up at the bakery in Shepherdstown that makes them all day."

I did hate biting into any food and having something unexpectedly squirt into my mouth. It was freaking gross, but I wasn't focused on that aversion.

Sitting atop wax paper really were large glazed doughnuts.

It was so simple. Just glazed doughnuts. Nothing fancy or spectacular. But he *remembered*, and I didn't know why that meant anything to me. I was sure serial killers remembered things about their victims, but I felt some of the tension easing out of my stiff muscles as I blinked back sudden hot tears.

Gah, I was so over-emotional. It was just doughnuts. "Thank you." I cleared my throat. "That's really nice."

His gaze flew to mine, and I hastily lowered my chin, walking past him into the kitchen. "Jillian—"

"You're eating one if I am," I said, snatching several sheets off the paper-towel roll. God, I was such a damn mess, but I . . . I missed this—missed having someone in my life who knew me inside and out, because no one, *no one* knew me like Brock had. I turned around only when I was sure I didn't look like I was seconds from exploding into tears, and went to the island, placing the towels on the counter. "I mean, I'm not going to eat three gigantic doughnuts."

"Since when?"

A strangled laugh escaped me. "Well, I'm not seventeen anymore."

"I can see that."

A fine shiver coursed over my skin as I looked up. There was an intense, almost predatory glint to his stare, one I didn't understand. And it suddenly struck me, really hit me, that after six years, Brock Mitchell was standing in my apartment, in *my* world, and I would never in a hundred years have expected this.

But there he was, larger than life itself, turning what was a roomy apartment into something that now felt entirely too small. He was a one hundred percent grown man who was not just breathtaking to behold, but a walking legend in the world of mixed martial arts. More than that, though, he was a man who overcame such a terrible childhood, beating statistics and naysayers. Demolishing everyone's doubt as he rose through the ranks, suffering a career-threatening injury to come back and win it all, over and over.

Brock had fire in him.

He always had.

And that was what had drawn me to him from the moment I'd seen him in the living room, glaring up at my father even though he was afraid and hungry.

The kitchen island separated us, but he reached over it with one long arm. The Henley stretched against his muscles as he swept his thumb along my skin, right over the deep indentation left in my cheek.

I sucked in a startled breath as that touch burned its way through me. My senses shorted out and a wild heat swept down the entire front of my body, tightening the tips of my breasts. He was only touching my cheek, my scar, and my body was flipping out.

Brock held my stare for a moment too long and then exhaled heavily, dropping his hand. I had no idea what he was thinking as he shifted his gaze away from me, but he had touched the scar, and I could only imagine it was something I probably didn't want to hear.

Unnerved, I grabbed the ends of my cardigan and yanked them together. Time to get this conversation back on track. "So, why did you—"

"Damn," he cursed, eyes narrowing. "What in the hell just darted across your floor?"

I turned just in time to see the tail end of Rhage's brown and white butt scurrying behind the couch. "Oh, that's Rhage, my cat. He hates people, so it's best to pretend like he doesn't exist."

"Rage?" He looked back at me, brows raised. "That's an interesting name."

"It's based on a vampire—a book character."

"Glad you clarified it was a book character," he teased as he reached over and grabbed a paper towel. "Did you get enough of these? We might need one more."

"Shut up." My lips twitched as I realized something else about Brock hadn't changed over the years. He loved to tease. Never maliciously, but he was always playful.

"For a second I thought you had a rat." He moved to one of the barstools. "Sit with me."

"Do you want anything to drink?"

"A water would be fine."

Of course he would ask for a water while eating a doughnut, I thought as I grabbed myself a Coke, because why would I purposely drink water when I had carbonated goodness within reach? I grabbed a bottle of water and placed it in front of him as I walked around the island and sat on the barstool that forced him to sit on my left.

I hopped up, only realizing then that my hair was pulled back from my face. I started to reach for the pin securing the length in place, but stopped myself. What was the point? Not like he hadn't seen it—and seen it when it had been a hell of a lot worse than this. Plus he'd just touched the one scar, so . . .

Annoyed with myself, I bit into the doughnut and nearly moaned as my taste buds practically orgasmed. It had been so long since I ate the fried, sugary yumminess.

"You like?" Brock asked, his heavy hooded gaze on me.

Mouth full, I nodded.

His smile was swift and wide. "Good." His gaze flicked away from me a moment. "You know what this reminds me of?"

I raised my brows since my mouth was full.

"When we used to sit in the kitchen late at night, because you decided you wanted brownies or cake," he said.

Swallowing the sticky goodness, I picked up my can of soda. I didn't want to reminisce with him, but I couldn't stop myself. "Actually, *you* wanted brownies or cake."

He chuckled. "That's a revisionist history of events."

I cast him a sidelong look.

"Okay. I was the one who wanted to eat the *baked* brownies or cake, but you wanted to make it because you wanted the raw cake and brownie mix." His thick lashes lowered. "You still do that?"

"Never." I did just that two days ago.

The look on his face said he knew the truth. Neither of us talked as we finished off the doughnuts, leaving one in the carton—one that I would definitely eat once he left.

"So, I came here to talk to you." Brock wiped his fingers off on the paper towel as his gaze slid in my direction. "Because I'm disappointed."

I frowned as I cleaned the stickiness from my fingers. "In what?"

"You."

"Excuse me?" I leaned back.

Rolling the towel up, he dropped it in the brown paper bag. "When you decided to stay and work with me—"

"For you," I corrected.

"*For* me." He dipped his chin and grinned, peering up at me through those impossibly thick lashes. "I didn't think you would spend the entire time hiding from me."

Oh crap.

I fixed a blank expression on my face. "I don't know what you're talking about."

"Really?" His tone was sly. "The only time I see you is when we're in a meeting with the staff."

"That sounds normal," I argued.

"And whenever I happen to walk out of my office, you're suddenly on the phone."

I bit the inside of my cheek. "Well, I'm making a lot of calls, checking the prices of advertisements and trying to find—"

"Uh-huh. And it's real convenient those calls only seem to take place when I'm not in my office."

I forced a casual shrug.

"And how do I know that?" He rested his chin in his palm, looking way too smug. "I checked today. I called Steve. You know, he sits directly in front of you, and I asked if you were on the phone."

Oh no.

"He said no, but guess what?"

I said nothing.

Brock waited.

Sighing, I folded my arms. "What?"

"You were on the phone a second after I stepped out of my office."

"How coincidental," I murmured. "You have some really bad timing."

He arched a brow. "That's bullshit."

"*Language*, Mr. Mitchell," I mimicked.

Surprise flickered over his face and then he threw his head back and laughed, exposing his neck. And who knew a neck could be so attractive? I didn't, but his was.

Without warning, Rhage jumped up on the island.

Brock lowered his chin. "Well, hello there."

76

The cat looked at him, ears perked and then twitched. He stared at Brock like he had no idea why another male was in the house. It would be a valid thing to wonder about.

"Sorry. He has really bad manners." I sighed. "Rhage, get down."

Plopping his butt down on the counter, he lifted one leg and slowly licked his paw as he eyed Brock.

"He listens well," Brock said dryly as he reached toward him.

"Don't do that!" I warned, but it was too late. His fingers were already within biting and scratching territory. Cringing, I waited for the inevitable claw swipe.

It never came.

Rhage lowered his paw and stretched his head out, sniffing the tips of Brock's fingers. Then Brock moved. Rhage stayed still as he scratched him behind the ear. After a few seconds, Brock removed his hand and Rhage hopped down, his kitty claws clicking as he pranced down the hall, toward the bedroom.

"What the hell?" I whispered, awed and a bit annoyed. "He hates everyone. Including me."

"Odd. Seems like a pretty chill cat." Turning back to me, Brock rested his arms on the island. "Anyway, you're avoiding me."

I was still fixated on the fact Rhage didn't bite him or at least hiss at him. My cat was a traitorous bastard of the worst sort.

"And I want you to stop."

"Huh?" I blinked, focusing on him.

He leaned in, his gaze locked with mine. "I get there is some ... there is some shit between us, and God knows if I could go back and change things, I would. You have no idea how badly I wish I didn't have my head stuck so far up my own ass back then. I can't go back though. Can never do that."

I clammed up, my jaw locking down so hard I was surprised I didn't undo all the work doctors had invested in repairing my face.

"But you know, when Andrew said you agreed to the job, I was so . . . so *fucking* relieved, because I knew then I was going to not only get to see you, but finally talk to you." He sat back and slowly shook his head. "Reconnecting with you means a lot to me, Jillian. I know I'm now your boss, and I know how this sounds, trust me, but I want to be friends with you."

I had no idea what to say.

"And I know we can't go back and pretend that I didn't . . ." A muscle flexed in his jaw as his gaze moved to the opposite wall lined with cabinets. "That I didn't let you down in all the worst ways. I know I've apologized before. I said I was sorry a hundred times."

Brock had.

"But those apologies aren't enough," he added.

I studied his profile, dread building as I started to understand him. "You don't have to be friends with me because of what happened, because you feel guilty or—"

"It's not that. Not what I mean at all." His gaze flew to mine and he leaned in toward me, leaving only a few scant inches between us. "I don't want you to come to work and stress about having to avoid me. I want you to be comfortable there." A lock of brown hair fell forward, brushing his forehead. "I know what I'm asking for is a lot. I know that there's a good chance I don't even deserve it, but I want us to be friends, Jillian."

Friends.

God, at one time, hearing him say that would've shattered my poor heart into smithereens, but now? I didn't know how to feel about that. Brock and I, as silly as it sounded back then with the age difference, *had* been best friends. Losing all that girlish hope that one day we'd have that romance-book happily-ever-after had been terrible. Ending the friendship had hurt worse, because when I cut him out of my life, I lost my closest friend—my partner in crime and adventure.

"Can we do that?" he asked. "I'm being for real. When I said last Monday this felt like a second chance, I meant that. Can we at least try?"

Honestly, I wasn't sure—had no idea if I could truly be friends with Brock. Not because he hadn't returned my feelings once upon a time. It didn't even have anything to do with what had happened to me the night Brock claimed he'd let me down in the worst ways possible, because I didn't blame him for what happened.

But I wasn't sure if we could be friends without me . . . without me falling deep again, slipping under, and catching the kind of feelings for him that would inevitably end in another heartbreak.

It wasn't that I was that weak when it came to the opposite sex, but Brock had a kind of magnetism that drew you in, even when you resisted. It was that teasing playfulness of him, the way he doled out affection once he got to know you and how he easily, with no effort, made you feel like you were the most important person in his world. It was how he made you forget that all those things didn't necessarily make you a special snow-flake. It was just how he was, and even the brightest and strongest women out there could be sucked in.

But Brock wasn't available. He was engaged. There was a barbed-wire-covered wall between us, a deep line in the sand that would never allow me to even ponder those thoughts. Not that I was thinking them now.

"And if you think we can't, what do I have to do to change your mind?" His jaw softened. "More doughnuts? I'm sure you still like Reese's Pieces. I can include a weekly supply as a part of your employment package."

I started to smile, so I curved my fingers over my mouth.

"What do you say?" he asked, nudging my arm with his.

Glancing up at him as I lowered my hand, I decided I could at least try, because it would make working together easier. I *was* getting tired of pretending I was on the phone. "Okay."

The smile that spread across his face proved a man could be masculine and beautiful, because that smile robbed the air right out of my lungs, and I immediately had to picture those barbed-wire-covered walls and the mile-deep line in the sand.

*Friends.*

I could do this.

# Chapter 9

"I know what I'm doing."

"No." Brock, who was currently hovering behind my chair Friday morning, reached around me and snatched the mouse out from underneath my hand. "I think you need to click that."

"No, I don't." I smacked his hand away, taking control of the mouse as I tried to move the graphic over so it was centered. Brock's sigh stirred the hair along my left cheek, sending a shiver curling down my spine.

"All you have to do is click on the centering button."

"Yeah, I already did that." I leaned to the right when he tried grabbing for the mouse again. I swatted his hand again. "Don't you have something better to do?" I asked, scooting my chair back, which forced him to step aside. I looked up as he moved to lean against my desk. "Approving advertisements is my job. I would already have this done if you weren't in here trying to backseat computer click me."

"Backseat computer click?" His forehead creased. "That sounds kind—"

"Don't even say it."

An innocent look crossed his face. "Apparently it's not me who has their mind in the gutter. I was going to say it sounded like a video game."

"Uh-huh." Slowly, carefully, I moved the mouse just a fraction of a centimeter, successfully centering the block of text. "Ah-ha! Done."

"You're so talented."

I shot him a look, and he grinned.

Paul appeared in the open doorway. He was a tall and lithe, middle-aged man with fair blond hair and bright blue eyes. Dressed in the Lima Academy polo and black nylon pants, he blended in with any number of the sales associates out on the floor, but he was one of the trainers from the second floor. He'd been here since the Academy opened.

I didn't know him very well since the trainers and scouts were mostly Brock's responsibility, but whenever he looked at me, like he did now, I had the strong impression that he thought my position was pretty useless.

Most of the employees appeared to accept me, like Andre had insisted would be the case, but Paul looked at me like I was about as wanted as a cold sore.

He also reminded me of that dickhead who used to work in Philly, the one who cornered me in the supply room.

"Mr. Mitchell, do you have a moment?" Paul asked, his glacial gaze moving from me to Brock. "I have a couple of new students that I'd like you to check out." He raised a file. "And see if you'd like to get them on film."

"Be right there." Tapping the bridge of my nose like I was five, Brock rose as he winked, and then swaggered out of the office.

Of course I watched him.

I couldn't help myself. He gave good rear, which was annoying. I mean, where did he get those trousers and why did they fit his ass so well? Why?

Shaking my head, I turned my attention back to the computer

and finished tweaking and approving the ads that had been submitted.

A couple hours later, after the daily sales meeting in the back conference room, I was gathering up the reports from the table when Brock asked, "So, you got any big plans for the weekend?"

I glanced over at him. His head was bowed as he scanned one of the sales reports that Jeffery had turned in. "Um, tonight, I'm babysitting Avery and Cam's kids. It's their date night."

"That's nice of you to do on a Friday night," he remarked and then asked, "Is that how you normally spend your Friday nights?"

Cradling the stack of papers to my chest, I stared at the top of his dark head. "Not usually."

"So you normally go out?"

I started to frown. "Sometimes." Okay, that was a total lie, but the last thing I wanted Brock to know was that I was sitting at home with my mean, traitorous cat, alone and eating brownie batter. "Tomorrow I'm going to see an art exhibit."

Brock slowly lifted his head. His eyes narrowed until only a thin slit of obsidian could be seen. "An art exhibit? That sounds . . . stimulating."

The mocking, teasing tone pricked at my nerves. "Yes. I'm going with Grady."

"Grady? That little guy you were at dinner with?"

Little guy? "He's not little."

"He's little."

"Maybe compared to your gigantic, Godzilla-sized self, he's little, but by normal human standards, he's not."

A smirk graced his full mouth as he leaned back in the chair at the head of the table. "I always thought you liked my gigantic, Godzilla-sized self. If I remember correctly, you loved that I could pick you up and throw you several feet in the air and into

83

the pool." He tapped the corner of his lips. "And I could do that because of my size."

My cheeks flushed as I hastily glanced over my shoulder, grateful that none of the employees were anywhere near the conference room. "Yeah, well, I'm not ten anymore, Brock."

"Huh." He folded his arms on the table and leaned forward. "I also clearly remember doing that when you were twenty."

The heat in my cheeks continued. "Is there a point to this conversation?"

He chuckled, glancing back at his paperwork. "Not really."

Eyeing him, I started to turn and then stopped, facing him once more. We were . . . friends now. Friends meant I got to ask him about his weekend. "So, do you have any plans?"

"After work, I'm heading back to Philadelphia," he answered, still looking down at the pages.

I guessed he was going home to Kristen. Or maybe she was at his home outside of Shepherdstown. They were engaged, so I imagined they lived together. "Are you keeping the house in Pennsylvania?"

Brock shook his head. "No. I'm in the process of selling it."

"So, the move down here is permanent?"

"It's looking that way."

A weird little burst of happiness lit up my chest, and I ignored it, not even wanting to look into the reasoning behind it. I wanted to ask him about his fiancée, but it seemed too weird to do so. "Well, have a good weekend, Brock."

"You too," he said, and when I turned and reached the door, he spoke again. "Is the little man known as Grady someone you're seeing seriously?"

Rolling my eyes, I twisted back around. I wasn't sure what was going to happen with Grady, but he didn't need to know that. "I'm looking forward to seeing him tomorrow."

Brock looked up just then, a slight smile on his face. "I know. I can hear all the excitement in your voice. Have fun looking at . . . artwork."

I had this distinct feeling he was baiting me, but I really didn't understand why. "I *will*."

His head tilted to the side. "You deserve better."

"What?"

Putting the papers down once more, he held my gaze. "You deserve better than him."

For a moment, I couldn't even respond, and then I laughed. "Are you feeling okay?"

His jaw tightened. "I'm feeling perfectly fine."

"I'm asking because you're telling me I deserve better than a man you don't even know anything about." Anger, sweet and empowering, rushed me. "And frankly, it is not your place or your business to even suggest something like that." On a roll, I lifted my chin. "And if you really want us to be friends, you can't say crap like that to me."

Silence stretched out between us and then he spoke.

"I don't know you anymore," he said quietly, and when I didn't respond—couldn't because the statement caught me off-guard—he tipped his head back. "I know the old Jillian. Could sit here all day and tell you about her, but this Jillian? I don't know her." A wry grin appeared. "But I want to."

Thinking maybe something went wrong with his brain, all I could do was stare at him.

"By the way, I want something to be clear between us," he said, holding my wide gaze. "There is not a single moment in the last two weeks that I've looked at you and seen the little girl I used to throw in the pool. I see a woman—a beautiful woman. Don't tell yourself otherwise."

\*    \*    \*

That night, as I lay in bed, unable to force my brain to slow down long enough to fall asleep or to get engrossed in the book I was reading, I stared up at my ceiling, slightly obsessing over what Brock had said to me before I left.

It wasn't the beautiful part.

Brock tossed out flattery like it was going out of style. Considering what had happened to my face, I wasn't bad. I could be passably pretty on a good day. Beautiful I was not.

No, it wasn't that at all, even as nice as it had sounded coming from those well-formed lips. It was the part where he said he didn't see a little girl when he looked at me, and all I could think about was the day I'd thought I was going to change that between us.

*Standing in my old bedroom, I didn't need to look around to see that it looked exactly like it had when I left three years ago.*

*Little girl bed.*

*Little girl dresser.*

*Little girl nightstand.*

*Posters of my favorite books that had been adapted into movies were tacked to the wall. An old teddy bear sat on the window seat, nestled between blue and pink throw pillows, their colors still vibrant as the day my mom had placed them there. Bookshelves lined the entirety of one wall, breaking only in two sections to allow entry to the closet and the attached bathroom.*

*Hundreds of books were stacked into those shelves, meticulously organized by genre and then by author's last name. Mom had started my love of reading when I was a teen, and I devoured historical romances, and those old, musty-smelling paperbacks were stacked one on top of the other, three rows deep. An entire bookcase was dedicated to young adult and then another held all the adult romances I'd collected, or hoarded, ranging from sweet to downright blush-*

*inducing steaminess. The final, the fourth bookcase, was half-full. It contained a few thrillers and old textbooks I didn't sell back, but also didn't have room in my dorm at Shepherd to store.*

*Being in this bedroom brought back a lot of good memories. Me curled up on the window seat reading. Me lying on my side in the double bed late at night with only the small lamp casting just enough light to read. Me standing at the other window, the one that over-looked the driveway, watching Brock drive away after he was over for one of the many family dinners.*

*Being in this room also made me feel like I was still that little girl that was never going to grow up and leave, but I wasn't her anymore. I'd done just that.*

*I walked over to the dresser, where I placed the Saint Sebastian medallion I'd found in a hippie store in Shepherdstown. It was about the size of a quarter, dangling from an old sterling silver necklace. I'd once read that he was the patron saint of athletes, so whenever I came across one, I always picked it up for Brock. Carefully gathering it up, I placed it in the little zipper pocket inside my purse.*

*Stepping in front of the full-length mirror, I barely recognized the person staring back at me. I'd left my hair down, spent about an hour with the curling iron so the thick hair fell in waves. I'd managed to coax my bangs to the side and they were held in place with about a can of hair spray.*

*I was actually wearing eyeliner, which had taken about five tries to get right, and I still wasn't sure I'd applied it to my upper lid correctly after watching several thirteen-year-olds giving tutorials on YouTube.*

*Nothing makes you feel inept more than seeing a tween apply makeup better than you.*

*But shimmery lilac eyeshadow warmed my brown eyes, the red lipstick made my lips look fuller, and the bronze highlighter on my cheeks complemented my darker skin tone.*

*Gone were the usual baggy, shapeless shirts and skirts I usually wore. I'd bought this dress specifically for tonight, and I'd never worn anything like it before. It was black and tight around the chest, showing off what I normally hid. The waist gathered under the breasts and was loose around the belly and hips, camouflaging the rounded hips no amount of cardio would get rid of. The flirty hem of the dress skimmed the top of my thighs.*

*I was even wearing heels—black heels with all these straps.*

*There was a good chance I'd break my neck tonight, but I felt . . . I felt pretty. Maybe even . . . sexy.*

*Heat invaded my cheeks, and I rolled my eyes at myself. Fiddling with the bangle around my wrist, I turned and checked the time. I'd need to leave soon. My stomach dropped a little, and I forced myself to take a deep breath as I turned back to the mirror.*

*Tiny little balls of nerves filled my stomach. I'd spent so much time with Brock, years really. Spending time together in the pool in the backyard, when the summer days were long and the nights even longer. Sharing dinners with my family and sitting side by side on the porch swing. Chasing after him and my younger uncles when they left to play ball or headed to the Academy to train. Katie had been right earlier. I had been Brock's shadow since I was eight and he was fourteen. Most boys his age would've been annoyed with a girl snapping at his heel every waking second he was around her, but Brock never made me feel like I was unwanted or that he was annoyed.*

*In spite of our age difference, he'd become my closest friend. When my uncles or cousins didn't want me tagging along, he was there to stand up for me and always made sure I was included. He talked to me about things—about his father and his mother—things I knew he spoke to no one else about, especially the girls he hooked up with. We shared secrets and stories. When high school became . . . became hard, he was a shelter whenever I saw him. He never treated me a certain way because of who my father was or what my family did. And when every guy at my school had been too afraid to ask me out because of said crazy family, it had been Brock who had escorted me to my senior prom after I'd said I wasn't going.*

*I smiled at the memory.*

*Prom had been insane. I was seventeen and he had just turned twenty-three. Besides the fact that he was the oldest guy there and that alone would've been super weird, Brock was already quietly famous among those who watched the fights. Pretty sure he spent more time posing for photographs than we did dancing, but if I hadn't been in love with him before, I fell hard and fast then.*

*He'd been like a brother to me up until, well, I started staring a little too long at the way his arms flexed or how his bottom lip was fuller than the top one. And then he'd gotten his first tattoo at seventeen, one of many, and I stopped thinking of him as a brother. He just never stopped seeing me as a little sister.*

*But tonight would be different.*

*"I'm ready," I said out loud, to my reflection. "I'm more than ready."*

I had been ready that Saturday night, ready to change how things were between us, except that night ended with him . . . with him meeting the girl who would become his fiancée and me . . . with me ending up in the hospital, almost dead.

Grady was holding my hand as we walked out of the exhibit hall and into the rapidly cooling evening air of early October. It was later than I had thought I'd be out. We ended up grabbing a light dinner from one of the restaurants on German Street and then we'd stopped to get coffee before heading to the Center for Contemporary Arts.

It had been a nice night, really nice.

The conversation had been easy and it seemed like we never ran out of things to talk about. He told me about growing up in western Maryland and spending his summers helping his grandfather on their family farm and how he still went back there quite often. I explained what it was like to grow up in the Lima household. Even though he knew nothing about mixed martial arts or anything remotely like that, he was genuinely interested in what I had to say.

And now as we were walking to where we'd parked, my head was in a weird place. It was strange being back on the campus since I'd dropped out with three semesters left to graduate. Looking around now, with the students milling about between the dorms, I remembered what it was like before the weekend I came home and after I'd finally returned to college.

I found myself thinking about the time I learned that Brock was engaged to Kristen. Since I'd avoided keeping tabs on him, I was usually successful in zoning out my family whenever they talked about him. This time I hadn't been so successful.

It had been right after I'd made the decision to leave college. After nearly dying, and that wasn't an exaggeration. I'd seriously almost died, like dead, dead. I had the scars to prove it. I couldn't bring myself to waste away hours sitting in the class-room and studying, learning things I'd never apply in life. Looking back now, removed from the intensity of everything, I knew it wasn't really a thirst to live life that drove me to with-draw from classes.

I'd been depressed.

It was common, I'd discovered later, that after a traumatic event, people became depressed, oftentimes years after the event. I'd been restless, with no desire to go to class, to be around people, and even unable to read for any long period of time. Nothing had interested me.

I'd dropped out of college, returned home, a bittersweet homecoming for my parents since I knew they wanted me there but not under those circumstances.

Mom had pulled me aside one evening, after dinner, to tell me that Brock had proposed to Kristen and she had accepted. It had been two years after *that night*.

Two years and . . . Brock was on Pay-Per-View. He was engaged to the girl he'd flirted with that night, and it finally hit me then that there had been nothing that Brock had to get over, because he hadn't had those kind of feelings for me. None. He was moving on, because nothing was holding him back.

His life was exploding in all the best ways while mine . . . mine had imploded, and everything I'd ever wanted—a degree, working for my family, traveling, being happy, and being in love—had felt like it was out of my grasp.

So I stayed home for six more months, found the job at the insurance firm, and moved back to Martinsburg.

And now I was starting to get back those things I once wanted. I was happy. I was working for my family and I . . . Drawing in a shallow breath, I peeked up at Grady.

We stopped by my car, and we stood facing one another.

He was not *little*.

Grady was at least an inch or two taller than me, so I could still wear normal heels, but yeah, he was short compared to Brock. He had to be close to six foot three. Obviously not Godzilla-sized, but—

Oh my God, I was not thinking about *him* while I was on a date with Grady.

"So, I was wondering," Grady said, and the centers of his cheeks pinked. Adorable. "If you'd like to grab dinner sometime this week?"

I started to smile, and ducked my chin a little. "That . . . that would be nice."

"So that's a yes?"

I nodded.

"I'm glad you said yes." He squeezed my hand. "I was prepared to grovel to get another date."

Another date? That sounded . . . really nice. "Groveling not necessary."

"Well, it's . . . it's getting late," he said, his gaze finding and holding mine.

"It is."

He stepped in to me, and his hand coasted away from mine, running up to my elbow. The breath he let out was shaky. Grady tilted his head to the side, lining up his mouth with mine, and I knew then he was going to kiss me.

He was really going to do it!

It had been so long since I'd been kissed, even been in the position to be kissed, and this was going to happen. His pale lashes had lowered. His eyes were closed. His mouth was coming right at mine.

Grady leaned in, slightly lowering his head, and I closed my eyes.

At the last second, without thinking, I turned my head, and Grady's lips brushed across my cheek. Warmth hit me, a mixture of embarrassment and disappointment. Why had I done that? He wanted to kiss me. I wanted him to do that.

Didn't I?

Yes, I told myself as I opened my eyes and met his questioning ones. I was just gun shy. I forced a shaky half-smile, one that probably looked more like a grimace. "I had a really good time today."

"Truly?" he asked.

I nodded. "I did."

His gaze searched mine and then he smiled a boyish, charming smile. "Then it's dinner next week? Wednesday?"

"Wednesday," I confirmed.

This time when Grady leaned in, I didn't pull away, but it was because he was giving me a hug. I returned it, telling myself that if he tried to kiss me again, I wouldn't turn away.

I *wouldn't*.

# Chapter 10

The massive omelet was steaming hot and full of nearly every meat possible—sausage, Italian sausage, bacon, Canadian bacon, and ham. Of course, I squeezed some veggies in there. It had peppers and mushrooms.

And cheese.

Lots of cheese, and I didn't care that cheese wasn't a veggie.

I'd never been more excited about anything in my life.

Avery went the steak and eggs route with a side order of extra crispy bacon. And it was a *huge* T-bone steak. Across from us was a very pregnant Teresa who had a stack of pancakes, a side bowl of fruit, and an order of sausage links.

I loved that these women ate as much as me.

Sunday breakfast was a tradition that had started back in Pennsylvania and had carried over to the West Virginia girls. I'd been invited to join them the moment I showed up at Shepherd all those years ago, because I'd met them through mutual friends. I'd bailed on them more than I joined them, but that was something I was actively changing.

I dug into my omelet as Avery's phone lit up. She placed her knife down and picked up the phone, laughing softly. "Oh man."

Avery extended the phone to the center of the table and there was a picture of Jack, Jase's son from a previous relationship, who was currently giving a very happy Ava a piggyback ride.

Jack was somewhere in his double digits of life. I was terrible at figuring out how old kids were. I guessed it was something that came along with producing them. He looked so much like Jase it made you do a double take. Rich russet-colored hair and beautiful gray eyes, he was a baby heartbreaker in the making. Next to them were two leashed tortoises. It looked like Jack had been trying to walk them when Ava climbed on his back.

"Oh, Ava is in heaven." Teresa popped a piece of watermelon into her mouth and then looked down as a bit of juice plopped on her swollen stomach. She sighed.

"Ava's in love with Jack," Avery explained to me and then grinned at Teresa. "Whenever Jack comes over, Ava is literally one step behind him, like his little shadow. It's so adorable."

"It is," Teresa agreed, stabbing a sausage link with a fork. "Which I'm sure Cam will be thrilled with once Ava gets older."

Avery rolled her eyes. "He's going to be one of those dads. You know? The kind that cleans a shotgun in front of the boys Ava dates."

Teresa arched a brow. "Does Cam even own a gun?"

"No, but I bet he will once Ava hits sixteen."

I laughed as I cut another large section of the omelet.

"Thank you again for watching Ava and Alex for us," Avery said for the hundredth time. "You have no idea how hard it is to get out on time when you have kids." She pointed her fork at Teresa. "At least with Jack, he's always been old enough to not need constant attention. Just wait until the baby comes. Getting laid becomes an Olympic sport. Thanks to Jillian, we were finally able to hopefully *not* make baby number three."

Chalk that up to things I never needed to know happened when I watched their kids.

"Yeah, but we have built-in babysitting," Teresa replied. "Jack."

"True," Avery said.

Teresa giggled as she rubbed her swollen belly. "Either way, if there's a will, there's a way," she said, dipping the sausage link in a pool of syrup. "By the way, Jillian, don't think we didn't notice how you skimmed the details on your date."

"Mmm?" I mumbled around a mouthful of egg and cheese.

Avery raised her brows. "So, you said you had a good time and that you guys were getting dinner on Wednesday, but did you guys, you know . . ." She elbowed me in the side. "Did you kiss? Did you do more?"

"Did you have sex?" Teresa asked.

I coughed, nearly choking on a piece of diced bacon. "No. No sex. Not that there is anything wrong with sex on the first date," I hastily advised, because seriously, I saw nothing wrong with that. It just wasn't how I moved since that seemed fast and I was like a three-legged turtle when it came to relationships. "He did try to kiss me."

"Try?" Teresa's brow creased.

Reaching for my glass of Coke, I shrugged a shoulder. "I turned my head when he leaned down. I didn't mean to. I just wasn't thinking."

"Oh," Avery said, sounding disappointed.

"What?" I asked.

"Nothing." She cut off a piece of steak.

I took a drink and then placed the glass down. "That didn't sound like nothing."

"I think it was more of a '*if you want to be kissed by someone you don't turn your head from them*' kind of thing," Teresa explained.

"I want to be kissed by him!" I exclaimed, and then flushed when the snowy-haired woman across from us looked over at me. "I do. It's just . . . I don't have a lot of experience."

Teresa's eyes widened like blue saucers. "Are you——?"

"No. I'm not a virgin," I said, shifting uncomfortably. "I've only been in one relationship."

"That guy was a dick," Avery said.

"Yeah, I know that, but there wasn't anyone before that? After him?" Teresa asked.

I shook my head. "It's not easy for me . . ." I trailed off as I scooped up a huge piece of omelet. What was I about to say to them? That it wasn't easy because I wasn't entirely comfortable with the way I looked?

God, that sounded lame when you said it out loud. Hell, I hadn't been exactly comfortable *before* everything. Would they truly understand that? Teresa and Avery were very pretty women, beautiful in their own ways.

"I just suck at the whole dating thing," I continued. "I have really bad taste in guys. I mean, I'm not saying Grady is bad. It's just that . . . I don't know what I'm saying. Please ignore me."

Teresa glanced over at Avery and then leaned forward as far as her belly would allow, which wasn't far at all. "We all sucked at dating. Especially Avery."

"True," she said happily, slicing off another section of meat. "There are times when I look back, I'm still shocked that Cam and I got together. I was . . . well, I was totally closed off to the idea of dating anyone. He was just determined to change that."

She leaned against the seat, her hand going back to her belly. "You know, I don't think I ever told you this, but the guy I dated all the way back in high school was a real dickhead. He hit me."

I nearly dropped my fork. She hadn't told me that. "I didn't know."

"And let's just say, when Cam found out, things went down shit creek with no paddle. But the point is, I've had crappy taste in guys too. It's nothing to be embarrassed about, especially not when you've recognized you had that issue—*had* as in past tense. And it's okay if you turned your head when Grady was about to kiss you. Maybe you're just not ready for the relationship to get to that level."

Nodding slowly, I poked at what was left of my omelet. I wasn't nineteen anymore. I was twenty-six, four years from thirty. So when in the holy hell would I be ready? At exactly what point would I be . . . be *normal*?

Thank God the conversation moved away from me, and they started talking about their desires to offer their own dance classes. I hated feeling this way—acknowledging that, at times, I had such little confidence in myself. Embarrassing wasn't even the word for it. No one liked a woman who looked in a mirror and didn't love what she saw.

Which was so damn ridiculous if you thought about it.

Pulling a mushroom out of the omelet with my fork, irritation pricked at me. I remembered when Abby had first reconnected with Colton and she'd been so uncomfortable with herself. The mere idea of becoming intimate with him terrified her and she'd been embarrassed to even admit she felt that way. What had I said to her? That not having the greatest confidence didn't make her any less of a person or something to feel bad about?

It made her normal, average even, because the average woman out there didn't look at herself every day and say "damn, I'm amazing." Everyone had moments when they doubted themselves and had trouble looking at their reflections for reasons that went beyond the physical.

I'd always felt that being told you should be more confident was like getting slapped in the face. How was being told that supposed to help you feel better?

I needed to cut myself a break. Seriously.

Shoving the mushroom and another chunk of omelet in my mouth, my ears perked up when I heard Avery say, "We would just need the space for a studio. Honestly, at this point, we'd just need a large room, but every place I'd looked at in town needed a lot of work and the rents were ridiculous."

"What are you guys talking about?" I asked.

Teresa was toying with a napkin, folding it into a tiny square as she said, "You know how Avery and I have been wanting to open up our own dance studio, starting small with just offering a few classes since I'm obviously out of commission for a while." She patted her belly. "So we just need a space, but what's available in town is ridiculous."

"It's either too big or too small," Avery confirmed. "And almost always overpriced for the kind of work required to convert the room into an appropriate studio."

An idea hit me, and I couldn't believe I had never thought of it before, because I had heard them talk about fulfilling their dreams to start up their own dance company. Then again, I'd never been in this position until now.

"We have quite a bit of space available at the Academy, on the first and second floors, that we're currently looking at renting out," I explained, looking between the two. "Most of the space is completely empty. Would obviously need some work to make it ready for a studio, but I know my father wants to expand the kind of services we offer. I know you guys are looking at doing your own thing, but—"

"We'd eventually love to do our own thing, but we know we don't have the type of capital or reputation right now," Avery said, practically bouncing in her seat. "Partnering with an organization like the Lima Academy . . ."

"Would be beyond anything we'd expected." Excitement filled Teresa's eyes. "Do you have to get permission from your father?"

"Not yet. I just need to talk to . . ." My brows lifted. "I just need to talk to Brock and see what he thinks. If I can convince him, then we might have a space for you. We could have you guys come in, look around, talk about what would need to be done, and how much it would cost."

"That sounds amazing," Avery said, exchanging a delighted look with Teresa, and for the first time in a long time, I let myself smile without trying to hide it.

I was full of nervous excitement, waiting for Brock on Monday. The moment I saw him walk past my office, head down and attention focused on his cellphone, I all but flew from my chair. However, the fact that he didn't pop his head in or wave as he walked by, like he'd done every day, was odd.

I sat back down, deciding I should wait for a bit.

Not to mention I should probably give him a few minutes to get settled in. It *was* Monday morning, after all.

Half an hour passed before I grabbed my cup of coffee and started toward his office and then pivoted around, heading to the break room. I totally saw nothing wrong with buttering him up with a fresh cup of coffee.

Knowing that he'd liked his coffee black, I grabbed one of the clean, Lima-branded coffee mugs from the cabinet overhead and poured him a cup. I topped mine off after adding another packet of sugar. Turning, I jerked back a step when I saw Paul standing a few feet behind me. Hot coffee sloshed over the rim of the cup, spilling along the top of my hand.

"Ouch," I muttered, resisting the urge to flail my hand and spill more coffee.

Paul smirked as he stepped around me, walking to the fridge to grab a protein shake. No *I'm sorry*. No *hello*. Nothing. I watched him pivot around and walk back out of the break room with my mouth hanging open.

"What an asshole," I muttered.

Pushing the run-in with Paul to the back of my mind, I made my way to Brock's office. The door was open, so I called out, "You got a few minutes? I brought you coffee."

Brock lifted his head and a faint smile tipped up the corners of his mouth. He had several days' growth of a beard on his cheeks and there were smudges under his eyes, as if he hadn't gotten a lot of sleep this weekend.

A weird feeling tugged at me. It was curiosity. I wanted to know why he looked so bad.

Closing a file he was looking at, he motioned me in. His gaze flickered over me, and I felt a flush travel over my skin. I was wearing dress pants and a sweater, but that quick glance of his made me feel like I was walking around in lingerie, which was one hundred percent due to my over-active imagination.

"I always have time for you, Jillian."

It was on the tip of my tongue to point out there had been many times in the past, when we'd gotten older, that he hadn't. Luckily, I had some common sense and realized how incredibly bitter that would've sounded.

And completely unnecessary.

So I came into the office and placed the cup on his desk, careful not to spill. "Did you have a good weekend?" I asked, sitting down.

"Long," he said, reaching for the mug. "It was a very long weekend."

I eyed him over the rim of my cup. "Looks like it."

Brock did look tired, but he still managed to look incredibly . . . well, incredibly sexy in his white dress shirt that was unbuttoned at the neck.

He eyed me. "You, on the other hand, look well rested. I'm guessing your date with that little guy didn't turn into a weekend adventure."

Slowly, I lowered my mug. "My date with *Grady* went very well, thank you very much, and for the last time, he's not little."

"Uh-huh," he murmured, sipping his coffee.

"And how does one date turn into an entire weekend?"

He raised a brow as he placed his mug back down. "Obviously you haven't been on a really good date then."

Heat blasted my cheeks. I guessed I hadn't. Nice of him to point that out to me. *Jerk.*

"Because a really good date with me doesn't end with an *art exhibit*," he said silkily. "A really good date won't end until the next night. Not until I've spent hours making sure it's the kind of date my woman never wants to end."

Oh.

*Oh* gosh.

Flustered, I squirmed as I stared at my coffee. I had no idea what that would be like, to be the sole focus of the kind of man like Brock *all* weekend long.

"You guys going out again?" he asked.

I lifted my gaze, feeling oddly hot, like I'd been sitting out in the summer sun. "We're having dinner Wednesday night."

Rising, he walked around the desk, and I tensed, having no idea what he was up to when his dark eyes held a wealth of secrets. "That's a shame."

Confusion swept through me. "How so?"

He walked until he was in front of the desk and leaned back

against it. "You're not going to be able to have dinner with him on Wednesday."

"And why not?"

Stretching out his long legs, I tensed even more when his knee brushed mine. Deep in my chest, my heart fluttered like a hummingbird taking flight. "Because you're going to dinner with me."

# Chapter 11

I opened my mouth, but immediately snapped it closed because my heart was suddenly entering cardiac territory. Was he . . . was Brock Mitchell seriously asking me out? Well, not asking me, but telling me we were going to dinner, like him and me? Us? But that didn't make sense. He had a fiancée—a real life fiancée.

"What?" I croaked out, a mix of wild emotions slamming into me from every side. Despite knowing he was engaged and there being that barbed-wire wall and mile-deep line that I knew he would never cross, a sweet burst of anticipation lit up my chest. Seconds later, a bitter acid washed it away, because I was not *her*. I was not the kind of woman to get involved with a man who was already with someone else, not even if it was the man I'd spent the vast majority of my life being in love with.

Not that I was still in love with him or anything.

He knocked his knee off mine. "We have a dinner date."

"I heard that, but I . . . I don't understand."

"We're going to that steakhouse in Martinsburg. The one right on Queen Street?" he explained. "We're going to leave work and head straight there."

I put my coffee down on his desk so I didn't drop it, because my hand was starting to tremble. "Okay. I have no idea why you think we have a date, because I clearly do not remember you asking me, and you have—"

"Just-found out about it this morning actually," he explained, and my eyes narrowed in confusion. "Two potential endorsers are visiting the Philadelphia location today and tomorrow, and they would like to see this location on Wednesday before they head back out West. We'll be taking them to dinner."

Oh.

*Oh.*

He wasn't asking me out on a *date* date. Duh. I mean, why would I even think that he was? He was engaged, and Brock had never been interested in me in that way. It was just a momentary lapse of intelligence.

Feeling about seven different kinds of idiotic, I tucked my hair back behind my ear and muttered, "Well, I guess I'll be canceling my date then."

"You'll thank me later for it." He winked when I looked at him. "Trust me."

"Okay. This conversation has gone way off track," I said.

"Those are the best kind of conversations." He reached behind him and curled his large hand around the mug.

I ignored the comment and refocused. "The reason why I'm in your office is because I wanted to see you—"

"It's about time you admit that," he replied smoothly, and those eyes of his, dark and endless, took on a lazy quality that had my pulse once again pounding all over the place. "Have I told you lately how much I like it when you wear your hair down?"

"No," I whispered.

"I do. You have beautiful hair." His jaw tightened. "Never noticed that before. You always had it pulled up, didn't you?"

"Um."

"Yeah, that's right. Always pulled up." With one hand still wrapped around the coffee cup, he picked up a piece of my hair, running his fingers along the strand. His voice deepened when he said, "You've always been a pretty girl. I know I've said that to you before, but you've become such a beautiful woman."

I wanted to laugh, to ask him if he'd been drinking this morning, but my heart was beating too fast. I had no idea how to process what he was doing and saying. Brock had told me I was beautiful before, but he'd always said it back then in a way that it was just a passing compliment, one tossed out and not really meaning anything. Hearing it come from his mouth now was nothing like before.

Lifting my gaze once more to his, I found that I was unable to look away. Brock was one hundred percent a grown man now and he never, ever had looked at me like he did in this moment, like he was . . . he was starving, and I didn't understand how he could be staring at me like that. It didn't make sense, not in the world we lived in.

Brock let go of my hair and his fingers brushed over the curve of my cheek. My skin tingled from where his fingers had touched, like an electrical jolt to my system. His gaze slipped from mine, coasting and lingering over my mouth before going even lower, and a sweet, heady flush of heat spread. Under the sweater, I could feel my nipples hardening.

Slowly, torturously, he dragged his gaze back up to mine. A shadow passed over his striking face and he swallowed once more, then lowered his chin. "Jillian, I—"

"Am I interrupting?"

I jumped at the sound of an unfamiliar female voice. A flicker of surprise skated over Brock's face and then his jaw hardened. I glanced over my shoulder, and nearly fell out of my chair as I whipped back around, my eyes wide.

It was the fiancée.

Kristen Morgan.

Oh my God.

My face caught fire, and I immediately wanted to explain that however this looked didn't mean whatever she could be thinking, but I didn't get a chance because Brock was rising and when he spoke, his tone was as hard as a polished diamond.

"What are you doing here, Kristen?"

Oh wow, that did not sound friendly at all, and I couldn't remember a time when I'd heard him sound like that.

"Is it really that much of a surprise?" she asked, her tone just as snappy, and I thought it was a really, really good time for me to exit his office.

"I'll catch up with you later," I said to Brock, whose gaze flitted to mine. His expression was now locked down, completely unreadable.

Picking up my coffee, I took a deep breath and turned, finally laying eyes on Kristen for the first time in many, many years.

We both gasped at the same time.

Obviously for different reasons.

Time had been extremely kind to Kristen. She was more beautiful than I remembered. Tall and slender, her shoulder-length blonde hair was cut in a trendy way, slightly longer in the front than in the back. Her features were flawless—high cheekbones and a perfect, pert little nose, and smooth golden complexion. She was wearing white skinny jeans. Never in my life would I ever squeeze my ass and thighs into that pair of white pants, but she did it and did it wearing flats and a tight turtleneck.

And she looked damn good while doing it.

Ugh.

"It's good to see you, Kristen," I mumbled, stepping around her.

She didn't respond as she stared at me, her china-blue eyes wide.

I didn't let myself think about why she looked so shocked when she saw me as I stepped out of the office. It didn't matter, and I refused to spend a second stressing about that.

Walking back to my office, I closed the door behind me and went to my desk, placing my mug on the coaster.

"Well," I said out loud, resting my forehead in my hand. "None of that went as expected."

Seeing Kristen reminded me of the first time I'd seen her. It was the last thing I really wanted to think about, but her presence brought back memories of that night, replaying them over and over in my head like some kind of twenty-four-hour humiliation network. That was the night that Brock had . . . had kind of chosen her over me.

*"He's going to get laid tonight," the girly, sing-songy voice sang in my ear. "Probably more than once and probably with more than just one of those horny as hell chicks."*

*I tensed. The flush hit my cheeks first before racing across my face and then down my throat. "No, he's not."*

*"Yes he is," whispered an evil voice in the back of my head.*

*Nope. I refused to listen to that stupid voice. This weekend was different and this night wasn't going to end in Brock's bedroom turning into a one-night-stand train station. We were going to dinner. We were just running a little late. That's all.*

*Squaring my shoulders, I looked over at Katie. Her glossy bubblegum-pink lips were turned down at the corners as she stared at the bar. I didn't dare look further south than her face even though it felt like I was compelled by some kind of dark magic to do so. She was barely dressed. Like, all she was wearing was a bra and shorts that were tinier than the underwear I normally wore. She was on break—an early break I was guessing since it was only a little after eight.*

*"We're going to be leaving soon," I insisted, turning the bracelet on my wrist. "He just hasn't seen those guys in a while."*

*"Uh huh. Girl. Honey child. Little boo boo babe," Katie cooed, leaning forward. And I was afraid that her boobs would suddenly spill out onto the high-top table between us. "Open your eyes and look—really look."*

*Part of me didn't want to, but I did, because I couldn't help myself, and when I looked, I saw Brock first. I always saw him first.*

*He was the most handsome man I'd ever seen, and that was saying something, because Jax, the co-owner of Mona's, was behind the bar, and he was stunning. And Brock was standing there with two of the hottest cops in the state—Reece and Colton Anders.*

*But they didn't compare to Brock's rugged attractiveness.*

*He had his hip propped against the bar, his head tipped back as he laughed at something Colton had said. Dressed in faded blue jeans and a tight black shirt that showed off the muscled forearms and defined pecs, he'd just gotten his brown hair cut again. It was cropped close on the sides and was longer on the top, standing straight up.*

*My gaze shifted to the left, to where a group of college-aged girls dressed for a night of partying was lingering. I wanted to think they weren't a part of the conversation with Brock, but I would be lying to myself. Reece and Colton weren't paying them any attention, but Brock was.*

*One of the girls I recognized. Her name was Kristen—Kristen Morgan. I hadn't seen her in ages, but we'd gone to high school together. She was my age, and she was beautiful. Sandy blonde hair and bright blue eyes, she had a body that matched her face.*

*Her top exposed her midriff, revealing a navel pierced with something shiny and dangling. I wanted to grab her by her curly hair and haul her ass out of the bar. She was touching Brock, touching him in a way that said she was familiar with him or she wanted to be. Her pale hand was on his arm as he turned to her, a half-smile on his lips. Kristen leaned into him, pressing her chest to his biceps. Brock was smiling at her, and it was a smile I'd seen before, many times before, but never directed at me.*

*My breath caught as my chest squeezed. Kristen's hand had moved from his arm and was now on his stomach—his stomach!*

*"You see what I'm seeing?" Katie asked.*

*Squeezing my eyes closed for a moment, I swallowed the rapidly forming knot in my throat. "We'll be leaving soon."*

*"Oh, Jilly," she murmured.*

*I shifted in my seat, embarrassed by her tone. I knew what she was thinking. I was foolish and naive. My heart started racing as I glanced back at the bar. Brock was paying attention to Reece and Colton once more, but Kristen ... His arm was wrapped loosely around her tiny waist.*

*The twisting in my chest increased.*

*"I have to leave soon. Got to head back to work," Katie was saying, and I dragged my gaze away from Brock. "I can walk you out."*

*The knot returned, crawling up my throat. "That's ... okay," I said hoarsely. "We'll be leaving soon."*


We hadn't left, though.

I wasn't even supposed to be at Mona's that night. Neither was Brock. If he'd done what he'd promised, so many things could've been different. He may've never crossed paths with Kristen, and perhaps our friendship would've remained the same over the years. Or if I had listened to Katie and left with her? Who knows what would've happened?

But I wouldn't have been there, and what happened later that night could've happened to someone else or not at all. I'd never know, because I couldn't go back.

I could never go back.

It was Tuesday afternoon before I got to speak to Brock about expanding Lima Academy into uncharted territories. He'd disappeared with Kristen on Monday, and didn't return until later that day, slamming the door shut behind him.

I'd wisely left him alone.

Monday night I'd made two phone calls. First was to Grady, telling him that I wouldn't be able to make it to dinner Wednesday night because of a work commitment. He'd sounded disappointed, but graciously offered to take me out the following weekend. We'd tentatively made plans for that Saturday.

I'd felt bad for canceling, but I didn't feel . . . excited about the rescheduled date. Maybe I would once it got closer. Maybe I would make a bigger deal out of it. Get a new dress. Do something special with my hair. Shave my legs.

Bringing out the big guns there.

The second call had been to my mother. We'd chatted for a bit, about how I was settling in at work, and she asked about my date with Grady. We'd talked for close to an hour, and before I'd hung up she finally asked me about Brock.

"How is everything with him?" she'd asked, her voice cautious.

I'd been playing with Rhage, dangling one of those feather-mouse toys. "Things are okay."

"That doesn't sound entirely convincing, hon."

"Well, they actually have been okay. We're getting along," I'd told her. "We're kind of friends . . . again, I guess."

"Oh, honey, it's good to hear that. Your father didn't tell me he was taking over as GM. He knew I would warn you," she'd explained. "He wants you two so badly to . . ."

I'd stilled. "To what?"

There'd been a stretch of silence. "To just get along. He knows that with you two at the helm in Martinsburg, it will be no time before it's as successful as the one here."

It had been nice to hear that, to know my father believed in me, but I also knew, because I wasn't dumb, that wasn't the only reason why either of them was asking about Brock and me.

I'd never admitted my feelings for Brock, not to my parents, not to Abby or Katie. Doing so always felt like I could never take it back, but as I'd stared at the muted TV screen, I'd been suddenly so tired of not . . . of just not being honest.

"Mom, I was in love with Brock from the moment he stepped through the front door of our house."

Even though half my hearing was shot, I'd swear I heard her sharp inhale. "Jilly . . ."

"I know you've always known that. Hell, everyone knew it. But we're . . . we're okay now. It's—" I hissed, yanking my hand back. The damn cat had latched his claws into my fingers when I stopped moving the toy. Rhage glared up at me. "I just want you to know that you don't have to worry about me . . . and him."

"Baby, I never worried about you two."

My brows had lifted as I'd shaken my stinging hand. "Really?"

"Not in the way you think," she said mysteriously. "Look, your uncles are outside and about to pile out of their cars, looking to be fed. When are you coming home to see us?"

"Thanksgiving," I told her.

"That's so far away," she complained.

A slight smile tugged at my lips. "Mom, that's only a little over a month from now."

"Too long," Mom countered. "I love you."

"Love you, too." I'd hung up the phone, feeling strangely lighter, having admitted to something that was so incredibly simple but so heavy.

And now it was Tuesday afternoon, and once again I was walking to Brock's office, hoping this time the conversation didn't veer into Crazyville. Rapping my knuckles off his door, I waited.

"Come in."

Taking a deep breath, I opened the door. He was watching TV. I started to frown, but I quickly realized it was a video of one of the recruits from the second floor. "Do you have a couple of moments?"

"Your hair is down again," he murmured, glancing over at me. "I approve."

I made a face at him as I closed the door behind me. "Thanks, but I wasn't looking for your approval."

A brief grin appeared and then he picked up a remote and paused the video. "What's up?"

Sitting straight, I folded my hands together. "I wanted to talk to you about possible expansion. It's not something that the Lima Academy would typically get involved in, but I think it's something worth looking into."

His gaze centered on me. "Go on."

I ignored the way his heavy stare made me feel, like there was no space between us. "Right now, the Lima Academy is very male-centric. Of course, with the exception of the gym and the few women we have training in one of our martial arts or self-defense classes. Now, we can always bring more women and young adults into our standard classes, something I am focusing on, but I think we can do more." My shoulders rose. "You remember Avery, right?"

"Cam's wife?"

I nodded. "And you've met Jase Winstead? His wife is Teresa. They're about to have a child—a baby boy."

The look on his face said he wasn't exactly sure how that worked into expanding Lima Academy.

"Anyway, both Teresa and Avery were . . . *are* dancers, professional dancers. Teresa was actually with one of the most well-known dance companies before she injured her knee, preventing her from having a career in dance. For quite some time, they've wanted to start offering dance classes, since there aren't many dance companies in this county or in the tristate. They want to eventually open their own studio, but they're a long way away from being able to do that."

Two fingers pressed to his lips as he rested his chin in his palm. "Okay."

"What they've been looking at is space for classes, but as I'm sure you know, space isn't easy to come by and neither are the type of funds necessary to start a studio from the ground up," I explained. "What I was thinking is we have a lot of space available, large rooms that could probably be easily converted into dance studio space."

Brock studied me for a moment. "You're basically suggesting that we rent out some of our space for dance classes?"

I shot him a dark look. "You don't need to say it like that. Some of those dancers are more badass than our fighters. Especially when you get into the tumbling and gymnastics aspect, which by the way, gymnastics would also probably be a great route to go down eventually." Scooting forward, I gripped the arms of the chair. "And offering classes like that doesn't just appeal to girls. A lot of boys are into dancing. There can be a lot of different age levels and styles. And not only that, we can upsell gym memberships to parents," I told him. "And maybe even a few self- defense classes."

Brock appeared to contemplate this for a couple of moments. "And we could probably get a couple of our lower-level martial arts classes out of cross-selling." His eyes narrowed. "But if your friends are interested in eventually opening their own studio and potentially taking their clients with them, what long-term benefit is there for us? Because it seems like we'd be footing most of the cost to convert the space."

I'd planned for that question. "If they do decide to leave and open their own studio, and that is an 'if' at this point, we bring in different dance teachers," I responded. "We could also make it worth their while to stay with Lima, which would probably be eventually taking on more of a sponsorship role and allowing them to run it, but that's neither here nor there at this point. With or without them, this could be a very successful endeavor and it's not something we've ever done before."

"Hmm." He tapped his fingers on the corner of his lips. "This is different, going in a direction I doubt Andrew was thinking of, but your father is innovative." He paused. "So are you."

Fighting a grin, I nodded.

Brock appeared to mull it over for several moments and then said, "I'm not a hundred percent on board with this, but I think it's worth looking into. What I would like to see is who our competitors will be, what they're charging, and what kind of profit we can expect to make after the expense of converting spaces."

It took great effort to contain my excitement. "I can do that."

"Well, let's set up a time when both of them can come see the space and we can figure out what they were thinking would be needed to meet their standards," he said, lowering his hand. "Have them bring their husbands."

I lifted a brow. "Why?"

"Because I'm pretty sure I'll zone out at some point during that conversation, and I can use the guys as an excuse and show them around the facility." He grinned when I rolled my eyes. "Hey, I'm just being honest. Plus, the six of us could grab dinner afterward. One big happy date."

Now both of my brows were inching up my forehead.

He chuckled as he sat back in his chair. "If only you could see the look on your face right now. Cute."

"Cute?"

"Very cute," he murmured.

I gave a little shake of my head, not allowing myself to think much of that. "I don't think that would be wise—the one, big happy date thing."

"And why not?"

"Well, yesterday is a good example," I found myself saying.

His head tilted to the side as his brows furrowed together. "What about yesterday?"

"Well, you know, when Kristen showed up."

He started to frown. "I'm not really following what she has to do with us having dinner with your friends."

For a moment, all I could do was stare at him. Sure, people who were involved with others had dinner with all sorts of random people all the time, but that wasn't the same here. I wasn't a random coworker. I never would be. Brock knew that.

I glanced around, wondering exactly how obvious I needed to be. "Kristen seemed very unhappy yesterday."

"That's pretty much a constant state of affairs for her," he commented wryly.

Okay then. "Well, perhaps as her fiancé, you should help fix that then, instead of making it worse?"

"What?" Brock laughed, shaking his head in disbelief. "Her fiancé?" As his laughter died off, a look of understanding settled into his expression. "Oh. I see."

"You do?"

His eyes seemed to darken as his thick lashes lowered. "Kristen and I are no longer engaged. I broke things off with her about a year ago."

# Chapter 12

"What?" I shrieked, and then cringed when Brock blinked. Yikes. "I'm sorry. That was loud. I just . . . I'm surprised."

"I can tell." A slow grin played across his lips.

He wasn't engaged? My thoughts whirled at a hectic pace. "Why?" I blurted out and then blushed. "I'm sorry. That's probably none of my business."

"I thought you already knew. I'm kind of surprised your parents haven't said something," he said, leaning back in his chair.

"Obviously, they haven't." Mom hadn't even mentioned it last night. Why wouldn't they say something? Then it hit me. Probably because she was afraid I would fall back in love with him if he was available. Geez. Did they really think I was that . . . predictable? Or pathetic. Either "P" word would work. "What happened?"

He drew in a deep breath. "We just grew apart."

"That's . . . that's all?" I blinked. I couldn't believe what I was hearing. Brock was and had been unreachable and untouchable for the last six years. I had long since accepted that he was going to marry the beautiful, shiny Kristen. They would have kids, a whole cargo van full of kids. They'd practically grow up at the Academy. My parents would dote on them, because Brock was like a son to them, so their kids would be like grandbabies, and I would be okay with it. I had been okay with it, because there wasn't a choice to not be.

I sat back, utterly shocked. "You were together for—"

"Almost six years. I know," he said, fingers tapping on the arm of the chair. "It wasn't meant to be."

And that's all he said.

Realizing that he obviously didn't want to talk about it, I let it drop. "I'm sorry to hear that."

He studied me a moment. "That's nothing to be sorry about, Jillian."

My breath caught a little, and his large office suddenly felt entirely too small, so I started to rise. "Thank you for hearing me out about the potential for expansion. I'll call them and see when they have some time available."

Brock waited until I reached the door and said, "Don't forget to tell them to bring their husbands and to plan to grab dinner afterward."

Slowly, I faced him.

He smiled at me as he picked up the remote. "One big, happy date, Jillian."

"I'm just a girl, standing in front of an oven, asking it to hurry up and bake my pizza."

Sighing, I all but planted my forehead on the oven door. There were still twenty-some minutes left. That meant forever. Turning away from the oven, I watched Rhage chow down, his tail sliding across the floor like he was angry-eating. I glanced at my phone as I nibbled on my lower lip. The desire to call Abby and talk to her about Brock was burning through me.

Brock wasn't engaged.

Was this common knowledge back home?

And even if my mom thought knowing Brock was now single would somehow send me down a path to heartbreak number five hundred, how could she or my father not say anything?

My heart started jumping all over the place as I folded my arms across my chest and leaned against the counter. Brock was a flirt, teasing and playful. He'd always been. He was the kind of guy you shouldn't take seriously when he showered you with attention. I had done so foolishly before and I wouldn't make that same mistake. Not when it was so easy to blur the lines of friendship with him, but him being engaged had helped keep my head on my shoulders and my heart firmly secured far, far out of his hands.

Not that I was trying to give my heart to him.

So really, him not being engaged meant absolutely nothing.

Nothing at all.

Brock was actually single again.

That barbed-wire wall was gone, as was that mile-deep line in the sand. I wanted to pretend they were still there, but that required a whole lot of lying to myself. Too much effort right there. Brock was available. He could still be dating Kristen. He'd gone back to Philly over the weekend and she was here on Monday. Though he hadn't seemed exactly thrilled to see her, but I hadn't poked around with questions, so—

"Oh my God," I muttered, unfolding my arms and rubbing my hands down my face. Thank the Lord I'd washed the makeup off first or I'd look like that dude with the melted face at the end of one of the Indiana Jones movies.

I could call Abby, but it was close to dinnertime, and talking about Brock to her, to anyone, would make them think—

My phone rang from where it sat on the counter, startling me. I walked over to it, seeing an unfamiliar Pennsylvania number. I almost didn't answer it.

"Hello?"

"Hey, it's Brock."

My eyes widened as my heart did a dumb, stupid jump in my chest. Thinking about him and having him call out of the blue made me want to look around to see if there were hidden cameras in my apartment.

"Heeey." I drew the word out.

There was a deep chuckle on the other end of the phone. "I realized something. Since we have the dinner tomorrow night, it would make sense that I pick you up in the morning."

"What?" I so did not see how that made sense.

"There's no point for both of us to drive to work and then to the restaurant. Parking in town is terrible. So I can pick you up."

My thoughts raced to catch up with what he was saying. "But you'd have to drive past the Academy, come clear out here to pick me up."

"It's not clear out there. It doesn't take that long and I like driving," he replied. "I'll be there at eight-thirty. Be ready."

"But—"

"See you in the morning, Jillian."

And then he hung up and I was left staring at my phone like an idiot. I could call him back, but once Brock had his mind made up about something, there was no talking him out of it.

"Why?" I said out loud.

Rhage meowed in response.

I looked over at the striped cat. He was sitting in front of his empty bowl, staring up at me like he actually thought he was going to get more food. "Not happening," I told the little devil.

Glancing at the time left on the pizza, I then saved Brock's number in my phone. I stood in the center of the small kitchen for several moments, unsure of what I was supposed to do now. Call him back and tell him no? And would that be me making too big of a deal out of him giving me a ride? Should I just leave before he got here and pretend I forgot? That would probably make me an ass. Or should I just go with the flow and stop stressing over it, because stressing led to reading between the lines?

And the last thing I needed to do was read between the lines.

I was extremely skilled at taking a simple statement and creating an entire paragraph of unspoken words out of it.

That was the last thing I needed to do right now.

"I need more than pizza," I decided, pivoting around and walking toward the fridge.

I opened the freezer and pulled out a carton of Reese's peanut-butter ice cream. I didn't even grab a bowl. Just a spoon. It was going to be that kind of night.

Hours later, I jerked up in the middle of the bed, gasping for air. The sudden movement had sent Rhage scurrying from the bed and racing out of the bedroom.

Several minutes passed as I sat in the dark room, confused and struggling to make sense of why I was awake and feeling like I'd just run up a flight of stairs.

Then slowly, painfully, it came back in pieces. Shattered images of the night . . . It had been a nightmare, but the emotions that nightmare awakened in me lingered like the bitter smell of gunfire. The feeling of helplessness as I stared up—stared up at the skinny, dirty man, not fully believing what was happening. The terror had been stark and all-consuming, obliterating my ability to understand that every breath I'd been sucking in erratically was counting down to the last one.

Hand shaking, I lifted my arm and ran the tips of my fingers over the deep indent in my left cheek. I squeezed my eyes shut, hearing the deafening popping sound. The flash of pain had been so quick, intense and fiery, and there had been nothing . . . nothing except this.

I ran my tongue along the inside of my mouth as I dragged my fingers to the other side of my face. Sometimes I thought if I pressed hard enough I could feel the implant, but that could've been my imagination.

Lowering my hand, I opened my eyes, and as my vision adjusted to the darkness, I could make out the shapes around me. Back in my parents' house, there were wall-to-wall book-shelves. They'd been my collection, a source of wonderful memories and new worlds.

I only had one bookcase here.

Most of the books I read were now on my Kindle, as they had been back then, many Kindle generations ago, but I'd still collected print books. I'd liked being surrounded by them, being able to reach out and touch them.

I didn't know why I hadn't done the same here, converting the guest bedroom into a library of sorts.

Drawing my knees up under the covers, I wrapped my arms around my legs. A question plagued me as I sat in the darkness with only the sound of a nearby fan running.

What would I've done if I hadn't gone to Mona's that night?

The question picked at me for years, because I . . . I couldn't answer that question. I mean, I'd wanted to work at the Academy. I'd wanted to finish college. But those were surface things, and I didn't have . . . a deep sense of self, of who I truly was before the shooting and who I became afterwards because of it.

I'd only been twenty when everything had changed for me. My life was paused before I got the chance to really discover what I wanted or who I was outside of being Andrew Lima's daughter or the girl who was Brock "the Beast" Mitchell's shadow. The remote control of life had slowly lifted its pause button, but . . .

I really should be asleep.

Tomorrow would be a long day—a big day. I would be meeting with potential investors, and not only was I representing the Lima Academy, I represented my father. The last thing I needed to be was half-asleep while trying to pay attention to what everyone was saying.

But there was too much noise—noise inside my head.

Lifting one hand, I folded it over my left ear and pressed down. The whirl of the fan faded until I could barely hear anything. True silence. I closed my eyes again and held my breath. In the stillness of my room, I acknowledged that I had wasted years of my life after being on the receiving end of a second chance. That was something hard to face even though I'd been doing just that over the last couple of weeks. To know one was only existing and not living.

I was starting to live, though. Truly. I believed that. Tears pricked my eyes. I could try harder, and I would . . . I would buy more bookcases. Then, when I was home over Thanksgiving, I would bring some of my most favorite books back.

I could do more.

I needed to do more.

Then, finally, my thoughts quieted, and for a few blessed seconds, there was nothing outside or inside me. Nothing.

My lungs started to burn, and only then did I draw in another deep breath. Lifting my hand from my ear, I touched the scar again and then shook my head. Cheeks damp, I pressed my lips together and didn't move for a long moment.

Throwing off the covers, I crept out into the shadowy living room. "Rhage?" I whispered. The dull overhead lights over the island cast a soft glow into the living room. I saw Rhage sitting by the end table.

"Sorry," I said. His ears twitched. "I didn't mean to scare you."

I knelt and extended my arms. Rhage didn't move for a moment, but then he rose and darted to my arms. I picked Rhage up, holding him to my chest as I turned and walked back to bed. I climbed in and laid him down beside me. Maybe he sensed I needed kitty cuddles, because he didn't run away from me or try to bite me. He curled up against my stomach and quickly fell asleep.

It was a long time before I dozed off, haunted by memories of a long-ago night that now seemed like yesterday.

# Chapter 13

Staring out the window at the rapidly darkening sky, I opened and closed my hands over and over as Brock pulled out of the parking lot of the Academy.

The whole day had been . . . weird. My mood was somewhere between eating a bag of Cheetos in one sitting and randomly wanting to paint and redesign my entire apartment. Eating the Cheetos would've felt amazing at the time but would've ended up making me feel gross. Painting was a no-go since I didn't own the apartment. And I sucked at interior design, but yeah, that was my mood all day.

The only thing I managed to do was lock down a time when Teresa and Avery could bring the guys and come to the Academy. Excitement poured through Avery's voice on the phone at the prospect of achieving what had long since been a dream of hers and Teresa's, and she also couldn't wait to tell Cam he would be having dinner with his idol.

Scheduling things with people who had kids or were ready to pop one out proved to be difficult. We were looking at the second week of November, a Friday evening.

And now I was on my way to this dinner with the investors, and all I wanted to do was eat that bag of Cheetos while curled up on the couch, marathoning old episodes of *Supernatural*.

That wasn't going to happen.

"You okay over there?"

Tearing my attention from the window, my gaze flickered over the interior of the extremely expensive car. I'd never really paid attention to the cars in the parking lot, and since I usually arrived and left before Brock, I didn't know what he drove.

But I wasn't surprised to see that it was a sleek, black two-door Porsche waiting for me Wednesday morning. Seeing the car made me want to ask Brock once more why he'd taken this position. I knew he'd agreed that he could live comfortably without working, so it wasn't like he'd blown through all the money from his fights and sponsorships like so many athletes did.

I glanced over at Brock and felt an unsteady flip in my chest. His eyes were on the road as he turned left, onto Route 45.

I'd never been a facial-hair kind of girl. Ever. But the scruff of his was filling in, and it looked *good* on him. *Way good.* I couldn't help but think what it would feel like when he kissed—

Okay.

So didn't need to think about that.

Bad life choice right there.

"Yeah," I answered, focusing straight ahead as I smoothed my hands over the pencil skirt I'd worn. "Just got a lot on my mind."

"Like what?"

I widened my eyes. Not like I was going to tell him exactly what was on my mind, but I said, "I'm nervous."

"What's got you nervous?" he asked, and when I glanced over at him, I saw that his gaze had been briefly on me before he refocused on the road.

"This whole . . . wining and dining thing is not my forte," I admitted.

"Oh, I think it's up your alley."

I snorted like a little piglet, one of those tiny, fat ones. "I think you're on drugs."

"And I don't think you're giving yourself enough credit," he replied. "You grew up with these guys coming in and out of the Academy. You know how to talk to them. You know how to handle them."

I turned back to the passenger window as a reluctant half-grin pulled at my lips. "It's not the same as then, though."

"How so?" he challenged.

Fiddling with the strap on my seatbelt, I decided I could be honest about why I was nervous. It wasn't easy. As soon as I started speaking, my cheeks heated. "You . . . you remember that I can't hear out of my right ear?" I kept going, not giving him a chance to say something. "When I'm with groups of people and there's a lot of background noise, it can be hard for me to follow the conversation. The meetings at the office aren't too bad," I added in a rush. "It's quiet, so it's not hard to follow, but restaurants sometimes can be the worst."

"I know," Brock said after a moment. "I wasn't thinking the Friday I saw you at the restaurant and stood on your right side. Sorry about that."

I glanced at him sharply, having forgotten that he'd done that. "It's okay. People forget. It happens."

"That wasn't cool of me," he continued, one hand draped over the steering wheel. "I took that into consideration. We have one of the more private booths in the back of the restaurant where it should be quieter. I'll be sitting to your right, so our guests will be to your left and across from you."

I opened my mouth, but I didn't know what to say. Part of me was relieved to learn he had taken my hearing into consideration, lessening the possibility of that becoming an issue. The other half of me was embarrassed he had to take that into consideration. And all of me was annoyed that I was embarrassed in the first place. My partial hearing was a fact of life now. I shouldn't be ashamed.

Annoyed, my fingers tightened around the strap. "I hate that I'm embarrassed by it," I admitted, unable to stop myself.

"You shouldn't be."

"I know. I know I shouldn't. I guess . . ."

"You don't like the attention it brings," he said, surprising me because he hit the nail right on the head. "You were never big on being the center of attention."

A dry laugh parted my lips. "I prefer to be an observer." Feeling his hand on mine, I stopped talking and looked down. His fingers were gently working mine from the strap. Sucking in a shallow breath, I looked over at him.

Brock was still focused on the road. "If you keep twisting the seatbelt like that, you're going to twist it right off."

"Sorry," I mumbled, because that was all I could say. He'd lowered my left hand to my thigh and hadn't let go. His large hand completely covered mine and the tips of his fingers were resting against my upper thigh.

My heart leapt in my chest, slamming against my ribs as I stared at his shadowy profile. My mouth dried, and I didn't pull my hand out from his. I was mostly frozen, except for my mouth. Unfortunately. "Are you and Kristen still together?" I wanted to smack myself upside the head the moment I asked that question, because I really didn't need to know the answer.

"I told you we weren't engaged." Brock shot me a wry grin.

He had. "But that doesn't mean you're not still seeing each other. You went back to Philly this weekend and—"

"I want back there to sign paperwork for the sale of the house," he explained. "I did see Kristen. She still had things she needed to get out of there. It's taken her a year. I told her if she didn't get her stuff out this weekend, I was donating the shit."

"Oh." My eyes widened.

"She wasn't exactly happy about that." His thumb moved over the side of my pinky, sliding up and down. It was such a slight touch, but my entire being focused on it. "It was a long weekend."

Gathering my thoughts, I recalled how tired he'd looked Monday morning. "So . . . why did she come here?"

"You know, I wish I knew why. None of the reasons she gave me made a damn bit of sense, all things considered." His thumb still moved over my hand. Did he realize he was doing that? I was pretty sure that wasn't something a boss did with their employee or friends, because that would get weird quick. "But to answer your question, no, I'm not seeing Kristen in any shape or form."

"Oh," I whispered.

The Porsche coasted to a stop at a red light and he looked over at me, his eyes hidden in the darkness of the car. "I'm not seeing anyone, Jillian."

My lips parted, but I couldn't get any words out, and my heart was really going crazy now. I lifted my gaze to his and I was snared. For a few brief seconds, there was no past, no yesterday and no tomorrow. There was just now, just Brock and me in this car, his thumb tracing invisible lines over my hand.

Then the light turned green.

A car honked behind us.

A boyish, almost sheepish grin curved his lips and he hit the gas pedal. I looked at our hands. What was he doing? What was I allowing? Biting down on my lip, I slipped my hand free of his.

For a second, his entire hand was flush with my thigh, the weight burning through the thin material of my skirt. Heat pooled low in my belly. His hand was just there for a few seconds, but my body's reaction was sharp and swift. Arousal pounded through my veins.

Then Brock seemed to realize that his hand was actually on my thigh and he jerked it back.

I exhaled softly, turning my gaze to the window once more. Houses blurred past as we drove down the main street in Martinsburg. I willed my body to get itself back under control.

"Jillian?"

"Hmm?"

"Are you seeing anyone?" he asked.

The question caught me off-guard. I started to say no, but realized that wasn't exactly true. "I kind of am."

The grin of his went up a notch. "You sure about that?"

I didn't answer.

Because I wasn't.

Through what turned out to be a three-hour long dinner—the longest dinner of my life—there were only two instances when I had difficulty following the conversation of the two fast-talking gentlemen from the west.

Brock had noticed immediately that I hadn't picked up on what they were saying. I don't know if I had a "WTF" expression on my face or if he was somehow just tuned into me, but he smoothly repeated their statements or questions.

The two men didn't seem to realize I had any problem hearing them, and after the initial double take I received and expected from most people, they didn't stare.

They wouldn't.

Both men respected my father too much for their stares to linger, and frankly, they were too in awe of Brock to really notice I was there.

So I ordered a glass of wine.

Or two.

Tyler James, the older of the two men, was most eager to see the Martinsburg facility. "We definitely have some time tomorrow. Our flight isn't until the afternoon."

Brock, who'd stuck to drinking only water, took a sip as he glanced over at me. "That would be perfect."

Holding onto the stem of the wine glass, I nodded. "We actually have two higher-level mixed martial arts classes in the morning, if you'd like to take a look at them."

Both men agreed they'd be interested in seeing some of the training in action, but the big surprise was when Brock mentioned my idea for expansion, advising that we were looking in the direction of offering dance and possibly gymnastics down the road.

"A lot of untapped potential you have there," Mr. James said as the check arrived. "We are definitely interested in potentially working together in the future."

Shocked that he'd even bring it up and that he would credit me with the idea, I was bowled over when both men, whose company specialized in high-protein drinks and bars, wanted to be kept in the loop about the possible endeavor.

It was close to nine-thirty when we stepped outside into the much cooler night air. The men said their goodbyes to Brock and then me, shaking my hand. It was Tyler James who spoke. "I'm really excited to hear more about the possible expansion." He smiled. "I think you got something very interesting brewing there."

"Thank you," I said, bubbling with elation. If Brock was on board and if possible endorsers were interested, then getting my father on board shouldn't be so difficult. "I think so, too."

I could barely contain my excitement as the two men climbed into the car they had rented. It had been a long time since I felt like I was actually accomplishing something I cared about at work.

Without thinking, I spun around and sprang forward, throwing my arms around Brock. It wasn't until I was hugging him that I realized exactly what I'd done. He was just sort of standing there, arms at his sides, still as a statue and obviously shocked by the unexpected gesture from me.

Okay.

We were friends now and while Brock didn't act like a boss should toward an employee, maybe we hadn't hit the hugging stage yet.

Feeling like a giant idiot, I started to pull back. I didn't make it very far, because Brock finally moved, folding his arms around my waist. A gasp parted my lips as he pulled me more firmly against him, and suddenly it wasn't just a normal, excited hug. Oh no, it was so much more. My breasts were pressed to his chest, my lower belly to his hips. There wasn't an inch of space between us, and when Brock drew in a deep breath and his chest rose, I felt it shudder through him.

His fingers tangled in the ends of my hair as I felt him lower his chin until it rested atop my head. Brock didn't hug me back. He *held* me to him, and yeah, that wasn't the same as a hug. They were vastly different things.

Cars passed us on the street. The distant hum of conversation drew close on the sidewalk and then passed us. A wild, raw emotion crowded my senses, dredging up old, familiar feelings of the way things used to be. A cyclone of passion and yearning whipped through me as I rested my chest against his, right above his heart. I could almost pretend like we—No. I couldn't pretend. That was starting down a road only someone who was a glutton for punishment traveled. I pulled back and looked up at Brock.

He stood still, the epitome of relaxed, but there was a coiled intensity to the way he stared down at me. It was unnerving and provoking. It made me think that if I stretched up on the tips of my toes, I could maybe kiss him.

*Oh my God*, what was I thinking?

Slipping free, I was thankful he couldn't see how red my face was becoming. "I'll pick up some pastries tomorrow," I decided, wrapping my arms around my waist as I shivered. Wind lifted my hair, tossing the strands around my shoulders.

Brock was quiet and still.

I drew in one breath and then another. "We should also give Paul a heads-up about them coming in since I believe they are his classes."

"They are." Brock shrugged off his black sport coat and draped it over my shoulders, apparently not even phased by the weirdness that had just gone down. "We have three prospects in those classes. I know your father is interested in having them come up to Philadelphia so he can get a read on them."

"Thank you." I gripped the edges of his jacket, holding them together as we crossed the street. "Which guys are you looking at?"

As Brock rattled off their names, he fished out his car keys. Hitting the unlock button, he opened the passenger door for me. I slid in, keeping his jacket around me, mainly because it was warm and . . . and when I inhaled deeply, I caught the scent of woodsy cologne.

"We did good tonight," Brock said as he closed the driver's door and hit the ignition button. Air blew out of the vents, quickly warming up.

"Yes. We did." I glanced over at him.

Sitting back against the seat, he eyed me in the shadows. "We make a good team."

"We do." A smile pulled at my mouth, so I turned to the right.

"Why do you do that?"

"Do what?" My smile faded as I looked back over at him.

He leaned over, curling his fingers around my chin. My breath caught and my eyes widened. "Every time you start to smile, you either stop or look away. Why?"

"I . . ." Our gazes locked, and I had this crazy sense of falling under. I don't know what made my mouth move. "I can't smile right."

His gaze searched mine and he didn't speak for a long moment. "Nerve damage?"

"Yeah." I tore my gaze from his. "It's weird. You'd think it would be my right side since I had . . . I had to have that part of my jaw replaced, but it's the left side. I guess it . . . just hit the right place."

Brock's gaze dropped from mine, to my mouth. "I can't . . . I can't remember the last time I saw you smile."

I tensed.

"Well, actually I do." He dragged his thumb along my lower lip, sending a wave of shivers over my skin. "I remember."

My eyes closed as his thumb made another sweep. The gesture affected me more than it should have.

"I know your smile now has to be as beautiful as it was before," he said, voice low. "Don't hide it, Jillian."

Then, my eyes still closed, I felt his lips against my cheek—against the deep scar. I sucked in a startled breath, shocked to the very core. It was such a sweet kiss, definitely not the first time in my life that Brock Mitchell had kissed my cheek, but it felt very, very different now. The way his lips felt, the brush of the hair on his chin and jaw caused my skin to prickle with heat.

How his nose dragged along the curve of my cheek as he lifted his mouth and pulled away scattered my senses.

It was just a kiss on the cheek, chaste and harmless, and I wanted it to stay that way, where it was safe, but my heart was thundering and my pulse pounding, and there was nothing, *nothing* safe about how that felt.

# Chapter 14

Brock slipped the car into gear and pulled out of the parking spot while I sat back against the seat, fingers aching from how tightly I was clenching his jacket. We didn't talk on the drive to my apartment.

"I'll walk you up," he announced, coasting into a spot near the front.

"That's not . . ." I trailed off as his fingers brushed my hip. He was unbuckling my seatbelt. I blinked and Brock was already climbing out of the car and walking around the front. "Okay then."

He opened the passenger door and extended a hand. Eyeing him curiously, I grabbed my purse off the floor beside my feet and stepped out. "You really don't have to do this," I stressed.

"I want to." Brock walked beside me, hands shoved into the pockets of his pants as we headed for the stairs. Luckily, I was on the third floor. Any further, I so wouldn't have taken the apartment. He looked around, scanning the parking lot and the apartments with soft glows illuminating from their windows. "It's quiet here."

"It is." Holding his jacket closed, I trailed my hand along the railing as we climbed the outdoor stairs. "I imagine at your new place it *really* is."

"The only thing you hear are birds and what I'm convinced is a bobcat or some shit."

I laughed. "A bobcat?"

"I'm telling you, sometimes in the middle of the night, you hear some weird shit. Other than that, it's pretty amazing." He paused as we rounded the second level. "You should check it out."

Glancing over at him, I wasn't sure how to respond to that. Was it a friendly offer? Or more? And why would I think it would be more? I had no idea, so I just nodded.

He didn't say anything as we reached the third level and headed down the wide hall. My apartment was all the way to the end, on the corner. We stopped, and for some reason, my heart started pounding like I'd climbed way more than three flights of stairs.

"Well, thank you for . . . um, walking me up here." Dipping my chin, I dug my keys out from the bottom of my purse and then looked up. "And for . . ."

I trailed off, because Brock stepped into me, so close that the toes of his shoes brushed against mine.

"And for . . . ?" he queried softly.

I had no idea what I had been about to say. A little dazed, I shook my head to clear my thoughts. "For driving me around today like my own personal chauffeur."

"I enjoyed it." Brock's smile was brief as he glanced at my door, and then his shoulders rose with a deep breath. "I think I missed my calling."

"Really?" I said wryly.

"Yeah. I could quit my job as GM. Get one of your uncles back down here and just dedicate my entire life to driving you around."

I shook my head. "You know, that doesn't sound bad actually. I hate driving."

One eyebrow rose. "I thought you liked driving?"

"I used to, but now I pretty much only drive just to get back and forth from work, and that kind of sucks the fun out of it."

"I can see that." He paused. "You tired?"

"Um . . ." I was so articulate.

His grin returned. "If not, I thought maybe we could share a . . . drink."

"I . . . I don't have anything good to drink. I mean, I have a bottle of wine that's unopened, but it's like the cheap wine that really doesn't do anything other than give you a headache," I rambled on, pulse pounding. "I also have some soda and coffee, but—"

"Water or soda would be fine," he said with a laugh.

I opened my mouth and my lips moved wordlessly for a few seconds. "Are you wanting to . . . wanting to come in?"

"Yeah. I'm wanting to come in, Jillian."

He wanted to *come in*, and my mind took that down a long and dirty road. I looked up at him and I had to crane my neck, because he was standing that close. A sudden thick tension sprang alive, filling the tiny space between us. Our gazes locked once more. Neither of us moved or spoke. His lips parted on a quick, shallow inhale. My chest rose in a deep, shaky breath. What was happening here? I didn't know, but I wasn't completely naïve. He was looking at me in a way he hadn't when we were younger, and that didn't make sense.

And I had a feeling if I let Brock in, I would begin to see things that were there, and that was so dangerous for us—for me.

Wetting my lips, I looked away just as his gaze sharpened. "It's really late."

"It's not too late," he said in a voice that stretched my nerve endings.

My heart leapt into my throat. "I just . . . I don't think it would be smart."

One side of his lips kicked up. "Some of the best things start off as not being very smart. Like when I tried to rob your father."

A surprised laugh burst out of me. "That wasn't smart, and you're lucky that worked out in your favor."

"So true." His head lowered, and I tensed, thinking that he just might be getting ready to do something really not smart.

He pressed a kiss to my forehead.

So not something a boss should do.

But I didn't really care about that as I stood still before him.

His warm breath danced over my cheek and then it stirred the wisps of hair around my temple. "But you're right."

Relief and disappointment battled inside me as I found myself nodding jerkily. I let myself in, not daring to look at him as I closed the door behind me and locked it. Only then, as I rested my forehead against the door, did I realize his jacket was still draped over my shoulders.

"Shit," I muttered.

Somewhere behind me, Rhage meowed pitifully.

I didn't move, because a part of me was still out in the hall, standing there, seriously considering letting Brock in. And that part of me was an incredibly stupid part, because I was desperate to know what would've happened if I had let him in.

My stomach felt jittery and nervous as I walked into my office Thursday morning and sat behind my desk.

I didn't know how Brock was going to behave today after asking to come into my apartment. I'd had a hell of a time trying to fall asleep last night, because my mind wouldn't shut down.

There was a good chance that I'd read something that hadn't been there when he asked to come in. That wasn't unlikely. I'd been a pro at doing that in the past. Maybe he just wanted something to drink and wanted to hang out like normal friends do, and I'd made it weird.

I always made things weird.

But that hadn't been a normal hug.

And he also hadn't acted like a friend. Not when he'd kissed my cheek and then my forehead. Friends didn't kiss each other on the face. I mean, I saw that happen a lot on TV shows, but never in real life, thank God, because hello, personal space. He'd also agreed coming in wouldn't have been wise.

Last night, I'd turned this stuff over and over in my head until I got so annoyed that I picked up my Kindle and forced myself to get lost in a historical romance about the illegitimate son of a duke who had become a pirate.

Now I was back to being anxious and worked up, probably over nothing, as I stared at an email that had come in overnight, containing a list of employees who were due for an evaluation. Several minutes passed and I had no idea what the hell I'd been reading, so I had to go back and start over, and then I realized HR was asking for Brock's and my input.

"Morning."

My head jerked up, and I saw Brock striding into my office. I tensed. First thing I noticed was that he was wearing black nylon pants and an old Lima shirt from one of his matches, which was so different from how he'd been dressing since I started. Second thing was the white paper cup he carried. Starbucks.

"Good morning," I mumbled.

Brock grinned as he placed the cup on my desk. "Pumpkin spice. Still steaming."

I glanced from the cup to him. "For me?"

"Do I look like a white girl in America? No. The pumpkin spice isn't for me."

Slowly, I wrapped my fingers around the warm cup. "Thank you."

Nodding, he started to turn. "I'm going to be on the second floor with the classes. Once our guests arrive, come get me."

"Okay."

I watched him walk out and then looked down at my yummy pumpkin spice latte. *Do I look like a white girl in America?* A grin cracked my lips and then I laughed.

The two potential endorsers showed up not too long after he left. They were impressed with what we had and the space available for growth. Both Brock and I had suspected we'd be hearing from them soon. We hadn't discussed anything with my father yet. I figured it was a conversation to have over Thanksgiving, when I was face to face in a couple of weeks.

On Friday, Brock brought me another latte along with two slices of pumpkin bread before, once again, disappearing and spending most of his day on the second floor.

That Sunday, I'd gone to the nearby Target in search of a bookcase. I'd been immediately drawn to the really cool ladder ones, but you couldn't really stack books rows-deep on them. I ended up buying two of the standard tried and true ones and spent an ungodly amount of time getting them out of my car and up the three flights of stairs.

This is when having a man around would come in handy.

But I managed all on my own. I even unpacked the pieces, but I didn't put them together. I ended up realizing there was a *Walking Dead* marathon on, and since I didn't have a TV in my guest room, I'd plopped my butt down on the couch with Chinese take-out and didn't move for most of the night.

Monday morning, Brock was late getting into work. There were no lattes or slices of delicious bread. Admittedly, I'd been disappointed . . . up until he disappeared around eleven-thirty and reappeared with a carryout bag from Outback.

"You might've packed lunch," he said as he walked into my office, carrying the wonderful-smelling brown bag. "But if I remember correctly, you could never turn down cheese fries."

"Never," I breathed, my stomach grumbling. I'd brought one of those not so bad Lean Cuisine dinners, so there was no way in hell I was turning down cheese fries.

He sat in front of my desk and pulled out the white cartons, then plopped down a little container on a napkin. "Sour cream."

My brows flew up. "Your memory is rather impressive."

Brock chuckled as he pulled out a salad—a *damn* salad. "How could I forget you having an epic breakdown every time you ordered takeout from there, but they forgot to give you sour cream?"

The corner of my lips twitched. Nothing sent me into the pit of despair and rage quicker than not having the correct dipping sauces on hand.

I had just happily popped open the container when I saw Paul walking by the office. He appeared to be heading to Brock's, but stopped and then looked into mine. Seeing where Brock was, he shook his head, and I couldn't tell, but I was damn sure he'd rolled his eyes.

What in the hell was this dude's problem?

Brock frowned as he looked over his shoulder, but Paul had already disappeared. He faced me. "What's that look on your face about?"

"Nothing," I mumbled, shoving several cheesy fries into my mouth.

After lunch, my cell started vibrating on the desk. A quick glance and I saw it was Grady. My finger hovered over it as I debated whether or not I wanted to answer it, which was such a jerk move.

Feeling guilty, I answered before it went to voicemail. "Hello?"

"Hey, sorry to bother you at work," Grady said.

"It's okay." I glanced at my open door. "I have a few moments. What's going on?"

"I hate to do this, but I'm calling to reschedule our date for this weekend," he said, sounding genuine. "I just heard from my parents. With my grandfather being ill, they need me to help out."

"Oh." I fiddled with my pen. "I hope it's not too serious."

"He's just getting way up there in age and doesn't know when to slow down." Grady laughed. "Things are kind of crazy over the next couple of weeks with mid-terms and then finals, but when things calm down, I really want to do that dinner with you."

"I understand." Flipping the pen, it shot from my fingers and rolled across the desk, dropping off the other side. I sighed.

"Are you sure? I feel like a jerk—"

"It's totally okay. I had to reschedule on you, so please don't stress about it." I rose and walked around my desk, grabbing the pen. "I'd love to grab something to eat when . . . when things calm down."

"I'm holding you to that."

I raised my brows, unsure if he actually planned on following through on that. I mean, it seemed kind of weak. He was going to be that busy from now until some undetermined time?

"Okay," I said as I plopped down in my seat. "Talk to you then."

"Bye, Jillian."

Hanging up the phone, I didn't know what to make of the call. Truthfully, I wasn't exactly disappointed or relieved. I was sort of apathetic about it, but I didn't expect him to call again. I guess after turning my head when he tried to kiss me and canceling on the original dinner date, he was looking for a way out. Couldn't really blame him.

Tuesday saw the return of the pumpkin spice latte. On Wednesday and Thursday, those lattes were once again reunited in my belly with pumpkin spice bread and an amazing slice of pound cake.

On Friday, Brock took me out to lunch, to this new sushi place in town. Brock asked about my upcoming weekend, and he'd told me he had some work to do at his place. We didn't talk about work or our past. I told him about the bookcases I'd bought but hadn't put together yet. He offered to assemble them for me, but I didn't take the offer too seriously.

On the way back to the Academy, we stopped at a flower nursery. I stayed in the car while he darted across the gravel driveway, entering one of the tented buildings, since he said it wouldn't take that long.

About five minutes passed before he returned, carrying two bushy flowers, one with burnt orange blossoms and another that was deep violet. He placed them on the floor of the backseat.

"Mums?" I asked when he climbed into the driver's seat.

"Yeah. What about them?"

"Why did you pick up two mums?"

"Why not?" A sheepish grin crossed his face. "I like them."

Brock was absolutely the last person I'd ever expect who would like mums, or any flower to be honest, but there were two of them sitting behind me, proving me wrong.

Proving there was something new about Brock I never learned. Something almost ridiculous . . . and so damn cute.

He glanced over at me as he backed out of the parking lot. "Almost had it."

Looking up at him in confusion, I asked, "Almost had what?"

"A smile," he said, watching me for a few seconds, and then he eased the Porsche down the gravelly road. "Almost got a smile out of you."

*"Love is a fire. But whether it is going to warm your heart or burn down your house, you can never tell."*

—Joan Crawford

# Chapter 15

A week turned into two, and Halloween came and went as November was ushered in. The air grew chillier with each passing day, and the weatherman on the local news warned this would a record-breaking winter, colder than the last several years, with feet of snow. *Feet*. Not inches.

I still hadn't put the bookcases together.

I didn't hear from Grady except for the occasional text from him checking in, which I always responded to. He didn't bring up dinner and my earlier suspicions were confirmed.

Thinking about Grady, I wished that I . . . that I was upset, because at least then I'd have known that I actually felt something for someone that was more than a passing interest. I guessed it wasn't to be, because I wasn't spending time with wishful thinking, hoping he'd make good on the promise of dinner.

However, I was spending a decent amount of time with Brock and things . . . things were really okay. We worked well together, in and out of meetings. There'd been no more dinner meetings or random appearances at my apartment, but every day he either showed with coffee, lunch, or dessert, and sometimes all three things in one day.

I began to wonder if he was trying to fatten me up.

Not that he needed to try. I did that all on my own.

But it was sweet of him, and I guessed maybe it was his way of making up for what had happened in our past or him trying to make up for lost time, because he used to do things like this years ago. Not as often, but he'd come to my parents' house when I got home from school, carrying a slice of pie or cake from the bakery down the street from the Lima Academy. Instead of delivering coffee to the office, he'd bring smoothies and milkshakes to my bedroom.

Things were kind of like before, but not.

Brock flirted like he used to, which meant he had this amazing ability to turn almost every comment into something that dripped sex. And it might've totally been my interpretation, because seriously, I currently existed in a several years long dry spell, so there were moments when I could turn almost everything into a sexual thing. Like seriously. I could be watching *Walking Dead* and suddenly be fixating on Daryl's biceps or Rick's baby blue eyes a little too long.

But the difference was I resisted letting myself get wrapped up in the way I thought I'd catch him looking at me. I didn't fixate on how it seemed like his hand brushed mine whenever we walked to the conference room together. I refused to pay attention to how his fingers grazed mine and lingered when he'd hand me my coffee or whatever treat he'd brought me. Those moments were often.

What I hated about those moments was the fact that the simplest touch from him could elicit a heady and nearly overwhelming reaction from me. My body instantly took notice and flushed. An achy heaviness would fill my breasts, and I would be left wanting . . . wanting so much, because something inside me was opening, an awakening, rising and searching.

Needless to say, the old trusty "magic wand" was getting a workout.

Several times over the course of the last couple of weeks, I'd find that whatever sleep I could get was either fitful, full of nightmares or I was too restless to sleep at all. I would think of the way a certain set of arms had felt around me, how strong they were and how hard the chest was under my cheek, and those thoughts would give way to fantasies.

Fantasies I tried to keep faceless. Fantasies where I imagined my fingers or the toy were replaced by a real hand or mouth. Fantasies where I pictured myself against a wall, flat on my back, on my belly in the bed, or bent over slightly, grasping the counter . . . or a polished, cherry-wood desk.

I'd give in, slipping my hand or the wand below the covers. I'd try to keep my mind empty as the acute throbbing would begin and this invisible cord inside me would spin tight, but it never failed. Just before release pounded through me, just as the cord unraveled, pulling all the muscles in my legs taut, I would see dark brown eyes and full, knowing lips.

I'd come seeing Brock's face.

And each time afterward, with my heart rate slowing, I wanted to smack myself upside the head. Picturing him while doing *that* to myself seemed wrong.

Yet it felt incredibly good.

Even though I didn't want it to, it always felt beyond amazing.

The Wednesday before Avery and crew were coming to the Academy, I learned from a quick call with her that the guys wanted to try out a new bar in Shepherdstown that also served dinner, and I was obnoxiously nervous about this.

I tried to hide it, because it was so stupid.

As lame as it was to admit, I hadn't been to a bar since that night all those years ago, and knowing it would be the first time

I'd stepped into one had me dwelling on how my last trip to a bar had turned out. Sitting in my office, I was thrown back to that night.

*Katie held my gaze for a moment and then uncrossed her slender, bare arms from her bedazzled boobs. She reached for the drink she'd brought with her over to where I was sitting. "How are you even in this bar? You're only, like, eighteen."*

*"Twenty," I corrected her with a sigh. I looked sixteen on a good day, but tonight . . . tonight I thought I'd looked my age. "I'm actually twenty."*

*"Still not of legal drinking age." The little sparkles and beads jiggled as she lifted the double shot and tossed it back in one impressive swallow. "If Jax or Calla catch you in here, they're going to flip."*

*Calla wasn't at the bar tonight. At least I hadn't seen her, and Jax didn't seem to have noticed me yet. Not exactly surprising. I tended to blend right in.*

*The door opened and some guy strode in, shouting Brock's name. I tensed and then deflated when Brock pushed away from the bar. "Hey!" he shouted in return. "Where've you been, man?"*

*"Yeah." Katie shook her head. "You sure you don't want to me walk you out right now?"*

*I nodded, not exactly trusting myself to speak at the moment, because there was a good chance I might start hurling curse words at everyone and anything.*

*Katie walked over to where I sat. Her fruity perfume reminded me of the drinks my mom drank whenever we went to the beach. She kissed my cheek. "Tonight's not going to be any different, Jilly. I know these things." Straightening, she tapped her finger on the side of her head. "It's a gift, but right now, it's a curse. He still sees you the way he did when he took you to prom. That's not changing tonight. You should go home."*

*I sucked in a sharp breath. That hurt—really hurt, cutting deep into my chest, through bone and marrow.*

*Katie left then, and I sat on the stool for several moments, not moving and barely breathing as I watched Brock. I'd barely gotten a chance to talk to him since I got here. He'd seen me. He'd looked at me in surprise and he'd eyed me—eyed me up and down. Brock had hugged me, and then he told me we'd be leaving soon. Then Colt and Reece showed up, and I'd retreated to the table before they remembered I wasn't twenty-one.*

*Grabbing my purse off the table, I pried it open and dug out my phone. I saw that it was now getting close to nine. Oh God. Would we still be able to go to the steakhouse? I wasn't sure what time they closed. My gaze flicked up as anxiousness burned a hole straight through my stomach. I had no idea how long I sat there, but when I checked the time again, it was past nine.*

*This wasn't happening.*

*Tonight was supposed to be different—special.*

*I couldn't let this happen.*

*Gathering up every ounce of courage that existed inside of me, I slid off the barstool and started walking forward. At the very last minute, I veered to the left and before I knew what I was doing, I was walking to the ladies' room.*

*Oh God, I sucked.*

*Once inside the obsessively clean restroom, I dug around until I found the tube of red lipstick. I reapplied it with a shaky hand as I gave myself a little pep talk. I was going to leave the bathroom and walk right up to Brock. Wasn't like I was interrupting him. I would ask if we were leaving soon, and he would then realize the time and how long I'd been waiting. We'd leave and tonight—tonight would get back on track.*

*I grabbed the little bottle of perfume, gave myself a spritz, and then smiled at my reflection. My bangs had fallen back over my forehead, dammit. Nothing could be done about that.*

*Slipping the strap of my bag over my shoulder, I walked back into the bar. I passed the group of girls, and luckily, Kristen wasn't attached to his side when I reached them. She was standing there, though, her head bowed alongside another girl's. They were whispering and giggling about something. Reece saw me first. His brows lifted and, my heart pounding, I touched Brock's arm.*

*Brock turned sideways and looked down. He was well over six feet, and I was barely pushing five foot six. He towered over me, and I barely came up to his chest. "Jillybean," he said in that deep, rough voice of his. "Where in the world have you been?"*

*"Um, I've been talking to Katie," I said. "She had to head back to work."*

*He grinned as he reached behind and picked up his beer from the bar. "She didn't even come and say hi to me."*

*"Well . . ."*

*Brock dropped his arm around my shoulders and drew me against his side. He smelled wonderful. A fresh, crisp scent that reminded me of the outdoors. My entire body shivered. "I was just looking for you, actually. Thought you ran off without me."*

*"No." I couldn't stop the smile racing across my face.*

*"Good to hear that." He squeezed my shoulder. "It would've hurt my feelings."*

*Colton turned from Reece and he had that look on his face, that off-duty cop look. "Hey, Jillian."*

*"Hi," I squeaked out, because Brock's hand was moving on my arm. Well, it wasn't his entire hand. It was just his thumb. He was tracing a circle along my skin.*

*He lifted his bottle. "Didn't realize you'd turned twenty-one."*

*"Um," I mumbled.*

*At that exact moment, Jax appeared behind the bar. His eyes widened when he saw me standing next to Brock. "Hey," he said, crossing his arms. "You know I got mad love for you girl, but you can't be in here. Twenty-one and under is only on Wednesday nights . . . thank God," he added under his breath. "When did you even get here?"*

*I sighed inwardly. Considering I'd been here for two hours, it was kind of embarrassing how easily I went unnoticed. I could probably strip naked and no one would see me.*

*"Oh hell." Brock slid his arm off my shoulders and put his beer on the bar. "Didn't even think about that."*

*My face was burning as he looked down at me. "It's okay. We were—we were leaving anyway, right?"*

*Brock's brows knitted together. "What? Oh! Shit. What time is it?"*

*"Um." I started to dig my phone out, but he'd already pulled his out of his back pocket.*

*"Here," a soft voice interrupted, and I looked up. It was Kristen. She was holding two shot glasses. "Do one with me, Brock."*

*Brock glanced down at me, still holding his phone.*

*"Come on," she coaxed, and I stiffened as my fingers tightened around the strap of my purse. "You promised me."*

*"I did." He took the shot, but he didn't drink. His eyes, so dark they were almost black, met mine. "Damn, Jillybean, I'm sorry. I didn't know it had gotten so late."*

*Fully aware that Kristen was waiting, like, right beside us, I said, "It's okay."*

*His gaze flickered beyond me, and an odd shiver coursed down my spine. He was looking at Kristen. "What are you doing tomorrow evening?"*

*Tomorrow evening? I blinked slowly. I was planning to head back to Shepherd, and he would be leaving with my father and the Lima Team. So why was—?*

*"How about we grab something to eat tomorrow? Yeah." Brock's smile could stop traffic. Right then it stopped my heart. "That would work better."*

"*What?*" *I breathed, thinking I didn't hear him right, because he wouldn't be home tomorrow. He wouldn't have time.*

"*We can grab dinner then," he continued, lifting the shot glass with an easy grin. "Spend some one-on-one time together."*

*My body flushed hot and then cold as realization sank in. He was ditching me. He was ditching me for his friends and for Kristen, and there'd be no dinner tomorrow night, because he wouldn't be here. He was flying out with Dad, and Dad liked to get to the airport early.*

"*Jillian," Jax said, his brows lifting.*

*Flushing to the color of my lipstick, my gaze darted around the group frantically. Reece was looking away—looking at his long-time girlfriend Roxy, who was down at the other end of the bar. Colton was studying his shoes. The guy I didn't recognize was smiling at the group of girls, oblivious to everything except the girls. And Kristen . . . Kristen was looking at me the way every girl looks at* that *girl, the one who has no clue—the one who gives you second-hand embarrassment.*

*Oh God.*

"*Yeah. Um, that's cool." I backed up, blinking back the sudden tears in my eyes. This was so humiliating. I needed to go. I needed to leave right now. "Tomorrow is fine," I croaked out, knowing that tomorrow wasn't going to happen.*

*Tonight was no different than any other night, and I'd been so dumb to think otherwise.*

"*Jillybean." He turned to put the shot on the bar. His mouth was drawn in a tight, flat line. "Hey, let me walk you out."*

*I smiled, kept on smiling even as his face began to blur. "No. That's not necessary. It's okay. I have to go anyway."*

*Brock started to frown as his eyes narrowed. "Jillian—"*

"*Bye!" I chirped out, giving Colton and Reece a quick wave. "See you guys later."*

*They might've said goodbye or they could've said nothing. I didn't know. Blood pounded in my ears, and I couldn't hear anything as I hurried through the bar, dodging the crowds of people talking and laughing. My hands shook as I pushed open the door and raced out into the balmy night air.*

A light tap on the door dragged me out of the memory. Feeling shaken and sick to my stomach, experiencing all that messy and raw heartbreak like it was seconds ago instead of years ago, I looked up and saw Brock standing there like he'd been called up out of the mists of the past.

Why did he have to be here right now? Why? Because seeing him right now was just as bad as seeing him immediately after masturbating to thoughts of him. Painfully fucking awkward.

He took one look at me and concern pinched his features. "Hey, you all right?"

"Yeah." I swallowed down the knot clogging my throat as I watched him walk into my office. "I was . . ." I trailed off. I didn't have a good excuse as to why I was sitting at my desk, staring at the wall like someone had kicked my cat into oncoming traffic. Lifting a hand, I tucked my hair back. "You haven't been standing there long, have you?"

"Long enough."

I tensed.

Brock's dark gaze roamed over my face, missing nothing. He said nothing as he came forward and then sat in the chair across from my desk. Several seconds passed and then he said, "Sometimes you get that look on your face. Like you're a thousand miles away. As if you're someplace else. And I think I know where."

Oh God.

My eyes widened.

"And I've seen that look before," he continued, his gaze finding mine. His broad shoulders tensed. "Because I . . . I put that look on your face before."

Sucking in a sharp breath, I pushed back from the desk using my toes. I gripped the arms of my chair. "I wasn't thinking about that. Not at all. I was just lost in thought. Seriously."

His brows lifted in surprise, and he stared at me like I'd just admitted to secretly being Batgirl or something. "You . . . you never cease to surprise me."

I laughed nervously. "I'm not sure that's a good thing."

Shaking his head as if he was almost stuck in a bubble of wonder, he then leaned forward, pressing his hands together. "You protect me."

"What?"

"You *protected* me back then," he said, his voice oddly hoarse. "And you are still doing it now, aren't you? You don't want me to think about that night, because you don't want me to be upset."

My God, was I that easily readable?

"Even though I know it still fucks with you. It still fucks with me. It *always* fucks with me, but you were the one hurt. I was the one who screwed up, and yet you still try to protect me."

I was going to break the arms of my chair.

"And I don't deserve that," he said, a muscle flexing along his jaw. "I sure as hell didn't deserve it then, and I still don't deserve it now."

Squeezing my eyes shut, I struggled to get air into my lungs. "Brock . . ."

"But I'm going to change that," he promised, and my eyes flew open. "One day, one day real soon, I will change that."

# Chapter 16

"This . . . this would be so perfect." With one hand on her protruding belly, Teresa turned in a slow circle. "I can almost see the mirror over here, across the wall. The bars right across from it."

Avery nodded as she stood next to her friend. "God, this is . . . this is even more than what we expected."

I allowed myself a small smile as they roamed the cavernous room lit up by industrial overhead lights. We'd already lost the guys. Jase and Cam had disappeared with Brock about five minutes into the meeting.

I stood back and let Avery and Teresa do their thing. There were a couple more spaces that were empty, but I felt this one would work better since it was large enough to be sectioned into more than one space. I'd already gathered part of the information Brock had requested, pricing other classes in the area and their average class size. As I explained to Brock before, there wasn't a lot of competition.

"So you think this space would work?" I asked.

Avery glanced over her shoulder, her eyes bright and warm. "Yes. This would definitely work."

"Some of the spaces we looked at before were literally just rooms above businesses that were kept cool by ceiling fans," Teresa explained. "And let's not even talk about the condition of the floors in those places."

"All right, so at least we know this space could work." I clasped my hands together as I tapped the pointy toe of my heeled shoe. "The next step is getting as close as possible an estimate for how much it would cost to convert this space into a dance studio. That's where you guys would come in," I explained. "I've spent some time looking at floor plans and material, but I figured you two would know exactly what you would need to make this work. So what I would want is an estimate."

They exchanged looks and Teresa said, "We can do that."

"Easily," Avery agreed. "When would you need the information?"

"We have time. We're nearing the end of the year, so we're moving into the budgets for spring. If we were to greenlight this project, we'll need to get permits and all of that lined up. Once we have the estimate, then we're one step closer."

Excitement glimmered in Avery's eyes. "Do you think this is going to happen?" she asked me.

"I think Brock is on board. He does have some concerns about cost and profitability, which is normal, but I think there is a lot of growth potential here," I answered truthfully. "The trick will be getting my father to sign off. He's open to new ideas, but this is not something he's ever considered before. I want to have everything lined up before we go to him. We want to position this so it doesn't even cross his mind to turn it down. I think we can make this work."

Avery hobbled from one side to the other, which I guess was her version of her happy dance.

Giggling, Teresa raised her arms and shook them before waddling over to where I was standing. "Thank you." She stood on my left side and placed her hand on my arm. "Seriously. I know nothing is official yet, but thank you for wanting to help us and trying to make this possible. Dancing has been such a large part of our lives, that to be able to seriously get involved in it again is nothing short of making a dream come true for us."

"No problem." Blushing a little, I glanced over to where Avery was smiling at us. "So what do you guys think about possible timing if this pans out?"

"The timing is perfect if we're looking at the spring before anything starts to get moving," Avery said, looking toward Teresa. "You're due by the end of December—"

"Thank God," Teresa muttered.

"By the time classes would be ready, we'd probably be looking at mid-summer, right?"

Teresa nodded. "Right."

There was a sudden burst of male laughter followed by the sound of something fleshy hitting what sounded like a mat.

Teresa glanced at the double doors with a slight frown. "I really hope Brock isn't showing them moves."

"God, I hope not, because I'm really hungry and don't want to spend the evening in the emergency room," Avery agreed.

I laughed. "If he is, he'll be gentle with them." *Kind of,* I added silently.

The look on Avery's face said she knew better. "Maybe we should go find them."

"Not necessary," a male voice announced from the door, and I twisted at the waist. Jase was striding through the doors, his gaze fixed on his wife. "I know you guys were bereft without us, but we're back."

Teresa snorted. "I don't think bereft is the right word."

A second later Cam and Brock entered, and I bet Avery was relieved to see Cam appearing to be in one piece and not limping. He immediately joined the redhead, draping his arms over her narrow shoulders. Speaking too low for me to hear, I guessed by the sudden pink tint to Avery's cheeks that whatever Cam had said to her was something she was glad I didn't overhear.

Jase walked up behind his wife, and looped his arms around her, his hands resting on her extended stomach. "Everything good?" he asked, kissing her cheek.

Closing her eyes, she nodded as she leaned back into him. I felt a tug at my chest, and lowered my gaze, feeling like I shouldn't be gawking at them like a creeper. The love they felt for one another was palpable, the same as Avery and Cam. It was good to be surrounded by such happy couples, but sometimes it was hard not to be a wee bit jealous. I felt crappy for feeling that way, but it was hard to imagine myself where Teresa and Avery were. Well, I mean I could imagine it, but that was all it was. A fantasy at this point.

I peeked over at Brock. He was checking out his phone, his jaw clenched, and I felt my stomach take an Olympic dive. He'd been out of the office most of Thursday and today, in various meetings, so I hadn't seen much of him since that afternoon in my office, when he made his promise—a promise I didn't fully understand.

He'd picked me up this morning, using the same excuse he'd said before, and I was a bit nervous about the drive home. Hell, the drive *anywhere* at this point, because he hadn't been very talkative this morning or the few times I'd seen him.

"Everything look good?" Brock asked, lowering his phone.

Teresa and Avery practically exploded into a chorus of enthusiastic yeses, and a small grin curved up the corner of Brock's lips while both husbands smiled more broadly.

"Good." Brock glanced over at me, his expression unreadable. "Then let's hit the road."

*     *     *

Staring at what I believed was my second shot of Jameson, I tried to figure out how I got to the point where my belly was full, the blood in my veins was warm, and all the muscles in my body were decidedly relaxed.

It had started with wine.

Squirreled away in the small restaurant-bar, we had commandeered a large booth in front of the windows, and Teresa who obviously couldn't drink had somehow weaseled me into drinking for her. Something about living vicariously through me.

Now, I was typically a "one glass of wine and done" type of girl. Very rarely did I drink two ... or four, and especially not around other people. The thing with getting buzzed, you tend to forget things about yourself, and while that could be awesome, I liked to be spatially aware of my surroundings ... and my weird mouth.

But before I knew it, and through no fault of my own, I drank a couple of glasses of wine, and I *think* one shot, and I wasn't thinking about my mouth or the scars, or the conversation Brock and I had had Wednesday, or the night Brock broke my heart and I ended up with said scars. I wasn't really thinking about any of that nonsense, and it was *wonderful*.

I should drink more often.

Now I stared at the second shot, wondering how it had shown up in front of me. Buzzing, my gaze bounced from the amber-colored liquor to Jase. Wait. Was this the second one? Or the third?

I think it was the third.

"It wasn't me." He held his hands up.

Avery, who had also indulged a bit, giggled. Her face was so flushed, I could barely make out the freckles. Cam wasn't drinking, so he was loading her up on drinks. Granted, she deserved to let loose. Raising kids had to . . . My thoughts trailed off, and then I remembered I was trying to figure out how the shot got in front of me.

I turned and looked at Brock.

He was sitting to my left, arms resting on the table. He shrugged a shoulder as he picked up his glass of water. "Thought you looked like you needed another one."

I studied him for a moment. "Are you trying to get me drunk?"

"Never." He widened his eyes innocently. "I'm just trying to get you to relax."

"I *am* relaxed." I picked up the glass. "Totes relaxed," I murmured.

"You're normally as tense as a damn cobra," he responded, and I had no idea if cobras were tense. I was going to have to take his word for it. "Drink up."

I drank up.

The liquid burned my throat and watered my eyes. Gasping for air, I squeezed my eyes shut. "Oh my God, it burns."

Brock chuckled and leaned into me, his entire right arm pressing against mine, and I liked it. A lot. "It's the good kind of burn, though. Puts hair on your chest," he teased.

"That's hot," I replied, my gaze dropping from his face to his chest. "You have a nice chest."

Another laugh rumbled out of Brock. "Well, thank you."

In the back of my head, I knew I was experiencing the worse case of word vomit, but I couldn't seem to stop myself, or care. "Do you still have tattoos on your chest?"

His smile was wide as he stared at me. "Since I'm not willing to subject myself to hours of laser removal, yes, I still have tats on my chest, Jilly."

I nodded, happy to hear this. "I really liked them. Especially the . . . the cross one. Yeah." Pausing, I easily pictured it in my head. "It's all Celtic and . . . shit."

"Celtic and shit." Jase laughed. "I like the way that sounds."

"Me too." I gave him the nod of approval I just knew he was waiting on.

"Look!" Teresa suddenly smacked Jase's arm. "I am so glad I'm not the only pregnant person here."

Jase chuckled. "It's a restaurant *and* bar. Last time I checked, pregnant women were allowed to eat in places that served food."

"Yeah, but it feels weird," she replied. "I feel like everyone is looking at me, secretly judging me."

"Fuck 'em. You don't know them. They don't know you," I said and then my mouth dropped open. "Sorry. That whole 'fuck 'em' part was kind of rude. I'm a bit buzzed."

Her eyes widened and then she grinned. "I like buzzy Jillian."

Buzzy Jillian liked her too. I refocused on Brock. "You . . . you know what?"

He took a sip of his water and then was leaning into me again, and I really, really liked that. And I also liked that his dark eyes warmed when he looked at me. "What?"

"You seem chill." I lowered my voice.

"Chill?" He dipped his chin toward me, his dark eyes glittering. "When wasn't I chill?"

I shrugged. My shoulder knocked into his. "You were all stone face earlier. You know, jaw clenched and quiet."

"Stone face? That's a new description." His gaze flickered across the table before settling on me. "I was just dealing with some stuff."

Oh. That sounded so dramatic. "What stuff?"

"Stuff," he repeated, and somehow his mouth ended up closer to mine. So close that I could feel his breath on my lips. "I'll tell you about it later. Okay?"

I was staring at his mouth. "Okay." I had no idea what I was agreeing to, but those lips were lush and curved up.

Brock chuckled again, the deep rich sound that made me feel giddy. Well, giddier than I already felt. Wait. Was giddier a word?

Avery leaned into Cam and tilted her head back as she gripped the front of his shirt, pulling him down to whisper something. His eyes widened slightly and then a knowing grin stretched his lips.

"It's time for us to leave." Cam raised his hand, looking around for the waiter.

Teresa arched a brow as Avery giggled again, and all I could think was someone was definitely going to get laid tonight.

Lucky.

The waiter appeared and a couple of blurry minutes later, Avery and I were clinging to one another, saying goodbye, and I tried to hug Teresa, and then I was sitting in Brock's car.

"Your car is so fancy," I told him, reaching for the seatbelt. I missed it and reached for it again. "So fancy-smancy."

Brock laughed as he shut my door. I managed to get myself buckled in by the time he was behind the wheel. "You doing okay over there?"

"I'm doing perfect." I plopped my purse in my lap, cuddling it close. "Avery and Teresa are really excited about the space . . ." I spent the trip to my apartment going into detail about how excited they were. Brock listened, and whenever I looked over at him, he was grinning as he concentrated on the road. It seemed like it took only seconds to get to my apartment complex. I blinked, and we were in the parking lot, and I was staring up at my darkened window. Unease crowded the happy buzz in my veins. It was early, not even ten o'clock, and the only living thing in my apartment was Rhage, and it was a Friday night. Being alone on the weekends sucked, because everyone else was out there. I didn't know where exactly, but they were *there*, and I was over here, doing nothing.

"I'm walking you up," he announced, turning off the car. He twisted toward me. "You think you can manage those stairs?"

Offended, I swung my head around and nearly toppled over. "I can walk."

Even in the dark interior I could see the amusement etched into his face. "Are you seriously going to sit there and act like you're not drunk?"

"I am a . . . little tipsy."

"I never would've guessed that," he replied dryly.

"It's your fault," I grumbled, opening the door. I started to get out and then choked myself with the seatbelt. "Damn it."

Brock laughed. "I'm not denying that."

It took me a couple of moments to get out of the car. "But I can fully walk up those stairs." I pointed at them just in case he had no idea what I was talking about. "I don't need your help."

Grinning, he slowly approached me. "Okay. You don't need my help, but how about I offer it to you anyway?"

I stared up at him, eyes squinty. "When did you become such a gentleman?"

"I'm not a gentleman." He took hold of my hand. "Trust me."

"I don't know about that." I let him guide me across the parking lot. "Wait. You know what would be great? Ice cream." Slipping my hand free, I wheeled around and started heading back to his fancy car. "We could go get ice cream."

"Come back here," he said, laughing. Circling an arm around my waist, he turned me back around. "Let's wait on the ice cream. See if we want to eat that in a little bit."

"Why?"

"Might make your stomach a bit upset after drinking the whiskey."

"Hmmm. That sounds legit." I stopped talking because I found we were in front of the steps and I needed to concentrate. They proved more difficult than anticipated.

At my door, I slipped my purse off my shoulder and found my keys where the hall swayed a bit. I pulled them out and promptly dropped them.

Brock swiped them off the floor, moving ninja-fast. "I got it."

"Yes." I watched him unlock my front door. "Yes. You do."

Shaking his head, he opened the door. "Get in."

I stumbled in, throwing out my hand and hitting the switch on the wall. Soft buttery light flooded the living room. My gaze immediately landed on Rhage. He was sitting on the coffee table and his little yellow cat eyes were full of judgment.

"Stop staring at me," I muttered, trudging forward. Then I stopped, remembering that Brock was there. I turned. He was still standing in the doorway. "You coming in?"

"You want me to?" he asked.

"Yes." Then I nodded, just in case he was confused.

Watching me with that grin on his face, he stepped inside and closed the door behind him. Then he walked over to the island and placed my keys on it. "You got water in the fridge?"

"I got water in the faucets, too." I toed off my heels and kicked them against the wall. Sighing, I wiggled my toes.

Brock snorted as he walked to the fridge. "You got any pain relievers?"

"Why? You got a headache?" Feeling warm, too warm, I walked toward the window, about to open it when I realized that would require a lot of effort at the moment. I looked down at myself and remembered that I had a tank top on under the sweater-blouse.

Listening to cabinet doors open and close, I reached down and peeled the sweater up over my head, letting it drop on the floor. Cooler air washed over my arms. Feeling a million times better, I turned around.

Brock found the stash of pills in the cabinet near the fridge and was doling out aspirins into his palm. With the bottle of water in his other hand, he turned around and went rigid.

I started to say something, but forgot whatever it was as his gaze swept over my face and then dropped, traveling over the thin straps of my top. The tank was tight, like a second skin, and it was low cut, showing off the swells of my breasts. I knew this, because that was where he was looking.

Pleasant warmth replaced the almost suffocating heat from a few seconds ago, but I didn't want to shed that feeling. Not when he was walking toward me, his eyes darker now, like a heated night sky.

Swallowing, I tipped my head back as he stopped in front of me. I don't know why I said what I said next. It just came out of my mouth. "Grady never took me out to dinner."

One brow rose.

"He had to reschedule, but he's been busy with his grandparents' farm and midterms and finals and . . ." I shrugged, and his gaze dropped again. "I don't think I care."

"Of course you don't. Told you, you deserve better than him. Take these and drink the water," he ordered. "You'll be grateful that you did when you wake up."

Knowing he had experience in these things, I did as I was told while he walked past me and picked up the remote. Rhage hopped down and pranced over to where Brock stood, winding his body around his ankles.

Traitorous asshole cat.

Brock turned on the TV and started flipping through the channels, settling on what appeared to be a Jason Statham movie where Jason Statham was playing . . . Jason Statham.

Placing the remote on the end table, Brock walked over and turned off the light, and then he sat down—no, he laid down on his side. Apparently I'd missed the moment he'd taken off his shoes and socks. He propped his head on his fist and looked over at me. "Come here."

I didn't move for a second. In the back of my mind there was a small voice that was starting to pick up in volume that was warning me not to go to him—to ask him to leave and then go face-plant the bed—but I told that voice to shut the hell up, and I went to him.

Brock extended his hand, and feeling dizzy, I placed mine in his. "Watch this movie with me? Then I'll leave."

Watch a movie with him? I . . . I could do that.

He tugged me down so I was lying stretched out on the couch beside him. He'd let go of my hand, so I was facing the TV. My back was against his front and there was the tiniest space between us.

It reminded me of other days, days long ago, when we'd lie like this at home. Touching but not. Several moments passed, and I felt his hand settle on my hip. I jerked at the touch and then bit down on my lip.

My heart pounded in rhythm with the gunfire echoing on the TV. His hand didn't move, but his thumb did. It glided back and forth. My body zeroed in on it as I stared at the TV, not seeing what was on it. I started to move.

"Jillian," he groaned, his hand flattening on my hip. "Lay still and watch the movie."

Pouting, I exhaled heavily. I didn't want to lay still. Not when he was here. Not when his body was long and warm and hard so near mine.

"Brock?" I turned my head so I could hear him.

"What, babe?"

I stared at the ceiling. "Is this . . . is this weird that we're here, right now?"

"Weird?" I felt him shift, and then suddenly he was staring down at me. The flicker of the TV cast shadows over his face. "There's nothing weird about this. If anything, it's right."

Right.

This was *right*.

My eyes searched his. "Did you . . . did you miss me this whole time?" I drew in a shallow breath. "I missed you."

Brock's gaze held mine. "Missed you every fucking day, Jillian, with every ounce of who I am."

# Chapter 17

I awoke to a dream.

That was the only explanation for why I was nestled up against a warm, male body—a body that I instinctively knew was Brock. It was his hand that was under the back of my top, flat against my lower back. It was his chest that my cheek was resting against, and his thick leg that was cradled under mine.

I awoke to a fire.

My body was overheated and lava had replaced the blood in my veins. The slow, sluggish pulse picked up, and my hips shifted, pressing the most intimate part of me against him. The friction was nearly immediate, like it was when I touched myself and thought of him. I moved against him, seeking release as my fingers curled into the material of his shirt.

I'd been dreaming of him—of his large body moving over mine and then in me, kissing and nipping at my naked flesh. The dream felt like now, and in the fog clouding my thoughts, I couldn't make sense of what was then and what was now.

But now he tensed against me, his hand spasming against my back. "Jillian?"

His voice . . . it sounded so real that I moaned and I lifted my upper body. There was a flash of his face and then I was moving my hand from his chest to the rough line of his jaw. I kissed him—I kissed him as I rocked against him, seeking and searching.

The arm around my waist tightened and then he was kissing me back—hard and wet, and there was nothing artful or slow about it. Our teeth gnashed together. Our tongues tangled, and this—*it's not a dream, not a dream*—didn't feel real.

His mouth moved over mine as I twisted my hips against his leg. The tension was coiling into a knot, but it wasn't enough, this wasn't enough. I whimpered into his mouth, my movements becoming more frantic.

Brock seemed to know what I needed.

"I got you." He pulled back, speaking in that deep, husky voice.

In a flurry of movement, he reached between us as his teeth grazed the sensitive skin under my ear, his nimble fingers catching the button on my pants, unhooking it. He worked the zipper down, loosening them. *Not a dream. Not a dream.* I was out of breath and my heart was pounding all over the place as his large, hot hand slipped into the opening of my pants and under the band of my panties.

The moment the tips of his fingers brushed over the tight oversensitive nerves, I cried out, throwing my head back. I didn't care if this wasn't a dream. I didn't care what tomorrow would bring. "Please," I begged, moving my hips against his hand. "Please, *Brock* . . ."

"Fuck," he grunted, his mouth hot against my neck as I felt his finger sink deep into my wetness. "Fuck, you're tight."

My body was out of control. I gripped his arm, holding his hand to me as he pumped his finger in and out. My hips were moving faster and he did something with his hand, twisting his palm and it was everything—his mouth against my neck, his hand in my panties, between my thighs, his finger inside me—I clenched and then broke apart, crying out as sharp pleasure shattered my senses.

My body went lax as I slumped down, half on him and half against him. In my chest, my heart slowed and I was barely aware of his finger easing out of me. Sweat dotted my brow as I closed my eyes.

"Fuck," I heard Brock say, and it was the last thing I heard.

I woke to my head throbbing and my left arm dead. I was also hot, like I'd been sleeping under a ton of blankets during the dead of summer.

Something furry brushed along the bottom of my foot, tickling me and causing me to jerk my leg. Confused, I pried open my eyes and immediately winced at the bright sunlight streaming into the living room. My head felt like a drummer had set up camp inside and my mouth felt like a desert and I . . .

I was not alone.

The first thing I saw was Rhage sitting on the arm of the couch, staring at me with his tail swishing back and forth. Slowly my gaze traveled up my leg and then got hung up on the very large hand resting on my hip. For several seconds I couldn't process it, then I turned my head and saw Brock. His profile was relaxed, hair messy and lips slightly parted. The white button-down was wrinkled and half un-tucked, revealing an impossibly flat and ripped lower stomach. My gaze flew back to his face, and it all came crashing back— dinner last night, the two or three shots of whiskey on top of three glasses of wine, coming home and passing out next to Brock.

Waking up in the middle of the night and—oh my God.
*Oh God.*
Oh God, what had I done?

I flushed hot and then cold, and immediately I knew I needed to move. Carefully, with more grace than I knew I had, I slipped out of his loose embrace, sprang from the couch like I was made of coils, and then darted down the hall. I reached the hallway bathroom and flew inside it, closing the door behind me. I backed up until I hit the low rim of the tub and then I sat down.

Oh my God.

Squeezing my eyes shut, I let out a pitiful moan. I'd dry humped Brock's leg. I totally did that—I dry humped his leg in the middle of the night, half-drunk and half-asleep.

And I'd done more than that. He'd done more than that. Glancing down at myself, I saw that my pants were still unbuttoned, unzipped. The hot-pink cotton panties peeking through.

Oh no, no, no.

I could still feel his finger inside me, pumping and sliding. I could hear my own breathy cries. Jumping up, I quickly buttoned up my pants and then turned, stopping halfway between the toilet and door.

"Holy shit," I gasped. "Holy shit."

I was never drinking again.

Ever.

Like fucking for real, I could not be trusted with alcohol.

"Okay," I whispered to myself. "Okay. Focus, Jillian."

He was still out there. I was going to have to face him. I had no idea how, because I had no idea how to look someone in the eye after practically molesting them while they slept.

I mean, when he woke up he seemed to be a willing partner, but still, this was going to be awkward, so awkward.

Turning on the faucet, I cupped the water and splashed it over my face. When I lifted my head, my face was still hot. What was I going to do? I slicked my hair back with wet hands, fighting the urge to sit down and have a really good cry.

Heavy footsteps sounded out in the hall, and I pushed away from the sink, quickly locking the door. Then I stared at it, holding my breath.

"Jillian?" Brock's voice was rough with sleep, and I turned my head so my left ear was to the door. "Are you in there?"

Clasping my hands together, I mulled over what to do.

"I hope so," he continued. "Because your cat is staring at me like he wants to be fed, and I feel like if I feed your cat, I'm crossing some kind of line," he added with a laugh.

That was crossing a line? Pretty sure riding his leg and then his hand in a drunken stupor was crossing a line.

"Jilly," he called again.

I had to answer. "I'm . . . I'm in here."

There was a stretch of silence. "Are you okay?"

No. No I was not. "Sure."

"Do you need anything?"

"No." Then hope sprang alive, because maybe, just maybe, I could get him to leave. "I'll be fine. You can go ahead and leave."

"What?"

Sliding my hands over my hair, I tugged on the ends. "Thank you for driving me home last night and making sure I got in okay. I really appreciate it. I'll—I'll see you on Monday."

There was another patch of silence, and I strained to hear what he was doing out in the hall. I thought I heard Rhage meow pitifully somewhere.

"Jillian," he said, and this time there was no lightness or teasing to his tone. "Come out here."

I scrunched up my nose. "No, thanks."

"*Jillian.*"

"Seriously, I'll see you on Monday—"

"You are not going to hide in the damn bathroom," he cut in. "You're going to open this door and come out here and talk to me."

Yeah, that was not going to happen, and when I didn't respond, I saw the knob turn.

Brock cursed. "Jillian, come on."

Nope.

"Okay," he said. "If you don't want to come out, then we can talk through the door. I'm not stupid. I know why you're hiding in the bathroom."

My eyes narrowed at the closed door.

"There's no reason to be embarrassed over what happened last night," he started and I lost it.

"Really? I think there's plenty of reasons to be embarrassed," I said, dropping my hands. "I got drunk and I—"

"Used me to get off?" he supplied.

"Oh my God, seriously? Thanks for putting it bluntly."

"I didn't mind."

My mouth dropped open and I just stared forward. I had no words. None. Zip. Nada. Then I shook my head. "How could you not mind? I practically molested you."

Brock's deep laugh made its way into the bathroom. "First off, if I didn't want you doing any of that last night, I would've stopped you. I wouldn't have made you come."

I slapped my hands on my hips and nearly doubled over. *Made you come.* Oh God, he had *so* done that. I couldn't deal with this. My head was still clouded from the devil's nectar known as whiskey and wine, and I needed coffee, and I needed him *gone*.

"Okay," I said after a moment. "Can we just pretend like that didn't happen last night?"

"Are you serious?" he asked, and shock colored his tone.

"Yes. I am serious. I don't want to think about it. I don't want to acknowledge it," I said in a rush. "And I want to go on like that never happened. We can do that. It's better that way. So you don't have to be okay with it or worry that it'll happen again or that I think anything stupid." I drew in a ragged breath. "Things will be normal."

"Open the door," Brock said calmly, way too calmly.

I shook my head. "You can leave."

"Jillian."

"I think you need to leave," I said this time.

"Open the goddamn door or I will fucking break it down."

Well then.

Casting my gaze to the ceiling, I let out a ripe curse and then unlocked the bathroom door, because I didn't put it past him to do it. "Better?" I shot back.

Brock stared at me, his jaw working, and damn it all to hell, he looked so rumpled and *sexy* with his hair nearly standing up and one tail of his shirt hanging loose. "Were you completely unaware of what you were doing last night? I need you to be honest with me, Jillian. Did you have no idea what you were doing?"

Part of me wanted to say that I was, but that wasn't completely true. I'd been aware. I woke up from a dream and I'd wanted him, and he was there and . . .

"I knew you were buzzed, but I had no idea you were that—"

"I wasn't *that* drunk," I whispered, knowing I could never let him believe he somehow took advantage of the situation when he hadn't, just to save face. "I knew what was happening, but I . . . I just wasn't thinking. I knew. Honest."

His eyes searched mine as some of the tension eased out of his shoulders. "Now I want you to listen to me and I want you to listen real good. If you think for a second I can go around and pretend that I didn't have my fingers in you and you didn't come all around them, you have another thing coming."

"Oh my God!" Horrified, I pressed my hands to my cheeks. "Can you not be any cruder?"

"Crude?" He smirked as he leaned against the door jamb, effectively trapping me in the bathroom. He crossed his arms. "You sure as hell didn't have a problem fucking my hand last night—"

"I was drunk. Like, I thought I was still sleeping," I argued.

"So do you normally dream of me then?"

My nostrils flared as I inhaled deeply and counted to five. "I do not dream about you."

A smug half-grin appeared on his face, and I wanted to smack it off. "Yeah, I'm going to have to call bullshit on that."

"You can call bullshit on your face for all I care," I fired back, and his brows flew up. That sounded lame to my own ears. "The point is, I didn't mean for that to happen last night and it shouldn't have."

A muscle flexed along Brock's jaw as he eyed me. "I know you didn't mean for it to happen, but it did. And maybe it shouldn't have happened like that, but it *did*."

I inhaled sharply as I blinked. Tears threatened to erupt, and with this headache, without coffee, and considering what had happened last night, it was going to be an epic meltdown. "Please," I asked, begged really. "Please, can we just forget this? Can you just leave?"

For a moment, I didn't think Brock was going to leave. I thought he was going to stay there, standing in the doorway of the hallway bathroom forever, but then something crossed his features. His jaw softened, as did those dark eyes of his. "Okay," he said, pushing off the door and unfolding his arms.

"For now, I'll let this go, but I don't want you acting fucking weird over this. What happened out there, on the couch, isn't something I'm ashamed about. You shouldn't be either." He stopped, drawing in a breath. "Don't let this screw up what we've got happening here. Okay?"

I wanted to ask what exactly he thought was happening here, but all I could force out was a weak, "Okay."

# Chapter 18

Somewhere between the weekend and Monday morning, I realized that something I'd fantasized and dreamt about since I was old enough to know what those sex scenes in the books I read were really describing had actually happened.

Brock had kissed me.

Well, I had kissed him and he'd kissed me back. It wasn't a long and passionate kiss. When I was younger, I'd dreamt of the kind of kisses that curled the toes and stole your breath. This kiss had been brutal and fast, and not only that, but he'd touched me—a part of him had actually been *in* me.

I couldn't even wrap my head around it, because it didn't . . . it didn't count. It wasn't real. I'd been out of it and he'd been half-asleep when he woke up, discovering me rubbing all over him like a cat in heat, and Brock . . . Brock responded like most men would've. And he hadn't even gotten anything out of it. I'd fallen back asleep almost immediately.

What happened had meant nothing.

It couldn't have, because we ended up being a disaster once before and we'd be a total catastrophe now. I had to guard my heart and I had to listen to my head. There was too much at risk for me to travel down that path again with Brock—my job, what I was hoping to accomplish for Avery and Teresa, and most importantly, my happiness.

I needed to keep my distance, so when my phone rang Sunday night, and it was Grady, not only was I surprised he was calling, I was *almost* eager to answer.

"You busy?" he asked when I answered.

"No. I was just reading," I told him, glancing at the Kindle on the couch next to me. The screen had long since faded out and Rhage currently had one paw resting on the black edge as if he were daring me to try to pick it up.

"So, I'm going to be home this Saturday," he said, and I couldn't help thinking that even Brock would've asked what I was reading. The moment that thought popped into my head, I wanted to smack myself with the Kindle. "And I was hoping you'd be free and we could finally catch that dinner."

"Really?" Surprised, I winced.

Grady laughed. "Yeah. You sound shocked. Did you think I wasn't going to keep my promise?"

Yeah, I really hadn't thought he would. He hadn't texted since last Wednesday, and that had just been a generic "hey, how you doing" kind of thing. "I just thought that maybe you were just really busy."

"I am, but I'll be free Saturday night. So what do you think?"

An acidic taste coated the inside of my mouth—the same mouth that had been locked on Brock's a little over twenty-four hours ago. Going out with Grady afterward seemed gross and wrong, like I should—

Wait.

Wait a freaking second.

I was not dating Brock. There was nothing between us, and it wasn't like he had professed any sort of feelings for me. What had happened between us was . . . was a *mistake*. He'd known how I felt about him back when we were younger and that hadn't stopped him from being the Academy bicycle.

There was absolutely nothing wrong with going out with Grady. Nothing at all, and actually, it was probably the best thing I could do.

So, I took a deep breath and said, "I would love to go out with you on Saturday."

Come Monday morning, I did my best to act as normal as humanly possible when I saw Brock, having decided I wouldn't think about it for one more second. We were grown adults—two sexually active, grown adults. Okay. I wasn't really sexually active, but I was sure he was. Either way, we were adults. These things sometimes happened, and it had nothing to do with our past or even our present.

Brock was my friend and he was also my boss.

I could handle this and not make a big deal out of it.

When he strode in, bringing my pumpkin spice latte, all I could think about was how his hand had felt against me, and I could feel my face burn like the seven circles of hell.

His lips twitched as he placed the cup on my desk. "Good morning, Jillian."

"Good morning." I focused on his chest and then thought about how I'd slept on it. I averted my gaze to his hands, and that was the wrong move, because then I was thinking about him using that finger of his. Good God, there was no safe place to look.

He lingered, because of course. "How was your weekend?"

"Good. I just hung out at home." I stared at his collarbone. That seemed like a safe place. "You?"

"Mostly boring," he said. "Except for Friday night and Saturday morning. That was far from boring."

Oh dear, he was going to go there? Sucking in air, I looked up at him. I was going to gloss right over that. "Well, that's good to hear. I have some phone calls to make, so . . ."

Brock folded his arms, stretching the dress shirt until I feared it would rip right off and slip from his body. "Make sure your schedule is cleared around noon. We're going to lunch."

My stomach twisted. The idea of going to lunch with him filled me with a mixture of dread and excitement, but I remembered that I was going to distance myself. I was going to be smart, for once, about this. Spending one-on-one time with him right now wasn't a smart move. "I have too much to do today."

One eyebrow rose. "You have time for lunch."

"I packed it."

Leaning forward, he unfolded his arms and placed his hands on my desk. "You can eat your packed lunch tomorrow."

"I can't," I said. "It's a salad. It will go bad."

His eyes narrowed. "Since when do you eat salads?"

"Since *forever.*"

He was quiet for a moment. "And if I go back into the break room, what's the likelihood of me finding this salad?"

Oh hell, he wouldn't, would he? Yes, he would. But there had to be a salad back there. I worked with a ton of fitness nuts. Someone must have packed a salad. "You'll find a salad."

"That actually belongs to you?"

I clamped my mouth shut.

Brock smirked. "What if I said, as your boss, you're going to lunch?"

My hand curled around the pen I held, clenching it so tightly I feared it would snap. "Then I would say that's kind of an abuse of your position over me?"

He laughed. "That's a reach."

I forced a casual shrug. "I don't think it would be right."

"And why is that?"

My heart thumped against my ribs. "I just have a lot of work to do—"

"It's because of this weekend," he interrupted. "Even though I told you not to let this shit get in the way of what is happening?"

My gaze flew to the door. It was open, but no one was nearby. Still, I kept my voice low. "There isn't anything happening, and it has nothing to do with this weekend," I said, and that was a lie, but then I went with a bit of the truth, telling him something that I hoped he'd take as a hint. "Anyway, I'm going out with Grady on Saturday, so . . ."

Brock stared at me for a heartbeat and then said, "The guy you said on Friday had been too busy to take you out and you didn't care?"

"I didn't say that."

"Oh hell yes, yes you did. I was sober. I remember what you said." Those midnight eyes met mine. "I remember everything you said and did."

Heat exploded across my cheeks. "Well, congratulations."

"Where is he taking you?"

"I guess to the steakhouse," I said dismissively. "He wanted to go somewhere nice."

Brock's full lips pursed. "You're really going out with him on Saturday?"

"Yes." I glanced at my computer. "So, is there anything else you need?"

His gaze hardened and a look of almost disbelief settled into his face. "You're really going to do this?"

"Do what?"

"Is this how it's going to be?"

I held his stare. "I don't understand what you mean by that question or the one before it."

Pushing off my desk, he straightened to his full height. "Oh, I think you do." And then with that, he pivoted around and stalked out of my office.

And I would barely see him over the rest of the week.

Saturday evening, I stood in front of the mirror attached to the inside of my closet door. I hadn't ended up buying a new dress. Instead, I dug one out that I'd bought when I'd been with Ben. It was this simple, but pretty black dress I'd planned on wearing to our anniversary dinner.

A dinner he hadn't showed up for.

He'd claimed that he'd stayed behind at work and lost track of time, but looking back, there'd probably been a good chance he was just having drinks with some other chick.

I'd tried not to linger on that relationship other than using it as a wakeup call—a rather painful and oftentimes embarrassing one. I didn't think about Ben a lot, but wearing the dress that had been meant for our anniversary, I couldn't help but wonder what he was up to now.

And then realized I honestly didn't care.

The dress was a little tighter than I remembered around my breasts, which were showcased in the heart-shaped neckline. The sleeves were quarter-length, and I liked that, because I'd never been a fan of my upper arms. Ever. The dress followed the curve of my hips and ended just above the thighs.

It had been a long time since I'd worn a dress.

It had been an even longer time since I wore a *tight* dress.

But I was doing it tonight and I thought I looked pretty amazing. Maybe even hot. Like h-a-w-t hot. My hair was down, parted to my left, and fell in cascading waves. My eyeliner was on point and the matte red lipstick promised to stay on for the next hundred years.

I felt good. Great, even.

Stepping away from the mirror, I walked into my bedroom. The only problem with tonight was that when I thought about my date . . . I didn't feel *anything*. No nervousness. No anxiety. Definitely not even a drop of anticipation. It was like I was getting ready to go to the grocery store while looking like the bomb diggity.

And that was just lame, really lame of me.

But if I thought about those early, dark moments with Brock, my stomach fluttered like a nest of birds taking flight, and that was wrong, really wrong.

Like so wrong I needed to bang my head on the wall.

I wasn't giving Grady a chance. I knew this as I slipped a plain gold bracelet on. I'd even thought that he hadn't been interested and was just coming up with excuses, but he obviously had been. Tonight would be different, because I would be a hundred percent focused on him, and if he tried to kiss me, I would let him.

And it wouldn't be a drunken kiss in the middle of the night either.

Snatching my black purse off my bed, I walked past the small low-back chair by the door, dragging my hand over Brock's jacket like . . . geez, like a total freak. I hadn't given it back. I'd totally forgotten about it when he was over last Friday, and he hadn't asked for it back, so I'd kept it.

Not my proudest moment.

Grabbing my military-style jacket out of the hall closet, I swooped down and scratched Rhage on the top of the head. "I'll be back soon." I pulled away before he made mincemeat out of my hand. "Or maybe I won't be back at all tonight."

Rhage's ears flattened.

After making sure there was a bowl of kitty food in the kitchen, I left my apartment. Grady was waiting for me just inside the very same steakhouse Brock and I had been at with the potential investors. There weren't many options for sort of upscale restaurants in the county.

A wide smile broke out across his face as he opened his arms. "You look amazing."

"Thank you." I gave him a quick hug and then stepped back. "So do you."

He glanced down at the loose khakis with a shrug; they were the kind of pants I couldn't imagine Brock wearing.

Whoa. Why in the hell was I thinking about that?

Grady took my hand as the hostess appeared, guiding us down the narrow aisle toward our booth near a roaring, crackling fireplace. The table was long enough to seat four people, but still somehow dainty with its white linen tablecloth, flickering tea candles, and delicate wine glasses. When I'd been here with Brock, we'd been seated in the dining area beyond the fireplace, where there were tables and no booths and less foot traffic.

I sat across from Grady, and when he ordered a bottle of wine, I thought that might be a good idea. During the drive here, I'd become oddly tense.

"I'm glad we finally made it," he said. "I was so disappointed to have to push this back. I really wanted to see you."

"I am so sorry about when I had to reschedule," I said automatically. "The work dinner was a last-minute thing."

"Tell me about it," he requested with genuine interest.

So I did as the wine arrived and we placed our orders. When our food arrived, a chicken breast for him and a filet, of course, for me, I'd managed to shake the weird tension and found I was enjoying myself without having to down half a bottle of wine.

Grady was beyond nice. And he was *smart*. And kind.

I totally should kiss him tonight, I decided as I took a sip of my wine.

Candlelight flickered off Grady's face as he picked up his glass of wine. "What are your plans for Thanksgiving?"

"I'm heading home to visit my family on Wednesday. Our offices close Tuesday evening and don't reopen until the following Monday," I explained, kind of shocked that Thanksgiving was next week. *Holy crap, where had the time gone?*

"That's nice. You staying up there the whole time?"

I nodded as I chewed on a piece of tender steak. "I don't visit my family as often as I should, so I'm going to spend the time off with them." Which meant capturing Rhage and shoving him in the kitty carrier, which was as pleasant as plucking hair off my lady parts with rusty pliers.

"You doing any Black Friday shopping?"

I laughed. "No. My mom is the kind of woman who doesn't even go to sleep Thursday night. She gets herself hocked up on caffeine and then goes and buys, well, mostly stuff for herself. I mean, she gets everyone gifts too, but I know half of those bags she'll be bringing home are for herself." I started to smile at the memory of Mom yelling at Dad to get the bags out of the car while I stood on the porch, trying to see if there were any Barnes and Noble bags.

Turning my cheek to hide the smile, I immediately thought of what Brock had said that night in his car. He hadn't wanted me to hide my smile, but he really didn't understand. Maybe Grady would, but six years of habit were hard to break. I bit back a sigh. My gaze flickered back to Grady, but stopped on the hostess desk.

There was a man standing there, his back to where we sat. He was tall and broad shouldered, and there was something about the way he stood that caused my stomach to dip like I was on a rollercoaster, about to drop down a steep hill.

My eyes narrowed as Grady talked about raising sheep or milking cows or something. The man at the desk . . . There was something so familiar—

*No. No way in hell.*

I felt my heart stop as the hostess approached the waiting area, her eyes all big and doe-eyed, and the man turned sideways. I saw the profile, and about fell out of my chair.

It was Brock.

It *was* really Brock.

"Oh my fucking God," I whispered.

Grady's chin jerked up, but I barely saw him. "Excuse me?"

I didn't normally take the Lord's name in vain, but I had a feeling Jesus and Moses and Mary and everyone at this point totally understood my response.

What was he doing here? Had I mentioned where I was having dinner with Grady? Possibly? I mean, I could've in random conversation. I had to have, because I couldn't picture Brock being that much of a stalker, because that was like leveling up in the stalker arena.

"Jillian?"

Blinking, I focused on Grady as my heart felt like it was trying to crawl its way out of my throat. "I'm sorry?"

He frowned as he leaned forward. "Are you okay?"

Clearing my throat, I nodded as I hoped and prayed Brock didn't see us. "Yeah. I'm sorry. I just, um, remembered something I needed to do for work."

A small smile played over his lips. "Sounds like it was important."

I glanced over his shoulder, spying Brock talking to the hostess. "Yeah. It's really important."

"Hopefully it's not another work dinner you've forgotten about."

Had I? Because that was most definitely Brock and he was by himself—oh my God, was he turning this way? I almost wanted to dive under the table, but that would be weird, so I hastily looked down at my plate, upping my prayers that he wasn't coming to the table. That there was no way Brock would be—

I peeked up through my lashes and saw his dark head over the high walls separating the tables, getting closer and closer, and I knew deep in my very core that Brock was coming to this table.

# Chapter 19

Like a toddler, I was of the mindset that if I wasn't looking at Brock, he couldn't see us. Like he wasn't truly there, so I fixed my gaze on my nearly empty plate, and prayed I was having hallucinations.

"Well, hello," came the smooth, deep voice that never failed to slip over my skin like heated silk. "What a surprise."

God. Damn. It.

I lifted my gaze at the same time Grady did, and I saw surprise flicker across his handsome face as he caught sight of Brock towering over our table.

"Hi?" I forced out.

Brock's full lips slipped into a half-smile as he looked down at Grady. "We meet again."

"Yeah. We do." Grady was nodding as he glanced between us. "This is a surprise."

"I know." Brock's dark eyes glimmered. "Such a coincidence."

My eyes narrowed as I picked up my wine glass. A coincidence, my rosy red ass. "So, what . . . what are you doing here, Brock?"

"Oh, I was just in the area and thought I'd swing by and grab something to eat."

"By yourself?" I asked, because this wasn't the type of

restaurant you wandered into by yourself. So what in the world was he up to?

"I do a lot of things by myself, Jillian." His amused gaze centered on me.

I widened my eyes at that and took a healthy gulp of my wine, because my mind really took that to a place that was really inappropriate since I was on a date with another man. I suddenly heard his heated words in my ear. *I got you.* And that made me think of his hand slipping between my legs . . .

Grady cleared his throat. "So, do you come here often?"

"Actually, I was here not too long ago." He was still staring at me, his lips curved into a rather delighted smirk. "Remember? Our dinner date?"

"Dinner date?" Grady parroted, sounding confused as his pale eyes settled on me.

I sputtered, nearly choking on my wine. I placed the glass back down before I threw it. "The *business* dinner," I reminded Grady. "The reason I had to reschedule our date. Brock, my *boss*, and I brought the potential investors here."

"Your boss," Grady murmured, sitting back in his chair. The air of confusion faded as his lips thinned. "And childhood friend, right?"

"We did grow up together." Brock chuckled as he planted a hand on the back of my booth. "Saying 'childhood friend' seems to belittle what we were to each other."

*What in the holy hell?*

"That sounds perfectly correct." I glared at Brock, but now he was busy eyeing Grady with that unnerving stare of his.

Brock ignored my comment. "Did she ever get around to telling you about the first time we met?"

"He doesn't want to hear about that," I cut in, forcing a dismissive laugh that came out a bit crazy-sounding.

"Actually," Grady replied coolly. "I would love to hear about that."

My mouth dropped open.

Before I knew it, Brock was settling into the booth beside me. Sitting so close that the entire length of his right side was pressed against my left. "So I was fourteen, I think, and you were eight." He gently elbowed my side. "Right?"

"Right," I murmured, eyeing the wine glass and thinking that my whole *never getting drunk again* thing sounded like a dumb idea right now.

"I'd been hanging around her father's Academy for a while. Every kid growing up in that neighborhood knew who the Limas were. We'd all loiter outside just to catch a glimpse of her father or one of his brothers."

"So your family is a bit famous?" Grady speculated, obviously forgetting Cam's reaction to Brock and all of that.

"Something like that." Fully aware of Brock's body against mine, I eyed my wine glass with fervor.

"She's just being modest. That's how Jillian is," Brock said in an infinitely familiar way, and I swallowed a groan. "Anyway, let's just say I was a bit of a punk back then."

"Was?" I muttered under my breath.

Brock grinned, obviously hearing me, and I hated that grin. It wasn't cute or sexy or charming at all. Nope. "I tried to rob Andrew, her father, one night."

"What?" Interest filled Grady's gaze as his hand halted, the wine glass several inches from his mouth.

"Yep. I'd left home. Was starving and it was cold. Needed money, and I was a fucking idiot," he explained, and Grady flinched at the curse word. "Tried to rob a man who could end my life in about six hundred different ways." Laughing softly, Brock shook his head. "But Andrew didn't kill me or beat the crap out of me like he easily could. Didn't call the police. He'd noticed me hanging around the Academy, knew that I was fighting in some of the underground circuits—"

"At fourteen?" Grady sounded stunned. The poor country boy had no idea.

"You'd be surprised by what goes on in the cities that no one ever knows about," Brock replied, leaning back in the booth.

I stiffened.

He draped his arm along the back, right behind me, and I tilted my head to the side, stuck somewhere between wanting to laugh at the outrageousness of him right now and wanting to throat punch him. "Andrew brought me to his house that night, offered me a hot meal and a place to stay."

"Wow." Grady's smile was faint when he looked at me. "Your father is a saint."

"My father saw raw talent and that's what he went for," I said, even though I knew that wasn't exactly the only reason. My dad had grown up on the streets of Natal, Brazil. Brock had a hard childhood, but it paled in comparison to my father and uncles. My dad saw a kindred soul in Brock . . . *and* a son he never had.

"It was pretty late when her dad brought me to the house and he left me in the living room very briefly. I'd never . . . never been in a house like that before." A distant look glazed over his eyes. "It was just outside the city, huge and yet still somehow *warm*. No cockroaches crawling on walls or rats scurrying in the dark corners. It was the kind of house I'd never dreamed of entering."

Grady was riveted as he slowly lowered his glass to the table, and I swallowed hard, thinking of the deep well of dark memories Brock had of his life before my father opened up our home to him.

"I was about to follow him into the kitchen when I looked over at the stairwell. You see, they have this half-enclosed stairway that empties into the front room and atrium. It was dark, but there was a little shadow plastered to the wall, peeking around it." A slow grin appeared on Brock's face. "All I saw was this hair—dark brown hair—and big eyes."

Scooting forward, I placed my elbow on the table and rested my cheek in my hand.

"It was little Jillybean." Brock laughed while I rolled my eyes. "She was eavesdropping on us and her father had no idea she was up. We made eye contact and I half-suspected her to run up the stairs, because I had just . . . well, I'd just gotten into a fight before running into her father. I was looking pretty rough."

I sat there and wondered in a daze what in the hell had happened. Brock had successfully commandeered what was left of my date, beguiling Grady with tales of our *childhood*.

I was going to seriously kill him.

"You didn't run?" Grady asked me.

I didn't answer. I couldn't. I leaned back once more, dropping my hands into my lap as I sucked in a sharp breath. I felt Brock's fingers suddenly tangling in the mass of my hair.

What was he doing?

"No, she smiled at me and then gave me this little wave." Brock slid me a sidelong glance. Our eyes met, and the air around us felt heavy as his fingers sifted through my hair without Grady seeing. "It was . . . adorable."

Oh my.

"After getting food, he set me up in this guest bedroom and went to bed. Was like the man saw right through me and decided I was trustworthy enough to have in his house like that. I still find it unbelievable." Brock's fingers made their way through my hair and now were tracing little circles against the center of my back, obliterating my ability to focus. "Still blows my mind."

"I can't believe it," Grady murmured, and it was then when I really hoped Brock would just stop, that he wouldn't continue telling this story.

But I wasn't lucky.

Nope.

God hated me.

"About an hour had gone by, and I couldn't sleep. My head was all over the place. The house was too damn quiet. I wasn't used to that. Wasn't used to people actually sleeping at night, and not yelling or car horns blaring," he continued, and I started to lean forward once more, to avoid those damn fingers, but he snagged a thick section of my hair, holding me in place. My eyes widened slightly. "I remember sitting in this room, the nicest room I'd ever been in at the time, thinking I needed to leave. You know, that I didn't belong in this house," he continued as if he wasn't using my hair as a damn leash at the moment. "And then there was this quiet little knock on the door. I had no idea who it could be."

"It was you," Grady said, brows raised as he glanced over at me.

I closed my eyes as Brock's finger slipped back through my hair, making patterns against the thin material of the dress. My entire being was focused on the burn of his fingertips.

"She brought me her teddy bear," Brock announced, and I opened my eyes, letting out a sigh. "What did you say when I opened the door and you shoved the furry old thing in my hands?"

I couldn't believe he was bringing this up. I also couldn't believe he actually remembered it. "I said you looked like you needed a friend."

Brock wasn't smiling as he met my stare. "She then ran off, going back to bed, I guess." A faint smile appeared. "I knew Andrew had a daughter. Even seen her a few times from a distance, but . . . never expected she'd give me, a complete stranger, a damn teddy bear." Dragging his gaze from me, he looked over at Grady. "From that point on, we were close."

I really, really needed him to stop touching my back.

"I can tell," Grady commented wryly.

"I've been her shadow ever since."

My gaze swung to his sharply. That was *not* how people related the story. I was his shadow. Never the other way around.

"Even took her to her senior prom," he finished, and that was *it*.

Lowering my hands under the table, I reached over and grabbed his thigh through his jeans, pinching until his arm jerked back.

His mouth twitched as he stared at me.

Satisfied now that his hands were in his own space, I let go. "He took me to prom because the boys who were my age were too scared of my father."

"Huh." Grady toyed with the stem of his wine glass. "Should I be afraid of your father?"

"No," I affirmed.

"Yes," Brock answered. "Hell, I'm still afraid of him."

I exhaled heavily, noisily.

Grady nodded like he understood, but it was clear he didn't, and then a seriously awkward silence stretched out between the three of us. I was seconds away from pitching myself under the table when Grady excused himself to use the restroom.

Part of me feared as he rose and walked off that he may not come back, and then I felt a measure of relief, because maybe, at this point, that would be better.

But Brock and I were alone, so I whipped toward him. "What are you up to?" I hissed.

He fixed me with an innocent look. "What do you mean?"

"You know exactly what I mean. Why are you here?"

"Hmm." He popped his chin in his fist, and my gaze dropped to the thin silver chain around his neck. "I just happened to be in the mood for a juicy steak and thought I'd pick one up."

"Yeah. And I just happened to be in the mood for a piping hot crack pipe," I snapped back. "Why are you doing this?"

Brock arched a brow.

"You're trying to ruin my date," I accused.

"I don't think I have to try," he drawled, grinning.

I glanced at where Grady had disappeared as anger flushed my skin. "What does that mean?"

He smirked. "You two have as much chemistry as tap water does."

"That's not true." I leaned away from him as my breath caught. My first thought was that he was right. My second thought was he didn't know what he was talking about.

"Really?"

"Yes!" I nearly shouted and then took a deep breath. "Grady is attractive—"

"So cute." He waggled his brows.

I seethed. "And he's funny and smart. And he's nice."

"Nice?" Brock laughed. "Exactly. Proves my point."

"What is your point?" My hands curled into fists. "That nice people are bad people?"

Brock inched closer and tapped his finger off the bridge of my nose. I smacked his hand away as he said, "You list his attributes like you're talking about someone who is interviewing for a job to watch over a kindergarten class."

"I did not." Taking a deep breath, I struggled to rein in my patience. "What are you doing, Brock? This—this doesn't make sense."

"It doesn't?" His brows rose. "Are you seriously going to pretend like you don't know why I would be here?"

I shook my head. "I don't know why."

He studied me for too long and then said, "He's not what you want."

Oh my God, I couldn't believe we were having this conversation. I met his heavy-hooded gaze with a glare. "You need to leave. Now."

One side of his lips kicked up. "If I know anything, I know what you want and you'll realize that by the time this night is over."

There were no words.

"But I actually do have another reason to see you. I wanted to talk to you about Thanksgiving. Since we're both going to your parents' house, we should drive up together."

Oh, holy shit balls on Sunday, *what*? "I need a second to process this."

His lips curved up. "Take your time."

"First off, this couldn't have waited to, oh, I don't know, any other time? And secondly, why are you having Thanksgiving at my parents' house? You haven't done that in years."

"To answer your first point, it was on my mind right now to discuss," he replied smoothly. "And why am I having dinner at your parents' house this year? This year is different, but we'll talk more about this later."

I opened my mouth.

"I'll let you get back to your oh-so-exciting *nice* date." He slipped out of the booth; his gaze drifted over me. "I really wish I could see the rest of you in this dress, because what I see so far is fucking amazing. You look beautiful."

My mouth continued to hang open.

"Have a *nice* evening."

Winking, Brock sauntered down the aisle, passing Grady on the way out. They stopped, exchanged a few words I probably didn't want to know about, and then Grady was walking toward the table.

He sat down with an odd little laugh. "Well, all that was . . . unexpected."

All I could do was shake my head helplessly. "I'm sorry. I have no idea what he was doing."

"I think . . . he was checking up on you." Grady rubbed a hand over his chest. "He was checking up on *us*."

I opened my mouth, but I didn't have anything to say, because Brock had never done anything like that before. Ever. Not even on the rare times I had dates when we were young and I'd tell him about them, obviously hoping he'd get jealous and realize he wanted me before someone else had me. Then he didn't even bat an eyelash.

"How did he know we were here?" he asked.

"Coincidence?" I repeated dumbly.

"You sure about that? Because he just left without picking up any food."

Oh my God, he *hadn't*. "I might've mentioned we were going here, but he's just—I mean, he's really . . ." I swallowed hard, struggling to explain what had just happened that didn't involve me spewing curses everywhere. "He's overprotective."

Grady nodded slowly. "Can I ask you something?"

*Please, no.* "Sure."

"Have you two ever been involved with one another?"

"What?" I forced out a laugh. "No. We haven't." And was that really a lie, because I wasn't counting what happened last

Friday, and me being in love with him for like ten years or so didn't count.

He looked over his shoulder and then back to me. "Maybe he's into you."

I laughed again, but this time it wasn't forced, because that was just unprecedented ridiculousness.

But was it?

I thought about him wanting to come in that night for a drink. Then all those lattes and the lunches, and he told me I was *beautiful,* and he wanted to drive me home for Thanksgiving, and I . . .

And then there *was* what happened between us that Friday night. I didn't want to think about it, had managed to stop myself all week whenever my thoughts drifted there, but it *had* happened. Brock hadn't wanted to pretend like it hadn't happened. He'd said he didn't regret those brief heated and dark moments. Could he—?

My heart started pounding fast, too fast, and I felt dizzy at the mere idea that someone else thought he could be interested. I was so used to everyone telling me he wasn't.

Grady finished off his wine.

The conversation kind of, well, sucked from that point. It was idle and mindless, and when the check came, he paid for it with a quickness a ninja would be proud of.

Grady walked me to my car, which was parked around the corner, behind a bank. He didn't hold my hand, but he hugged me goodnight. Not a full body, chest to chest hug that made me feel shivery and wanting. Definitely nowhere near a kiss.

"I'll call you," he said, stepping back.

I nodded. "I . . . I had a good time."

"Me too." He lingered for a moment, his gaze searching mine, and then he turned. "Have a good night, Jillian."

I stood there for a moment, watching him walk away, and I knew he wasn't going to call me again.

And I wasn't going to call him.

Avery was going to be so disappointed.

# Chapter 20

Not exactly comfortable lingering in dark areas at night for obvious reasons, I immediately locked my car doors and turned on the engine. Then I sent Brock the quickest text message possible.

Meet me at my place. Now.

Yes, it was a demanding text, one I probably would've never seen myself ever sending Brock, but I was *pissed*. I had no idea what Brock had been up to when he stopped by the restaurant. Wanting to talk about Thanksgiving? Utter bullshit.

My hands clenched the steering wheel as I eased out of the small parking lot and turned onto the street, immediately hitting a red light. I didn't hear my phone ding and I also didn't check if he had responded, fearing that if he had and gave some excuse for why he couldn't talk now, I'd drive my car into something.

I fumed the entire drive home. The little part of me that had been left breathless earlier over the fact someone else thought Brock was interested in me had quickly been burned away in fiery irritation.

What he'd done tonight was not cool.

Arriving at my apartment, I climbed out of the car and slammed the door shut. Scanning the parking lot, I didn't see his car and as I hurried through the chilly air, under the starry night sky, I yanked my phone out of my purse.

Of course, no response.

"Asshole," I muttered, stomping up the stairwell.

Yeah, there really hadn't been much of a spark between Grady and me, but that was none of Brock's business. Not even remotely. And maybe tonight could've been the night that something developed between Grady and me, but that hadn't happened. Brock showed up, took us all for a quick trip down memory lane, giving Grady the impression that what we had going wasn't worth investigating further. Reaching my door, I unlocked it and yanked it open, wanting to tear it from the hinges.

Stripping off my jacket, I tossed it over the back of my couch and grabbed the chilled bottle of wine from the fridge. Working the cork out, I took a nice long gulp, forgoing a glass.

Forget the whole not drinking thing for right now.

A small part of me knew that even if Brock hadn't busted all up into my date like the Kool-Aid dude, a spark wouldn't have magically appeared between Grady and me. After reading a crap ton of romance books—after knowing what I had for Brock at one point in my life—I was a firm believer in if that special *it* wasn't there on the first real date, it most likely was never going to appear.

And that wasn't even taking into consideration that the nights when I couldn't sleep and I slipped my hand between my own thighs, it hadn't been Grady's face that appeared in my mind.

But still.

I was pissed.

Raising the bottle of wine to my lips again, I jumped and dribbled a little on my chin as I heard a knock on my door.

My heart felt like it was on a trampoline at the same moment my eyes narrowed. Wiping my hand along my chin, I placed the bottle on the island and stalked toward the door, pulling it open.

Brock stood outside, lashes lowered, shielding his gaze.

"That was quick," I snapped.

His full lips twitched. "Let's just say I figured you'd be wanting to see me tonight, so I hung around this end of town."

"Is that so? You're psychic now?"

Brock lifted his gaze and his lips parted. "Damn," he exhaled. A strange look crossed his chiseled features, like he was seeing something hidden for the first time. Something he knew always existed but was out of reach. "You and that dress . . ." He stepped into my apartment, forcing me to back up as he closed the door behind him. "I knew you would look beautiful."

Beautiful?

There was that word again, a word I was sure he knew what it meant.

Skin flushed as I glared at him. "I don't want to hear you say that. I don't even want to know that you think that."

Brock appeared to ignore that statement, because he asked, "When did you get those curves, Jilly?"

Emboldened by my anger, I held my ground. "Oh, I don't know. When I was *nineteen*. But you didn't notice them then, did you?"

"No." He shook his head, almost in wonder. "I didn't want to notice."

My brows flew up. "You didn't *want* to? That makes no sense."

"It doesn't?" Those dark eyes pierced mine. "You were Andrew Lima's *little girl*."

"I'm still his daughter, the last time I checked."

"True," he murmured, and then his gaze swept over me once more, starting at the tip of my head down to the pointy tips of my heels, then swept up again, lingering on my chest. "But not so little anymore."

Despite my anger, I felt my nipples harden. I crossed my arms and lifted my chin. "Are you drunk?"

Brock blinked and his gaze shot to mine. "I haven't touched a drop of liquor since that night."

I sucked in a sharp breath.

"Not one fucking time since that night."

"Well, okay." Feeling a little chagrined, I dropped a bit of the attitude. "Look, I didn't text you to come over and talk about my—my dress or how you've suddenly noticed I'm not a child anymore. What the hell was up with tonight?"

Not answering, he glanced around my apartment. Spying Rhage sitting on the arm of the couch, he brushed past me, shoving the sleeves of his V-neck sweater up his forearms, revealing the brightly colored tattoos on his left arm.

"Well, just help yourself to my cat. That's not—" I stopped as Rhage rose, stretching his kitty head toward Brock's large hand, rubbing against him. Disgusted, I shook my head. That cat was also an asshole. "That's bullshit."

Scratching Rhage behind the ear, he looked over his shoulder at me. "Your language is burning my innocent ears."

"Oh, shut up. You cuss worse than a drunken sailor tossed overboard into a swarm of tiger sharks." Unfolding my arms, I walked over to the wine.

He raised an eyebrow as I took a drink from the bottle and then murmured, "You're going down that route again? If so, I am so glad I'm here."

Eyes narrowed, I clutched the bottle to my chest. "Okay. It's time to get real. What was the purpose of tonight, and don't tell me it's because of Thanksgiving. You had ample opportunity to talk to me about that. There was no reason for you to hunt me down on a date, interrupt it, and ruin it."

"I ruined your date?" He laughed as he straightened, facing me. "That guy didn't have a chance in hell with you."

"How would you know?" I fired back.

He took a step toward me, and I stepped to the side, keeping a safe distance between us. He kept coming in a slow, measured approach, causing a dizzying flutter in my chest. "I just do."

"That's laughable." I kept inching away from him as he slowly followed my movements. "You even admitted that you didn't know me anymore."

"That's not exactly what I said, Jillian." His eyes glimmered as he lowered his chin. "You tell me one thing about little Grady that excites you."

Excites me? My pulse was all over the place at the moment, and it had nothing to do with Grady or the wine I'd just guzzled. "I'm not having this conversation with you."

"Why?" One more step and he was about a foot from me.

My apartment wasn't that large, so I found myself with my back almost against the wall. "Because it's—it's inappropriate!"

"Inappropriate?" His laugh was deep and rough. Sexy. A fine series of shivers danced down my arms. "Why in the hell is this inappropriate?"

"Because—because you're my boss."

"I am not just your boss. Have you forgotten that I literally had to carry you upstairs and put you to bed after you got into your dad's liquor cabinet and drank for the first time?" he asked. "Or the fact that you've been there for me, for some of the darkest moments of my life? Helping me change into clean clothes because I was too fucked up on pain meds and alcohol to even know what year I was in?"

I drew in a stuttered breath. Oh my God, we never talked about that time—about those months after his chest wall injury.

"Or let's talk about how not that long ago you were riding my fingers until you came? Just a boss? Come on, Jilly, you can do better than that."

"Don't call me that," I snapped, thrown off-balance. I struggled to breathe as Brock left what remained of the space between us behind. He towered over me, so close that his right leg brushed against my left one.

"It has nothing to do with me being your boss. Us working together isn't even a drop in the damn bucket of our life," he said. "You don't want to answer the question, because you know there is none."

"That's not true," I swore, and then stiffened as he pried the open wine bottle out of my hand and placed it on the small table beside us. "What are you doing?"

Placing both of his hands against the wall, on either side of me, he leaned in and lowered his head so we were nearly eye to eye. "Tell me one thing that excites you about him."

"Why?" I whispered, my chest rising and falling sharply as my gaze dipped to his mouth.

"Because I want to know . . ." One of his hands left the wall and curved over my shoulder. I shuddered, and his head tilted to the side. "I want to know why, after what happened between us, you'd actually go out on a date with another man."

My heart was beating so hard I could feel it in every part of my body. Senses overwhelmed, I had no idea how we'd ended up here, him slipping his hand down my arm, to my hip. I had no idea how his other hand was suddenly on the other side of my waist. All my being zeroed in on the warmth of his hands burning through the thin dress. A sharp ache hit low in my stomach, throbbing and intense.

"Jillian?" he said my name in this soft way that did crazy things to my brain cells, melting them together like they were nothing more than butter.

I wet my lips. "He's nice. Grady is really nice."

"Nice?" His hands glided up my sides, and my body reacted without thought. My back arched and my breath hitched as he lowered his mouth to my ear. His breath was hot against my skin as he said, "You don't want *nice*. *Nice* doesn't excite you."

My hands found their way to his chest. I pushed at him at the same time my fingers curled into the front of his sweater, holding him in place.

"I'm sure Grady is a nice, little man," he went on, and his hands were on the move again, one coasting back down to my hip. The other stayed over my ribs and each swipe of his thumb brought him into contact with the lower swell of my breast. "I don't have anything against him, but if he excited you, if he brought this very same blush to your cheeks?" His hot mouth coasted over said cheek. The coarse hair of his jaw elicited a sharp gasp from me. "If he excited you, if you were really into him, then I wouldn't have ruined your date. You'd be with him right now. And I sure as hell wouldn't know what it felt like for you to come."

I wasn't sure that logic worked, but my mind seemed to have checked out, because it was all about the way I felt. A languid heat invaded my bloodstream. The throbbing increased in certain areas of my body. My breasts grew heavy and achy, and those feelings only intensified when I felt his breath on my lips, turning my blood to molten lava.

His lower body leaned into mine, and my breath came in short inhales as I felt him against my belly, thick and hard. Holy crap, there was no denying that, no hiding his reaction. Sharp arousal loosened and tightened my muscles all at once. Our mouths were now lined up perfectly, his lips so close to mine.

I'd never felt anything like this before.

Never.

Brock was going to kiss me, and this time, it would count.

And I wasn't going to turn my head away.

I was thinking Brock wanted to do a hell of a lot more than kissing.

Realizing that, knowing I would let him kiss me and I would ultimately let him do whatever he wanted to me, cleared some of the fog from my thoughts.

*What was happening here?*

It had only been, what, almost two months since we'd re-entered each other's lives? Two months after years of no contact—years of my life falling apart and his living something like a *Forbes* success story? He'd even gotten engaged and broken up, and he . . . had broken my heart. But now he was back in my life as my boss, my *freaking* boss, and I was barely beginning to figure out who I was.

My fingers flattened against his chest. "What . . . what are we doing?"

Brock stilled, and for a moment I wasn't even sure if he was breathing or not. Then he shifted slightly, resting his forehead against mine. "I . . . I really don't know."

That bitter mixture of disappointment and relief swelled once more. Swallowing hard, I pushed against his chest even though I wanted to say screw it and climb him like a damn spider monkey.

"But," he rasped, and then the hand at my back slid to my hip, gripping it. "But I do know, Jillian, that I want you."

# Chapter 21

Brock wanted me.

He'd actually said those words. It wasn't my imagination or wishful thinking. Nor was it something I made up in my head after reading between the lines. He'd just said it, and I could *feel* that he wanted me, and that alone did funny things to my body.

The hand at my hip tightened and the one under my breast stilled. His forehead was against mine, and when he made this raw, masculine sound of need, a shiver worked its way through my body. He pressed in, forcing my back flush against the wall.

He wanted me, but was it six years too late?

Based on the way my body had responded to his with him barely touching me, I was going to say *no*, it wasn't too late.

But was it wise to even indulge the idea? That was the question.

He shuddered and then I felt his lips press against the corner of mine, the side that didn't move right due to the nerve damage, and I gasped at the contact, my body flashing cold and then hot.

I blindly turned my head toward his and his lips brushed over mine, a soft sweep as gentle as a breeze. There was no pressure behind it, and the kiss we'd shared in the middle of the night had been a whole lot deeper than this, but this soft touch of his mouth undid me in a way no other kiss had ever done before.

Brock pulled away just an inch and our gazes connected and held. He then took my hand and pulled me away from the wall. He led me to the couch, and when he sat, he pulled me down so I was in his lap and my legs draped over his. Feet dangling, my heels slipped off and fell to the floor.

Startled by the sound, Rhage dove off the arm of the couch and scurried down the hall toward one of the bedrooms. Or maybe he was heading for the hallway bathroom. Rhage had lately taken to sleeping in the sink in there for some reason.

But I quickly stopped thinking about the weird cat.

My heart was pounding erratically as Brock kept one arm around my waist, securing me in place as he lifted his other hand, catching my hair and tucking it back behind my ear. He tipped my chin up, and his gaze searched mine and every inch of my face.

"I don't know what is happening," I blurted out.

"Me neither." He cupped my jaw, moving his thumb just below the scar.

"That's reassuring." I placed a hand on his chest, needing a bit of space between us. He dropped his hand, but he didn't let me out of his lap. "This is . . . this is crazy."

"Crazy can be good," he replied, one side of his lips kicking up.

"Or crazy can be the kind of crazy that ends really badly," I reasoned, trying to grasp onto sanity. "We just can't do this."

"And why not?" His other hand fell to my bare knee. The contact caused me to jerk in his arms.

I thought there were plenty of reasons why. "We . . . we work together, Brock. If we do this and it blows up in our faces, we have to keep working together. I can't let my dad down," I said. "I . . . I can't let myself down."

"Why do you think it will blow up in our faces?" His question sounded genuine. "Do you think that I would be here if I thought it would hurt you in the end?"

I stared at him, wanting so badly to believe his words, but I never thought he'd hurt me as badly as I'd *allowed* him to before. "Why?" I asked. "Why now, after all this time?"

"It . . . it just changed. I don't know exactly when it happened," he said, voice rough as sandpaper. "If it was the night I saw you at the restaurant, or your first day at work, when you cocked major attitude at me. That wasn't the Jilly I knew, and it threw me through the damn loop, because it was fucking hot. I don't know if it was when you hugged me after that dinner, because that was the Jilly I knew, but you didn't feel like her in my arms."

I couldn't think, could barely breathe, as his words washed over me and his eyes closed. The hand on my thigh slid all the way up, over my stomach and then my breast, and a ragged sound left me as his palm grazed the aching tip, but kept moving until his fingers circled the base of my neck, his thumb resting against my wildly beating pulse.

"Or maybe it happened before I even saw you again," he said, appearing to be talking to himself, but that statement didn't make any sense. His eyes opened and shone like polished obsidian. "Maybe it was seeing you finally relax and laugh the night we went out with your friends. It could've been falling asleep with you lying against me. Hell, what we did that night had a lot to do it with it."

My gaze searched his tense, strained features.

"It could've been all those minutes and more, but I knew that morning, when I woke up and found you hiding in the bathroom, that I wanted you. And there wasn't a damn day that went by that I didn't think of you, Jillian. I should've told you that the first night I saw you."

Air halted in my lungs.

"I always wondered about you, about what you were doing, how things were going for you . . ." His eyes opened and they were dark. "I wondered if you found someone. And I asked about you—I asked often."

"What?" I breathed.

"Your mom . . . she kept me, well, informed. You didn't know that?"

I hadn't. A burst of anger lit up my chest, because Mom really shouldn't have been keeping Brock up to date on my life, especially without telling me.

"I knew when you dropped out of college. I knew when you got the job at the insurance firm," he explained, and my lips parted on a sharp inhale. "I knew when you started dating someone. I also knew you never brought him home to meet your parents, so I knew it couldn't be that serious."

Holy crap.

Thunderstruck, the anger gave way to surprise. "Why didn't she say anything to me?"

"I asked her not to. I was . . . I was sure you wouldn't want me to know any of those things. You had made it clear the last time we had talked that you didn't want me in your life."

A twinge of regret blossomed in my chest. It had been that last holiday I spent with him and my family. "You . . . you brought her to the house."

I think that was what broke me the most about Brock back then. The girl he'd been flirting with, the girl he'd ditched me for, wasn't just some one-night stand who was forgotten the moment he walked out. It was the girl he ended up getting involved with. It was the girl he finally settled down for. It was the girl he proposed to.

He turned his head slightly, looking away as if he couldn't go eye to eye with me. "I wasn't thinking."

A knot formed in my throat as that night came rushing back. It had been the Christmas after everything had happened and Brock had come to Christmas dinner. He hadn't come alone. Roughly four months after he'd broken my heart and my life had literally imploded, he'd brought Kristen to *my* family dinner, and I . . . I'd lost it.

Face still practically a wreck and healing, my mental state nowhere near stable, I'd come downstairs for one of the rare times to join my family, and I could still remember it like yesterday.

I'd made my way into the large dining room, my weary gaze tracking over the familiar faces, and I'd seen Brock first. He'd been staring at the door, and for a moment, I thought maybe he'd been waiting for me, looking for me. Although he had dealt a death blow to my emotions that night at Mona's, tiny seedlings of hope had formed in the weeks afterward during his visits.

But then I'd seen who he stood next to, and seeing her, knowing that he brought her to the dinner, meant she was important to him. No one-night stand. No drunken hookup. He'd never, ever, brought a girl to my parents' house.

Kristen was his girlfriend. Not me. Never me.

I'd pivoted right around and gone back upstairs, managing not to flip my shit in front of my entire family. It hadn't mattered, though. They all knew. And that mortification and raw hurt from the night at Mona's had resurfaced in a messy explosion of emotion.

Brock had come after me like he had a hundred times before then, like he *hadn't* the night at Mona's.

He'd come to my bedroom, and I'd *yelled* at him. I was pretty sure I called him a "selfish, conceited whore" at one point and I'd told him that I never wanted to see him again. I'd said other things, terrible things, and I could still see his face and the shock that had been etched into his features. The pain I didn't want to see, and especially the guilt I didn't want to acknowledge.

It was like almost dying all over again, but looking back, I knew it hadn't been all his fault. He shouldn't have had to live his life worrying about hurting the kind of feelings I had for him. It wasn't fair to him, and that had taken a whole lot of soul searching to realize—painful, brutal soul searching.

His thumb massaged my pulse, tugging me out of the past. "Jillian?"

"I'd . . . I'd overreacted. I mean, I was . . . fuck," I said, letting it all out. "I was jealous. I was so jealous, Brock, because I wanted to be her. I'd lo—" I cut myself off as tiny bundles of nerves formed in my stomach. I pulled so his hand was no longer touching my throat. "I just wasn't in a good place."

"Don't take the blame for this," he told me.

"I'm not. Well, I'm taking partial blame for the . . . the fuckery known as us." Desperately needing space to think about this clearly, I slipped out of his hold and off his lap. Standing, I thrust the hair back from my face and moved until the back of my legs touched the coffee table. "I was young and—"

"And I didn't want to see what was right in front of my face." He scooted to the edge of the couch and stared up at me. "I just wanted you to think of me like you would a brother."

Uncomfortable about where this conversation was going, I edged away from the coffee table, moving so I was standing in front of it, my back to the TV. "Brock—"

"But I knew that wasn't the case. I wasn't a fucking idiot."

I stiffened.

His hands hung between his knees. "And I wanted to just think of you as someone who was like a baby sister to me."

"You did. You didn't once treat me like I was anything other than that."

"I told you. I couldn't let myself. You were six years younger than me. Now? Not a big deal. Then? Not to mention jailbait, but your father would've murdered me. Hell," he grunted, a wry grin on his lips. "He still might kill me. You were too young and I was . . . I was too caught up in my own head. All I had were my dreams—be this big UFC star. Get a shit ton of endorsements. Work hard and party fucking harder, and you—"

"I didn't fit into that," I said without an ounce of bitterness, because I hadn't. I'd been a child compared to him, full of silly dreams and hopes.

And there was a part of me that still felt like her sometimes. That I could be easily swept off my feet again, sucked back into Brock just when I was finally, finally starting to live my life.

"But I always knew," he said, lowering his gaze. He let out a ragged breath. "I fucking knew how you felt."

Crossing my arms across my chest, I shivered. I didn't know what to make of that confession, what to make of any of this. A huge part of me was in shock. When you've spent a good part of your life wanting something and then another decent chunk of your life accepting you'd never have it, to now have it seemingly within reach was hard to comprehend.

I glanced over at him, and my stomach dipped in the most pleasant way. What would it be like to be with him, with our past no longer between us, and just *now*? My skin flushed with sweet anticipation, but at the same time, a part of me held back.

A part of me wanted to run screaming for the hills.

"I just . . . I really need to think about this. I mean, I don't even know what you really want, if you just want to get laid—"

"If I wanted to just get laid, I'd already have someone in my bed right now. That would be easy."

"Wow," I muttered.

"I'm not saying that to be an ass. It's true, but I don't want that. Obviously." His jaw tightened. "If I just wanted that, I wouldn't be here."

I bit down on my lip. "So . . . what are you saying?"

"I'm saying that I want you," he said. "That is what I want, and I don't know what's going to happen. I have no idea, but I'm sure as fuck not going to deny what I feel and want just because it may turn out to be shit."

Except if it turned out to be shit, we had to face each other every day, and if it turned out to be shit, how would we really move past that a second time? How could I?

Taking a deep breath, Brock rose from my couch and approached me. I eyed him warily as he walked around the coffee table and stopped in front of me. Before I knew what he was doing, he cupped my cheeks in his large hands and tipped my head back.

"Walking out of this apartment is not what I want to be doing." He lowered his mouth, stopping a hair's breadth from mine. "What I want to be doing is taking you back to the bedroom, stripping you bare, and fucking every single doubt from your mind."

Oh *goodness*.

"But I get it. You've got to wrap your head around the way things are now," he went on. "I'm going to give you that time. All right?"

"Okay," I whispered back, because what else was I supposed to say? His mouth was so close to mine, and I was absolutely thrown through a loop.

Then Brock kissed me.

Really kissed me.

His mouth came down and his lips moved against mine like he was committing the feel of them to memory. My arms unfolded and somehow my hands were back to his chest. He nipped slightly at my lower lip, startling me. I gasped, and then his tongue slipped through the seam of my mouth.

Now *this* was a kiss.

Hot. Hard. Wet. His tongue slipped over mine, and he didn't so much kiss me as he did devour me. The scratch of his beard and the softness of his lips, the prick and satin, was such a heady mixture, dragging a throaty moan out of me.

"Fuck," he groaned, lifting his mouth. "That sound."

I couldn't speak. I opened my eyes and gazed up at him dazedly. I was officially going to count that as our first kiss. Yep. Sounded good.

Brock held my gaze and then he let go of me. "Hardest thing I'm about to do is walk out of here," he murmured. "Dream of me tonight."

Then he was gone, walking out of my apartment and closing the door behind him, and I was left standing in the center of my living room, my lips tingling from his kiss and my body a riot of unfulfilled desires.

*Go after him.*

I started to but stopped, because I . . . I was scared. Truly terrified by what was happening, because I had lived for so long no longer hoping Brock would wake up interested in me, and now he was. On what level and how deep, I had no idea. I wasn't sure even he knew, but I wanted him—wanted him more than I ever wanted anyone, because I'd *always* wanted him and he had *never* wanted me.

Until now.

And what terrified me was the knowledge that if I fell for him again, I would fall deep, and I'd never recover. If I loved him again, I'd be lost forever.

# Chapter 22

Sleep had not come easily Saturday night. Not with my body wishing it was still pinned between Brock's hard body and the wall. My mind would not shut down.

It was close to three in the morning when I finally found a few hours of sleep, and then I rose at the butt-crack of dawn, disturbing a disgruntled Rhage. I let the coffee percolate as I showered, leaving my hair to air dry while I grabbed a can of fancy food for him since I felt bad for waking him early.

Rhage appeared to accept my offer of apology by shoving his entire whiskered face into the bowl. Cringing, I watched him, knowing he was going to smell like fake fish or whatever was in that food.

Taking my cup of coffee with me, I curled up against the arm of the couch, trying not to think about Brock holding me in his lap last night as I picked up my phone. It was early, but I knew my mom would be up.

She answered on the second ring and immediately assumed the sky was falling. "Is everything okay?"

"Yeah." That wasn't necessarily a lie. "I know it's early, but I . . . I talked to Brock last night."

There was a beat of silence as I sipped my coffee, and then she said, "Well, hon, I assume you talk to him quite frequently now."

Lowering my mug, I rolled my eyes at her blatant obtuseness. "Mom, he told me you've been telling him everything about me over the last couple of years."

"I haven't been telling him *everything*," she responded blithely. "That's an exaggeration."

"Is that really all you have to say?" Needing more caffeine to deal with this conversation, I took another drink. "Why didn't you say anything? He said he told you not to, but Mom, come on."

"I didn't think it was wise to tell you that he was asking about you," she replied.

"Why? Because you thought if I knew he was asking about me that I was going to be obsessed with him?"

"Obsessed? Honey, hold on a second. Your father is about to come in here, and I don't think he needs to hear this conversation," she said, and I raised a brow as I chugged my coffee. "Okay," she said with a heavy sigh, and I figured she was in the sunroom, surrounded by various plants. Mom had a true green thumb while I was the black death to greenery. "Why in the world would I think you'd be obsessed with Brock?"

"Mom," I groaned. "Come on. You have eyes."

"Yes. I have two functional eyes. You had a crush on the boy growing up, Jillian."

A crush didn't truly represent what I had felt for him, but whatever.

"I didn't tell you about him because you made it clear more than once that you didn't want anything to do with him."

Finishing off my coffee, I rose to get a refill and passed Rhage, who was sitting by the coffee table, licking his paw. "If you knew that, then why would you tell him anything?"

"Because he cared about you—he's never stopped caring about you. Because he was a part of your life for over a decade, and he's family to us," she answered as I poured myself a new cup. "Jillian, I'm sorry if you feel like I shouldn't have talked to him, but when he asked about you, it was always coming from a good place."

Turning, I leaned against the counter and curiosity got the best of me. "What . . . what was he asking about me?" I knew what Brock had told me, but there was a small part of me that needed to hear Mom validate it.

"He always wanted to know that you were okay. That's where most of his questions were leading. How you were doing at Shepherd. When you dropped out, he wanted to know what you were planning to do. He'd asked if you had friends," she said, and I exhaled sharply at the bitter burn in the back of my throat. "I think he needed to know that you were okay and you weren't alone."

Pressing my lips together as I held the phone to my left ear, I slowly shook my head. Truthfully, I wasn't mad at her. I got why he asked about me. I'd cut him off and out of my life with a rusty butter knife. I got why she told him. Brock had become like a son to her.

"So what were you two doing having this conversation on a Saturday night?" Mom asked slyly. "Because I'm sure you weren't at work."

"He hijacked a date I had last night."

"He did what?" She let out a surprised laugh.

I sighed. "You remember the guy I was telling you about? Grady? Well, I was on another date and Brock showed up and basically ruined it."

"Oh no," Mom murmured, but it was too subdued. Like I could practically see her grinning from ear to ear.

"Well, he didn't really ruin it. I mean, if I was being honest—"

"And you should be."

Wrinkling my nose, I folded an arm across my waist. "Anyway, Grady is nice but . . . it wasn't going to work out anyway."

"Of course not," she replied.

"What does that mean?"

"Let me ask you a question, Jillian. Why are you asking me about Brock? Besides the fact that he told you he was obviously still thinking about you all these years?"

I shifted my weight from one foot to the other. "Because . . . because he came over last night and—"

"Did you two have sex?"

"Oh my God, Mom!" I shrieked, startling Rhage and causing him to jump like one of those Halloween spook cats.

"What?"

"*What?*" I repeated dumbly. "Okay, like I don't want you ever asking me that again. Ever."

She sighed heavily in my ear. "It's human nature, Jilly. Your father and I have a very active—"

"Stop. Please stop." I threw up a little in my mouth. "I don't want to hear any of that."

"Fine. So Brock came over and there was no sex. Did you guys quilt a blanket? Watch *Beaches*? Did you two even cuddle, because I think he's the type that likes to cuddle."

"Oh my God," I moaned, close to hanging up on her. "You need to focus."

"I am focused."

"We just talked—talked about things, and he . . . he seems to be interested in me like more than just friends, and he's not at all worried about us working together."

"Well, why would he be worried about you two working together? Not like the Limas have ever separated work and family before," she replied dryly. "Brock has been asking about you for six years, honey."

"Yeah, and for most of that time he was with someone, so that's not an indication of anything."

"If you say so."

I sighed. "Mom."

"If you think that means nothing then I'm sure there are things I don't think he's talked to you about."

"Like what?" I demanded as unease brewed.

"That's not my place to go into, hon."

"Oh!" I threw an arm up. "It's not your place to tell me his business, but you told him mine?"

"Not the same thing," she repeated.

"Whatever."

"So are you two finally getting together?" she asked.

Taking a deep breath, I counted to ten before I responded. "No, Mom. We're not."

"I'm confused."

I tipped my head back and groaned, "Why?"

"You love him."

I sucked in a sharp breath. "I was in love with him, Mom, but that was a long time ago. I'm not that girl anymore."

"You may be a woman now, but that doesn't mean how you feel about someone has changed."

My gaze flipped to the ceiling.

"And this Grady fellow you went out with, he was a good man, I'm guessing? Attractive. Smart. Interested in you? But you felt nothing for him and it was going nowhere?"

"Yeah." I frowned, thinking I knew where this was heading, and this conversation was so not turning out the way I expected it to.

"You sure you still aren't in love with Brock? And if it's not love anymore, you're not interested? You don't think about him?" Mom paused. "I want an honest answer."

Walking away from the counter, I shuffled out to the living room. "I . . . I don't know."

"That's not honest." When I didn't speak, she said, "Jillian, you've been through a lot. I know this, and you've been hurt. If I could take that hurt from you, I would."

"I know." I walked to the window and pulled back the curtain. I stared at the woods behind the apartment complex.

"And that hurt—the kind Brock laid down on you *and* the kind you physically suffered—obviously would have you hesitating," she said as I watched the bare branches sway in the wind. "I don't blame you for that. No one would, but it shouldn't stop you from taking risks."

Chewing on my bottom lip, I said nothing because going there with Brock was a *huge* risk.

"Living is all about taking risks, Jillian. Isn't that what you're trying to do? To start living again?"

Part of me wished I'd never told her that when I'd left home for good, because she had a point, damn it.

"Do you still like him?" she asked again.

"I . . . I don't know," I whispered a bit lamely.

Mom laughed quietly. "Honey, I think you know how you feel."

I thought I did too, because truth was, no matter what, even when I hated him and I hated everything we'd ever shared, I still liked him. I never stopped liking him.

"Are you driving up with him for Thanksgiving?" she asked.

"I don't know, Mom."

Her laugh brought a wry smile to my face. "I'll see both of you soon, and I have a feeling at the exact same moment too."

Hanging up the phone after I told her my plans for the day, which involved finally putting together bookcases, I let the curtain fall back in place. Mom made it all sound so simple, but it wasn't.

But she was right.

Living meant taking risks.

Just after three in the afternoon, when I was about to finally put the bookcases together, there was a knock on my apartment door.

I stepped out into the hall, my stomach flip-flopping around. I wasn't expecting anyone, but intuition sprang alive. Hurrying to the door, I didn't bother with the useless peephole. I cracked open the door.

"Brock," I whispered.

"Hey," he replied with a grin.

"What are you doing here?" I asked, glancing around like the outside hallway held all the answers.

"Visiting you."

My brows lifted.

"I'm actually here to do my good deed for the day."

Having no idea what he was talking about, I stepped aside. "And what would that good deed be?"

Brock walked into my apartment, and as he passed me, he swooped down and kissed me before I could even process what he was doing. It was sweet and all too brief, but still left me standing there stunned.

"Kissing me was your good deed?" I finally asked, closing the door.

He looked over his shoulder at me. "I kind of like the way you think, but no. I'm here to put together your bookcases, because I'm sure you still haven't done that since you mentioned buying them."

"I haven't," I admitted. "You remembered that?"

Brock faced me. "I remember everything, Jilly."

A shiver curled its way down my spine, and I looked away. "You seriously came over to put together my bookshelves?"

"Yep." There was a pause. "And I wanted to see you."

I peeked at him, unsure of what to say.

"I know I said I'd give you time," he said after a moment.

"And this is you giving me time?"

"Yes." That half-grin was back, doing funny things to my stomach. "So where are the bookshelves?"

"In the second bedroom down the hall." Deciding that if he wanted to put the shelves together, he could have at it. I had no problem supervising.

*Aaand* I was kind of, okay sort of, really interested to see him here.

"I'll grab some drinks," I offered, then pivoted around, hurrying off before I could change my mind and ask him to leave, even though I knew I wanted him to stay.

Gah. Sometimes I made no sense to myself. At all.

Once I had two bottles of water, I led him into the guest room. It was pretty barren. Just a narrow, single bed that was barely used, a desk in the corner, and a nightstand.

Brock didn't comment on the lack of design as he walked toward the pieces of the shelving system. "Where's your cat?"

"Probably in my bedroom, under the covers. That's where he takes his afternoon naps."

Brock laughed. "I like that cat."

"Yeah, he likes you. Which is weird because that cat hates everyone."

"Your cat has good taste." He slid me a sidelong glance. "Then again, everyone likes me."

"Ha. Ha." I stared at his back and suspicion blossomed. "Did you talk to my mom today?"

"No." His brows flew up. "Why? Should I have?"

I shook my head as I picked up the packet of hardware. Sitting on the bed, I watched him rummage through the boards. I liked how he was dressed, casual in jeans and a fitted thermal. My gaze got hung up on the clear definition of his chest and arms.

I started thinking.

Which probably was bad, but whatever.

Picking up the instructions, he sat on the left side of me, on the bed. "Well, this shouldn't be too difficult."

"It's not. I'm just lazy."

One side of his lips quirked up. "I'm surprised you don't actually have any bookshelves overflowing with books, to be honest."

Turning the packet of bolts and screws over in my hands, I shrugged. "I . . . I just haven't gotten around to it."

"And you've lived here how long?"

"Shush it," I murmured, fighting a grin.

"But you're now doing it?" He dropped the paper on the bed behind him and rose. "Interesting."

I had no idea why he found that interesting. "I plan on bringing back a ton of books when I come home from Thanksgiving."

"How many is a ton?" he asked while he laid out the shiny gray boards.

"A crap ton."

That grin spread, and damn it all to hell, it was truly a sexy grin. Who had I been kidding when I thought it wasn't? "Well I hope a crap ton fits in the Porsche."

My eyes narrowed. "I never agreed to ride with you."

"You will."

"You're awful sure of yourself."

The look he shot me screamed he had reason to be. Feeling a little flustered, I eventually stopped supervising and helped as he told me how he was renovating his kitchen.

"You didn't buy a newer house? Or have one built?" I asked.

"Did buy a new house. Wanted something different. Plus, there wasn't a lot of land available where I wanted," he explained, spinning the hex key like a pro. "Also wanted to get my hands dirty."

I arched a brow as I picked up the shelf and held it in place for him. "Seriously? Since when are you into construction and renovation?"

"Hey, I know how to use these hands." He glanced over at me, lashes lowered. "Trust me."

My cheeks heated as my stomach wiggled. Yes. Yes, he did. "Why do you have to make everything so . . . so perverted now?"

Brock laughed. "You think that's perverted? You haven't seen anything yet."

"Yay. Something to look forward to."

Shaking his head, he screwed two pieces together. "Some of the stuff I'm not going to be able to do. I've already demolished the kitchen, so it's been carryout and grilling."

"It's kind of cold for that, isn't it?"

"Nah. Doesn't bother me." Turning the shelf upright, he rose. "Where did you want this?"

I showed him. "So is the kitchen completely gutted?"

"Almost." He carried the shelf to the wall across from the bed, then turned to the second one and began working at that. "I'm going to try to rehab the cabinets, so they have to be taken down carefully."

Surprise flickered through me as I watched him work to put the shelves in. This was something new about him.

"You don't need to look that surprised."

"Sorry." I sat back down on the edge of the bed. "I just didn't know you were into doing stuff like that."

"There's a lot I'm into that you don't know about."

There he went, saying something that so didn't sound like a normal comment.

"This isn't the first time I've used these hands for good." He picked up the other packet of hardware and ripped the little bag open.

I flushed hotly.

"Get your mind out of the gutter." He laughed. "I was thinking about the time I taught you how to pick a lock."

Since he was focusing on the bookshelf, I grinned freely. "Yeah, you did do that. When I was twelve. A total useful skill for a child."

He laughed. "You never know when you'd need that. Besides, putting these shelves together is the least I could do for you."

Bending over, I picked up the board marked A. "How so?"

Brock was still for a moment and then he looked up at me from where he knelt on the floor. "After I was injured, I was a fucking—"

"Mess?" I supplied helpfully.

His grin was small as he nodded. "I thought my career had ended. My head was in a really bad place."

It had been in a really bad, dark place.

"But you were there for me the whole time. When no one else could stand to be around me, you were there," he said, taking a deep breath. "I lost count of how many times you showed up in the middle of the day or even at night and helped get me to bed when I was passed out on the floor. Cleaned up after me when I had too much to drink." Disgust filled his voice. "Or when you'd bring me food and make sure I actually ate it. You stayed even when I was piss drunk and was getting on my own damn nerves.

So, yeah, putting together some bookcases is the least I could do."

I lowered my gaze as I sucked my lower lip between my teeth. Was that why he was here? Why he . . . he wanted me? To atone for the past? That seemed silly, though. "Brock . . ."

"You know, there's something I need to say—something we need to talk about. Okay?" He waited until I met his gaze. "That night you were hurt, the night you almost died, I wasn't there for you. It happened to you because of me."

"Stop." My heart twisted something painful in my chest as I scooted closer to him, still holding the board. "You didn't—"

"I didn't try to rob you? I didn't pull that trigger?"

# Chapter 23

Hearing those words spoken, words I barely allowed myself to think about, caused me to flinch as those memories came roaring back. It was like a plug pulled from a water-filled sink. There was no stopping the deluge.

*I didn't remember walking across the packed parking lot.*

*All I knew was that I was standing in front of my car with my hands slapped over my eyes. Oh God, he totally bailed on me. Brock had me drive all the way up here to spend time with him, with just him and me, and he was inside of Mona's with everyone else—with those girls. That totally just happened. Brock had seriously bailed on me.*

*My shoulders shook as a sob rose in my throat. Brock didn't even see anything wrong with ditching me. I saw that in his face. Not for a single moment did he think there was anything wrong, and I was so, so stupid.*

*So fucking stupid in my dumb dress and dumb makeup. No wonder he'd looked at me like he had when he first saw me. It hadn't been because he finally saw me as something other than his Jillybean. It was because I looked ridiculous. Compared to the girls in there—to Kristen—who were wearing skintight denim skirts or jeans, I looked like I was playing dress up.*

*Tears streamed down my face as I lowered my hands and slipped my purse off my shoulder. Katie had been right. Brock would get laid tonight. He wasn't going home alone while I was—*

*"Excuse me?"*

*Sucking back tears, I turned around. A man stood there—close, too close. I took a step back, bumping into the side of my car. There wasn't enough light in the parking lot for him to see my tear-stained face, thank God. But I also couldn't see much of this man. What I could see wasn't good. His cheekbones appeared gaunt. His eyes were shadowy, and when I breathed in deeply, I smelled the pungent scent of sweat and greasy food. His hands were shoved into the pockets of what appeared to be dark work pants.*

*Unease blossomed in the pit of my belly. "Can I help you?"*

*"Yeah." He turned his head slightly to the side and barked out a dry cough. "Do you have a dollar?"*

*I don't know why I answered the way I did. I had a dollar, but my head was shaking no. "I'm sorry. I don't," I said, turning back to my car.*

*The man moved fast.*

*One hand shot out and his fingers caught in my hair. I let out a startled shriek as my head was jerked back. I acted out of instinct, and I started to swing my bag at him, but I froze—stopped moving, stopped breathing. For a split second, I didn't believe what I was seeing. I couldn't even process it, but it was real and it was right there.*

*He held a gun an inch from my face.*

*"Oh my God," I whispered, mouth drying.*

*"Don't move," the man ordered. "Just give me your purse and you aren't going to get hurt."*

*I immediately lifted my purse, fully prepared to give him every cent I had on me, right along with the credit cards. Pain flashed across my scalp as he shoved my head forward. Thrown off-balance, I stumbled to the side and, too panicked to catch myself, I fell to the ground.*

*My knees scraped off the rough pavement, tearing open a scream. A harsh grunt of air exploded out of my lungs as the panic erupted like a bomb inside me.*

*"God dammit!" the man spat. "I told you not to move."*

*"I-I didn't mean to." I reached for my purse and in my hurry, the contents fell out, scattering across the ground. I reached for my wallet. "Here! Take it. You can take it."*

*Clenching the gun in one hand, he ripped the wallet out of my hand. I stayed where I was, not daring to move. Bile rose swiftly into my throat. I was going to be sick. I was going—*

*"Only sixty dollars? That's all, bitch?"*

*I squeezed my eyes shut. "I-I'm sorry. That's all I have. That's—"*

*"Give me your car keys." The end of the barrel grazed my cheek, and I nearly vomited. "Now."*

*Falling forward, I dragged my hand across the pavement, skimming over the tiny, plastic bottle of perfume and the beaded coin purse my vovó gave me for Christmas a couple of years back, before she passed away. My fingers brushed over the thin chain of the necklace I'd stashed in my purse—the gift I hadn't given Brock. I found the keys, snatching them off the ground. With a shaky hand and my heart pounding against my ribs, I lifted them up to the man. "H-Here."*

*He ripped the keys out of my hand and started to back up rapidly, the gun still pointed in my direction. I didn't dare move. I held my breath, praying that he'd leave, that I would walk away—*

*Several things happened next.*

*The door to the bar opened and music poured out into the balmy night air. The man cursed. A car horn blew and there was a deafening pop. Red hot pain flashed through my entire body, lasting a second—only a second.*

*Then there was nothing.*

Brock's tortured gaze held mine now, and I knew . . . I knew he was reliving the same night. "You shouldn't have even been there, Jillian. You think I don't remember the events of that entire weekend? I was supposed to take you out to celebrate my big comeback." He barked out a harsh, biting laugh. "I was planning to. I really was, but I got there . . . and I have no real good excuse, and trust me, I've searched for one. Over and over, I tried to explain why I chose to stay there and let you walk out, why I didn't follow you. No reason I had is good enough—will ever be good enough."

Brock laid the board down and thrust his hand through his hair. The soft ends flopped forward. "I know I never said these things to you afterward. I should've. You didn't want me saying anything to your parents about why you were there, and I honored that, but I got to tell you that shit *ate* at me. I was out there, fighting matches, winning money, and seeing your dad, after everything he'd done for me, was still doing for me, and you were lying in that hospital bed, because I was a fucking jackass. I let you down and that's something I can never forgive—"

"Don't say that," I pleaded, realizing I couldn't bear to hear him say he couldn't ever forgive himself for it. "Yes. You ditched me. That hurt—that really hurt, but you're not responsible for what happened to me. I don't blame you for it."

"How can you not?" he asked, voice as sharp as ice.

There was a point in my life I had. That point hadn't lasted long. I didn't blame him. He hadn't been the guy hooked on heroin, desperate for money and tweaking like crazy. I couldn't hold him responsible for that and I didn't care if some people thought I should. But I hadn't let go of all the hurt from that night, and obviously neither had he.

Then it hit me with the force of a speeding semi-truck.

How were we still living like this?

I was afraid of getting hurt again. He was carrying the guilt for not returning my feelings when I was a *teenager,* and feeling responsible for me . . . for me getting shot, something he hadn't done? Neither of us was really living.

What in the actual fuck had we been doing?

"We need to let it go," I whispered, and that moment, the very second I said those words, they rang true with a kind of clarity that was earth-shattering.

Brock needed to move on from that night, and God's honest truth, so did I, because I hadn't. For six years, I really hadn't let any of it go. And how could I move on, be truly happy and gain my life back, if I didn't?

How could it really work between Brock and me if we both didn't?

I sucked in a soft breath.

In a daze, I lifted my hands to my face, pressing one finger against the deep indent in my cheek. You'd have no idea that a bullet had entered my left cheek and then gone straight through to the other side of my mouth, somehow not touching my tongue, the roof or the floor of my mouth, before blowing through my right jaw, practically exploding it to smithereens, and in the process, taking out some of the necessary parts needed for hearing in my right ear as it exited.

God knows I was so damn lucky.

Besides not being severely disfigured, I'd actually survived. I barely remembered being conscious after being shot. There were flickers of memories—of panic and not being able to breathe, of the metallic taste of blood as it was pouring down my throat, out of my mouth and nose as I heard yelling—screaming. That was all I remembered until I woke up in the hospital with a tracheostomy tube, unable to talk at the time or hear out of my right ear.

It had been a long recovery from that point.

I remained under observation for nine weeks, re-entering the hospital multiple times for the reconstruction parts. It had taken a year for me to leave home and come back to Shepherdstown.

And it had taken six years to fully acknowledge that we both were still standing in Mona's, stuck in that moment of me walking away and him not following. It was a moment that had lasted too long.

"What are you thinking?" he asked.

Wordlessly, I stared at him, realizing we were on the cusp of something I had never believed possible. It was like walking up to the cliff's edge and staring down. Could I take that leap again? I wanted to try, because I was tired of denying how I felt when I looked at him. I was tired of fighting it. I wanted . . . "I want . . ."

His gaze was bright and endless as he stared up at me. "You want what?"

Air constricted in my throat. "I want to let it all go. I do. And this is still scary as hell for me, but I want to start really living. I want to take risks and I . . . I want you."

Saying it out loud was like slipping off a too-heavy blanket, one that was rough and itchy. Like opening your eyes and seeing how blue the deepest part of the ocean could be and how bright the sun was when the ground was covered in snow and ice.

Tears blurred my eyes as I whispered the words that made me feel incredibly vulnerable. "I want you, Brock."

He moved incredibly quickly, snatching the board out of my hand and letting it hit the floor. Grabbing my hands, he hauled me down onto his lap as he sat on the floor. My knees slid on either side of his hips, and when he kissed me, it was like the goodbye kiss from the night before.

Senses spinning all over and mind reeling. I trembled and shook in his arms as he nipped at the corner of my lip and then flicked his tongue over the little bite, soothing it. He coaxed my lips open, keeping the kiss, tasting me—claiming me, but I'd already been claimed by him.

I'd always been his.

The kiss deepened as he drank me in, and there was a brief second where fear sprouted in my stomach. Brock had the power to hurt me again, but the threat was lost in the primitive rumble that rose up from his chest. He broke off the kiss, and my lips felt swollen in the most delicious way.

"I want to know something," he said, smoothing the hair back from my face. "Something I've been wondering about longer than you realize—longer than I should've been."

"What?" I asked, trying to calm my breathing.

Those hands slid down my body, coming to rest on my hips, and when he spoke, his lips moved against mine. "I want to know how you taste."

Taste?

I knew what he meant by that. Goodness, did I ever. The request sort of shocked me. I mean, we hadn't even been on a date and we'd just kissed, for the first time, last night. And he wanted to do that already?

And I wanted him to do that. My body really wanted him to do that, like it was one hundred and ten percent on board, but it had been a really, really long time since I'd even been kissed.

Suddenly, I felt incredibly naïve and wholly out of my element. With my hands on his shoulders, I leaned back, putting some space between us. "Brock, I . . ."

"What, babe?" His hand grasped my hair, gathering it against my neck. He kissed the corner of my mouth.

I shuddered as my hands slipped to his chest. "It's been . . ." Cheeks heating, I tried again. "It's been a really long time since I've done this."

The hand on my thigh stilled and Brock drew back so he could look me in the eye. "How long?"

"A really, really long time," I repeated, squirming slightly. "It's been years since I . . . since I've even been kissed, let alone anything more than that."

Those dark brown eyes nearly turned black.

"I feel like I'm practically a born-again virgin," I said, forcing out a laugh.

"Fuck," he growled. "That just makes me want to do it so much more. You have no idea."

My hands spasmed against his chest, clutching his thermal as my heart worked overtime.

"Let me do this for you." Brock's dark eyes glinted with bright desire. "Let me make you come, Jillian. Please, let me help you start really living."

I lost my breath as I shuddered again. How could I refuse that? For real. I was aching for him in a way I had never felt before. My body wanted him. My heart and soul did. There was no reason to refuse this. Nothing but shadowy doubt and deeply rooted insecurities.

Living is all about taking risks.

Yes. Living was taking risks. Living was putting yourself out there, sometimes jumping without looking, but I had a safety net. Brock would catch me. I didn't doubt that.

"Okay," I whispered, feeling like I'd agreed to go skydiving.

He pressed his lips to my forehead. "Thank fucking God."

I giggled. He was really excited about going down on me. The humor slowly evaporated, because his mouth claimed mine once more, and it was hot and deep. His tongue slipped over mine and flicked the roof of my mouth. He kissed me until my head was spinning and I was melting in his arms. Then he moved, his lips coasting over my chin and over the side of my jaw that had literally been pieced back together. I started to stiffen, but I felt the tip of his tongue trace the line.

My fingers were going to rip right through his shirt as his mouth traveled down the side of my neck, blazing a trail of hot kisses. He nipped and licked as the hand on my thigh moved to my breast. The tips hardened, and I wanted more, wanted to be bare, but then he was moving again.

His hands dropped to my hips and he lifted me up, startling me with his strength. I was no small chick by any means, but he moved me around like I weighed nothing.

My back was on the floor before I knew it, wedged between the bed and surrounded by half built bookcases. He caged me in and I stared up at him with wide eyes, my pulse racing.

"I've wanted to do this for . . ." His hands dragged down my stomach, over the thin sweater I wore. He pushed up the material, exposing my lower stomach. "Hell . . ."

Emboldened by his stare, I wet my dry lips and asked, "How long have you wanted this?"

"Long enough that when I woke up last Friday and you were rubbing all over me, I wanted to get my mouth between these legs," Brock muttered, hooking his fingers under the band of my leggings and tugging them down a few inches. He groaned. "No panties?"

My face flushed, but I lifted my rear when he tugged again and watched him rock back as he drew the pants down my leg. I had this horrible habit of not wearing undies when I was home and in leggings or yoga pants.

They ended up somewhere behind him.

And then he was staring at me, staring at the most intimate and private part of me. The look of stark hunger on his face stole my breath. Any thought of stopping him had dive-bombed out the nearby window.

"You're beautiful," he said in a rough voice, and the way he said it made me believe he truly meant it. "So fucking beautiful."

My heart slammed in my chest as his hands ran up the outside of my calves and then crossed over at my knees, slipping along the insides of my thighs. He stopped just before the crease between my hip and thigh, gently easing my legs apart. Cool air brushed over me, and my breath caught. Instinct demanded that I close my legs, but his heated gaze locked onto mine.

"I need to do this." His voice rumbled through me. "It's all I need right now."

Drawing in a shallow, stuttered breath, I relaxed.

The promise in his gaze said I wouldn't regret the decision. His head dipped as he kissed the space below my navel, and then he dropped lower, settling his broad shoulders between my legs, spreading me wider.

I couldn't swallow or breathe as his lips moved against the inside of my thigh, leaving a wet path upward, closer and closer to where I throbbed. My hands flattened against the carpet. The hair on his jaw scratched my skin in the most amazing way.

"So damn beautiful," he murmured.

Completely exposed to his gaze, I trembled as his hand slid over my pelvic bone and dipped down. This was nothing like what we did in my dark living room. I'd done *this* before. Twice. It really hadn't done a thing for me, and I had never been able to understand why some women were so into it, but the intense way he focused on me without even having touched me there yet had already surpassed my past experiences.

He licked his lower lip as he looked up, his gaze piercing mine. "Do you trust me, Jillian?"

Oh God, my heart swelled in my chest so fast and so big it felt like I was going to float right off the floor. "Yes."

Brock smiled at me and then he was on me. That was it. No warning. No fooling around. His mouth was on me, and the contact jerked my body. My back nearly came clear off the floor as heat flooded my veins.

His tongue dipped in, and the way he kissed me there was hot and wet and deep and shattering. His tongue moved like he'd kissed me earlier, slipping in and out until my head fell back, and I couldn't watch him anymore.

I reached down, threading my fingers through his hair with one hand. He growled against me as my grip tightened. "Oh God."

Raw and primal sensations pounded through me as my hips moved, meeting the strokes of his tongue, and when he stopped, I cried out in dismay.

Brock chuckled, and then I let out a strangled moan, because his mouth closed around the tight bundle of nerves as he worked a finger through the wetness and deep inside me.

"God," I gasped out, incapable of saying anything else as I tugged at his hair.

My brain checked out as my body took over. I was rocking against his finger and mouth, and when he slipped in another finger, filling me even more, I started panting and making these sounds, these tiny moans I'd never, ever made in my entire life— sounds I would've normally been embarrassed over but not now. There was no room for embarrassment or thoughts or our past.

There was nothing but what he was doing in me, stirring and building inside me. There was just his mouth and his fingers, and the way my body rocked and moved. Passion burned through me, igniting a spark that quickly grew into a flame as he went deeper and faster.

I burned—burned for him in a way I never had when I was younger. Oh no, what I was feeling now was beyond anything I'd ever imagined.

"Brock," I breathed.

God, he was unbelievably good at this.

My body was coiling tight and my eyes flew open. My other hand flung out blindly, smacking into the side of the small bed. Brock made that sound again, that deep growl, and it threw me right over the edge. Crying out as every muscle in my body tensed and then released. Brutal pleasure poured through me, liquefying bone and tissue. I was lost to the storm of pulsing and throbbing.

Unable to move much and beyond sated, my arms flopped to my sides as I watched Brock lift his head from between my thighs. A fully male, smug smile graced that beautiful, talented mouth of his.

I gasped as he slowly withdrew his fingers from me and brought one to his mouth. He licked his finger.

Oh my good God.

Breathing pitched, my eyes widened. He was . . . there were no words. None.

Brock rose, prowling up the length of my body and planting one hand beside my head. His lips glistened. "So I'm driving us home for Thanksgiving, right?"

I couldn't help it. A grin tugged at my lips and I laughed softly. How could I say no after that? "Yeah, you're driving us home."

# Chapter 24

There was a small part of me—okay, that wasn't true. There was a rather large part of me that wondered how things would be at work. Would Brock act like nothing had changed between us, or would he have no problem with public displays of all kinds of things? I had no idea if he wanted our relationship known to our coworkers.

Then again, I had no idea if we were in a relationship. Just because he went down on me, giving me the most amazing orgasm I'd ever experienced in my entire life, and told me he wanted me didn't necessarily mean we were officially doing the boyfriend/girlfriend thing.

I was thinking I should probably clarify that.

Brock stopped in my office Monday morning, one hand holding his phone to his ear and the other holding a latte for me. He winked and then walked back out. Of course, my face started flaming the moment I saw him.

He'd put the other bookcase together and then spent the rest of the day watching a mini-marathon of Will Ferrell movies with me. We hadn't talked about that night or what happened to me anymore. We'd ordered a pizza and then he'd left around eight. His goodbye kiss made me wish it were a hello kiss.

After he blew my mind yesterday afternoon, he hadn't let me return the favor. He'd rolled off me, found my pants, grinned

244

like a cat in a shop full of canaries while he helped me pull them back on, and then got back to work on the bookcase. I wanted to return the favor, but because I was an idiot, I hadn't been able to work up the nerve.

With Ben, I hadn't been the one to initiate any action between us, and since he had been my only relationship, that meant I'd never actively seduced anyone.

I couldn't even picture myself doing it.

But I wanted to.

Around ten that morning, I gathered up a stack of reports and headed for the conference room for our Monday meeting. Cradling the papers to my chest, I stepped out of my office just as Brock came out of his. I waited, feeling as nervous as I would have all those years ago.

His lips curled into a smile as he approached me. "Love the skirt," he said in a low voice as he leaned in, speaking into my left ear. "Shows off your amazing ass."

My eyes widened as I glanced around. The cubicle walls were too high to see over, but I didn't think anyone overheard him. I still tripped over my own feet, though.

Brock chuckled as he folded his hand around my forearm, steadying me. Shaking my head, I started to tell him to stop looking at my ass while I committed this gray skirt to memory so I could wear it again or find more like it, but just then Paul stepped out from behind one of the cubicles.

His light blue eyes flickered from Brock to the hand curled around my arm. Something tightened in his expression, but it smoothed over so quickly that I wasn't even sure I noticed it.

Paul nodded in my direction before turning his attention to Brock. "I got a rundown from the trainers in Philly on the guys we sent up there."

Letting go of my arm, Brock took the paper from him. "Thanks, man." He fell in step beside me as we continued to the office. "We're going to check in on them when we're there this week."

"Sounds good." I glanced over at Paul, who was walking a few steps behind me, to my right. "What's the game plan with them?"

"If your father likes the way they're turning out, he'll keep them on up there," Brock explained. "If not, they'll be sent back down here for more training."

I nodded as we rounded the line of desks. Several staff members were waiting outside the door and were chatting. I felt Brock's hand on my elbow. I glanced up at him questioningly and his thick lashes lifted, shooting a pointed look in Paul's direction. The other man was staring down at me, and I realized he must've spoken.

"I'm sorry," I said politely, surprised I hadn't heard him direct anything to me since when he spoke to Brock I could hear him. Had he lowered his voice? *No*, I told myself. I wasn't even sure he knew I had hearing problems, and if he had, that would be a micro-dick move. "I didn't hear you."

Paul's expression was stoic as he repeated, "Do you have the new membership reports?"

I frowned slightly, wondering why he was asking for that. "Yes. Is there a reason you need to see them?"

Brock had stepped ahead, already entering the conference room, and Paul stopped as the rest of the staff followed him in. "Do I need a reason to see them?"

I started to point out that I was well within my authority to question whatever the hell I wanted, but the statement died on the tip of my tongue. I took a deep breath. "I just don't understand why you would need to see them as that is not your department."

246

"Actually, it sort of is." Paul folded his arms as he stared down his long, aquiline nose at me. "Chase Byers, one of the guys who works the front desk, wants to transfer to training, so I need to evaluate his performance and make sure he's earned the transfer." He paused, features sharp. "I'm pretty sure Brock mentioned this to you?"

I opened my mouth as I glanced into the room. I was pretty sure he hadn't.

"Jillian," he said, touching my arm. "Did you hear me?"

My gaze swung back to his. Okay. There was no way he'd just spoken or I was totally losing my mind. "What?"

"Do you have his report?" he asked.

Hating that I could feel my cheeks burning, I looked down at the reports I held and thumbed through them until I found Chase's weekly activity sheet. I pulled it out and handed it to him. "Sorry. Here you go."

"Thanks," Paul said, but sure as hell didn't sound like he meant it.

"No problem," I responded, irritated more with myself than him. I was his manager, and yet I was the one apologizing? *What the hell?*

Paul didn't respond as he walked into the meeting. I didn't get this guy and the problem he had with me. Frowning, I looked up and met Brock's stare. His brows were raised. He was waiting for me and I was just out here standing around, staring at the floor.

Lovely.

Sighing, I shoved Paul's attitude aside and walked into the conference room, closing the door behind me as I told myself that next time I was going to put Paul in his place.

Tuesday afternoon, close to three, my office phone dinged, signaling an internal call. I glanced over and saw the GM button was lit up. A smile tugged at my lips as I picked it up.

"Yes?"

"Need to see you," Brock said through the phone and then promptly hung up.

I shivered at the sharp bite of desire. Telling myself to chill and that his need to see me surely was work-related, I locked my computer as I toed my heels back on and then rose. Standing, I smoothed the skirt of the beige dress I'd found in the back of my closet.

I really needed to go shopping for clothes.

Brock had stayed late at the Academy last night, so I hadn't seen him after I left work and before I returned this morning. He had texted last night, telling—not asking—me to have nice dreams of him.

It was so corny that I laughed out loud when I saw it.

The text, the kiss yesterday he stole while he came in my office before I left, the entire weekend and all that he'd done—none of it felt real. Which was why, when I chatted with Abby last night and made plans to see her when I was home, I hadn't mentioned what was happening with him. Maybe by then I could.

The floor was mostly quiet as I walked the short distance to Brock's office. At this time of day, most of the staff were either on the gym floor or on the second level, but since the offices had closed tonight for a long five-day weekend, I was sure some had already snuck out. Tucking my hair back behind my right ear, I slipped into his office.

"Close the door behind you," he ordered when I stepped in.

Stomach flipping all over the place, I did as he demanded. "What's up?"

Brock hit a few keys on his keyboard and then pushed his chair back from the desk. His gaze drifted over me, and he had this way of looking at you that made you feel like you were stripped bare and completely exposed.

He didn't say anything. He just sat in his chair, his position the epitome of arrogant laziness, as he eyed me.

I stopped by one of the chairs, feeling my cheeks start to warm. "You getting ready to train with the guys?" I asked, noting the nylon pants and Lima shirt. He hadn't been wearing that the last time I'd seen him.

"For a bit," he answered, resting his arms on the chair and clasping his hands together. "But that's not what I want to talk to you about."

"Okay?"

A mysterious, sexy little half-grin appeared on his lips. "Come here."

I hesitated. "I *am* here."

"Closer," he added, nodding toward his desk.

My gaze flew to it. Did he want me to sit on the desk? Well, that seemed wildly inappropriate.

His chin dipped and he waited patiently while I worked up the nerve to either make my way over to him or run out of the office, my face the color of a tomato.

"I'm not going to bite." He paused and then added, "Not right away, at least."

My lips pursed together and then I glanced over at the door. It was closed. No one would walk right in. No one here would dare barge into the Beast's office.

Brock was still waiting on me.

Calling on every ounce of courage I had, I forced my legs forward. To some, this wasn't a big deal, but with Brock, I was way out of my element. Hell, with most guys I was way out of my element. The whole time my heart pounded. I walked around the edge of the desk and stopped in front of him. My gaze dipped, and I sucked in a deep breath that went nowhere.

Brock was hard.

I could totally see that, because his nylon pants did nothing to hide all that he had going on down there. My gaze flew to his.

The grin on his face spread. "So, I've been thinking about something."

"You have?" I asked doubtfully. With that massive of an erection there was probably only one thing he was thinking about.

"Laid awake most of the night," he said, tipping his head back. "It's about something you said to me this weekend."

I'd said a lot of things this weekend. Leaning back against his desk, I folded my hands over the smooth edge. "I'm going to need a little more detail."

"You said you wanted to start really living. I want to help you do that."

My heart turned over heavily in response to his statement. "I'm pretty sure you already did."

"Yeah. I did. But that was just one thing. Don't get me wrong. I thoroughly enjoyed it. Can't wait to get my mouth between your legs again," he told me, and my jaw nearly hit the floor. Holy crap, he said that like we were discussing the weather or something. He leaned forward, unclasping his hands. "What have you done since you left me?"

*Left him?* Did he really think that I left him? I never thought of it that way, but I guess he could. "I don't know what you mean."

"You went to school for a little while and you've worked. I know that. What else have you done?"

I opened my mouth to tell him, but I came up empty. There was nothing to tell him. Nothing. It was like I was this blank canvas. Nothing on the outside or inside. A knot formed in my throat and my eyes suddenly burned.

"Hey," he said quietly, clasping my hips in his large hands. "It's okay."

"Yeah. Of course." I cleared my throat. "I'm okay."

His solemn gaze searched mine. "I'm not asking that question to upset you."

"I know." And I did.

Brock's hands tightened. "Do you remember sitting out on your parents' swing and talking about all the places you wanted to visit?"

Not trusting myself to speak, I nodded jerkily.

"Did you see those places?"

I shook my head no.

"You still want to see those places?" he asked. "I think I remember some of them. You wanted to see the Pacific Coast Highway and travel overseas. Scotland, right?"

"Right," I whispered. My heart was doing back springs and cartwheels.

"And I think, if I remember correctly, you wanted to take a road trip on the old Route 66? Something about the world's largest bottle?"

A soft, shaky laugh shook me. "The world's largest ketchup bottle."

He shook his head. "I still have no idea why you want to see that—"

"It's a giant catsup bottle!" I explained. "Who doesn't want to see that? They even have a festival!"

The grin was back, the kind of grin that always, *always* held sway over my heart. "You're . . . adorable."

I thought I might cry.

There was a good chance.

"Even though going to a catsup festival isn't on my list of things to do, I would gladly take you there." He stated this like it would happen just because he claimed it would. "We have a lot of time to do these things and we're going to—"

I moved without thinking.

My brain just shut right down, and for one of the rare moments in my life, I wasn't all about thinking and little else.

Bending at the waist, I cupped the sides of his face, welcoming the prickly tickle against my palms, and brought my mouth to his.

*I* kissed Brock.

Kissed him like I'd wanted to at eighteen and kissed him in a way I never would've imagined at that age I'd one day be capable of.

Brock was no submissive recipient. He wouldn't sit there and let *me* kiss *him*. That just wasn't in his blood. He quickly took over. His hand wrapped around the back of my head and he returned that kiss fiercely. Blood immediately turned to lava in my veins. I broke the kiss, pulling back far enough to see him, and realization slammed into me. Damn it all to hell.

I was so in love with Brock again.

*"From a little spark may burst a flame."*

—Dante Alighieri

# Chapter 25

Oh Christ.

I really was in love with him, and if I was going to be honest with myself, I'd probably never stopped loving him. Not completely. It was why, after two months of being back in my life, he could worm his way into my heart, firmly cementing himself there.

Realizing how strongly I felt was scary as hell, but I didn't want to dwell on it. I didn't want my fears and crap to hold me back in this moment, because I wanted to do something incredibly naughty considering where we were.

I don't know what gave me the idea. Maybe it was knowing how hard he was when I walked in. It could've been what he said about helping me get out there and live. Or it could've been the fact he'd actually take me to a festival that centered around an exceedingly large catsup bottle.

It could've been all those things, because what I wanted to do wasn't like me. Not at all, but I didn't want to think about that, because what was "like me" didn't matter.

I moved before rational thought could stop me or I could fear that someone, anyone could bust through the door. I moved before I let myself truly process that I was opening myself up to a whole world of hurting by acknowledging that I was in love with Brock.

Dropping down to my knees in front of him, I placed my hands on either side of his knees and spread them apart. His ragged inhale was like a shot of thunder as I slid my hands along the inside of his thighs, and I took a deep breath. I cupped him through the pants. He was hot and hard, straining the thin material.

"Fuck," he groaned. His hands dropped to the arms of the chair, and when I peeked up, I saw he was white-knuckling it. He breathed heavy as I lifted my gaze to his, wondering if he'd stop me. "I'm all yours," he gritted out.

The statement excited me beyond belief, but knowing that *my touch* was doing this to him, setting his jaw in a hard line and making his chest rise and fall powerfully thrilled me.

Lowering my gaze, I stroked him through his pants, reveling when he let out another rough sound. A strange and wonderful warm haze invaded me as I reached for the band. My hand shook as I tugged on his pants.

Brock rose, aiding me along as I inched his pants and the tight, black briefs down, exposing the rather impressive length.

Holy wow . . .

He was thick and long and perfect, and I . . . *I* wanted to taste *him*.

"You keep staring at me like that, this will be over before we even get started."

The right side of my mouth curved up. "We . . . we wouldn't want that, would we?" I wrapped my hand around the base of his cock. He kicked against my palm, burning hot and smooth like silk over steel.

His head fell back and his hips punched into my grasp. I moved my hand, slowly dragging it up and then back down. Awed and fascinated, I felt him from the base to the gleaming tip. He breathed heavily and ground out my name: "Jillian."

Tiny hairs all over my body raised as a far-off part of me never foresaw this, never could imagine that I'd be on my knees in an office, about to do what I was getting ready to.

Stretching up a few inches, I lowered my mouth, closing my lips around the tip. The salty taste of him teased my tongue. Hoping I was doing this right, I moved my hand as I brought him deeper into my mouth.

"Fuck," he growled, hips flexing as I swirled my tongue along the broad head of his cock. "Jillian, I . . ." He seemed to lose track of what he was saying, because he swore again and his large, powerful body tightened.

I dragged my hand and tongue all the way to the tip and then I lifted my mouth. "Am I . . . am I doing it right?"

His midnight eyes were blazing. "You couldn't do it wrong, Jillian. There is no way you could do this in a way I wouldn't love it." My lips curved into a smile, and he throbbed in my hand. "Christ. You holding my dick, sitting there and smiling up at me without worrying about it, is going to kill me."

Heart thumping, I let instinct take over. His hips jerked again as my mouth closed over him once more. Heat swamped me, and I ached as if he was doing this to me, and the arousal heightened when I felt his hand close around the back of my head, his fingers curling through my hair.

His grip tightened and a prick of heat coursed over my scalp, dragging a moan out of me that reverberated through him. His hand stilled. "You liked that?"

"Mmm," I murmured, realizing that I did like that little bite of pain.

"I'm going . . . to have to remember that," he said.

The illicit promise spurred me on, and his hips powered up. Brock shook as he gripped the nape of my neck, trying to pull me off or hold me there, I wasn't sure, but I wasn't going anywhere.

His entire body tensed around me and I heard the harsh punch of air coming out of him seconds before he pulsed into my mouth. When he finished, my jaw ached a little, but it was worth it. I kissed the blunt tip and then carefully let him go. Grabbing his pants and briefs, I inched them back up until he was covered.

Then I lifted my gaze to him.

His eyes were half-closed and his striking features completely lax. A long moment passed and I realized it was the first time I'd seen him like this in a long, long time, and he looked so beautiful, so at rest.

Then those eyes opened, and Brock moved wicked fast. One minute he was standing and the next, he towered over me, a hand at the back of my head and his mouth on me.

Brock kissed me deeply, branding my lips and scorching my senses, and then pulled me to his chest, folding his strong arms around me. "Now that is how I want to end every work day."

"Every?"

"Every."

Three hours and twenty-two minutes after I'd left Brock's office, it sort of sank in that I'd given Brock, who was really my boss, a blow job, on my knees, in his office . . .

Of what was technically my father's business.

*Holy shit.*

I'd gone—God, how long? With the exception of that Friday night, three years with only mechanical action, and I literally went from zero to porn star status in like forty-eight hours. That was crazy.

And kind of impressive.

A tiny, hidden part of me was kind of proud. Knowing what I did in there made me feel empowered—*sexy*. I hadn't felt sexy in like, well, forever, it felt like.

But it was Brock's influence. He just had that magnetism that had made a score of really smart women willingly do really bad and not so smart things. What if someone had walked into his office? What if it had been Paul? He already had about a pinky's worth of respect for me.

I was going to blame Brock for my behavior.

As I packed Tuesday night for the trip home, I was a little nervous. It wasn't that long of a drive. A little over three hours, so the chances of Rhage doing something horrific to Brock's Porsche were slim. At least, I hoped, but I was more worried about how my family would perceive what was going on between Brock and me. Us riding up together already had to have the whole group gossiping like a bunch of old women.

Mainly because we hadn't labeled what we were, even though Brock obviously had plans for us in the future—plans that involved catsup bottle festivals.

So I figured we'd play it cool. Like we were friends and nothing more at this point. Maybe I'd tell my mom we were dating. That didn't sound too serious. I just didn't want them to think we were together, *together* in case everything spectacularly blew up in our faces.

Like I couldn't help but expect it to.

I hated that part of me, but that didn't change the fact that part existed nor erase the shadow of unease that warned me that what was happening between us wasn't real.

Brock arrived early Wednesday morning, a baseball cap pulled down low, shielding his face as he stepped into my apartment carrying a bag of fresh doughnuts and coffee.

"You're amazing," I told him, still half-asleep as I snatched the bag out of his hand.

"That I know."

Peeling open the carton, I practically moaned at the sugary goodness that awaited me.

"Since I'm amazing, I should get a kiss." He reached up, turning his hat so it was on backward. "Don't you think?"

I thought that maybe he didn't need a reason for a kiss. Tipping my head up, I waited but he stopped short. I opened my eyes.

"Smile for me."

I bit down on my lip. "Brock."

"Come on," he coaxed, grinning. "I brought you coffee and doughnuts. I get a smile and a kiss." When I didn't move, he placed his hands on my shoulders and squeezed gently. "Smile, Jilly."

Rolling my eyes, I didn't know why it was such a big deal for me, because I knew he'd seen my smile over the last couple of days. However, I hadn't really been thinking in those moments.

I could do this.

I could smile for him.

I mean, the guy had seen my vagina all up close and personal, so I really couldn't be embarrassed over my wonky smile. But I couldn't help but remember the girl who sat next to me in World History after I returned to school. She'd asked if I had a stroke. The question hadn't been malicious. She hadn't blurted it out. It seemed like it had been building in her for weeks to ask. She'd even followed it up by relating how her grandfather smiled after he suffered a stroke. I also couldn't help but remember how Ben had never asked me to smile for him.

But Brock wasn't the girl in my history class and he sure as hell wasn't Ben, so I did it.

I could feel the right side of my lips curve up while my left side simply twitched and did nothing.

Brock's gaze swept over my face and settled on my mouth as he slid one hand up, around my neck. His thumb massaged the space just below my pulse.

"I think there's something you need to understand," he said, his gaze flicking to mine. "Your smile was beautiful before. Could light up a fucking room and could bring a smile to my face seconds before I stepped into the Octagon. Your smile is different now, but even more beautiful."

"Come on," I said wryly, starting to pull free. My smile didn't make me an ogre, but it wasn't beautiful.

"It's true." He kept me in place with just a hand at my neck. "You know why? It proves what you've been through and what you've survived. That smile is a fucking miracle. Just like every breath you take is. That smile is nothing to ever be ashamed of. It's a smile to be fucking proud of."

Oh wow.

That was more than sweet. That was a *beautiful* thing for him to say.

"You feel me?" he asked.

"I feel you," I whispered back.

"Good."

Lowering my gaze, I didn't stop the smile that now tugged at my lips. I let it happen as I willed the knot in my throat to disappear. I cleared my throat. "First the doughnuts and now the whole beautiful smile thing? Are you trying to get laid?"

His richly colored eyes glimmered with amusement and something more, something lavish and promising. "Is it working?"

A laugh escaped me, and I shook my head. Rising up on the tips of my toes, I kissed him. His arm swept around my waist, holding me in place as the kiss deepened and consumed me. A wonderful heady warmth slid down my throat and over my chest.

Brock lifted his head, putting a little distance between us. "Yeah, we're going to have to stop."

"Why?" I asked, breathless.

"Because if we don't, we're never going to make it out of here."

I wanted to ask if that was such a bad thing, but I grinned and slipped free. After shoving two doughnuts in my mouth, I went and found Rhage hiding under the bed. It took some coaxing to get him out. Eventually I had to wiggle his toy mouse in his face and then I snatched him up once his upper body appeared.

He was not a happy camper, struggling in my arms as I walked out into the living room. I kept his legs pinned.

Brock arched a brow when he saw me. He'd already taken out the super-cute paisley print weekender bag. "You doing okay over there?"

"Yes," I sighed, walking to where his carrier was. "He's just an ass."

He chuckled. "Need help?"

"I got it." Having a ton of experience at shoving the cat into the carrier, I knew I just had to keep him from grabbing onto the sides. Once I had him in, I tossed his toy mouse inside and latched the door. A second later, Rhage's disgruntled face was pressed against the bars.

"It's like cat prison," Brock commented.

"This cat needs to go to prison." Rhage hissed as I picked up his carrier. "Ready?"

Brock's grin was small, but it twisted up my insides. "Been ready."

Normally, being a passenger during a trip that was longer than an hour would put me right to sleep, but I was more interested in talking to Brock than I was in dozing. We'd chatted about how we were going to broach the subject of converting some of the space into a dance studio. Avery and Teresa had gotten early numbers back to me, and I felt confident enough with them that we were ready to talk to my dad. Then our subjects turned to less serious things.

He peppered me with questions ranging from working at the insurance firm to what the last book I was reading was about. About halfway through the trip, I got a text message from Abby.

My stomach dipped as I read it and glanced over at Brock. "It looks like a bunch of people are going to Mona's tonight. Abby knows I'll be in town, so she's invited me."

Half of Brock's face was hidden by the cap he wore. "Do you want to go?"

I wasn't sure. I hadn't been to Mona's since the shooting. I had no idea what it would be like going back there, but I wanted to see Abby and everyone else. I planned on doing so anyway, but underneath the unease was a trickle of excitement. "Do you?"

"Not up to me," he replied.

"That's not real helpful."

One side of his lips kicked up. "Babe," he said, and a secret part of me sort of loved it when he called me that, because it was something he'd never done before. "If you want to go, we can go. If you want to stay home and chill with your family, we can do that. If you want to go by yourself—"

"I don't want to go by myself," I cut in.

He glanced over at me. "If you did, that's cool too."

Nodding, I glanced down at my phone. "Abby said Colton will be there. Roxy is working, so Reece will also be there. Obviously Jax and Calla will be there."

"Cool."

My fingers hovered over the phone. "I think Steph and Nick we are actually in Martinsburg with her mom, but everyone else will be there. Even Katie." I hadn't seen Katie in forever, it felt like. "It would be cool to see all of them."

"Totally up to you."

Nibbling on my lower lip, I was still for a second, and then I decided to act off the excitement instead of the dread. "I think we should go. For a little bit? I mean, that's if you really want to go with me."

"Do you really have to wonder if I want to go with you or not?"

I peeked over at him. "Well, if we show up together then people might think . . . things."

"Do I look like I care about what people think?"

No, he didn't, but I had no idea what he meant by that in terms of us being together or not. "Okay then," I murmured, sending Abby back a quick text saying I might be there. I didn't mention that Brock would be with me, because I didn't want to open that Pandora-size box of questions at the moment. "I guess we have plans for later."

"I guess we do."

Placing my phone back in my purse, I twisted in my seat and checked on Rhage. "So, I've been wondering about something," I said, looking to change the subject. "Why did you retire? You still have a couple more years left in you."

He chuckled. "The way you say that makes it sound like by the time I hit forty, I'm going to be useless and should be put down. You know, that's not a long time off from now."

"Well," I drawled the word, teasing him.

One hand on the steering wheel, he shrugged a shoulder. "I was . . . getting tired."

I stuck my fingers through the little holes in Rhage's cage, touching his paw. He immediately withdrew. "Physically or . . . ?"

"Physically and mentally," he answered as I gave up on the cat and twisted back around. "You know how it is," he continued. "The constant training that sucks up the entire day. The traveling wasn't bad, but worrying if you were going to lose your endorsements to the next big deal or if you were going to get hurt again can really wear on you."

All of that was completely understandable. I wasn't sure if fans knew how much of their lives the fighters gave up to fight even two or four times a year.

"And even if you're not worrying about serious injuries, you get tired of your nose likely getting broken once a year." He grinned as he reached up, feeling along the back side of his left ear. "Or cauliflower ear."

"Yours isn't bad."

"I'm lucky." His hand dropped. "But yeah, you know, in my last match I felt it—felt it in here." He placed his right hand to the center of his chest. "It was just a sharp, stabbing sensation. I didn't tear the muscle again, but damn, there was a second when fear punched the air out of me. Did not want to go through that again, and I knew that tiny bit of fear meant it was time for a change. You can't get in there with anything holding you back. The moment you find yourself hesitating, it's time to bow out."

The idea of him tearing that muscle again terrified me. It could still happen. Especially since he still liked to get on the mats with new recruits. "Do you miss it?"

"Sometimes, but I was ready to move on. And I think being ready when I left makes it all okay."

Something occurred to me as I listened to him. He'd said he broke off the engagement with Kristen about a year ago. His last match was probably six months to a year before that.

Asking about Kristen felt weird, but the curiosity was too much. "How did Kristen take you retiring?"

If my question caught him off-guard or if he was uncomfortable with it, his expression didn't show it. "I think she liked the idea of me being around more and we could actually do things together. When I was actively fighting, it was like having a ten to twelve hour a day job. I was always training, so it didn't leave a lot of time to go and do things."

I studied him closely. "You say that like once it happened it was a different story."

He grinned. "You know, Kristen and I were together for a long time, but we really weren't in the same place often. You really don't know each other—know their wants and desires—until you're spending a lot of time with them. Things change then."

"So . . . you two didn't get along?"

One shoulder rose. "I don't think we did. Not really. She didn't see it that way."

I wanted to ask him what was it about Kristen that made him propose marriage to her if he didn't think he knew her, but there was no way I could ask that question without it sounding incredibly bitter.

"What about you and that guy you dated?" he asked.

"There isn't much to tell." I tucked my hair back as I gazed out the window at the endless concrete of the turnpike. "We met at Shepherd. He asked me out, and I . . ."

"What?" he asked after a moment.

The reason why I'd gone out with Ben and stayed with him was embarrassing to admit, but since it was caring and sharing time, I forced out the truth. "I was just . . . I was just lonely. I wanted to be with someone and he was interested in me."

Brock was quiet for so long that I had to look over at him. His profile was stoic, made of marble and ice. "Did he treat you well?"

I squirmed. "That's a weird question to ask."

"You never brought him home to your parents."

"That's not an indication of how he treated me," I pointed out.

"Did he want to meet your parents?"

I looked away. "Not really."

"So did he treat you like you deserved?"

Uncomfortable, I folded my arms. "Most of the time it wasn't bad or good. It was just . . . somewhere in the middle. I don't regret the relationship. I learned a lot from it."

"Like what?"

"Like not to ever settle again."

It was close to eleven when we pulled up in front of my parents' house. My stomach was full of knots, but I was relieved to see there weren't five hundred cars in the circular driveway. At least we wouldn't have to deal with all my uncles and their wives and their herd of children.

I stared up at the double doors, excited to see my family, but also anxious. They could be . . . overwhelming at times.

Brock killed the engine, and a second later I felt his fingers curling around my chin. He guided my gaze to his. Leaning into me, he closed the distance and kissed me softly. It was a tender and sweet kiss, one that held infinite patience.

"You ready to head in there?"

Realizing he sensed the hesitation, I drew back and stared at him. I wanted to thank him. I wanted to kiss him again.

Rhage meowed pitifully from the back seat.

Laughing, I sat back and unbuckled my seatbelt. "I know who's ready."

We climbed out, and before I could grab the carrier, Brock already had it in his hand. Rhage was probably loving that. We walked up the driveway, leaving our bags to grab later.

The door opened before we reached it and out came my mom, a flurry of long brown hair and big eyes. One second I was standing on the porch, arm raised, and the next Mom was wrapping her arms around me, squeezing the living daylights out of me.

"Mom," I gasped, hugging her back. "I can barely breathe."

"Deal with it." She hugged me tighter.

I coughed out a laugh and then she pulled back, smoothing a hand over my hair, pushing it back from my face. Her eyes were watery as she smiled, then her gaze moved to Brock, and I winced in sympathy as she enveloped him in an equally suffocating hug. Somehow, he managed to hold onto Rhage's carrier. Brock laughed at her exuberance and returned the hug with one arm.

"Hon, let them get in the house." Dad's voice rang out from inside the house. "They've been in the car for hours."

"Hush it." Mom let go of Brock and then looped her arm through mine as we started inside. "You'd think by now he'd know how easily excited I am."

"You'd think," I argued dryly.

Mom laughed.

Warm air greeted us as we stepped in the foyer, and I saw Dad striding across the scuffed hardwood floors. His hair was more salt than pepper since the last time I'd seen him and the lines around his eyes had increased, but the man was still fit as a fiddle.

"Hey, Dad." Slipping free of Mom, I met him halfway.

Dad's hug was just as intense, but it didn't feel like I'd have cracked ribs afterward, so that was great. "Have any trouble driving up here?"

"No." I stepped back.

"There was a little traffic when we got close," Brock told him, placing the carrier on the floor. "But nothing too bad."

267

Mom stared down at Rhage. "You just had to bring Satan with you, didn't you?"

"I couldn't leave him at home."

"He's staying in your room," she warned.

"Of course."

"Am I seriously the only person this cat likes?" Brock asked as he dipped down, bravely sticking his finger through the holes.

Mom's shrewd gaze bounced between us, and I was sure she was wondering exactly how often Brock was around the cat. "Yes," I answered. "You are pretty much the only person."

Dad kept his arm around my shoulders as he eyed Brock. "It's good, real good to see you two together again."

"I'm glad to hear that," Brock replied as he looked up, his gaze straying to mine. "Because Jillian and I *are* together."

# Chapter 26

Well, at least now I knew where Brock and I stood; however I'd wished he hadn't quite dropped the bomb like that. I would've liked it to be in private, so I could've done a happy dance. And I wish it hadn't been in front of my parents, because things got a little weird after that.

Dad appeared smug and patted Brock's back like being with me was equal to him winning a tough match. Then Dad crossed his arms and nodded sagely as if he had always known this was how it would turn out.

And Mom . . . Good Lord, Mom looked about ready to cry, and not just a few tears. Oh no, she looked like she was about to sob like somehow Brock had discovered the fountain of youth and was about to give her directions on the location.

Truth was though, I was . . . I was pleased they were happy, and they really were. I had to look away, focus on the new painting in the foyer of a sandy golden beach and sky at dusk, vibrantly catching the blue and pink hues, so no one saw how shiny my eyes were getting.

Especially when Brock draped his arm over my shoulders and pulled into my side while Mom continued to gush on about how happy she was. It was a big deal to her. We were here for Thanksgiving, and tomorrow would be the first true family dinner in a long time.

And it . . . it really would.

Brock leaned in and whispered in my left ear. "You okay?"

I nodded and then looked down at the cat carrier. Rhage was hissing and carrying on while my mom stared all googly-eyed at Brock, probably already planning the wedding invitations while baby booties danced in her head.

Rhage withdrew from my finger and I sighed. "I'm going to take Rhage upstairs. He's getting—"

The front door swung open and a swarm of small people rushed in, a literal sea of tiny humans. I blinked, losing count once I saw the sixth dark-haired child, and I knew it was Uncle Julio, because he could seriously fill out an entire baseball roster with his own children.

I straightened before I was knocked over by the wave of children. Brock shifted closer and his arm went around me again.

Julio's wife came through, carrying the youngest on her hip, and miraculously she didn't look pregnant. "I told you Brock was here," Heather yelled over her shoulder. "That was his car out front."

"I know that's his car," my uncle shouted back.

"And Jilly is with him!" Heather drew up short, her gaze moving from my face to his and then to the arm around my shoulder. "And Brock has his arm around her!"

My brows rose.

Brock chuckled under his breath.

Beside me, Mom practically buzzed with eagerness to explain. "Oh Heather, dear, Brock and my baby girl are together."

"What?" yelled Julio. "Woman, they haven't . . ." His voice faded off, and I heard a childish, girlish squeal.

"Together?" Heather cocked her head to the side, and the small child, a boy or a girl, I had no idea, tugged on her long, blonde hair.

"We're seeing each other," Brock explained while I stood there like an idiot.

Mom let out a little squeak that sounded like Beaker from the Muppet Babies, and then Heather was hollering, "Brock and Jilly are seeing each other!"

"Oh my God," I murmured.

Brock squeezed my shoulders.

A second later, what I guessed was the last of their kids came running through the open doors. It was Hannah—I think—and she made a beeline for Rhage's carrier, cooing as she dropped onto the floor, sticking her little fingers toward the cage.

"I wouldn't do that—" I reached for the child.

"Don't let that damn cat out," Julio griped, and my gaze flew to the open door. "You remember what happened last time, Hannah-Banana. Nearly took off your finger and the cat got out. Took us half a day to catch him."

"That's an exaggeration," I said dryly.

Julio looked like he had the last time I'd seen him—a younger version of Dad. Still no graying hairs or skin creasing in the corners. He was a little taller, a few inches above me, and he was dressed like he always was, in black track pants and a Lima shirt. That was all. It was forty degrees outside and windy as hell, and that was all he'd wear.

"Look at you two." My uncle grinned as he strode across the foyer, managing to navigate the children as they appeared to be climbing all over everything—furniture, Mom, Dad, the walls. Julio stopped in front of Brock and patted his chest. "Name your first kid after me."

"Oh my God," I said again.

"I'm sure they'll name their first kid after me," Dad chimed in, grinning as his dark eyes sparkled.

"But what if it's a girl?" Mom asked quite seriously as Heather shuffled forward, giving Brock and me a one-armed hug. The kid on her hip ended up in my hair and it took four seconds to untangle the poor child.

"Can we not talk about having babies?" I asked, wrangling the last strand of hair free from the small child's death grip. "We really aren't at that stage."

"I want kids," Brock announced, glancing down at me, and the air stalled in my lungs. "Maybe not an entire soccer team like some."

"But you'll have fun making that soccer team." Julio grinned.

Heather turned her head to me. "But you will not have fun delivering said soccer team."

"Okay," I said, stepping away from Brock. My face was on fire. "I need to get—"

The child at the carrier fell back and Rhage flew out of the cage in a flurry of brown and white fur. Claws rapped off the wood floor as he shot into the living room. Mom shouted. Kids squealed and ran off.

"Damn it," I muttered, exhaling heavily as something somewhere in the living room crashed to the floor. "Not again."

Dad laughed as he walked up to my side and kissed my temple. "Welcome home, Jilly."

Later, after Brock caught the damn cat hiding in a bushy fern in the sunroom and brought him up to my bedroom, I sat on the corner of my old bed and waited for Brock. He was in his old room, getting ready for the evening.

We all had an early dinner and then Julio and Heather packed up the kids. They'd be back tomorrow with everyone else, and I was sure that would prove interesting. Or overwhelming. Brock and I planned on discussing the option of converting the space either Thursday evening or Friday.

I'd showered and curled my hair so it fell in loose waves down to the center of my back. I hadn't parted it like I normally would; instead I let it part naturally, straight down the middle.

I wore a thin V-neck sweater in deep red, because I knew it would be warm in Mona's, and a pair of dark jeans tucked inside the same boots I'd worn the night I'd first saw Brock in Martinsburg.

Getting ready had reminded me of that night so long ago, but as I sat on this narrow bed that would barely fit two people and gazed around my room, I couldn't help but think about how so much had changed since that night—how much I'd changed. Sometimes it felt like I was still that same girl who got dressed up one Saturday night, full of girlish hope, and other times I didn't even recognize her.

Though as my gaze roamed over the hundreds of books lining my bookcase, I didn't feel like I wanted to be far from this room. There was no slicing pain in my stomach or pressure in my chest. There were memories, but they didn't haunt me.

One side of my lips tilted up as I thought about tonight. A flutter started in my belly and spread upward. I was nervous, but in a . . . a good way. I was going out tonight.

I was going to Mona's.

I was going to see my friends.

That was a flutter of *excitement*.

A knock on my door drew me out of my thoughts. "Come in."

The door cracked open and Brock popped his head in. "Is it safe, or is Rhage going to make a run for it?"

I glanced to the open closet door. "He's hiding in the closet. Just shut the door in case he decides to make another run for it."

Brock slipped in, quickly closing the door. As I got a good look at him, the flutter in my belly increased until it felt like a swarm of hummingbirds.

The beard was gone.

His jaw was bare and the hard, chiseled line was on full display. So was the faint scar on his lip. I wanted to touch it—kiss it. He wore a black Henley and a pair of jeans, and somehow he looked like he belonged in his own personal jet. He wore those clothes. They didn't wear him, and he looked amazing.

"Really loving that top," he said, and I blinked, drawing my gaze back to his. He'd been checking me out as I'd been doing the same thing. He walked over to me. His finger skimmed along the collar of my sweater, over the swells of my breasts. "I really love this shirt."

"Perv," I murmured as I reached up and placed a hand on his cheek. "You shaved."

"Yeah, figured it was time. You like?"

"Like it either way." Biting down on my lip, I dragged my hand along his jaw. The skin was impossibly smooth.

Brock dipped his head and my hand slid back to the nape of his neck. The kiss was sweet and felt different since the beard was gone. "You sure about tonight?"

A faint smile tugged at my lips as I lowered my cheek to his shoulder and inhaled deeply.

"I mean, we can stay in." A hand slipped over my lower back and down the curve of my rear. "Wait until your parents go to bed, then I can creep into your bedroom like we're both teens. Keep you to myself."

I laughed. "I'm sure. I want to go." I looked up, searching his face as a seed of doubt blossomed. Maybe he didn't want to go . . . to go with me. "Do you want to go with—"

"Babe." The grip on my ass tightened. "If you're about to ask if I want to go with you, I might turn you over my knee."

I raised my brow. "I really would like to see you try that."

"I bet you would really like it."

Maybe, but that wasn't the point. I inhaled deeply. "If you want to go and so do I, then what are we waiting for?"

His grin was slow. "Then let's go."

My stomach churned as I climbed out of the car, the cute Coach wristlet dangling from my wrist. The parking lot was full. Not entirely surprising since it was the night before Thanksgiving and many would have the next day off, which meant many would spend Thanksgiving hung over.

But I wasn't thinking about drinking and spending the next day with a massive headache. Taking a deep breath, I stepped forward and without wanting to, without even trying, I found myself staring toward the side parking lot, where the Dumpsters were and where the staff usually parked. It wasn't that well-lit back there.

It was where I parked the last time I'd been here.

Cold wind whipped through the parking lot, lifting strands of my hair and tossing them around my face.

Ice settled in my veins and my stomach wiggled with a nest of snakes. I wanted to look away. I wanted to walk straight into the bar, unaffected by being here, but I couldn't.

"Jillian?"

I jerked to my left, not realizing Brock had joined me in front of his car. "I'm sorry."

"It's okay." Yellow light from the overhead lamp fell upon his face. Concern filled his steady gaze as he took my hand in his. "What are you thinking?"

My mouth dried. The door to Mona's opened and laughter spilled out into the parking lot.

"I'm thinking about that night." Brock squeezed my hand as he brought it to his chest. "I think it makes sense. It's okay if you are."

I wet my lower lip and then nodded slowly. "I never . . . I never drove past here again. I didn't come anywhere near here. I just . . ."

Brock circled his other arm around the nape of my neck, drawing me close. For several moments we stood there in silence, then he said, "You know, I haven't gone by the place I grew up since I was . . . hell, in my early twenties?"

Surprise flickered through me. "You haven't?"

He shook his head. "Not once since then."

All I could do was stare. Brock rarely talked about his past. He'd always been that way. "I thought you'd gone back."

"Just that once. Saw my father." He let out a heavy breath. "He was still drinking and he still wanted to do nothing but talk with his fists."

"You never told me you saw your father."

He raised a shoulder in a slight shrug. "There was nothing to tell. The man barely cared that I was even there, standing in front of him and alive. All he saw was that I was wearing nice clothes and driving a nice car. He saw me and saw his next bottle of whiskey."

Sadness filled me. "And your mom?"

Another slow shake of his head. "She wasn't there, but that wasn't anything new. She was never there."

His parents really were the worst. His dad was a drunk who had never been able to hold down a job. He'd stay out, come home, and even though Brock rarely admitted it, I knew his father used him as a punching bag.

Just like Brock's father had used his mom.

And which was probably why his mom was never there, but who could leave knowing what was happening to their child? I never understood. Never would.

"I don't drive down that street. Don't go into that neighborhood." He cupped my cheek, smoothing his thumb along the damaged jaw. "I understand why you never drove past here and I get why this is a big deal for you."

My gaze shifted away from his, to the side parking lot. "I'm . . . I'm okay. It's just—I don't know. I almost died here." I let out a shaky breath as I reached deep in and tried to see how I felt, but there was nothing really there. "I guess . . . I don't know. I felt like coming back here would be this eye-opening, epiphany moment, but I just kind of feel numb."

"However you feel, whether it's nothing or angry or sad, it's all okay."

I nodded as I dragged my gaze back to his. "Do you ever want to see them again—your parents?" I asked as a burst of cold wind caused me to shiver.

"You know, I don't even feel bad about saying this, but no. I don't." He shifted so his back took the brunt of the wind. "The only thing those people taught me was to survive, and they weren't even very good at that."

"But you did survive," I pointed out.

"Luck," he said, the corners of hips lips curling up.

I shook my head. "No, it's not luck. You have . . . you have fire in you, Brock. You were determined to do more than survive, to make something out of your life. To succeed and—"

"And you don't think you have that?" His eyes searched mine. "After what you've survived and where you stand today?"

I lowered my gaze, unsure of how to answer the question, because I wasn't sure if I had that same kind of fire Brock had, because I'd given up so much and he'd fought for so much.

And I really didn't want to think about any of this right now. "Let's get in there before everyone thinks we bailed on them."

He was silent for a moment. "We can leave whenever you want. Just let me know and we're gone."

"Okay." Thinking he deserved a kiss for that, I stretched up and brought my mouth to his.

Despite the cold wind, the kiss warmed me from the inside out. My lips parted and the kiss deepened, turned scalding hot. Brock kissed as if he was drinking every part of me in, taking long and deep drafts. My body melted into his, and I was rewarded with a deep, throaty growl.

"You sure we gotta go in there?" he asked, pressing his forehead against mine.

I let out a shaky laugh. "Yes."

"Then we better do this before I change my mind and find a very different way of spending our evening." He shifted his hips, and my eyes widened as I felt him against my stomach, hard and thick.

Blushing to the roots of my hair, I stepped back, but he kept me close as we turned to the entrance of the bar. Holding my hand in his, we walked into Mona's together, for the first time, side by side.

# Chapter 27

Mona's had really changed since all those years ago. Gone were the old floors that always looked dirty and possibly sticky no matter how many times they were cleaned. They were replaced with what appeared to be some kind of fancy tile that looked like slate. The bar was all new, still shaped like a horseshoe with two wells, but the bottle display was also updated with bright white light and lit blue tubes running underneath the clear shelves, showcasing the more expensive liquors. TVs were on the walls and hung from the ceilings in various places. The round high-top tables were all black and the stools had freshly cushioned seating.

There were a lot of people standing around the bar and the tables. I couldn't see toward the back where the booths and larger tables were next to the pool tables.

Mona's had gotten a facelift and the place no longer looked like the dive bar down the street. That had to mean that business was going well for Calla and Jax, the owners.

I'd seen Calla a few times over the years, but we'd never really talked about the bar, so I was beyond happy to see all the new additions.

Brock led me around an older couple, and the first familiar faces we saw were Reece and Colton Anders. They were leaning against the bar, watching one of the TVs hung on the wall.

Reece and his older brother, Colton, were police officers, and both of them, with their dark brown hair, classically chiseled features and startling blue eyes, could star in their own hot cop calendars.

Like, it could be just them, alternating each month, and no one would complain. No one.

I'd seen them since the shooting, especially Colton since he was always with Abby. I had no real memories of what happened after I'd been shot, just shattered glimpses, but I knew Colton and Reece had been there.

I was alive because of their quick thinking and experience, and the two would always hold a special place in my heart.

Colton spotted us first, and a wide smile broke out over his face. "Hey! You guys are finally here." He pushed off the bar, crossing the distance between his. "Real good to see you two."

Reece followed, spotting Brock's hand around mine, and his smile kicked up a notch. I could feel my cheeks heat as the guys did their weird one-arm man-hug thing and then I got the full hugs. From both of them!

"It's been forever since I've seen you," Reece said in my good ear, drawing back. "You look amazing."

"Thank you."

Colton moved in next, and I heard Brock grumble something under his breath that caused Reece to laugh. "You doing good?" Colton asked. "Abby said you are, but you know how she is, she worries about everyone."

"I'm doing good. Truly," I said, pulling back, feeling the bitter bite of shame. There were long gaps in time when I didn't talk to Abby, talk to anyone really, and I knew she had worried. "Where is Abby?"

Colton looked over his shoulder and tilted his chin up. "The girls have a seat back . . . there they are." With a hand on my shoulder, he pointed to one of the large round tables toward the back. "You see them?"

Stretching up, I thought I saw the back of Abby's head. I turned to Brock. "I'm going to go over and say hi."

"Cool," he replied, but as I started to step away, he caught my arm and hauled me back. My hand landed on his chest. "But first."

I opened my mouth, but whatever I was about to say was cut off with his kiss. It was quick but deep, and he kissed me like no one was standing right in front of us. When he let go, I swayed a bit and his grin was smug.

"I'll swing over there in a bit," he said.

"Okay," I whispered, feeling dazed. There was a good chance I would've agreed to anything at this point.

Brock lowered his mouth to my left ear and said, "Fucking cute as hell."

"What?" And then I realized he was acknowledging that I was still standing there and staring up at him like a doofus. Like a doofus who Brock found "fucking cute," but still a doofus. "I'll go now."

Brock chuckled.

Turning around, I wiggled my fingers at the incredibly hot cop duo and then navigated the throng of people. The partial hearing made me feel slightly unbalanced as I walked through the crowd.

I rounded the set of high-top tables and saw them. Abby was sitting at the table, toying with a straw in her drink. Standing beside her was Roxy, a bartender at Mona's who was married to Reece. I didn't know Roxy too well, but she was hilarious, extremely quick-witted and very talented. The woman could paint anything.

Sitting next to Abby was Calla. The tall blonde had her hair pulled back. The faint scars on her face were barely noticeable. She was laughing at something the absolutely stunning brunette sitting across from her was saying. Surprise filled me when I realized that Steph was there and Nick was standing behind her chair, his hands on the back. I figured they'd be in Martinsburg with her mom.

Roxy started to turn and she spotted me. "Hey! Oh my God, look at you!" Full of energy, she bounced over to me and enveloped me in a warm hug. "Ah, you made it here!"

"It's so good to see you." When she pulled back, I laughed. "I love the glasses and hair."

"Me too." She reached up, touching the green streak of hair that matched her glasses. "I know it's only Thanksgiving, but I'm getting festive already. Green reminds me of Christmas. Reece says I should've gone with red, but I'm thinking about saving that for Valentine's Day."

"You could also go white for Christmas," I said. "You know, for snow and Santa's beard."

Her eyes widened behind the glasses. "Damn. I didn't even think of that. I've actually never done white before."

I actually couldn't believe there was a color Roxy hadn't tried yet.

Abby let out a squeal and extended her arms, but she was blocked in. "Jillian! Finally!"

"Sorry. We were running a little late." I waved at her.

"Oh, the 'we' part is very exciting." Roxy bumped her hip into mine. "Very, very exciting."

Steph extended her arms from where she sat. "Look at you! Holy crap, you look amazing. Love the boobs."

I blushed as Nick dropped his head, shoulders shaking with laughter.

"What?" Steph turned around and shot the dark-haired Nick a look. "She looks hot. Women need to tell other women when they're looking hot. It needs to be a rule."

"Thank you," I said, laughing. Steph was possibly one of the most gorgeous women I'd ever seen in real life. She was bold and confident, spoke her mind often and freely, and she was also one of the most loyal and sweetest people I knew. I bent down to hug her. "I thought you would be in Martinsburg—oh my God, you're pregnant!" I froze halfway, realizing she had quite the little belly on her.

Steph laughed. "Yeah, that I am. I'm six months along."

"She didn't tell any of us for the longest time," Abby said. "Hell, she just started wearing really loose tops—"

"Which should've been a dead giveaway," Calla added dryly. Steph rolled her eyes.

"And stopped drinking," Abby continued. "I asked her, because she claimed she'd just gained weight and was on a diet."

Flipping her dark hair over her shoulder, Steph laughed. "We just didn't want anyone to know until we were a hundred percent sure this was going to . . . that it was going to last," she said. "We wanted to make sure we were basically out of the woods."

"It's why we stayed home this Thanksgiving," Nick explained, placing his hands on her shoulders, massaging them. "Her mom came up and we're having dinner here."

"I'm so excited for you guys," I said, wanting to clap like a seal. "Congratulations."

"Where is Brock?" Nick asked, speaking up to ensure I heard him through the hum of conversation and music.

I pointed to the bar. "He's with Colton and Reece."

"Haven't seen him in a minute." Bending down, he kissed the top of Steph's head. "You good?"

She nodded. "Tell him I said hi."

Nick kissed the side of her face and then walked by me, ruffling my hair like I was a five-year-old. I shot him a look, but his expression said he had no regrets as he swaggered off.

Calla popped up from her seat and we exchanged a quick hug. "It's so good to see you," she said, drawing back with a soft smile. "It's been a while."

"Yeah, a couple of years." I glanced around. "The place seriously looks amazing."

"Thank you." A proud look filled her eyes. "It's been a long process, and there are a few things Jax and I still want to work on. We got the kitchen upgraded, but we really want to do some sort of expansion. There's room to build out back, but we'd have to close down while that takes place, so we're trying to figure out a good time to do that."

"Wow. That sounds amazing," I said. "What are you planning to do with the expansion?"

Calla glanced at Roxy with excitement in her eyes. "We're thinking about adding some more tables, enough room for a couple of more pool tables, but we want to add a stage."

"That would be awesome," I said.

Roxy nodded. "Hell's yeah it would be."

"Take my seat." Calla stepped aside. "I've got to get back to the bar, because *someone* is on their lunch."

"That's me," Roxy chirped.

I sat down next to Abby, finally getting to hug her. "I'm so glad you're here," she said and then into my left ear, "And you are so going to have to fill me in later on what is going on with you and Brock."

"I will," I promised.

Smiling at me, Abby leaned back and said, "You know, she's not the only one having a baby."

My gaze darted between the three remaining women. "Which one—"

"Not me." Calla held up her hands. "Jax and I are happy being the cool aunt and uncle right now."

I looked at Abby and her brows knitted. "Don't you think I'd tell you?"

"I'd hope so, which leaves you . . ."

Roxy laughed, shaking her head.

"Then who?" I asked.

Steph laughed. "Your answer is right in front of you and she's lying."

"All right, it's me." Roxy straightened her glasses. "I'm about two months along."

My mouth dropped open.

"I still don't really believe it myself," she said, patting her practically non-existent stomach. "We weren't exactly trying, you know?"

"In other words, she forgot to take her pills one too many times," Calla explained, laughing when Roxy smacked her arm.

Abby shook her head. "I honestly worry about drinking the water here. It's like everyone is waking up pregnant."

"I heard you can catch it on a toilet seat," Steph commented.

I laughed, relaxing back against the booth. "Note to self. Do not use the restroom here."

"Yeah, but a Brock and Jillian baby would be so cute," Abby said.

"Shut up right now," I said, holding my hands up like I could ward off pregnancy that way. Not that I had anything to worry about at this point. I was on the pill and we hadn't even had sex yet. "Do not jinx me."

"Oh, look who's here," Calla said. "I told her you were coming by tonight."

Twisting in my seat, I looked across the bar and my mouth dropped open. At first, I wasn't sure my eyes were functioning correctly, but then I blinked, and I still saw her, and I knew it wasn't someone who time-warped out of the seventies.

"Katie!" I shrieked.

The blonde hadn't changed one bit since the last time I'd seen her. Her hair was pulled back in a tight, high ponytail. She wore sparkly pants that looked like bell bottoms. Pretty sure she was wearing platform heels, and the bright fuchsia shirt she wore kept sliding off her shoulder. She had to have at least a dozen bangles stacked from her wrist to her elbow.

"Hey, girl, hey!" She had a shot glass in one hand and a glass of dark liquid in another. "For you. It's Coke. Because I know you don't want to drink tonight."

I stared as she placed the fresh Coke down in front of me, slightly unnerved by the fact she knew I wasn't going to drink. "Thank you."

She grinned as she reached down and hugged me tightly. "I got something to say to you, Jilly," she said, and everyone at our table quieted, because when Katie had something to say, you listened. "Hopefully you listen to me this time."

Every muscle in my body tensed, because I knew what she was referencing and I should've listened to her last time.

"Still going to be rough at times, but he's worth it now," she said, holding my gaze with eyes the color of the ocean. "You just had to wait to discover that."

Um.

I didn't know what to say.

She was obviously talking about Brock. She had told me once that he hadn't been worth it *yet*, and I thought she had been telling me that he simply wasn't worth it at all.

"Holy shit," Steph exploded, leaning back in her seat. "Is that a wedding ring on your finger?" Her hand darted out and she snapped up Katie's arm. "That is a so a wedding ring."

"What?" Abby demanded. "When did you get married?"

"Who did you marry?" Roxy asked.

Calla, who hadn't headed back to work, shook her head in wonder. "And do we know him?"

Katie giggled. "Yes. I got married last weekend. We eloped to Vegas." Popping back a step, she wiggled her finger. "And you all don't know him," she said, "Not yet. But you will. And he will be your favorite."

Not a single one of us batted an eyelash.

"And when will we meet him?" Calla asked.

"Soon." She tapped Calla on the nose. "Very soon."

"I'm sorry. Hold on a second," I said, shaking my head. "How did you meet this guy?"

"Well," Katie said, lifting her shot. "Let's just say he was a very, very determined patron of the club." Winking, she took the shot and then lowered the glass. "And we have been together for like eight years. So it was about time we jumped the broom."

Steph's jaw nearly hit the table. "What? You've been with this guy since *then*?"

She shrugged a shoulder. "Yes."

"Why haven't you told us?" Roxy looked like she was about to hit Katie next.

"When did I have a chance to talk to you guys about my man? Y'all are a bunch of dramalicious bitches who constantly need my wise and sage advice." She planted a hand on her hip. "And it's not like I'd ever come to any of you for relationship advice. For realsies."

For some reason, I found that hilariously funny. Maybe because it was accurate. Tipping my head back, I laughed— laughed hard enough that I think I hurt my abs.

Steph was also laughing and she looked like she was seconds away from peeing herself. From that point, Katie told us about her man, who apparently none of us knew about, while I sipped my Coke. Time passed. Calla and Roxy returned to the bar. Katie stole someone's chair and brought it over to our table.

I saw the crowd parting, making way for Brock like he was some kind of extraordinarily hot Moses.

Within moments, I saw the glazed-over shocked faces of nearly every male in the bar once they realized they were in the presence of Brock Mitchell. If I had my complete hearing, I knew I'd hear the murmurings and gasps.

Brock nodded at the girls as he took my hand and pulled me onto my feet. Tugging me close, he said into my ear, "I was missing you."

Placing my hands on his waist, I laughed. "I haven't been gone that long."

"Long enough." He kissed my neck and then my jaw.

"You two are freaking adorable," Steph said as Nick came up behind her.

"That we are." Circling an arm around my waist, Brock drew me to him. I went, placing my hands on his chest as he lowered his head. His lips swept over mine and then he shifted his head, speaking directly in my ear. "You doing okay?"

"Yeah." I slid my hand up to his shoulder. "I'm glad we decided to come."

"I'm glad *you* decided to come."

Tilting my head, I smiled a little as I rested my cheek against his chest. Colton was placing a new drink down in front of Abby as he kissed her upturned face before straightening. I found Reece and Roxy next. She was back behind the bar but had her arms across the top, gripping the edge as she stretched toward Reece. He met her halfway, kissing her.

Calla was smiling at something Jax was saying. They too were behind the bar, standing in the center. She started to turn, but Jax caught her around the waist and laid one on her. The guys around the bar hooted, and when he let go of Calla, her face was as red as a cherry.

Nick was back to rubbing Steph's shoulders and she had this dreamy, peaceful look on her face. You almost couldn't believe she was sitting in the middle of the bar. She reached up, placing her hand over one of his and squeezing.

They all had their own struggles and stories to tell and they all made it to this point, happy and in love.

I looked to the right, and found the bright blue eyes of Katie staring back at me. She raised an eyebrow and nodded. She didn't have to speak. I knew what that look and nod meant, and I heard her words from earlier in the night.

*Still going to be rough at times, but he's worth it now.*

I turned into Brock, wrapping an arm around his waist. I felt his chin graze the top of my head, and he held me tighter as Colton shouted over the music.

Sometimes, like now, I really believed Katie just might be psychic.

I let out a happy sigh.

Deciding to come here was a huge decision, but I had no idea until that moment how badly I needed to do this—to retrace my steps in a way, and I had no idea how much it would affect me.

My shoulders were lighter.

My thoughts a little less heavy.

My heart a whole lot fuller.

Two fingers pressed under my chin and tilted my head up. Warm brown eyes stared into mine.

"You here with me?" he asked.

"I'm always with you."

# Chapter 28

I woke in the middle of the night, surprised to find a hard, unmovable body pressed against mine. The cobwebs of sleep lifted as I turned slightly. "What are you doing?"

"I missed you." Brock's arm tightened around my waist. "Plus, I behaved last night and stayed out of this room."

He had . . . much to my disappointment. I'd hoped he'd sneak into my room, but when we came back from Mona's we parted ways with what was a pretty chaste kiss.

Thanksgiving had been a chaotic crazy mess of awesomeness. My family behaved as expected. They were nosy and demanding and all around lovable as they asked one question after another.

Afterwards, Brock and I had talked with my father and my uncles about our proposal to convert the two rooms into a dance studio. My father and uncles didn't immediately scoff at the idea, but Andre looked doubtful. We laid out all the pros and cons for them, comparing cost to potential profit, and by the time the conversation was done and we lost half of them to the football game, I was feeling pretty confident about it. Dad had been eyeing those papers with that gleam in his eye, the same one he got when he saw a new recruit he knew he could shape into a winner.

"If my parents caught you in here . . ." I stopped, rethinking where I was going with that. "Actually, my parents wouldn't care. They'd probably applaud it."

Laughing softly, Brock nuzzled my neck. "You're right."

"Isn't that kind of weird?"

He kissed the space below my pulse. "A little."

Wiggling around so I was facing him, I threw an arm over his waist. "You are not going to be comfortable in this bed. You barely fit."

"I'll be fine." He kissed the tip of my nose. "Besides, we're just going to sleep."

"For real?" I said dryly.

"Yep." His nose brushed over my cheek. "As much as I want to get my mouth between those pretty legs of yours, we're in your parents' house. Not happening."

A surprised laugh left me. "You are being serious."

"Yeah, I am. Not going to disrespect your parents like that."

"Oh my," I whispered, giggling. "Look at you, being all gentleman-like and stuff."

"Shut it." He nipped at my lip.

Another quiet laugh left me. "So, I was thinking."

"Oh no."

I smacked his arm. "I thought the girls would be doing morning breakfast on Sunday, but they all are doing family things."

"The shame," he murmured, nipping at my jaw.

I grinned in the darkness. "I thought maybe we could head home Saturday. A day earlier, so we could—"

"So we could have some one-on-one time?"

"Yeah," I whispered. "What do you think? You could help me pack the books tomorrow and we can spend a little more time with my parents before heading back."

"I . . ." His hand slid down my side and over my hip. " . . . think that is a wonderful idea."

"I thought you might like that idea."

His hand slipped to my rear and he squeezed. "Now what gave you that idea?"

"I have no idea."

The damp musk of the river was the first thing to greet us when I climbed out of Brock's car Saturday evening.

On the way home, Brock had asked if I wanted to see his place and we decided I'd stay there. I had another change of clothing for the morning, and I was more than eager to see his home since I hadn't had the chance yet.

Dusk was settling as Brock grabbed our bags and I picked up Rhage's carrier. The cat hissed, and I rolled my eyes as I followed Brock up the wide set of stairs leading to a sprawling, bare porch.

"Does it go around the house?" I asked. "The porch?"

"Almost." He fished out his keys. "It stops at the French doors in the dining room and empties out onto a patio. There's a second-story deck you can access from the bedrooms upstairs."

"Wow," I murmured. His house was about fifteen minutes outside of Shepherdstown, down a dark and windy road that followed the river. All the houses we passed had been huge, so I wasn't exactly surprised when the massive two-story came into view.

Brock opened the door and somewhere in the house, an alarm beeped. Light turned on, flooding the area. The front door opened into a massive entryway. It was a somewhat open floor plan. I could see all the way back to the kitchen.

He put the bags near the steps that led upstairs and then turned to me. "Remember, the kitchen is a mess."

"It's okay."

"You say that now . . ." Grinning, he walked toward the back of the house, tossing his keys on a foyer table butted up against a wall.

I glanced up, taking in the exposed beams and deciding that the house had a rustic feel to it. Although Brock grew up in the city, the masculine simplicity fit him.

Brock turned the light on in the kitchen, and I got my first look at his remodel project. I was a bit awed. First off, the kitchen was huge. Like, it was the size of my kitchen, living room, and then some in my apartment. The counters were gone, but the positioning of the wide double fridge and unused, still-sealed wall ovens gave me an idea of how it would look once it was put back together.

Half the cabinets were off the wall, stacked side by side where a table probably normally would've sat. There was a large picture window above the sink.

I placed Rhage's carrier down and walked over to the window. "Wow," I said. "The view of the river is amazing."

"It's one of the reasons why I bought the house," he said. "Nearly every room has a view of the river or the woods. Not a lot of land with the property, but it doesn't feel that way."

"No." I moved to the doors leading to the patio. "You can't even see any neighbors. Just the lights from the houses across the river. It's beautiful."

"The kitchen's not much to look at, though," he said.

I faced him. "But it's huge, and once you get it finished, it's going to be amazing."

A slight smile appeared on Brock's face.

"You could have an entire football team in this kitchen and still have room."

The smile spread. "I don't know about that."

Brock set up Rhage's stuff in the kitchen by the door that led out onto the deck, and I let Rhage out. The cat crept forward, ears flat as he took in his new surroundings. He made it about two feet and then plopped his furry butt down, his tail swishing back and forth.

"Got to say. He does not look impressed."

I laughed as I rose. "He's a hard cat to please."

He shook his head as he turned to the fridge and grabbed me a drink. We lingered in the kitchen for a while, watching Rhage investigate every nook and cranny.

Eventually, Brock took me on the tour, through the dining room that was occupied by a dining set that had yet to be used. There were two living rooms. Well, according to Brock one was a living room and one was a media room, whatever that meant. I saw he had a huge-ass TV in one, and the other just had chairs and plants that could've been borrowed from my mom's sunroom.

There was a study he had set up, and in there were more photos from when he was fighting. They hung on the walls, beside another large TV.

"You still haven't unpacked completely, have you?" I gestured at the two large boxes in the corner. There had been a few in the living room as well.

He laughed as he led me out of the office. "I keep meaning to do it, but I've been focused on that kitchen." He slid me a long look. "And you."

A giddy smile tugged at my lips. "I should feel bad for sucking up your time."

"But you don't."

"Nope."

Brock picked up the bags he'd placed down earlier and led me upstairs. "There's four bedrooms up here. I have a guest room set up. Nothing too exciting in there. Eventually I'll do something with the other rooms."

Following him down the wide hall to open double doors, I

had to think this was the kind of house for a large family. And he wanted kids. Not an entire team of them like my uncle had, but he did want babies. I realized that maybe Brock was ready to truly settle down and start a family.

Brock moved ahead, turning on a bedside lamp, and I got my first look at his room. Like the rest of the house, it was a bit bare.

There was a wide dresser with a mirror beside doors that either led into the bathroom or closet. There was another dresser opposite the doors leading out onto the deck, and there were two nightstands. Other than a few wooden boxes on the dresser, the kind that looked like someone would stash fine tobacco in, there weren't many personal items.

Nothing truly looked lived in.

With anyone else, this might've concerned me, but Brock had never been into decorating. His room at my parents' house and his apartment when he was younger had been the same way.

My gaze roamed over the room and then stopped. I stared at the large bed in the center of the room and my stomach dipped. Tonight would be different. This I knew. I didn't know how. Maybe it was instinct. Who knew? But tonight was not going to be like any other time.

Little knots of anxiousness filled me as I crossed the large bedroom, approaching a bay window. Pulling the curtains back, I peeked outside. Beyond the trees, I could see the moon reflecting off the slowly churning waters of the Potomac.

Glancing over my shoulder, I watched Brock pick up a small candle from the dresser and light it. He grinned in my direction as he placed the candle on the nightstand.

After a few seconds, the scent of honeycrisp apples reached me. "Are you sure you're okay with Rhage running around?" Nervous, I fidgeted with the curtains, running my fingers over them. "He will use the litter box, but I can't promise he won't be into everything."

"It's okay."

"He'll destroy something. I'm positive."

"He'll be fine."

Turning to face him, I watched him strip off the loose sweater he wore, tossing it onto a chair in the corner. The plain white shirt came off next, and then there was his beautiful upper body, all on display.

My mouth dried as my gaze dipped, taking in those taut ripples and those amazing indentations on either side of his hips.

Why, with a body like his, was he interested in a body like mine?

That was a question no one would ever be able to answer.

He wore no belt so those pants hung indecently low, so low I realized I could see the band of his tight boxer briefs. My gaze moved over the tattoos. He had a wolf's head over one pec. The other side of his chest was the start of spreading wings that traveled over his shoulder and flowed into numerous designs that traveled down his entire arm. An archangel raising his sword, surrounded by flames. Underneath that, across his forearm, a skull. Red and black bands gave way to an eye above his wrist. He turned slightly, pulling his phone out of his pocket and placing it on the nightstand. I saw the edges of the phoenix rising from ashes and fire. The tattoo was huge, covering his upper and middle back.

I wondered if he'd get more.

"You like what you see?"

Flushing, I dragged my gaze back to his. "Do you really have to ask that question?"

One side of his lips kicked up and my gaze dipped once more, snagging on the silver chain around his neck. I started to look away, back to those amazing lower abs, but I saw what dangled from his neck.

My breath halted in my lungs.

My heart stopped.

My lips parted on a sharp inhale as my hand flew to my mouth, my fingers pressing against my lips.

Concern flitted across Brock's striking features. "Jillian, you okay?"

I couldn't speak as I stared at the tiny medallion hanging from his neck, and I felt dizzy, like I would fall right over. I recognized that necklace even though I hadn't seen it in six years.

"Jillian?" He strode toward me. "What is—?"

"The necklace." I let out a shaky breath. "You have the necklace."

For a moment, he looked confused as he lifted his hand and placed his palm over the medallion. Understanding settled. "You didn't know?"

"No," I whispered, blinking back sudden tears.

"I found it that night," he said after a moment. "After they took you away in the ambulance. Everything was hectic. Colton had you on your side, trying to keep the blood . . . keep you breathing until the EMTs got there, and then they did, and you were gone. I saw your purse on the ground, and I was think-ing . . . I was thinking how you would have hated to know your purse was there, getting dirty and shit."

Oh God.

My fingers curled against my lips as Brock lowered his hand, and I saw the sterling-silver medallion once more.

"I was gathering up your stuff and I found it on the ground," he said. "I knew it was mine. You were always finding these things for me. I meant to tell you I had it, but . . ." He trailed off.

But everything had happened.

Things had blown up and we blew apart.

But he'd found the Saint Sebastian necklace I'd found for him and had planned to give him that night we were going to dinner.

His eyes met mine. "I've worn it ever since."

He'd found it and he'd had it with him.

"For the longest time, it was the only way I could feel close to you."

# Chapter 29

Emotion cut off the strangled sound building in my throat. I dropped my hands and then I was moving without really thinking, crossing the small distance between us. I picked up the necklace, curling my fingers around it. I'd forgotten about the necklace. How, I had no idea, but I had, and he hadn't.

Brock made this sound that came from the back of his throat. "Why are you crying?"

"Am I?" I whispered, clearing my throat.

"Yeah." He cupped my cheeks, swiping away the tears with his thumbs. "How do you not know you're crying?"

"I don't know." I lowered my head, all but face-planting in his warm chest.

Brock let out a soft chuckle as he folded his arms around me. "If I knew the necklace was going to make you cry, I wouldn't have worn it."

"It's not that." I still held the necklace in my palm, probably strangling him with the chain, but I couldn't let go. "I forgot about the necklace and you didn't."

"I didn't." He pulled my head back, tilting it to look up at him. My blurry gaze met his. "I never forgot you. I never forgot anything you used to do."

He was going to make me cry really hard now.

Reaching down, he gently pried my fingers off the medallion. Then he lifted my hand to his mouth. He pressed a kiss to my palm. "I kept all the little charms. There in the box on my dresser. You can check it out—"

I pulled my hand away and stretched up, looping an arm around his neck so I didn't fall over as I kissed him.

I was pretty clumsy at it, the whole initiating a kiss thing, but Brock didn't seem to mind or even notice. The arm at my waist tightened, and the entire length of my body was pressed against his.

The kiss between us had started off gentle, a slow exploration of his lips and mine. We could kiss for a hundred years, but I would never grow tired of it. Never. And when the kiss deepened, my entire body roared awake and tingled. His tongue flicked over mine, and I felt him across my stomach, growing harder and thicker.

Deep in my core, an intense throbbing picked up as I drew back and looked him in the eyes. I could feel my cheeks heating, because I thought about his hand between my thighs and that wonderful, wonderful tongue of his.

The ache intensified.

His eyes darkened as he stared down at me. His throat worked on a swallow. He let go of my waist and slipped a hand down my side to the hem of the shirt I wore. "May I?"

Heart leaping into my throat, I nodded.

That half-grin was back, curling up at the corners of his lips as he gripped the ends of my shirt and tugged it up over my head. I didn't know what he did with the shirt, because I was too conscious of the fact I was standing in front of him in a plain black bra and jeans.

His gaze moved over me, lingering along the swell of my breasts. Heat traveled down my throat and my nipples hardened, straining against the cups of my bra. "I want to see you. All of you."

I let out a shaky breath. "I'm . . . I'm yours."

"Fuck," he growled, and then his mouth swooped down, claiming mine in a head-spinning kiss that left me breathless and wanting. I was barely aware of his quick fingers behind my back, making short work of the tiny clasps. The bra snapped loose, and as he tilted his head, taking the kiss to a whole new level, he slid the straps down my arms and then the bra fell to the floor. He was still kissing me as his fingers moved to the front of my jeans and unhooked the button. He tugged down the zipper and then his hands were on my hips urging down the jeans. They slipped a few inches before getting hung up on my thighs.

Brock lifted his head and stepped back only far enough for him to look down. His gaze roamed over my breasts in such an intense way it was almost like a physical caress. He knelt, dragging my jeans down with him.

My shaking hands landed on his shoulders. I steadied myself as I lifted a leg and then the other so he could remove the jeans. His calloused palms slid back up the outside of my legs. His fingers reached the band of my panties. I didn't even want to look down to see what I was wearing. I was pretty sure they were striped boy shorts. I could've worn something sexier.

He pressed a kiss just below the band of my panties as he slid a hand between my thighs. Then he tipped his head back and those lashes of his lifted. "This," he said, cupping me. I gasped, and I started to flush, because I knew he could feel how turned on I was. I was drenched. "This is also beautiful."

I wanted to laugh, but I couldn't make a sound as he dragged his thumb up the center of my core, circling the center of nerves. A wicked grin appeared on his lips as he leaned in, replacing his thumb with his mouth.

"Brock," I cried out as he sucked—sucked deep and hard, drawing me in through the thin material. "Holy . . ."

He chuckled against me, and the rumble stole my breath. "You liked that, right?" He inched his fingers around the band. "I bet you will love it without these in the way."

Oh God.

I didn't have to respond, because we both knew the answer to that question.

My breath caught as he brought his hands down, taking the flimsy panties along with them, baring every inch of my skin. Brock rocked back on his haunches and looked up at me.

I fought the urge to cover myself.

He'd seen a lot of me, but not all of me, and this was my first with him, with anyone. Ben and I never really got fully naked. A bra stayed on, or a shirt. It was always dark, and he never, never looked at me like Brock was.

Like he wanted to eat me up.

I was soft in all the places he was hard, a lot softer. When I sat, there were most definitely rolls in places you really didn't want to think about, but as he slid his hands down my arms and over my waist to my hips, he didn't seem to notice or care.

"You're beautiful," he said, and he spoke the words like he meant them. "Fuck, I could come just looking at you."

That sounded doubtful, but I liked hearing that. No, I *loved* hearing that.

Brock rose fluidly, dragging his hands up my legs and then over my waist. "Stay here."

I did as he ordered and watched him back up. He never took his gaze from me as he reached into the nightstand and pulled out a small foil package. He tossed it on the bed. Still holding my gaze, he undid his pants and stripped down until he was as naked as me, and . . .

Oh my God.

I felt a little dizzy.

His body was beautiful, an artwork of color and designs, of dips and planes. I'd felt him before, knew that he was very well-endowed, but I still marveled on how he was *that* thick and *that* large. It was rather impressive. His cock twitched as I stared.

"I like that," Brock said in a deep, husky voice. "I like you looking at me."

The breath I took didn't go very far as I forced my gaze to his. "You say I'm beautiful, but you . . ."

"I'm what?"

There were no words.

Walking to where I stood, he placed his hands on my hips. There was a glint to his deep brown eyes and a tilt to his sensual lips. The tips of my breasts grazed his chest. He lowered his mouth to my left ear and said, "I cannot wait to be inside you."

I shivered as my eyes drifted shut. "Don't wait."

His cock jumped against my belly as he drew his thumbs along my jaw, tilting my head back. Fueled by his response, I said, "I don't want to wait another minute."

He made the sexiest sound ever as his hands clenched my hips. "Damn . . ."

Brock kissed me, slow and deep, drawing out a pulsing ache between my thighs as he turned me. He walked me backward until my legs touched the bed. With controlled pressure, he guided me down so I was sitting. I opened my eyes as his mouth left mine.

I stared up at him, breathless.

Smiling, he cupped one breast and smoothed his thumb over the rosy nipple. My heart was racing as he placed one knee on the bed. I reached out, wrapping my hand around the base of his cock. He was like hot steel covered in silk. I explored him from base to tip, marveling at the feel of him.

Brock groaned as he picked up the condom. I stroked him until he caught my wrist, pulling my hand away so he could slide the condom on. I scooted away from the edge, leaning back on my elbows in the bed.

His gaze flicked up, meeting mine as he rose over me. He stopped at my thighs, kissing me as he nudged my legs further apart with his shoulders. His mouth crept and I felt his tongue along the seam of my thigh.

Pulse pounding, my head fell back as my hand floated toward him. I sank my fingers into his hair as his breath moved closer and closer. I tensed, letting out a low moan as his tongue dragged up the very center of me.

"I can never get enough of your taste," he said, moving upward, nipping at the skin below my navel. "I could eat you for lunch and dinner."

"I don't think I . . . I would complain about that."

"No." His breath danced over the sensitized skin of my breast. "No, you would not."

The head of his cock prodded at my entrance as his mouth closed over one breast and he palmed the other. I lost all ability to breathe as my body arched and I pressed against him. His tongue, his teeth, and those fingers sent stinging jolts of pure pleasure through me.

My grip on his hair increased as I curled one leg over his. "Brock," I panted, impatient.

He lifted his head, bringing his mouth to mine. He kissed me, and when he drew back, he caught my bottom lip between his teeth. The edge of the medallion he wore slipped between my breasts.

I lifted my hips. "Please, Brock."

"I love hearing you beg." His hand slipped between us. "But you don't need to beg me for this."

I jerked as he finally, *finally* pushed in, and I couldn't let myself think about how long I had wanted this from him, how long I had waited. There was such little room for thought as I had to see this, experience only this. I opened my eyes and watched as he entered me. There was something wholly sensual about doing so.

His lashes lifted and his gaze pierced mine. I was unprepared for the feral, possessive stare. "Keep watching," he rasped out. "Fuck. You're tight."

"I told you," I gasped. "It's been a really, really long time."

His body shook as he held still, and then he thrust in until his hips were flush with mine, and I cried out, nearly overwhelmed by the burning feel of him. It was almost too much—the stretching and the fullness. I lingered somewhere between intense pleasure and pain, and it spun me around.

"I love that sound." His lips moved over mine. "I'm going to make sure you're hoarse and can barely talk by the time I'm done."

And he did.

Brock started to move, and although it had been forever and it took a few moments to catch a rhythm, I pushed up with my hips as he pushed down. Our bodies moved in perfect sync. He caught my mouth as he planted one elbow beside my head. His hips swung and plunged, delving deeper and deeper, and the thrusts of his tongue matched his cock.

*It* started.

This deep tightening, a clenching of all the muscles in my body, and I was like a coil wound too tight. I whimpered as I lost the rhythm, my hips writhing against his and my nails digging into the taut skin of his back. I was close, so close I thought I'd die.

"Jillian," he growled, his large and powerful body trembling.

I knew in that moment he was holding back and I said words I never thought I'd ever utter, and later, when everything was done, I would probably be mortified, but in that moment, I didn't care.

"Fuck me," I whispered against his lips.

It was like a cage was unlocked. Brock got an arm under my waist as he rose up, planting one hand on my belly, holding me in place as his hips slammed into me, lifting me up with each plunge. He went deeper and deeper, and I couldn't move. He held me, and he . . . he *fucked*.

And I *loved* it.

My whole body shuddered as I wrapped an arm around his and grasped the blanket with the other. "Yes. Oh, my God . . ." I couldn't breathe. The tension spun and spun, and I became someone else. I tossed my head back, eyes wide and unseeing as words tumbled out of my mouth. "Faster. Please. Brock, please—"

Brock cursed as he thrust hard and deep, and I shattered, coming so hard I *screamed* his name. Red-hot pleasure swept over me like a fire burning out of control. My back arched as he came down on me, pushing me into the bed. His hips ground into mine as he said my name over and over like a prayer and a curse. I felt him tremble as he stilled deep inside me, his body finally spasming and mingling with the aftershocks still rocking my body.

Neither of us moved for several long minutes.

I couldn't.

My legs were jelly and my arms boneless.

Brock pressed a kiss to my shoulder and then my neck. I turned my head toward his and our lips met. The kiss was slow and heartbreakingly sweet.

"You okay?" he asked.

"I think I'm dead," I told him, sliding my hand along his back. "Dead in a good way."

Brock chuckled, but the laugh sounded shaky. He kissed my forehead and then eased out of me. There was a slight burn. "Be right back."

I rolled onto my side as he walked away from the bed, toward the bathroom, and I had a very nice view. Once he disposed of the condom, he came back to the bed.

"Do you need anything?" he asked. "Water?"

I shook my head. "I'm fine."

He stood there for a moment, simply staring at me, and then he got to tugging the blankets down, which was a feat since I was practically dead weight on them and not very helpful, but he managed. He climbed in, pulled them over us as he slipped one arm under me. He hugged me closer so I was resting against his side.

Several moments passed in silence and then he said, "This is going to sound corny as hell, but I have to say it." He paused. "It's never been like that for me. Usually it's just about coming, you know? Getting off. I didn't want to let go. Wanted it to last. Never wanted that before."

Pleased and feeling so warm, I bit my lip and then admitted, "I never asked someone to fuck me before, so it's a first for both of us."

Brock's entire body shook as he laughed. "Got to tell you, when you said that, I almost lost it right there. Fun would've been over before we got to the good part."

"The whole thing was a good part."

"Yeah," he murmured. "Yeah, it was."

We fell into silence again, and my eyelids drooped. Just as I was dozing off, Brock said to me, "I lied."

"Lied about what?" I whispered, sliding my hand over the tight dips and planes of his stomach.

There was a pause and then he said, "The night I ruined your date with that guy wasn't a coincidence."

A small grin tugged at my lips and I turned my face into the side of his chest. "I figured that."

"The first night—the first time I saw you at the restaurant wasn't a coincidence either." His fingers stilled along my upper arm. "Your mom had mentioned where you'd be. It was in passing. She probably doesn't even remember. I went there knowing you would be there. I hadn't planned on saying anything to you. I just wanted . . . I just wanted to see you, and I didn't want to wait until Monday."

I opened my eyes.

His chest rose with a deep breath. "And when I saw you, I had to talk to you. I was there because you were there."

I should've probably been irritated at Mom and him for that, but I decided I didn't care. "Creeper," I murmured.

Brock's arm tightened around me. "No regrets."

In the flickering light of the candle, I smiled and closed my eyes.

# Chapter 30

Everything and nothing changed between Brock and me in the days and weeks following Thanksgiving and the night at his place.

As corny as it sounded, it was like a fairytale come true, but my girlish fantasies of Brock and me being together was nothing like the real thing. Back then I had no experience in, well, anything, and what limited knowledge I'd gained from Ben had been repeatedly and amazingly blown out of the water each time Brock touched me—kissed me and took me to bed . . . or on the couch, the kitchen counter—against the wall. Brock was never sated, and neither was I. I'd never been like that before, where I spent a good portion of the day lost in thoughts about our time spent alone. My heart was in the clouds and my head was quickly following.

He spent many nights at my apartment, because I had a functioning kitchen, and I think he was growing attached to Rhage, even if he didn't necessarily admit it. Over the weekends, I'd gather up Rhage and we'd end up at Brock's, eating carryout and helping him the best I could with stripping the cabinets, which involved a whole lot of elbow grease and sanding off the old finish.

We exchanged keys and he knew I was on the pill even, but we still used condoms. At work he made it pretty obvious we were involved. He made no move to hide it whenever he kissed me before leaving for out of office meetings or whenever he would give me that smug, secretive smile during a conference if a quickie was stolen during our lunch break. The staff seemed to have no problem with it. Well, all except Paul. Unsurprisingly, his smirky face got even more smirky once he realized Brock and I were seeing each other. During one of the meetings when we announced that my father was considering converting the two rooms on the second floor into dance studios, his eyes rolled so far back I feared they'd roll out of his head. Whatever.

Things went beyond the physical with Brock—how everything changed.

I relaxed around him. When I smiled, I didn't think about how it looked and I worried less about what people thought. Instead of hoping people ended up on my left side during important meetings, I made sure that they were.

I added to the books I'd brought back with me, and it wouldn't be too long before I needed a new bookcase. I hoped Brock would offer to put that one together and I hoped it ended the way it had last time.

Everything had changed, but still, things remained the same in little ways. We didn't dwell on the night our lives changed. It wasn't exactly laid to rest. I think both of us acknowledged it was there, that it would always be there. It was a part of us, but it would no longer be between us, and Brock still didn't talk about his relationship with Kristen, not even when I poked around the subject. I couldn't help it. I was curious about why they stayed together. Why they really broke up.

Brock was skilled at evading all conversations that started to veer into territory about her, and I wasn't sure exactly why. Obviously, I had a feeling there was something there he wasn't fond of discussing. I didn't like it, but I did like the way he *veered* those conversations. It usually involved those talented hands and mouth.

With each passing day, the wiggle of doubt that this wasn't going to last, that what we had wasn't real, faded. It didn't haunt the time I spent with him or keep me awake like the nightmares used to. It *was* fading, but it lingered like the acidic scent of scorched wood.

The doubt remained the same, lessened and almost gone, but it was still there.

One Monday night, Brock helped me set up and decorate my artificial Christmas tree. We set it up in front of the window that overlooked the parking lot below.

It wasn't a huge tree, only about six feet tall and not very full, but it had the frosted tips that reminded me of snow and came with twigs and berries already attached.

"How do you keep Rhage from destroying this?" he asked, untangling the string of golden lights.

"He kind of does his own thing with the tree." I glanced over at where the cat sat. He was already within a few feet of the tree, his eyes wide and, I imagined, full of anticipation. "That's why I don't use bulbs. Even the kind that don't shatter would be pointless. He'd knock them off in seconds."

"He'll leave the tinsel and lights alone?"

"Yeah, he kind of only climbs about halfway up the tree and just sits in it, staring at you like some kind of wannabe jungle cat."

Brock chuckled as he plugged the strand in. I handed him the one I'd been working on.

Watching him wrap the tree with the lights, I couldn't stop the smile from forming on my lips. We did this a lot growing up, but this was our tree, and there was something incredibly magical about that.

"I'm surprised you didn't have this up before Thanksgiving," he commented, readjusting the lights on one of the lower branches.

I laughed. "I've calmed down a bit in the decorating department."

"Still kind of early."

"It is not early," I argued, digging out the silver tinsel from the bin. "It's December."

"It's December twelfth," he replied dryly.

"Whatever." I looked down as Rhage eyed the dangling tinsel. I grabbed the end so I didn't tempt him to prove me a liar. "Are you getting a tree?"

One shoulder rose as he picked up the star. "You know, we never did the Christmas tree thing."

"You . . . you and Kristen?"

He nodded. "We spent the holidays at her family since . . ."

"Since the last time you came to my parents?" It had been the night I'd lost my shit with him.

"Yeah." He glanced over at me. "Figured it was better that way. Didn't want to ruin your holidays."

Half of me felt bad, because Brock was a part of our family, and I felt like I might've robbed him of that. The other half didn't feel bad at all. I wasn't sure what that said about me.

"Anyway, we never really did a lot of the Christmas stuff at our place or even when we lived separately." He easily secured the star to the top while it would've taken me well over an hour and would've involved a lot of F-bombs. "We never did this. Not once."

"Really?" Surprise flickered through me. "That sounds . . . I don't even know how that sounds."

A wry grin appeared on his lips. "Doesn't matter how it sounds."

I stood there for a moment and realized he was right. Hanging the tinsel, I was careful not to step on Rhage's tail.

"You going to miss me when I leave on Wednesday?" he asked, stepping back to allow me to get the tinsel wrapped around the tree.

"Maybe," I said, tucking the edge of the tinsel back into the branch. Brock was going to be at the Philly branch with some new recruits my father wanted him to look at. He was supposed to come back Saturday afternoon. Straightening, I took a step back and admired the tree—*our* tree. "It's so pretty."

"I think I've found something prettier." He wrapped his arm around my waist, drawing me back against his chest. "And I'm also kind of offended that you said maybe."

Resting my hands on his forearms, I laughed. "Didn't realize you were so sensitive."

"I am." He shifted his head, causing me to gasp as his rough jaw dragged along my neck. He nuzzled the skin there. "I need my ego stroked."

Emboldened by his touch, I lowered a hand and reached behind me. My fingers roamed over the line of his zipper. My cheeks heated as I said, "Something else need to be stroked too?"

Brock's deep, husky chuckle sent shivers down my spine. "That always needs stroking."

"Is that so?" I bit down on my lip as I felt him harden against my hand.

He pushed his hips against me. "Mmm."

Hiding a grin, I slipped free and turned around, facing him. The way he stared at me, his jaw clenched and his eyes so dark they were nearly black, made me weak in the knees. My heart started pounding in my chest. I took another step back.

"Now where do you think you're going?" he asked.

I raised a shoulder. "I think I might get a piece of that pumpkin pie in the fridge."

Brock held my gaze as he slowly shook his head. "I'm thinking I want to have dessert now."

"You want a slice, too?"

"Yeah. I want a slice."

He moved so incredibly fast and was standing in front of me within a heartbeat. Before I could even process what he was doing, he dipped and had an arm under my legs. In a blink of an eye, I was up in the air and my stomach was coming down on his shoulder.

A wild-sounding laugh escaped me as he turned and started walking back toward the bedroom, leaving the softness of the twinkling Christmas lights. "This was not the kind of slice I was talking about."

"You sure about that?" His hand came down on my behind, causing me to shriek. "You liked that."

I did.

I really did.

Hair swinging in my face, I barely caught my breath by the time he placed me on my feet. Then his hands were all over me, stripping my sweater and leggings off at record-breaking speeds. Then the bra was gone, along with the undies, and I was completely nude, standing in front of him. Desire swirled inside me as I stared at him, leaving me feeling out of control and dazed. Thick tendrils of lust mingled with the raw heat as he reached behind him and curled his fingers along the collar of his thermal, tugging it over his head and off.

His body . . .

I could seriously drool over it.

Brock stepped into me, thrusting his muscled thigh between mine, and I lifted my hands, placing them on his chest. I marveled at the hard planes, over the abs that dipped and rippled.

He didn't kiss me.

His mouth went much lower, closing around the tip of my breast. His tongue rasped over my nipple. All thought fled as he tugged on my breast. My head fell back as raw, exquisite sensations zipped through my veins.

"This is the kind of dessert I want every night," he said in a smoky, thick voice as he lowered his hand to my hip, urging me to move.

My lips parted on a sharp inhale and then I cried out as his teeth caught my nipple in a delicious little bite. He didn't need to guide me. My hips rolled and rocked against his thigh. Tension quickly built, and I wondered if I'd come this way. It was quite possible.

But then we were moving. One arm circled my waist and he lifted me up, placing me down on the bed. His lips were hot against my neck and I wanted those lips on mine. My fingers sank deep into his hair and I tugged his head up to mine. The kiss was deep and consuming. I curled a leg around his and lifted my hips, grinding against him. The friction of his jeans did crazy things to my senses, but it wasn't enough.

"I want you in me," I whispered in the darkness of my bedroom, surprised by my own aggressiveness. "Now."

Brock made this deeply masculine sound against my lips. "You're going to have to be patient."

"No," I whimpered.

I felt his lips curve. "Do I need to teach you to be patient?"

My lips curled at the sensual warning in his voice. "Maybe?"

Suddenly, without any warning, he gripped my wrists, capturing them in one hand. He held my wrists pinned to my stomach as he moved down and down, kissing and licking his way from my mouth to my breast and lower, over my navel.

"Open up for me," he ordered, and I did, spreading my legs as my fingers curled helplessly around air.

I held my breath, drowning in pure sensation as I waited for him, for his mouth and for his tongue. I waited until I was straining against his grip, and then his mouth was on me, sucking deep as he slipped one long finger inside. I cried out as he worked my body until I was stretched to the breaking point, teetering on the edge, and then he stopped.

"Brock," I gasped, eyes flying open.

He said nothing as he rose, and with one hand, he undid his pants, shoving them down his thighs and freeing himself. Even in the darkness, I could feel his stare piercing me. My hands itched to touch him, but he still held them together as he came over me. A heartbeat passed, and I realized I wanted him like this, bare and raw. We'd talked about birth control and using condoms. He knew I was on the pill, but we still used one every time.

Except now.

I felt his tip against my heat, the hard and hot length of him pressing into me as he lifted my hands, pressing them down into the bed behind my head. The position arched my back, thrusting my breast into his waiting mouth. I felt the cool metal of the medallion hit my skin.

"Oh God," I whispered.

He lifted his head and his free hand traced over my jaw and then down the center of my chest. I could barely catch my breath as his hand coasted over my belly and then my hip. "I think I would love to tie you up. What do you think?"

I squirmed, breathless. "I think . . . I think I'd like that."

"Oh, babe, you would definitely love it." His hand curled around the base of his cock, and I moaned as he started to enter me.

"But I want to touch you," I said.

"I know." He pushed in slowly, tortuously. The stretch was there, so was the burn, and I reveled in it, wanting more and more. "Damn," Brock groaned, his body shaking as he controlled every inch he gained. "This is perfection."

Brock punched his hips forward, and my gasp of pleasure was lost in his heated groan. His presence, like before, was tremendous, almost too much, and when he started moving, I thought I would die.

I yearned to touch him, but I couldn't break his hold, so I gave in to him, to the almost painful pressure around my wrists, to this sublime torture. Fully seated in me, Brock held still for several moments and then he began to move, pulling back until just the tip of him remained, and then thrusting forward until there wasn't even a breath between us. The tug and pull of each thrust was building a cyclone deep inside me.

A fine sheen of sweat broke out all over my body as his rhythm increased. His hand went to my hip. "Wrap your legs around me."

Not needing to be told twice, I did just that, and it seemed impossible, but he went deeper. "You're killing me."

"Not yet."

And then he did.

Brock drove into me over and over, stopping to grind against me, and each time he did, he hit that spot. My head rolled from side to side as the knot of tension tightened and tightened, and then I broke. Release whipped through me, stealing my breath and my voice. I couldn't even say his name. I was thrown up to the heavens and he followed, his head burying into my neck as his body shuddered in a powerful rush.

It took a while before the storm passed, before he lifted his head and kissed the side of my neck, before he peeled his fingers from my wrists, and before he said, "Now I could really go for a slice of that pumpkin pie."

Laughing, I turned my head to his and kissed him. "With whipped cream?"

He stilled and then pushed up on his elbow. "You have whipped cream?"

"Of course," I murmured.

"Do not move. Not even an inch." He eased out of me and then rolled off the bed, popping to his feet. He was gone only a few minutes and when he returned, he had the pie and the Cool Whip.

The Cool Whip didn't go on the pie, though.

Brock spent the night proving there were much, much better uses for it.

# Chapter 31

My office phone rang early Thursday morning.

I'd just finished scanning the news headlines, not prepared for anything that required critical thinking skills until I finished my first work cup of coffee.

Seeing that it was an outside call from the Academy in Philly, I figured it was either my dad or Brock.

"Hello?"

"Hey, hon." It was Dad. "I got you on speaker. Brock's here."

"Miss me?" That was Brock.

I rolled my eyes as my cheeks turned pink. This whole relationship thing all open in front of my parents made me want to giggle like I was thirteen. "Not particularly," I responded, grinning.

"Ouch," he replied, laughing. "We're going to have to see about that when I get home."

My eyes widened. Did he just suggest what I think he suggested in front of my dad? I wanted to crawl under the desk, but I was also locked in place, because I could almost feel his hands around my wrists, pinning me in place as he . . .

Goodness.

I placed my forehead in my hand and cleared my throat, deciding to ignore him. "So, what's going on?"

"We thought we'd call you with some news," my father said.

I immediately straightened, my gaze swinging around my empty office and settling on the tiny three-foot Christmas tree I'd brought in that morning. I'd picked it up last night at Target. It was pre-lit and I'd splurged on another timer, hooking it up so it stayed on while I was in the office.

The only news I was waiting on was about converting space into a dance studio.

"Good news?" I asked, hopeful.

Brock chuckled. "If it were bad news, do you think I'd be in the office?"

Hope gave way to excitement. "You're going to approve the plan?"

"I'm going to approve the plan," Dad replied.

I jumped from my chair and danced in a small circle as I silently screamed into the handset. "Thank you," I managed to say calmly. "You will not regret this choice."

"You're dancing, aren't you?" Brock asked wryly.

Continuing to hobble around my chair, I said, "No. I am not."

"On one condition," Dad spoke up again. "Your friends need to sign a contract where they agree to not move their dance company for at least eight years. It's a lot of money we'll be investing in this. We don't want to spend it and then have them bail on us."

"Completely understandable." I sat down, brimming full of excitement. "I'm sure they will be agreeable to this."

"Get in touch with them today," Dad said. "If they agree, I'll get the contract written up next week and we'll get this squared away before Christmas."

"Will do." I squeezed the phone until I was sure it creaked. "Seriously, Dad. Thank you for believing in this."

"It's not this road I believe in. It's you," he said. "And it's Brock. I believe in both of you."

A knot sealed off my throat as unexpected raw emotion swamped me. My office blurred. Hearing him say that? God, I'd been waiting . . . waited for so long. I managed to say something that sounded kind of professional, and then it was Brock talking into my ear.

"You're off speaker," he said, and a moment passed. "You feeling good right now? Doing okay?"

"I'm feeling great," I admitted in a hushed, raspy voice, and then, because of everything we'd shared in the last couple of weeks and how wonderful I was feeling, I said, "I'd be feeling perfect if you were here."

There was a stretch of silence. "I'll be back as soon as I can."

"I know."

"Call your girls. Let them know."

I did just that.

I was able to get a hold of Teresa, who patched in Avery, and there were many, many shrieks to be heard. I was actually afraid Teresa would end up going into labor.

"Thank you," Avery said hoarsely, and I thought she might be crying. "You have no idea how much this means to us— means to me. You seriously don't."

My eyes were burning and blurry again. "I think I do. I'm just happy to help you guys do this." I took a deep breath and tried to chill myself out. "Okay. So are you guys okay with the contract of eight years?"

"Of course," she said in a rush.

"Yes," Avery agreed.

"That's what I thought. So, I'll let them know and we'll get the contract in hopefully next week," I explained. "Then we'll move on to getting some contractors out here to look at the space."

Getting off the phone after that proved a little difficult, because if they thanked me one more time, I would be a blubbering mess. We made plans to get breakfast on Sunday—if Teresa didn't have the baby by then—and they promised they'd be out of hugging.

There was no erasing my smile that day. No way. Not when I knew I was helping two special people make their dreams come true. Not when I knew my father believed in me.

Friday, just after lunch, I looked up to find Paul coming into my office, carrying several pieces of paper.

He didn't knock.

He didn't announce himself.

Just walked right in and said, "Can you get these to Brock ASAP?" And then dumped the papers on my desk.

My brows flew up as I glanced down to what he had so disrespectfully placed on my desk; I was about to point out that, even though I would see Brock before Monday, he wouldn't be seeing these papers before then, when something on them snagged my attention.

I snatched them up, quickly scanning them. "What is this?" I asked. Paul was almost out the door. I had to call him back, and when he came in, he stared at me pointedly. "What are these sales plans and estimates for?"

The look on his face shifted. "What does it look like?"

Oh man, the not often used bitch switch that existed at the nape of my neck was so, so close to being flipped. "It looks like a proposal for the space on the second floor—for rooms C and D."

"That's what it is," he replied lazily, crossing his arms.

I tilted my head to the side. "You do realize that I already had a proposal in place for those rooms."

"For that dance thing? Yeah, but come on, that's not going to happen."

Then he laughed.

He *laughed*.

I counted to ten and made it to two. "It hasn't been announced yet, but that dance thing was already approved for rooms C and D. So this?" I picked up the stapled papers. "You're going to have to propose your smoothie idea for one of the other rooms."

He blinked and stared at me like I had two heads. "What?"

"I have the approval. The contract is coming in on Monday."

"I need those rooms."

"I'm sorry," I said, placing the papers on the edge of my desk. "Those rooms have been contracted. You can see about—"

"I need at least room D. It's the only one that can be converted to include a kitchen based on the wiring and floor plan," he shot back, cheeks flushing.

I shook my head, having no idea what to say to him at this point.

"This is bullshit!" Paul exploded, and I jumped in my seat, unintentionally flinching. He then barked out a harsh laugh. "Why am I even surprised? Seriously. Of course you got that stupid dance shit approved."

Paul started to turn away, and I don't know what exactly triggered in me, but my back stiffened as if a steel rod had been dropped down my spine.

*This isn't right.*

The way he talked to me. The way he looked at me. This man didn't have to like me, but he needed to respect me—respect my position and my authority. What had I told myself before? That I would not tolerate this. I was not the same nineteen-year-old Jillian who let people walk over her—who had been cornered by a guy before and had to be saved by Steph.

That was not me.

Oh hell no, I did not survive a gunshot wound to the mother-fucking face for this dickless prick to speak to me like this.

"Paul?" I called out.

He stopped and turned, impatience written clearly on his face. "What?"

The hair along the nape of my neck bristled. There it was. *That* tone. It made my skin feel like it was stretched too tight. "Close the door and please take a seat."

His eyes flashed. "I have a session about to start."

"Please close the door and have a seat," I repeated, refusing to allow him to excuse his way out of this. "Your session will have to wait."

Paul hesitated for a moment and then he turned. I saw his lips moving, and I knew he was muttering something under his breath as he closed the door. He took his sweet-ass time making his way to the chair and sitting. He met my stare a bit belligerently.

I drew in a deep breath. "As you may have realized, I'm partially deaf. I can't hear out of my right ear, but the interesting thing about losing a part of your hearing is that it forces you to pay attention to people when they're talking. You have to follow conversations closely, watch their lips, and read their body language."

Paul looked back at me like he was already bored with the conversation.

Clasping my hands together, I placed them on the table. "I don't need to hear the words you mutter or purposely speak too low to know that you have little to no respect for me."

A flicker of surprise widened his eyes. "Excuse me?"

"You speak to me as if you don't understand that I'm your boss."

His lips thinned as he shifted in the seat. "Brock is my boss."

"Yes and no. He's your boss and I'm also your boss," I said, keeping my voice steady. "Especially when he is not here. You don't have to like me. Not at all, but you need to respect me."

A faint shade of pink colored his cheekbones. "I don't know where you're getting that I don't respect you. I think you're being a little dramatic."

He was about to see "dramatic," because my head was seconds from spinning full circle. "Do not gaslight me, Paul."

Part of me wondered if he even knew what that meant. He inhaled roughly, flaring his nostrils, and a tense moment passed. "Respect is earned. It's not given."

I forced my expression to remain blank. "And how have I not earned your respect?"

"Your father owns this Academy," he shot back. "And you're sleeping with the boss. Exactly how have you earned this job?"

Whoa.

He did not just say *that* to me.

Anger whipped through me. My first response was to fire him on the spot, right then and there, because even though I did need to talk to Brock before I decided to end someone's employment, I was one hundred percent sure that he would back me on this.

But firing him was too easy.

"Let me explain something to you, Paul. I was born and raised in the Lima Academy. There is not one thing you know about this place that I do not. This is not just a job to me, but it is a part of my legacy. The blood that runs through my veins built this facility. If you had no problem with my uncle running this Academy, then you should have no problem with me," I said as my skin prickled. "I don't need to address your second comment, but I'm going to. Yes, I am going out with Brock. So maybe you should take that into consideration the next time you open your month and speak to me."

The pink faded from his cheeks, and Paul paled.

"While Brock doesn't make any concessions toward me because of our relationship, I'm pretty sure he and my father would not appreciate such insinuations, but most importantly, I don't. This is the one and only time I'm going to have this conversation with you," I warned, lifting my chin. "We can work together. We can continue to make Lima Academy a state-of-the-art training facility that includes an *amazing* opportunity that could expand my father's dream. Or you can find another job. That's your choice. Don't make me make it for you."

Paul was silent.

"That's all for now," I finished.

He sat there for a few moments and then he nodded curtly. I watch him rise from the chair and stiffly walk out of my office, leaving the door halfway open.

Once he was gone from my sight, I exhaled at the same point I laughed. It was shaky and strained, because a tiny part of me couldn't believe I'd actually done that.

I didn't just stand up for myself and my decisions, I delivered an epic verbal bitch slap. I sort of wanted to pat myself on the back.

Screw patting myself on the back.

I was going to eat a plate of cheese fries tonight.

Smiling, I turned to my computer and got back to work, feeling ... I don't know. Strong? Confident. Badass. I felt like I imagined how Steph felt, and that was *amazing*.

The grin stayed on my face for several hours as I got caught up on email. It was getting close to four in the afternoon and the little Christmas tree I'd brought into the office twinkled and shimmered in the fading afternoon light. I was about to go raid the vending machine when there was a soft knock on my door.

I looked up and my breath stalled.

Kristen Morgan stood in the doorway of my office. I blinked, thinking I was hallucinating, but it was her. Dressed in dark denim jeans and a white turtleneck that hugged her upper body, she looked like she just walked off a Macy's catalog.

Did she have the wrong office?

If she did, why in the hell was she here to see Brock?

"I know this is very unexpected, but I was hoping you had a moment," she said, curling one manicured hand over the door knob. "Because I really need to talk to you."

"About what?" I was absolutely dumbfounded.

She stepped inside, closing the door behind her. "I need to talk to you about Brock. You deserve to know the truth."

# Chapter 32

"Deserve to know what truth?" I asked, having no idea what the hell she was talking about.

Kristen gestured at the chair. "May I?"

So polite.

I nodded and then, as she sat and placed her purse on the floor, I snapped out of the shock of seeing her here. "Wait a second." I placed my hands on my desk, extremely wary of this. "What are you really doing here? We've maybe exchanged a handful of words our entire lives and you're suddenly here because you need to tell me the truth about something?"

"You have every right to be suspicious of my visit." She crossed one impossibly long leg over the other. "If it was you coming to me, I'd feel the same way." She smiled weakly, but it didn't reach her eyes. "I know Brock isn't here. That's why I came down today."

A chill settled over my skin. "How do you know that?"

"I was with him for *years*. We were engaged and we shared several mutual friends who work for your father," she explained. "It came up in casual conversation that he was there."

Casual conversation my ass. I did not like the idea that someone working there was keeping tabs on Brock and reporting back to Kristen. Instinct warned me that I needed this conversation to stop right now, before she could spew any "truths" at me.

328

I didn't know Kristen well. Brock never said anything bad about her, but I couldn't fathom that there was some altruistic reasoning behind this visit.

"I'm actually really busy today," I started. "So I'm not—"

"Did Brock tell you that I was pregnant?" she cut in.

I stopped—stopped talking and maybe stopped breathing. It took several moments for me to force out one word. "What?"

"I guess he didn't. I'm not entirely surprised." She tilted her head to the side. Icy blonde hair slipped over her shoulder. "You probably aren't even that surprised. You've known him since you both were kids, so you know he's not much of a talker."

Brock *was* a talker—with me, at least. The room felt like it was spinning. "You were pregnant?"

Thick lashes lowered as she slowly nodded. "It was not too long after we got together. Maybe a little over two years into the relationship. I was on the pill, but I wasn't exactly taking them regularly." She laughed softly. "I wasn't very responsible back then and . . ." She took a deep breath. "Since you're with Brock now, you know how he is. He likes to . . . *fuck*."

My stomach turned sour and a dozen mental roadblocks flew up.

"The pregnancy didn't . . . it didn't *stick*," she went on before I could respond. "It really tore me up. I didn't want to get pregnant back then, but once I found out that I was, I was happy, and he was happy. I wanted that baby, and I wanted Brock. I loved him, and when I lost the baby, I was a mess."

I didn't know what to say. Brock had never mentioned that Kristen had been pregnant and that seemed like something one would share. Then again. Brock rarely talked about Kristen.

"After I lost the baby, he proposed to me about three months later," she said. "As you know, I said yes."

I jerked in my seat. "I'm . . . I'm sorry to hear that you lost a baby. I didn't know, but I'm not sure why you're telling me this." And why Brock had never mentioned it to me.

"I'm telling you because when Brock proposed to me, I knew why he had. I managed to convince myself that it wasn't what I feared, but I was wrong." Her gaze met mine, and there was a fine sheen to it, as if she was holding back tears. "I wanted to believe he wanted to marry me because he loved me, but that wasn't the case. Brock asked me to marry him because he felt *guilty*. He felt responsible for me losing the baby."

"How . . . how did he feel responsible?"

"It was during a rough part of the relationship. He was traveling a lot, leaving me behind. I was stressed out. We were arguing a lot. It wasn't his fault, but he blamed himself," she said so sincerely that I wasn't sure how to process it. "And that's why he asked me to marry him. He wanted to make me happy again and he succeeded for a while, but I soon realized he was with me because he felt guilty. Not because he truly loved me. But that's his MO."

The chill returned, encasing my insides in ice.

"Brock felt guilty when it came to me, but it never touched on the guilt he carried because of you." Her gaze lowered and her shoulders tightened. "I was there that night. I knew who you were when you were talking to Brock. I could see how much you cared about him, and I could see that Brock barely even noticed that you were there." She shook her head, exhaling softly. "Anybody could've seen it. You left, and he stayed with me. I felt sorry for you."

Well, that was just lovely. My fingers curled inward. The nails dug into my palms.

"I was there with him when someone came running into Mona's screaming about someone being shot. We didn't go outside immediately. His friends did—Colton and Reece. They ran out. I don't remember how we heard it was you, but we did. He saw you on the ground. It was brief, because one of the brothers pushed him back, but I'll never forget the look on his face," she said, a distant look settling into her expression. "Like he blamed himself for me losing the baby, he blamed himself for you getting shot."

"It wasn't his fault," I was quick to tell her.

"I know that. You know that. But no one, not me and not even you, could change the way he felt, especially after that Christmas when he brought me to your house. I just want to let you know, I didn't want to go," she said. "I didn't want him to be there, because I knew what it would do to you and him."

My heart turned over heavily. "Kristen, I—"

"The entire time we were together that guilt festered. It was an open wound spreading into every aspect of our life," she interrupted as tiny darts of pain shot across my palms. "For six years, you were all that he would really talk about."

I sucked in a sharp breath.

Her cheekbones turned pink. "He was already around your family, but I know he talked to your mom about you. I overheard them on multiple occasions, and I never said a word to him about it. I thought that if he knew that you were okay, that you were doing fine, he'd eventually let it go and fully be a part of us—of our future. He never did. And he never stopped talking about you." She let out a bitter-sounding laugh. "How do you think that made me feel? It was worse than being with someone who was in love with someone else."

Unable to say a word, I pressed the tips of my fingers to my lips.

"Actually, I would've preferred that he had loved you. At least I would have lost him to someone he loved. Not to someone he felt this twisted sense of responsibility for." Her red lips thinned. "I even asked him, right before he ended the engagement, if he was in love with you—if he had spent six years with me loving someone else."

The room was still whirling, and I didn't want to hear what she was about to say, but I didn't stop her. The woman who delivered the epic verbal bitch slap was gone. I was frozen in my chair, unable to stop this train wreck.

"He said he didn't. Not in the way I was afraid of," she said.

My gaze flew to hers, and I got what she was saying. I didn't need to read between the lines. She just told me that Brock didn't love me. Truth was, she might be right. We hadn't exchanged those words, and finding out if he loved me or could love me the way I loved him, had always loved him, was mine to discover from him. Not from Kristen.

But it was too late.

"When he decided to retire and began talking to your father about coming down here to work, I knew he would find his way back to you—find some kind of way to make amends, assuage his guilt, and I'd had it." Anger colored her tone for the first time. "I told him I did not want him coming down here, because not for one second did I believe that he wanted to be the GM. He was trying to find a way to get close to you. I made him choose, and he chose you and he chose his guilt. That is why we broke up."

"Okay," I blurted out. "This sounds crazy, and I don't know what to say to you. I'm sorry things didn't work out—"

"You really think I'm making this up? You're telling me not once has he mentioned his guilt?"

Brock had.

Her chin lifted. "Has he even told you that I've contacted him many, many times since he moved here?"

"What?" I stiffened.

Kristen leaned forward. "I wanted to get back with him. I'm woman enough to admit that. We've talked it out. The weekend he came back to—"

"To finalize the sale of the house?" My stomach dropped to my toes. He'd returned looking like he hadn't slept. Kristen had followed him. Never once did he tell me that she was trying to get back with him or that she was contacting him. "Were you two together?"

She bit down on her lip. "Part of me wants to tell you yes, because maybe, just maybe, if you shut him out of your life for good, he'll be able to move on, to actually live, but I'm not going to lie. I tried." She laughed again, the sound hurting and cutting all at once. "It didn't happen and not from lack of effort."

I sort of wanted to hit her. For real. It didn't matter at that moment that Brock and I weren't together then. This woman who knew I was with Brock was sitting here telling me how she was still trying to seduce him.

"What in the actual fuck?" I said. "Do you hear yourself?"

"I hear myself. Trust me."

"Then why are you here?" I demanded. "What is the point?"

"The point is I'm trying to do you a favor. I'm trying to stop you from making the same mistake as me and stop you from making a fool out of yourself like I have."

My brows flew up. "Really? I'm supposed to believe that? You're sitting here telling me that you're in love with the man I'm with, and I'm supposed to believe you're trying to do me a favor?"

"I'm not still in love with him. I've learned my lesson," she said, eyes bright. "And yes, I am doing you a favor, because if you're still in love with him after all these years, you've wasted just as much time as I have, because he's not with you because he loves you. He's with you because he believes he ruined your life."

My mouth popped open.

"When he learned you dropped out of college? Screwed him up in the head. When he found out you were seeing someone that your parents never met, it messed him up. When he found out you were single again, living all alone, he was torn up. Everything that ever went wrong in your life since that night you were shot, he blamed himself for it."

Oh my God.

"You might think it's crazy. You may not even want to believe me, but he would go to the ends of the earth for you," she said, snatching her purse off the floor. "But not for the right reasons."

My hands were starting to shake. "You need to leave."

Kristen shook her head at me like I was a fool turning down a million dollars. "You need to ask yourself why now. Why is he with you? If he wanted you and loved you for all the right reasons, why did it take six years?"

There could be a thousand reasons why it took us six years to find our way back to each other. Each of them equally valid. But I knew Brock carried some heavy guilt over what happened to me. Everyone knew it.

"Not only does he feel like he's obligated to you. He feels like he owes your father. It's a double whammy for him. Getting with you is making up for how he believes he failed to be there for you and for your father."

I flinched, because I'd thought that myself. More than once. It was like she plucked it right out of my darkest thoughts.

Kristen rose. "Don't be like me. Don't spend years of your life convincing yourself that he's there for you because of the right kind of feelings." She turned and then looked over her shoulder. "Good luck, Jillian."

I sat there, not moving, long after Kristen left, unable to shake what she'd said to me. I couldn't laugh it off or disregard it, because . . . because it made sense.

It made too much sense.

*"Yesterday is ashes; tomorrow is wood. Only today does the fire burn brightly."*

—Old Eskimo Proverb

# Chapter 33

I didn't cry.

I didn't even flip out after Kristen left.

I didn't call Brock.

I finished my day at the Academy and then I drove home without getting the huge plate of cheese fries like I'd anticipated earlier.

I drove home and found myself standing in the second bedroom, staring at all the wonderful books I'd brought home.

Mostly I was just in a daze as I turned over in my mind everything Kristen had said. Never would I have expected she would show up and say those things. If only the part she'd said about herself was true, the bare-bones honesty was shocking. But some of what she'd said hadn't surprised me.

I'd always feared that Brock was here, back in my life and with me, truly with me, because he felt like he needed to. And that hurt, that cut so deep it was nearly a physical pain.

That fear made it feel like a gorilla was sitting on my chest. That fear stole my appetite. That fear swept the successes from the last couple of days right out from underneath me.

And I *hated* that.

Part of me just wanted to ignore what Kristen had said to me, and that was a huge part, because that's what the old Jillian would've done. The one who didn't have a flicker of fire in her.

The old Jillian would've *settled*.

That Jillian would've pretended that everything was okay, because it was easier and safer than facing the pain, but I knew I wouldn't be able to forget it. It had wormed its way into my head and it would stay there even if I forced myself to let it go, and it would haunt everything I did and every word Brock spoke.

Reaching out, I dragged my fingers across the smooth spines of the books and then dropped my hand.

But I wasn't her anymore.

The conversation with Kristen preyed on the doubts I'd buried deep over the last couple of weeks. They were now brought to the surface, leaving my skin and soul feeling raw and brittle.

I couldn't just pretend the conversation between Kristen and me had never happened. I couldn't wish it away. I couldn't be okay with that fear that had existed before Kristen walked through the door. I would talk to Brock. I just didn't know what he could say that would truly erase the doubt, because I worried that this was more than him.

That I was letting what Kristen said dig in deep, because of *my* own issues—*my* doubts, *my* confidence, *my* fears.

And I didn't know if it was all on me, and if it was, how I was going to fix that.

A hand slipped over my bare arm, to my hip, pushing the covers down my legs. The rough, calloused palm grazed my thigh, sending a rush of tight, hot shivers over my skin.

"Babe." A deep voice stirred the hair against my temple.

Feeling a hard warm chest press against my back, I blinked open my eyes. Confusion swirled as I turned my head sideways. "Brock?"

He kissed the corner of my lips. "You say that like you don't know it's me." The drag of his rough jawline along my neck caused me to gasp. "Who else would be climbing into your bed at one in the morning?"

Still half-asleep, I started to grin, to tease him that it could be anyone, but as the seconds passed and the more awake I became, the events of the day returned.

I scooted away, reaching for the lamp on the nightstand. Soft light flooded the bedroom. What was he doing here? He wasn't supposed to come back until Saturday afternoon.

"Where are you going?" He circled an arm around my waist, tugging me back and under him.

Before I could respond, his mouth closed over mine. With the touch of his lips, my body responded without thought. My lips parted, and the kiss deepened. His lower body settled onto mine, and I could feel him through his jeans, pressing against me. He rocked his hips into me, and my breath caught on a burst of exquisite sensations. Within seconds I was already throbbing. He could either turn me on that quickly, or I was always that ready for him.

"I missed that sound," he said against my lips. "Drove like a maniac to get here now instead of in the morning just to hear it."

I was seconds from being carried away by the pulse-pounding desire. If I didn't stop this now, I wouldn't be able to, and even though I wanted nothing more than to feel him, all of him, we needed to talk.

Calling on every ounce of willpower I could find, I placed my hands on his chest. "Brock—"

"Fuck." His hips rolled as his hand slid up over the loose shirt I wore, skimming the swell of my breasts as his forehead grazed mine. "That's another thing I missed here. My name on your lips."

339

My body flushed hot. Oh man, he really knew how to distract me, but I pushed lightly on his chest. "We need to talk."

"We can do that." His lips brushed over my right jaw and then his teeth caught the fleshy part of my lobe. "We can also do other things."

"No, we can't."

He chuckled. "It's called multitasking, Jilly."

"I can't multitask like this," I admitted. Already, my heart rate was all over the place.

His hand roamed over the crest of my breast, his fingers finding the hardened peak. "That's not my problem."

I wanted to laugh, but if I did, his persistence would sway me. My fingers curled into the sweater he wore. "Kristen came by the office today." Those words were like dousing Brock in ice water. His hand stilled, as did his hips. He lifted his head and stared down at me with dark eyes.

"Come again?"

"Kristen stopped by the Academy to talk to me."

"About what?"

His question sounded so genuine that I had to think he had no idea the kind of intimate details she'd shared with me. But maybe, just maybe, some part of what she'd said wasn't true.

I met his gaze. "About a lot of things."

He lowered his brows and then he shifted off of me so he was on his side, using his elbow to prop him up. His hand remained on my stomach. "Why do I have a feeling I'm not going to like what I'm about to hear?"

The tendrils of desires scattered. "Good question."

"Well, I can't imagine her visit was about homemade Christmas cards." He grinned—he actually grinned.

"You don't seem too bothered by her showing up to talk to me."

"Why would I be?" he asked, slipping his hand down to the edge of my shirt. "Honestly, I'm not happy to hear she was here. She has no business coming around you."

I studied his features, trying to decipher how he really felt about it. "You . . . you never really talk about her."

"What is there to say? We were together. Then we weren't."

"You two were together for years," I pointed out, dumb-founded by his statement. "You were engaged. It's not like you dated for a couple of months and then went your separate ways."

He was quiet for a moment. "What did she want to talk to you about?"

"A lot of things." I sat up. His hand slipped, but he kept his arm around my waist until I scooted back against the head-board. My gaze flicked to the doorway and I saw the slight frame of Rhage lurking in the hallway, trying to decide if it was safe to come in or not.

Brock waited. "Details?"

My gaze slid back to him. "Why haven't you told me that Kristen was pregnant?"

"She talked to you about that?" Surprise colored his tone. "What in the fuck?"

"So, it's true?"

"Shit." Brock thrust his hand over his head, scrubbing his fingers through his hair. "Yeah, it's true. She got pregnant a few years ago. She had a miscarriage. I never told you, because it's not something I really like to think about." There was a brief pause. "I also didn't tell you because I was sure that was something you really didn't want to know about."

My stomach twisted with a weird mixture of feelings. Pushing my hair back from my face, I had no idea what to think about that. I was relieved that he was being honest, dismayed that he hadn't told me, and I even understood why, in a way. The stupid, mindless jealousy that simmered low in my gut told me why he hadn't mentioned it.

I was ... I was jealous because he'd gotten someone else pregnant, and trust me, I recognized the ridiculousness of that. I realized how incredibly horrid that was. How wrong.

I drew in a deep breath. "That had to have hurt you—for her to lose the pregnancy."

Brock flopped onto his back, rubbing his hands down his face. "It wasn't good for either of us, Jillian."

"I'm sorry," I said.

"Nothing for you to be sorry about." His chest rose with a deep breath. "I wasn't ready to have a child. Wasn't even something I was thinking about when she got pregnant, but I grew to be happy with the idea." He dropped his hands to his chest as he tilted his head up so his gaze found mine. "Wasn't meant to be."

"She said that you felt guilty over it."

His brows furrowed together.

"That you felt responsible for her losing the baby," I said. "That your guilt over losing the baby drove you to ask her to marry you."

Those eyes turned to midnight. "What else did she say to you?"

He didn't deny it.

My heart sank. "She ... she told me that you never really loved her."

A muscle flexed in his jaw. "I have absolutely no idea why she told you that, but I cared for her. I think a part of me loved her, but I wasn't in love with her. That part is correct."

I winced. While there was a terrible, horrible little part of me which was pleased to hear that, to know his heart had yet to belong to someone, there was a greater part of me that could not fathom how he could spend six years with someone, get that person pregnant, ask for their hand in marriage, and still not be in love.

Then again, people stayed together all the time for a hundred reasons other than love. Finances. Children. Loneliness. Sometimes it was just easier to stay with someone, so why would guilt be so farfetched?

It wasn't.

But this was the person he'd picked over me that night. I'd let that go. At least, I thought I had. Sometimes I wasn't so sure. I guessed that would always be a work in progress for me, and there was nothing wrong with that as long as I truly worked at letting it go. But, what if Brock stayed with me for years and years and never loved me, never loved me like he should?

"What else did she say to you, Jillian?"

"She told me that she was . . . or had been trying to get back with you." A flash of anger lit me up. "Why didn't you tell me she was still contacting you?"

"Why would I?"

I cringed. "Seriously? Why? I'm your girlfriend—"

"Yes, you're my girlfriend, and because of that, I don't want you worrying about some woman who obviously didn't understand it was over."

That thrill of hearing the words "my girlfriend" was still there, but he should've told me. "I get that, but you should tell me if someone is trying to get with you. I have a right to know that."

He looked like he wanted to disagree, but then sighed. "And have you stress out over something that would've been irrelevant? Because that shit is not happening with Kristen. That shit is not happening with any woman. I know that, back in the day, I didn't do commitments, but you know me. When I'm with someone, I'm with them. You never have to worry about that with me."

343

Brock was loyal—sometimes to a fault. Him cheating wasn't something that concerned me. That wasn't the issue.

"What else did she say?" he asked. "Because I bet there is more."

There was. "She said that you felt guilty for what happened to me that night at Mona's," I told him.

His forehead creased. "Of course I've felt guilty over that. You and I have discussed that. I don't see—"

"Are you with me because you want to be with me, or because you feel guilty about what happened to me?"

He stared at me for a moment, almost like he couldn't find the words to say, and then he said, "Is that a serious question?"

"Yes. It is."

"I don't think I need to answer that question."

Frustration snapped at the seeds of dread sprouting in my stomach. "I think you do."

"Do you really believe that?" Brock sat up fluidly, thrusting a hand through his hair again. He clasped the back of his neck. "Seriously?"

"It's a serious question, Brock."

"And how does me wanting to be with you out of guilt make sense?" His eyes glinted. "What did she say to you?"

"She said that you stayed with her out of guilt and that you're with me because of guilt."

Brock cursed under his breath as he shook his head. "And you really, truly think that?"

"I don't know what I think." Tugging my hair back, I quickly twisted it and then let go. The hair spun loose. "I need time." And I needed space so I could think straight. "Look, it's really late. Maybe you should just go home."

His brows flew up. "You really want me to leave?"

I rose from the bed, snatching the long cardigan off the corner. I yanked it on. "Yeah. Yeah, I do."

"Well, I hate to break it to you, but I'm not leaving."

My arms fell to my sides. "Oh, yes you are."

He stared up at me from where he sat at the head of the bed. "There is no way in hell I'm going to leave when you've got that nasty shit crowding your thoughts, so you can talk yourself into whatever the hell it is you're so badly wanting to believe about me."

I gaped at him. "I don't want to believe any of this, Brock."

"Are you sure?" he challenged. "Because you seem damn quick to think that I'd actually be with you out of guilt. That I'd actually be *fucking* you out of guilt."

I cringed. "You don't have to say it that way."

"Really? You think that sounds bad? Try being on the receiving end of hearing someone say that," he shot back, and okay, he had a point. "I get why it would be easy for you to believe this, but you have to give me more credit than that."

Swallowing the lump building in my throat, I folded my arms across my chest. "I do give you credit, but how could you have not loved her?"

"How does what I felt for her have anything to do with us?" he fired back. "Jesus Christ, Jillian, I can't answer that question. I don't know why I never loved her enough to want to be with her. It just didn't happen."

"Did you ask her to marry you because she lost the baby?"

Shaking his head, he lowered his chin. "I don't know. Maybe I did. Maybe that was a part of it. I wanted to make her happy. I tried."

Tugging the edges of the cardigan together, I looked away. "She said you let the guilt of what happened with me—"

"Why in the hell does it matter what she fucking said to you?" he demanded as he moved to the edge of the bed.

"It matters, because I deserve someone who's not settling for me out of guilt!" I shouted. "And I deserve to be with someone who loves me as much as I love them!"

Brock stilled.

I don't think he even breathed.

And then I realized what I'd said to him.

Oh my God.

Blood drained from my face and then rushed back at dizzying speed. I'd just told him I loved him.

# Chapter 34

I hadn't just told Brock that I loved him.

I'd practically screamed it at him, actually.

Everyone and their mother knew that I'd been in love with Brock when we were younger. Even Brock, who had tried to not acknowledge it, had known. But that was back then, when I was naïvely young and he was this unattainable rising star who only allowed himself to see me as a little sister to him.

That was not now.

Not when I was old enough to know what those words really meant and how they felt.

"What . . . what did you just say?" he asked as he lowered his hands to his knees.

Oh dear.

I held the ends of my sweater tighter as I glanced toward the door like that was going to be of some assistance. "I said I deserve someone who isn't with me because they feel guilty."

"That's not the part I'm talking about," he clarified, voice dangerously calm.

My lip trembled as my heart pounded against my chest. The words burned on the tip of my tongue like ash. Those three words were easy to toss around. People said them all the time, but I thought—no, I knew—that when you truly meant those three words they were hard to speak.

347

The old Jillian never would've had the courage to repeat them.

I was not her anymore.

Squaring my shoulders, I lifted my chin. "I said that I . . . that I love you."

Something I couldn't decipher flickered across his face. "You love me?"

"Yes." I swallowed hard. "I loved you when I was eight. I loved you when I was twelve. I loved you when I was twenty, and I . . . I love you now."

Brock rose. "If you loved me all those times and love me now, then why haven't you asked me what I was thinking the first time I saw you at the restaurant? Why don't you ask me what I was feeling when I realized you were going out with that guy again? Ask me what it was like when I woke up the first time with you in my arms? Why not ask me how I felt the first time we kissed?"

A tremble coursed through me as he took a step forward. "You could've asked me what it was like the first time I got inside you and every time after that. If you loved me all this time, then why haven't you asked me if I loved you?"

Air punched out of my lungs as what he said settled over me like warmed silk.

He stopped a few feet in front of me. "I don't bring up Kristen because that part of my life is way over. The things that happened with her are a part of the past. They have no impact on anything that I do now and she sure as fuck has nothing to do with us. That might sound cold and cruel as fuck, but it's the truth. And you're right. I should've told you that she'd been calling and texting me. Then we could've talked and you would've been prepared for the kind of shit she was about to dump on you. I am sorry for that, because that's my fuck-up."

My fingers eased on the ends of the cardigan.

"I'm going to address the whole me feeling guilty over Kristen losing the baby. Did it upset me? Yes, it did. Did I feel bad for her—for her having to go through that when I wasn't even there? Because I wasn't. I was at a match in Australia when it happened. *That* I felt guilty over. Because I should've been there when she had to go through that, but I don't feel responsible for her losing the baby. I don't know what she told you to back that up—"

"She said you two were arguing often and that she was upset with you not being around."

A dry, humorless laugh broke the silence. "Maybe she thinks it's my fault. We weren't fighting bad. Just normal shit. Hell, who knows, but contrary to popular belief, I don't go looking for things to feel like shit over."

I let go of the cardigan and lowered my arms.

"And this whole I'm with you out of guilt?" His lips pressed into a thin, hard line. "I can't deny that guilt had eaten me up, and sometimes, there are moments where it still does. I know you don't blame me. There was a time where I wished you did, but I'm damn glad now that you don't. But for you to think that I'd get this involved with you because of that?" Brock stopped and closed his eyes, almost as if he couldn't continue, and I knew—I knew right then—that I had hurt him. I'd hurt this man who was so strong, both physically and mentally. I had wounded him with my doubt.

A bitter knot formed in the back of my throat, and I drew in a shallow breath. "What . . . what were you thinking when you first saw me in the restaurant?"

His lashes lifted. "I was thinking that I was glad I sought you out. I was thinking that you looked more beautiful than I could've possibly ever imagined. And I was thinking . . . I was thinking that even though it was risky approaching you and having you figure out why I was there, I just had to hear your voice."

The next breath I took was shaky. "What were you thinking when I said I was going out with Grady again?"

Brock's lip twitched. "I wanted to punch my fist through a wall."

"How did . . . you feel when you woke up with me?" I asked, my voice hoarse.

"Calmer than I've felt in fucking years," he said, his eyes warming. "Like I was waking up and I was *home*."

Oh.

Oh God.

My eyes blurred. "When you kissed me? And when you were finally with me?"

"Felt like it was the first time and the best and the last time." He took one more step, and with his long legs, he was right in front of me. I tilted my head up, and he slowly lifted his hands, cupping my cheeks. "I think there is one more question you need to ask me."

The lines of his face faded as tears filled my eyes. "Do you . . . do you love me?"

"I love you . . ." He lowered his forehead to mine, and a shudder rolled through me. "I love you like I wish I allowed myself to when we were younger. I love you because you're not just sweet but you're kind. I love you because you have this fire in you that you don't even recognize, but I do. You're strong and you're a *survivor*."

A tear slipped down my cheek, and he chased it with his thumb. I couldn't speak. If I tried, I knew I'd start sobbing. Hearing him say these words, these beautiful words, wasn't even from my wildest dreams. My heart swelled like a levee about to break. I wanted to laugh and cry. I wanted to dance and I wanted to hold him.

*He loves me.*

"There is not a single part of how I love you that has anything to do with guilt." He dragged his thumbs along my cheeks, catching another tear. "And I'm *in* love with you and I've never felt this way for anyone. You're my first," he said, pressing his lips to the deep scar in my left cheek. "You will be my only."

Brock kissed the left corner of my lips and then he tipped his head, kissing the right side of my jaw. "I love you, Jillian."

I was beyond words.

Clutching his shoulders, I turned my head, blindingly finding his mouth, and from there, everything spun beautifully out of control. My shirt came off. His sweater joined it on the floor. One after another, items of clothing fell away until there was nothing between us.

His hands flexed on my hips and in one powerful move, he lifted me up and had me on my back. I took a startled breath and then he was hovering over me, caging me in with his arms and his body.

Brock swooped down, claiming my lips in a feverish kiss that was full of so much love and passion. My heart fluttered unsteadily as molten lava coursed through my veins. "I love you," I said to him, cupping his cheeks and dragging his gaze to mine. "I will never stop loving you."

"You've never stopped."

Then there were no words. All communication was through lips and teeth, tongue and hands. He nipped at my breasts and suckled deeply as he trailed a fiery path of hot kisses down my stomach and below my navel, and he still went lower. He licked every inch of my skin and every breathy moan he drew out from me was an expression of love.

Intense heat built, turning into a glorious ache. Lust and love spread throughout me, and when his mouth closed over the tight knot of nerves, I screamed his name. My head fell back as his fingers plunged deep inside me. He worked me up and took me over the edge.

I was coming when he rose above me once more and planted himself deep, delving into my mouth with his tongue, and he thrust his hips against me almost savagely. I bucked under him, grasping his straining arms as I wrapped my legs around him.

As he moved, I no longer knew where I began and he ended.

My head thrashed as he thrust in and out, in and out, his mouth leaving mine so his hot breath panted in my ear. We were *fucking*. We were *making love*. Grinding his hips, he reached between us, and the tension spun tightly. Pressure built, and then it happened. I came again in a burst just as powerful and beautiful as the first. Tight, sensual spasms rocked my body as Brock's thrusts lost all rhythm. He moved so fast and so hard, pushing me across the bed. The thump of the bed against the wall filled the bedroom.

"I love you," he said, and then he was falling over the edge, surrendering to the bliss still echoing through my veins.

Skin slick with moisture, we held each other as the minutes ticked by. I don't know how long we stayed like that before he eased out of me and onto his side. He brought me with him, circling his arms around me and holding me so I was facing him, holding me in a way that said he was never going to let me go.

Brock kissed me in a way he never had before. At least that was how it felt. He kissed me slowly, tenderly, and so deeply that tears rose.

*Love.*

This kiss was what love felt like.

\*     \*     \*

Long after our bodies stopped moving and our hearts slowed, I lay awake beside a sleeping Brock, replaying his words over and over again. A crooked smile was probably permanently fixed to my face, and I didn't care. There was so much Brock had said to me that had brought that smile to my face. The fact he loved me was a big reason. Duh. But there was something else.

He'd said I had fire in me.

Hearing that and knowing he believed that meant that I had come so, so far from the Jillian he'd grown up with.

I was *loved*.

And I had *fire* in me.

Both were important and amazing, but the latter . . . God, it meant everything.

Because from the moment I decided to take the job at the Lima Academy, I'd been changing. Even before that. The process had been slow and painful at times, but the realization that I wanted to live differently, wanted to take more risks and experience life, had started before Brock reappeared. His presence had aided in the process, but it hadn't been him.

It had been me.

Some people were born with fire in them. They burned intensely bright, full of fiery drive and ambition for everything and everyone, but never fully committing one hundred percent to any one thing. They have *that* fire, but they burn out halfway through life, forever dwelling on what *should* have been and never what *could* have been.

Others have the same kind of fire in them from the start, their hunger and determination to succeed the cornerstone of every decision and choice they make. Their flame may flicker, but it never goes out. They never focus on what they *should* have in life, but focus on what they *could* have.

Then there were people who didn't realize they had that fire, that it lay kindled inside them, needing to be stoked into flame. I never would've believed that I had that fire, but I did, and sometimes it would flicker and fade and other times it would rage and burn.

But it would never be extinguished.

Never.

I looked down at Brock, soaking in his beautiful face and stunning body. He was more than all of that, so much more. Brock was intelligent and he too was a survivor. He was a good-hearted man and loyal, and when he cared, he did care deeply. That was why he felt remorse and regret. Those things weren't obligations. That was where Kristen had been wrong about us—about them.

And I'd been wrong to ever doubt him.

There was a part of me that wanted to search Kristen down and either smack her upside the head or explain in great detail about how wrong she was. Or do both of those things. But . . . why? Why waste one more second of my life on something or someone who was living in the past? I'd done that for far too many years, and I wasn't going to do it for one more second.

Lowering my head, I kissed the medallion I'd bought him so long ago, the necklace I'd planned to give him that night. The one he wore every day. Then I lifted my lips to Brock's and kissed him once more. I was rewarded with a sleepy little half-smile.

There were no more yesterdays.

There was only today.

There was only tomorrow.

*'The inner fire is the most important thing mankind possesses.'*

—Edith Södergran

## About the Author

Jennifer L. Armentrout is a Number One New York Times and internationally bestselling author. She lives in Martinsburg, West Virginia.

*Don't Look Back* was nominated as Best in Young Adult Fiction by the Young Adult Library Association. *Obsidian* has been optioned for a major motion picture and her *Covenant Series* has been optioned for TV.

For details about current and upcoming titles from
Jennifer L. Armentrout,
please visit *www.jenniferarmentrout.com*

Jennifer L. Armentrout

# Tempting the Best Man

**The addictively steamy first book in *New York Times* bestselling author Jennifer L. Armentrout's Gamble Brothers series . . .**

Madison Daniels has worshipped her brother's best friend since they were kids. Everyone thinks she and Chase Gamble would make the perfect couple, but there are two major flaws in their logic. 1) Chase has sworn off relationships of any kind, and 2) after blurring the line between friends and lovers for one night four years ago, they can't stop bickering.

Forced together for her brother's wedding getaway, Chase and Madison decide to call a truce for the happy couple. Except all bets are off when they're forced to shack up in a tacky 70s honeymoon suite and survive a multitude of "accidents" as the family tries to prove their "spark" can be used than for more than fighting. That is, if they don't strangle each other first . . .

# Jennifer L. Armentrout

# Tempting the Player

**The addictively romantic second book in Jennifer L. Armentrout's *New York Times* bestselling Gamble Brothers series . . .**

Chad Gamble, all-star pitcher for the Nationals, is one of the best players on – and off – the field. And right now, the notorious bad boy wants Bridget Rodgers. But with her lush curves and snappy comebacks, the feisty redhead is the kind of woman a man wants to settle down with . . . and that's the last thing Chad needs.

When the paparazzi catch them in a compromising position, Chad's manager issues an ultimatum: clean up his act or kiss his multi-million dollar contract goodbye. To save his career, his meddling publicist says he'll have to convince everyone Bridget isn't just his flavor of the week, but his girlfriend.

Being blackmailed into a fake relationship with Chad Gamble isn't easy, especially when the sizzling physical attraction between them is undeniable. With a month to go on their arranged pretence, it's going to take every ounce of willpower they have not to fall into bed together . . . or in love.

Jennifer L. Armentrout

# Tempting the Bodyguard

**The steamily romantic third book in Jennifer L. Armentrout's *New York Times* bestselling Gamble Brothers series . . .**

Alana Gore is in danger. A take-no-prisoners publicist, her way with people has made her more than a few enemies over the years, but a creepy stalker is an entirely different matter. She needs a bodyguard, and the only man she can ask is not only ridiculously hot, but reputed to have a taste for women that goes beyond adventurous.

Chandler Gamble has one rule: don't protect anyone you want to screw. But with Alana, he's caught between his job and his increasingly high libido. On one hand, Alana needs his help. On the other, Chandler wants nothing more than to take the hot volcano of a woman in hand. To make her writhe in pleasure, until she's at his complete mercy.

She needs protection. He needs satisfaction. And the moment the line is crossed, all hell will break loose . . .

Do you wish this wasn't the end?

Join us at www.hodder.co.uk, or follow us on
Twitter @hodderbooks to be a part of our community
of people who love the very best in books and reading.

Whether you want to discover more about a book
or an author, watch trailers and interviews, have the
chance to win early limited editions, or simply browse
our expert readers' selection of the very best books,
we think you'll find what you're looking for.

And if you don't,
that's the place to tell us what's missing.

We love what we do, and we'd love you to be part of it.

www.hodder.co.uk

@hodderbooks

HodderBooks

HodderBooks